STOLEN THUNDER

STOLEN THUNDER

David Axton

St. Martin's Press
New York

Library of Congress Cataloging-in-Publication Data

Axton, David.
Stolen thunder / David Axton.
p.   cm.
ISBN 0-312-09395-0
I. Title.
PS3561.O55S66   1993
813′.54—dc20   93-18506   CIP

First published in Great Britain by Bantam Books.

First U.S. Edition: May 1993
10 9 8 7 6 5 4 3 2 1

To Lisanne and Jane,
for keeping a difficult promise

Special thanks are due to (in no particular order): Chris Chippington of the Imperial War Museum, Duxford, for letting me clamber over the museum's B52D; David Haller and Phil Keeble of RAF Coningsby, for allowing me first-hand acquaintance with one of Her Majesty's Tornado F3s and for some graphic accounts of what they're like in the air; Jeff Ethell of Front Royal, Virginia, for patience beyond the call of duty in dealing with transatlantic phone calls demanding intimate details of B52s; the United States Air Force public-relations machine, in this case embodied in a bus that carted a suspicious alien (me) up and down Davis-Monthan; Dennis Topping, for the lore of the Old West; and to Ray and Edna Strayer of Tucson, Arizona, who introduced me to the Graveyard in the first place.

From 2 March 1965 to 31 October 1968,
US Air Force B52 bombers attacked targets in
North Vietnam. The campaign was called
ROLLING THUNDER

PROLOGUE

Heat was choking in the stillness inside the 747 and the only sound was the high sniffing of a stewardess who couldn't quite stem her crying. Stench from the overflowing toilets dangled in the heat amid the haze of cigarette smoke. There were people here who'd taken it up again after being off nicotine for years.

The youngest hijacker put the boot in the American again, the man huddled on his side on the platform by the forward door. Despite himself, the American moaned in pain.

All the hijackers laughed. They watched him, stirring with what little strength he still had, looking for some place to lie where he wasn't in anguish. There wasn't one. In the heat ripple around the shell-pocked terminal a mile the other side of Beirut airport, television crews and press photographers with long lenses propped on bipods were also watching. But the press crews couldn't see the detail.

Tariq Talal wasn't the real name of the bulky, bearded man who was leading the five hijackers. It was the name they all knew him by, the *nom de guerre* he'd chosen years before. It was a name that, if this bulky man with the folding-stock Kalashnikov on his shoulder had his way, was destined to become a force to be reckoned with in the Middle East.

This miserable, snivelling wreck of an American officer hadn't heard of Tariq Talal when they took over the 747. He had now.

The youngest hijacker, the one who couldn't really grow a beard yet, kicked the American again and this time the five of them heard another rib go. They murmured their approval. The American officer was fighting for breath now, his eyes open to slits and not seeing much. Blood mingled with his saliva.

He'd been a lucky find, Tariq Talal thought, leafing languidly through the man's passport. Hardly over thirty years old, fit, highly educated, an F15 fighter pilot from a squadron in Germany; a man who would have been destined for an illustrious career serving the Great Satan, America, had fate not led him into Tariq Talal's hands. Captain Edward Masterson, MSc. He didn't look so fit now; didn't look the proud fighter pilot any more. Fleetingly curious, Tariq Talal looked down at Edward Masterson's face and, for a moment, there was eye contact. The fear in the American's pain-racked eyes amused the hijacker.

Edward Masterson had gone beyond trying to under-stand the mind of a man who could derive amusement from torturing and humiliating another person purely on a racial basis; or, indeed, any other. The pain was worse than his inability to understand. They'd broken both his elbows, both his knees; the equally fierce hurting inside him told him he had internal ruptures; and now he was partially deaf and his vision was impaired.

Infinitely worse than this inescapable universe of pain was his sheer helplessness.

He'd wanted not to cry out. Not to show pain, not to show weakness. Not to weep. Not to give these terrorists the satisfaction of *seeing* that they'd humiliated an American officer. But he'd blown it. The pain, and the rising terror of more pain, had been too much. Edward Masterson had prided himself on not being a coward but he'd been wrong about himself; he'd been a coward all the time and hadn't even known it. Beyond a certain point, maybe everyone was.

Edward Masterson squeezed his eyes shut. He was

struggling not to shed more tears but he could hardly concentrate on that when it took so much effort to breathe while so many new pains kept spearing into him. He could taste blood.

Tariq Talal kicked Edward Masterson.

The young man rolled on his back, limp, eyes closed, lips parted. Tariq Talal watched him a moment, impassive. He looked for signs that he was still breathing but he couldn't see any. Quite slowly, he took the folding-stock Kalashnikov off his shoulder and cocked it. He pointed it at Edward Masterson's exposed throat. He paused a moment, but the young man didn't move.

Inside the 747, the single shot made a huge sound.

After some minutes, three of the hijackers picked up Edward Masterson's body and heaved it out on to the tarmac. It looked quite a long way down. It wasn't yet two in the afternoon and the day was very hot. A couple of minutes later, the control tower came on the radio, speaking to the 747's captain: could they send someone to collect the body?

No, Tariq Talal said.

He kept them waiting until early evening, and all that time Edward Masterson's body lay there in the sun. When he finally allowed them to send a pickup truck, he stood in the forward door where the television cameras could see him. He shouted down to the two men in overalls as they picked up Edward Masterson.

'The world shall know that Tariq Talal has triumphed over the Great Satan, America!'

The cameras caught that. They'd also caught the final bullet the man had put into Edward Masterson, through the open forward door, and the way the other hijackers had tossed him out of the aircraft.

Among the people who watched the replays, in their living rooms, was Edward Masterson's shocked, desperate widow.

CHAPTER 1

Almost two years later

Winter sun gleamed off the outward-sloping plate glass of the control tower at Davis-Monthan Air Base, on the southern edge of Tucson, Arizona. For January, it was mild. Mild in January in Tucson meant you'd probably need a light jacket or cardigan over your shirt. Two A10 tank-buster jets were taking off noisily, one close behind and to the left of the other so that, watching from the tower, all you could see was one aircraft that seemed to have too much ordnance slung underneath it. Sunlight gleamed on the camber of several hundred aircraft wings. Davis-Monthan is where the US Air Force stores the aircraft it hasn't an immediate use for but isn't yet ready to scrap.

The young woman who owned the old Volkswagen Beetle wasn't yet ready to scrap her car either. She felt sentimentally attached to the little vehicle and enjoyed feeling that way.

All the parking spaces outside the tower were taken, so she double-parked. She straightened to her full six foot, locked the car, adjusted her USAF uniform cap, tweaked her skirt, and walked in through the operations room. She got a couple of salutes and a 'Hi, Becks' from someone she knew. She acknowledged her with a grin and went up the stairs.

Big as it was, the glasshouse top was crowded. The operations officer of the day was a gnarled old major, pushing retirement age, and he turned with a look of annoyance to see who else was shoving in. His irritation

1

vanished as he recognized Captain Rebecca Laird whom he'd invited into his domain today to see the show.

'Why, Captain Laird. Come right on in.' The handshake was firm, the shy smile welcoming.

Becks Laird had been serving at Davis-Monthan for almost a year and she was fed up with Arizona. She'd been born a Minnesota country girl and she hankered after the sight of tall green woods and mountains with real snow on them. Today's event promised to be the most exciting thing to have happened at Davis-Monthan since they'd posted her here.

They called this place 'The Graveyard', after all those stored and forgotten air force aircraft. To Becks it felt just like that. For her, the place had two things going for it.

One was promotion. She'd had those captain's bars on her shoulders for very nearly three weeks now, which at twenty-six was a nice feeling; and she actually had a department of her own to run, albeit a small one. She'd been head of A2 – air force intelligence – here since the previous incumbent, an aging, lovably idle Bostonian, had retired from the service. She'd been his deputy up till then, a couple of weeks before Christmas; and she knew, fondly, that he'd had a hand of some sort in the choice of his successor.

The other thing Tucson had going for it was Professor Van Burkart of the University of Arizona. Van taught English literature to undergraduate students and he was Captain Rebecca Laird's lover.

'Thought you weren't coming, Becks,' the old ops officer said with his half-hidden smile. He was a man who kept a pet labrador and enjoyed showing Becks pictures of his grandchildren. He knew how bored Becks was with Davis-Monthan, even though she was far too shrewd ever to complain, and he'd invited her up here for the only sort of entertainment the base was likely to see for months. 'They're taxying out right now.' He

2

handed Becks a battered old service-issue pair of 6 × 30 binoculars.

They leaned on the rail, craning a bit into the angle of the outward-sloping plate glass. The ops officer had Becks's slim, tall form against one shoulder and a keen young black engineer officer against the other, and Becks had a pot-bellied master sergeant squeezing her other shoulder. Behind them there were desks with consoles and the Japanese-American woman ground controller was saying: 'Affirmative, Bright Angel, that is a *right* turn, intersection five, backtrack taxiway for holding point three one.'

'Bright Angel' was the departing aircraft's callsign. The departing aircraft was a USAF-surplus B52 bomber. Davis-Monthan was full of B52s. From where she stood, Becks could see one end of a row of them, with canvas covers over their engine intakes and cockpit trans-parencies. They stood alongside old-model F4 Phantom fighters and C130 Hercules transports and – the one that had surprised her when she first arrived here – early-series AV8As, the British-designed Harrier jump jet.

This B52 was different. It was a comparatively late G model, built in 1959, and they'd taken out the attack radars and bomb racks and sold it to an air museum in Perth, Western Australia. It would fly there unrefuelled, and they were hoping it might break a couple of records on the way, but after that it wouldn't fly again.

'BUFFs,' the ops officer reminisced. 'That's what they called 'em when I was on bomber wing in Guam. Big Ugly Fat Fellows.'

'Fellows?' Becks slid him a teasing glance. Undue delicacy amused her. She put a hand on his sleeve. 'Hey, why did they call it Bright Angel?'

The ops officer glanced at her. 'When that plane was flying in Vietnam, her captain was a guy born and raised in a little town near the Grand Canyon. You know the

3

Bright Angel Fault? It's the one runs right across the whole canyon, north to south, and carries the main rim-to-floor hiking trail, the one that comes up out at Grand Canyon Village.'

Then someone called out and the B52 came slowly into sight.

Davis-Monthan didn't often witness a B52 takeoff. They landed them here now and then but, once down, the B52s tended not to fly out again. It was a very American bomber: the first thing that impressed you about it was sheer size. Watching it now as it lumbered ponderously on to the taxiway, laden with all the fuel its tanks could take, Becks thought that the nearest comparison to its endless fuselage was a railroad freight car – except that the BUFF was longer. Its wings were so swept back you could see their sheer weight dragging on them; outrigger wheels kept the tips off the tarmac. It had eight engines in four twin pods under the high-mounted wing. In the 1940s, when this device had been designed, they'd had a job to get much over 11,000 pounds thrust out of a jet engine; by 1990, Boeing – which had built the B52 – was powering 747 airlines with four engines, each producing 58,000 pounds.

Bright Angel, improbably small in the far distance of Davis-Monthan's long runway system, turned slowly to the holding point. Hard outlines of the mountains stood smoky blue against the pale lemon sky and the desert floor stretched flat, league upon league. Laboriously the big bomber turned round, on to the runway.

'This'll be good 'n' dirty,' the ops officer told Becks. 'They use water injection into the cans for takeoff on those Gs and it creates one helluva lot of smoke.' By *cans* he meant combustion chambers. Becks lifted the borrowed binoculars.

Almost imperceptibly, Bright Angel started its run. Imagine the energy it took, Becks thought, to get that amount of mass moving. The thing weighed a couple of hundred tons and had 48,000 gallons of Jet A in its tanks.

'See the tail?' the ops officer said. 'That short fat one's how you tell the Gs from the Ds.' He indicated the row of stored, ex-Vietnam B52Ds with their tall, slim tails; the G's tail was stubby in comparison. The G's nose was different, too, bursting out in streamlined blisters that hid TV cameras and electronics antennae.

Someone raised a Pentax and the ops officer turned. 'No photos, now, boys 'n' girls. That there pilot's a Vietnam vet and he says photos before a mission bring bad luck. OK, now.'

They did as he said.

In the winter afternoon the desert landscape of Tucson was endlessly flat right up to the foot of the jagged mountains that formed the skyline and the huge, vaulting heaven above it where Bright Angel was bound. Its colours were soft pastel sapphire and mauve and apricot and the B52 in its menacing, hard black paint scheme slid through it like a snake. Sun flashed briefly on the cockpit windscreen. Becks was watching through the binoculars but the runway was half a mile from the tower at its closest point and you couldn't see detail, couldn't read serials or squadron emblems. Faint exhaust trailed from the jetpipes and she wondered when the thick black smoke from the water injection would start. Then it flew.

The wingtips came alive first, flexing up and pulling their outriggers clear of terra firma. After that, the B52 just came off the ground. It didn't rotate nose-up, the way any self-respecting aircraft might, it simply levitated, fuselage parallel to the runway, if anything a touch nose-low. The outriggers folded away quickly, and the tandem mainwheel bogies under the fuselage disappeared. Bright Angel lifted away into the dazzle towards the south.

'Left turn.' A different controller. 'Standard departure, cleared to FL four zero zero. Contact Los Angeles radar on one two eight decimal one five.'

'Bright Angel.' The voice on the speakers, acknowledging, was a languid, southern drawl.

Tiny now against the sky, the dark silhouette rolled into its climbing left turn to bring it round to the north, circling the Tucson urban area. For the last time Becks watched the profile of the savagely swept wing. Lowering the binoculars, she turned to the ops officer.

He was looking puzzled. 'I'll be darned,' he murmured. 'I sure thought he'd need that water injection.' Absently he took back the binoculars. 'Well, it ain't hot today, I guess. And without a bomb load, he won't have been anywhere near max gross weight.'

'Or maybe he was showing consideration for the environment,' Becks smiled. That was something else Tucson had going for it: lovely clean, dry air, so you could see for miles. 'Thanks for the invite.' She gave the ops officer a peck on the cheek and headed back to the old Volkswagen.

*   *   *

The man she'd double-parked was the pot-bellied master sergeant, and he was still ambling across to his minibus as Becks drove away.

It was five past five, only twenty-five minutes to the end of the duty day. Becks parked again and went into the A2 office. It had her name on the door now. Julio, her clerk, wasn't there, he'd been off somewhere else to watch the B52 take off. Becks unlocked the communications room. It was hardly more than a broom cupboard with no outside light and jam full of hot, smelly equipment.

Nothing off the computer screen, nothing off the printer, the telex or the fax. No messages, no mail.

Boring old Davis-Monthan, Becks thought, you don't change, do you? She leaned her long body back in the chair, reached behind her and pulled out a comb from her long, sandy-blonde hair. Then the phone rang.

She jammed the comb back in place. 'Davis-Monthan A2, Captain Laird speaking.' Her voice was bright, alert.

'Captain, where the hell've you been?'

No mistaking that high, metallic, indignant tone. Major-General Gus Hartmore was the sort of professional who had his airmen – and women – painting coal white if he caught them without enough shine on their shoes. He'd been base commander here hardly longer than Becks had been head of A2 and he left few folk in doubt that having a woman in that job was an aberration wished on him by his predecessor in a moment of inattention. Five foot eleven of hard muscle and energy, he hated knowing that Becks was an inch above his height.

'Sir, I was in the control tower.'

'What does A2 have to do with the goddam control tower?'

'Sir, I was expanding my knowledge of the air force inventory by observing a B52 takeoff.' Careful, Captain Laird.

'Your duty station, Captain Laird, is right there in that A2 office. Just because we are not launching combat missions outa here right now does *not* mean that Davis-Monthan is other than an operational US Air Force base with an important role in this nation's affairs. How're you gonna get the work done that you been neglecting all afternoon?'

There wasn't any work, only routine filing that could wait till next week. Tell Hartmore that, though, and it would be another nail in her coffin as far as keeping this job was concerned. 'Sir, I guess I'll stay on here until it's clear.'

7

'You better, Captain.' The phone banged down.

In the empty office Becks stuck her tongue out. *The hell with you, Gus Hartmore.* But she still gave it till half past five before leaving.

* * *

A prairie dog was digging busily in a patch of sandy soil as Becks parked outside her long, dull, whitewashed, two-storey quarters block. Becks watched the prairie dog a moment. It sat up and looked back at her, small paws hooked forward; checked her out; and went back to digging. Becks walked indoors.

Her quarters were an apartment she shared with a woman air traffic control officer and with Yeltsin, her pet rat. The first thing, as always, was to let Yeltsin out of his cage and play with him for a few minutes, then top up his food and water and put him back. Yeltsin was good company, he always made her smile. Becks hung up her uniform neatly in the wardrobe and went into the shower. She changed into blue Levis, snug on the hip, and a light woollen jumper. She pulled all the clips and combs out of her long, sandy hair and glanced herself over in the mirror as she brushed busily. Well, it *wasn't* all vanity, she *was* entitled to a spot of pride in herself; she *was* quite a reasonably attractive young woman. Round face, clear eyes, freckles, curves in all the right places. She snapped on a ponytail ring, put back the soft contact lenses that she'd taken out for the shower, then transferred a few things to her off-duty shoulder bag and picked up the car keys.

Heading out the door, she bumped into her ATCO room-mate. Ella was just shorter than her, just younger, fit and confident and effervescent. She was from a smart middle-class black family in Savannah, Georgia, and her mother owned a majority shareholding in a TV station.

'Hey, Becks, you wanna make up a tennis foursome?'

It was tempting, Becks thought, if only to be able to brag to friends in snowy Minnesota about playing tennis in January. But she had other plans for this evening. 'Sorry, Ella . . .'

The knowing grin spread across Ella's face. 'Ah, *ha . . .*'

* * *

The main gate at Davis-Monthan led out into Craycroft Road, one of the main crosstown streets, and Becks drove the Volkswagen a bit quickly for the likes of suburban Tucson at six in the evening. The main university campus was virtually in the downtown area, left from Craycroft Road as you drove out of the base, and Van lived almost as far as you could get the other side of town without vanishing into the Sonoran Desert. It was a street running up into the mountain foothills, off the Tanque Verde road, east Tucson, close to the Saguaro National Monument cactus forest, which was one of Van's chief delights. Van had been born and raised amid the salt spray of the coast of Maine but, unlike Becks, he loved Arizona.

Becks ran the Volkswagen into the car port and parked behind Van's totally impractical Porsche Targa sports car. The house was a low, whitewashed cube with a saguaro in the front yard, lemon and grapefruit trees in the back yard, and wooden window frames in need of a lick of paint. The kitchen door was open the way it always was when Van was at home. Van was right there, at the stove, wearing an apron advertising Italian pasta and cheerfully cooking up pancakes stuffed with prawns in wine sauce.

'Wow, hiya, Captain Curvaceous! You're right on time, beautiful!' He stretched out his beefy right arm, his left hand gripping the pan's handle, and she went to him and accepted the embrace.

She was never sure, with remarks like that, whether

9

he was betraying subtle male chauvinism. Any time she challenged him, he would always laugh and say he had a right to show he appreciated her; and she knew there was truth in that. She knew too that, joke as he might, he would ultimately always take her seriously.

Any other attitude and she wouldn't still have been with him.

She dragged her lips away from his. 'Stop shaking that goddam pan. What's more important, kissing me or cooking?'

'Yeah,' Van said, then ducked. 'Hey, Rule One in the kitchen, never bat the chef!'

'Till he's through cooking,' Becks finished off menacingly.

'You wanna fix margaritas?' Van said. Any season was margarita season, especially here, within spitting distance of the Mexican border.

Becks slid him a sidelong glance as she poured tequila over crushed ice and added lemonade – careful not to let him realize, or his vanity reading would go off the clock. Professor Van Burkart was a big, active man and Becks could picture the effect he had on eighteen-year-old girls straight out of high school. Thirty-eight years old, six foot three, athletic as well as artistic – he painted oils in that saguaro forest – bearded, intriguingly bald, divorced and virile.

She set the table. Van set down platefuls of what Becks told the whole of Davis-Monthan, but would never tell Van, was in her opinion the best cooking in southern Arizona. They washed down Van's pancakes with Becks's margaritas. Then they held each other close on the sofa and watched the news on TV. Van never missed the news.

CBS led off on violence in Panama, with US forces on alert, following with an analysis of the US-Japanese trade deficit and the latest incomprehensible twist in Middle

10

Eastern affairs. In Israel a rightwing extremist settler shot an Arab and, two hours later, the Libyan leader was accusing the US of the murder. Van switched off the TV with the remote control.

'It's their logic. No-one is ever going to understand the logical rules they apply to it.'

Come the day, Van and Becks alike were Republican voters. But neither of them was inclined to chase an idea through the frontiers of common sense.

'Doesn't matter what logic you use,' Becks said, 'once you believe a thing badly enough.'

'OK.' He had his arm round her shoulders. She had her head tucked into his chin.

'I don't use logic on you,' Becks murmured. 'Else I'd keep asking what a career girl like me's doing with a dinosaur like you.'

'Reason you don't use logic,' Van said, 'is, you'd soon figure out where it led.' Then he kissed her.

*   *   *

A lot later, with the kitchen door closed and the blinds down, and a touch of heat in the airconditioning as the early night gathered a chill, they lay close together, naked in the aftermath of love. Van, as usual, was the first to grow impatient; Becks simply drowsed as he held her. He jacked himself up on an elbow, disturbing her.

'Coffee or wine?'

Becks considered. 'Both.'

With a booming laugh, Van slapped Becks's bare bottom. It stung. He rolled off the couch and strolled across the carpet and into the kitchen. Coffee came first, and he heaped grounds into the filter.

He switched on the machine. The phone rang.

Van muttered. Still naked, he sauntered to the instrument. 'Yeah?' He paused. 'Yeah, sure. I'll call her.' He

11

set down the receiver and cocked an eye through the doorway. 'Becks, for you.'

Her first instinct was that she couldn't talk to someone on the phone if she had no clothes on. She grabbed Van's discarded shirt and wrapped it round her as she dashed to pick up the phone. The way the shirt fell, it was no substitute for decency.

'Hello?'

'Captain Laird?'

Who the hell did he think it was? She knew at once it was the base. Like any professional, Captain Rebecca Laird always left contact numbers.

'Hultlander, ma'am, duty officer at Davis-Monthan. Uh . . . can you come into base right away, ma'am?'

Something was wrong and the back of Becks's neck prickled. 'What is it?'

'Some kinda mix-up over that BUFF we launched today, ma'am.'

It was two minutes past seven, Tuesday evening.

CHAPTER 2

Three groundcrew in overalls were at different points under the far-flung extremities of the B52 at four-fifteen on Tuesday afternoon and the six flying crew, yards away from the ground guys, stood by the bomber's nose. They held their bone domes in their hands and their bare heads were bowed. All six wore air force olive flight suits, with black boots. The captain was a tall, rangy, cowboyish man with a patrician bearing that his grizzled, crinkly, short-trimmed hair set off impressively. He had the cowboyish name of Bat Masterson, although he'd been christened not Bartholomew – like his namesake from the Old West of a hundred years earlier – but Virgil. He'd been a conscientious Roman Catholic believer all his life and now he led his aircrew in prayer.

'Almighty God our Heavenly Father, we bow before You in worship of Your Holy Name. Bless this our mission as we devote ourselves to Your sole true righteousness. Bless these warriors of the Cross who now lay down their lives in Your Name. Grant them – grant us – victory, O God. In the Name of Jesus Christ, amen.'

The other five muttered their amens.

Bat Masterson jammed his bone dome on his head, ducked his tall body under the lower panels of the B52's nose, stepped on to the crew ladder, and went quickly up inside the aircraft.

Of the five people who'd joined in Bat's prayer, one in particular found it an odd invocation. But then, this man hadn't flown before with General Bat Masterson.

Captain Jerry Yeaver wasn't quite Bat's height but had

the same lanky, long-limbed build; belying a seldom used but still fierce physical strength. He was a bespectacled, studious man, with hollow cheeks, gaunt, bright eyes and a square, clean-shaven jaw. He was the B52's EWO – electronic warfare officer.

He didn't go next up the crew ladder after Bat. That was the privilege of Lieutenant-Colonel Mario Peroni, the co-pilot, like Bat a B52 veteran of many years' standing. Mario's strutting walk gave a hint of the pride he rightly held in himself and his abilities: he was a man of experience, a confident man. He was a New Yorker, proud of his Italian ancestry, a stocky, five foot nine with bushy brows, a hook nose and a weathered tan. A crucifix nestled in the thick, black hair at the neck of the T-shirt he wore under his flight suit.

The gunner went next, Lieutenant-Colonel Russell Feehan. He was the oldest of them, a man in his early sixties, wearing glasses; his once chubby face was today grey, drawn, almost translucent. Russell was a touch taller than Mario yet he seemed smaller, his appearance oddly shrunken, his limbs thin, his hands bony. Climbing the ladder, he seemed to be dragging a great weight.

Usually in a B52 crew the gunner is the only man who's not an officer. But Russell Feehan had been an expert shot all his life and his last job had been gunnery training officer in a Strategic Air Command wing.

Jerry Yeaver ought to have been the next man up the ladder, because he was the last of the four whose crew stations were on the B52's 'first level' – the upper deck of the twin-deck aircraft. Instead, Jerry deferred instinctively to the navigator, who was supposed to sit below on the 'second level'.

The navigator was a woman. It was even rarer to have a woman in the crew than to have an officer manning the guns; and she was the only person in the crew who wasn't American-born. Her name was Mrs Tamasin Penhale

Masterson, but she wasn't married any more. Her married name didn't come directly from Bat Masterson but from Bat's son, Edward. Edward was dead.

Jerry knew perfectly well that Tamasin Masterson wasn't on this flight for a jolly, she qualified on merit. She had experience and she had talent; she flew Learjets for a living. By the time she came to convert to jets she'd already had turbine experience in Britain in her University Air Squadron, a pre-training corps attached to the universities; she'd handled Royal Air Force multi-engine types as co-pilot, up to the C130 four-turboprop transport. Very few women anywhere in the world had actually handled a B52 in flight but Tamasin was one of them. On paper it had been a USAF-RAF officer exchange. The Penhale family were ancient Cornish squirearchy and the present couple of generations were lifelong friends of the Mastersons. Bat had pulled some strings for Tamasin, years earlier, when he'd been commanding a B52 outfit at Eielson, Alaska.

These days, Jerry Yeaver tended to wince at the mention of Eielson, Alaska.

'Go ahead,' Jerry muttered, shyly avoiding Tamasin's eye.

'No, you go.' She was a compact, sturdily built woman, at five five a lot smaller than Jerry, her charcoal hair cut very short. She wasn't naturally vain, she just took a proper pride in herself, and today her make-up was carefully understated, the way she'd have worn it if she'd been captaining that Lear with Donald Trump for a passenger. She liked to be taken seriously but she liked men who opened doors for her, too.

Still Jerry hesitated.

Tamasin laughed, and Jerry grinned warily, and the sixth crew member laughed heartily and clapped both of them on the shoulders.

15

'Well, if you guys can't make your minds up, guess I'll have to go!'

Colonel Chuck Brantley was the radar navigator and in any case he had to get into his seat before Tamasin did. He was a rotund, jovial fifty-two-year-old, five eight, with no white or grey in his rich black moustache, just a trace of nicotine stain, and he hopped up the crew ladder more nimbly than his pot belly might have led you to expect.

Jerry deferred to Tamasin and climbed the short, steep ladder to the B52's second level. Chuck Brantley, puffing a bit, was levering himself across the navigator's ejector seat and into the one next to it. He glanced Tamasin over as she climbed in after Jerry and slid in beside Chuck. She was a purposeful woman, rather intense right now. So was Jerry, and that was about the way Chuck wanted him. What Chuck noted about Tamasin was the feminine touches, the tiny earrings, the trace of perfume, the varnish on her efficiently clipped nails. Her deep, dark eyes were hooded, menacing, but Chuck wondered how she got a small hand like that around eight power levers when she flew the thing.

From the second level a vertical ladder ran up to the first and Jerry climbed it. It was as black inside the big bomber as it was outside; all the metal surfaces were black. After the endless spaciousness of Davis-Monthan's flight line it felt constricted and, for a moment, the dread of what was to come caught Jerry by the gut. He levered himself out on to the metal deck of the first level, ducking his head under the cables and tubing slung from the cabin ceiling, and climbed into the EWO station without a glance forward to see what Bat and Mario were doing, up front at the controls.

Jerry checked inside his flight case just once more, though he knew the provisions he'd brought were all there. He stowed the flight case, strapped into his ejector seat, and looked to his right as he settled his bone dome on his head. The EWO station and the gunner's were side by side and faced aft, and Jerry's eyes met Russell Feehan's. There was pain in Russell's.

'You OK?' Jerry murmured, concerned.

Russell gave him a wry grin. 'Guess I'll make it.' Then with his bony hand trembling slightly he swallowed a painkiller.

'Bright Angel,' Bat said on the radio in his lazy Arizona drawl. 'Groundcrew. Outside leads?'

Bat and Mario were the only two crew who could see out. Even they couldn't, sometimes, when they pulled the nuclear flash blinds down. Today what they saw was flat landscape all the way to the steely blue horizon and a cloudless, almost colourless, sky.

'Outside leads all detached,' the groundcrew chief said in Bat's headset.

'Hatches?' Bat said.

'All hatches closed.'

'Outrigger chocks?'

'Outrigger chocks removed.'

'Thanks, bud. OK, fellas, here goes, get your fingers in your ears.'

Bat fired the cartridge starter on Number One. They numbered the engines from left to right facing forward: Number One was the lefthand engine in the lefthand outer pod. At once, the needles swung up on the rev counter and the turbine temperature gauge. Bat moved the Number One power lever forward. He settled the rpm on 80 per cent. Jet engine rev counters give you a percentage of the maximum. In contrast with a piston engine, turbine speeds of 15,000 rpm are not uncommon, and percentages are easier to read.

Bat started Number Two. He went through the drills briskly, methodically, until all eight were running. On the radio panel he selected the ground control frequency. He thumbed the mike switch.

'Davis-Monthan ground control, good afternoon, sirs,

this is Bright Angel with all eight engines running good, outbound for Perth, Western *Oz*-tray-lie-ay. This is for radio check and airfield information, I thank *you*.'

Jerry Yeaver couldn't see the mountain skyline. In the rear-facing ejector seat he could see Russell to his right, that translucent skin, head back, a bit strained; and the radar scope and radio and radar and electronic countermeasures controls on the panel facing him; and the ribs and metal inner skin to his left. He could feel the tremble of power flooding through the airframe. He'd felt that plenty of times before but it wasn't so familiar that it lost its excitement.

As Bright Angel started to taxi, Tamasin Penhale Masterson was going through the most important action of the flight: fixing Buster in the coffee holder so he didn't fall out. Buster was a fluffy toy white rabbit and her best friend at school had given him to her on her seventeenth birthday, the day she flew her first solo, in a Cessna 152. Ever since that day, Buster had flown with her every time she'd gone up and he'd always brought her luck.

On her headphones she could hear Bat copying his airways clearance.

She was tense and she inhaled deeply. Navigation was a routine task and she knew she was good at it, she ought to be able to relax.

Today wasn't a routine day, though, and they all knew it.

The gyros on the inertial navigation system were running now and Tamasin started putting in the co-ordinates for the waypoints they would use. She started with the co-ordinates for Davis-Monthan itself: 110 degrees 50 minutes west, 32 degrees 15 minutes north.

'You know what it does to a guy,' Chuck Brantley said, 'when you take big sighs like that?'

Tamasin ignored him.

'Hm,' he said. 'Sure does.'

The nav and radar nav stations faced forward. Tamasin preferred it that way, despite all the flight safety arguments about rear-facing seats being better. She could feel the B52 rumbling ponderously along the tarmac and the thrill of excitement inside her was almost sensual. They'd *almost* done it.

Chuck's hand stroked her left knee.

'Hey, get off, man, I have work to do.' She didn't want to get too annoyed with him, too early. This flight was going to be quite long enough to have a good quarrel on.

With the afternoon sun of January in his eyes, Bat brought Bright Angel to the holding point and turned the big aircraft at right angles to the runway.

'Clear to roll, Bright Angel,' the controller said. 'Traffic is zilch.'

Mario Peroni didn't trust that, he was craning out the righthand cockpit window to look for A10 fighters on the approach. But there really weren't any.

'Bright Angel,' Bat said. 'Lining up.'

He steered the B52 right round to the left, on to the runway centreline, and pushed all eight power levers right to the stops with one big, battered hand. Full bore on eight hefty military jet engines shoved two hundred tons of Boeing engineering accelerating down Davis-Monthan's runway fourteen.

A long, long, long, long roll.

From the pilot's seat you couldn't see the wings without twisting round and losing the visual marker you'd picked for your takeoff run, but Bat knew B52s: he could always tell when the tips, the first things to fly, started flying. He kept his right hand jamming the power levers against the stops and his left hand tenderly cradling the chunky plastic control yoke to see when it started telling him things. After a long time testing it, he felt the movement as the tail came alive.

As one piece, like a lump of concrete levitating, the whole

aircraft drifted almost accidentally up off the runway, nose down as if having second thoughts about doing this in the first place. Never in his flying career had Bat known another aircraft that took off ass first. But this was it, *we have lift-off*, and he cleaned up flaps and gear, all the multifarious bits of it, aware out of the corner of his eye of Mario, lower lip jutting, beginning the routines that in another age, another aircraft, would have been the flight engineer's job: the fuel transfers.

'Davis-Monthan tower, sirs, we are in your debt. This is Bright Angel, en route for Perth, have one real good day on *us*!' Then Bat Masterson cut the outside radio and switched to intercom. 'OK, brave team. Ain't no turning back now!'

He'd known there'd be high spirits but he hadn't quite expected the uninhibited cheering that came back to him through the headset. Tamasin's voice was clearest with her feminine high pitch, but Chuck and Mario were whooping and Jerry was going *ra, ra, right on*, and even Russell was chipping in. And Bat knew the way Russell was feeling. They'd done it. They'd got into the air with 48,000 gallons of Jet A kerosene fuel, and a B52 to get it away in. Harness recklessly undone, Chuck threw his arms round Tamasin, smooched her, and forgot until the moment of impact the way the bone domes would intervene.

On the level above, Bat anticipated it. 'Wow, team, we did it! Radar, get your hands off the navigator, we need her working!'

Jerry Yeaver was looking sidelong at Russell Feehan because he liked the man and he was worried about him. Russell looked looser now. He was gently flipping worry beads that his wife had bought him years before in the Plaka in Athens.

'We're staying on station for this leg, crew,' Bat said. He had the B52 trimmed out and they were already climbing through 18,000 feet. He had the cabin pressurized and they wore their oxygen masks dangling loosely by their chins, putting them to their faces only when they wanted to use the intercom mikes. The rushing roar flooding the cabin was rock steady and the air over Arizona was calm.

Chuck lit a cigarette, grinned sideways at Tamasin, and blew smoke through his nose. Tamasin didn't grin back, she hated cigarette smoke.

'This is your captain speaking,' Bat said on the intercom. 'We're on our way. We can fairly safely say there ain't no-one gonna stop us now. We have the most difficult part of this behind us – the part that lies ahead is just the most dangerous, that's all.' He made it sound as if the dangers didn't matter. Maybe he was right, Tamasin thought. 'Every one of us on this team believes in our mission,' Bat said, 'and we're gonna kill this one. We have a long haul ahead of us but we're gonna surmount all those difficulties. Let's go for it, team! Make every bomb count!'

Again the whoops and the cheering.

Forty thousand feet. Bat levelled out. The afternoon sun was on the nose and it caught the small, metallic snaking of the Colorado river seven and a half miles below. They came over California.

'Los Angeles radar, good afternoon, Bright Angel is a B52 approaching you from Tucson, flight level four zero zero, en route via Hawaii for Western Australia.'

They had the flight plan. Clearance confirmed. Under the nose there was nothing to distinguish the California desert from the Arizona desert. The winter sun dazzled Bat and he put his shades on rather than lower his visor.

Mario was fidgeting with his fuel transfers, big, stubby fingers on the switches. Uneasy, distrustful, he toyed a moment with the crucifix at his neck. Bat knew of old that Mario was about to start checking up on people. It was a neurotic reverse side to the New York-Italian machismo.

'Gunner – anything on radar?'

21

'No, sir,' Russell said, deadpan.

'EWO,' Mario said, 'who has radar on us?'

'LA radar,' Jerry said.

Mario snarled: 'Who the hell *else*?'

Long body tense in the ejector seat harness, Jerry scanned the spectrum analyser again, scanned the frequencies. 'No-one else.'

'Goddammit,' Mario exploded, 'there *has* to be someone else! Goddam well find out!'

'Sir!' Rattled, Jerry searched harder.

'Radar,' Mario growled, 'what do you have?'

'A pain in the ass,' Chuck Brantley replied, '*sir*!'

That annoyed Mario, the way it was meant to, and Mario didn't yet feel like tangling with Chuck. 'Nav,' he snapped, 'how are we for time and track?'

'About on, sir,' Tamasin replied with languid confidence.

It was an English-style answer when what Mario wanted was American-style precision. 'OK, nav, then get us goddam well *right* on!'

Bat frowned at Mario, his hand resting on the yoke while the autopilot did the flying.

'*Co*-pilot,' Tamasin said icily, 'we are right on.'

'So why'n'cha say so straight off?'

Chuck laughed into the intercom. 'Looks like we need a phrase book to translate English into good American.'

Usually Chuck was good at reducing tension, but this time Tamasin wasn't so ready to be pacified. 'I am *trying*, co-pilot, to keep from overreacting to people who expect me to prove myself when I've proved myself plenty of times already.'

'But not on this crew!' Mario said.

That was true, Tamasin reflected. This crew had never flown together before and never would again.

This time when Chuck put his podgy hand on her knee

it was in genuine concern. Into the mike he said: 'Ease off, Mario, give the girl a break.'

'*Everyone* on this crew has to know their jobs,' Mario said doggedly. 'Everyone on this crew has to be able to take the rough with the smooth – and it's gonna be rough where *we're* going!'

Tamasin understood that message; she'd understood it all along. Mario had never flown with a woman crew member before and he had real misgivings about her. Well, he'd find out a few things, that was all.

Mario went back to Jerry. 'OK, EWO, who else besides LA has us on radar?'

'No-one, sir.' All these ranks were just so much fiction these days, since none of them was still in the military. Even so, Jerry couldn't suppress the old reflexes, especially with a man who'd put him on the defensive.

'You mean you can't find anyone.'

Jerry raised his voice. 'Sir, I mean there are no radar waves striking this aircraft other than the ones out of LA!'

'Jesus!' Mario turned to Bat but he'd left his intercom deliberately switched on. '*Now* do you see what I meant when I told you I wasn't happy about going into this thing carrying guys who have no combat experience?'

Tamasin heard that. She'd been meant to.

Jerry made a mistake. He defended himself, the protest audible in his voice. 'Listen, I have all the time I need in combat exercise; I have . . .'

'Combat *exercise*?' The scorn in Mario's voice rippled through the roar in the big jet's cabin. 'Son, you're talking to guys who flew Linebacker missions in '72 when North Vietnam airspace had more SAMs and MiGs and triple-A than anywhere in the world before or since.' Linebacker, Tamasin recalled, had been the operation to flatten targets around Hanoi, using B52s; Bat had flown on those missions and didn't mention them much. Triple-A was anti-aircraft artillery. 'Combat *exercise* is kindergarten compared with when guys are *really* trying to kill you. How do we know how you're gonna react when the SAMs start coming up at us? You have the attitude like you wanna chicken out right now!'

'Cool it, crew,' Bat Masterson said in his deep, patrician, lazy Arizona drawl. He gave Mario a look. Bat's theory of leadership was to treat all his team members as equal adults and he didn't like having to play the part of policeman. 'On this crew, we *all* have to function together as a team. And we will. I picked all of you, and Chuck down there helped me pick you. We're gonna kill that sonofabitch, OK? But we'll do it that much easier if we all get along just fine.'

Jerry yanked his mask away from his face and slumped over the panel so that his bone dome hit the hard transparency of his radar scope. Russell laid a hand on Jerry's shoulder. Jerry said something but in the noise washing round them Russell couldn't hear, and he put his face close to Jerry's to listen.

'I wish I could get off this plane and shoot myself right now.'

The older man strengthened his grip gently on Jerry's shoulder. 'No, you don't, buddy. We're all in this to the finish.'

Jerry said through the jet noise: 'The only good part about that is, we all get killed at the finish.'

Russell didn't have a ready answer for that. He kept his hand on Jerry's shoulder.

Below at the navigator's station, Tamasin slid Chuck a covert glance because it was true what Bat had said: Chuck was the man who'd picked half this crew. Chuck's contact network was a source of wonder to her.

Tamasin wasn't one of those Chuck had picked, though, because she and Bat were the two who'd dreamed this mission up in the first place. She reached out an index and chucked Buster, the fluffy rabbit, under the chin, while Chuck grinned knowingly and lit another cigarette.

In a pause between fuel transfers, Mario looked down. The coast of California was an intricate fretwork of golden brown, and the waves gliding in off the Pacific were as delicate as Venetian lace. The beaches slid under the nose and out of sight and the landmass of continental USA was behind them.

'Pilot, crew,' Bat said. 'Stand by to depressurize. Masks on. Oxygen check.'

Tamasin clipped up her face mask. Maybe eventually she'd stop noticing its pungent smell of rubber. The oxygen flowed, the intercom worked, the crew reported in to their captain. Bat cut the intercom and switched back to the LA frequency.

'OK, guys, this is Bright Angel ready to sign off, I guess.'

'Bright Angel, LA radar, good to've spoken to you. Contact Hawaii Oceanic.' The disembodied voice quoted the new frequency. 'Have a nice flight, now.'

The B52 was depressurizing already. Bat switched the intercom back in.

'Pilot, crew. Harness tight. Nav?'

'Ah . . . twenty seconds,' Tamasin said. 'Nineteen. Eighteen.'

Bat should have been on the radio to Hawaii by now. Instead he was on intercom, coolly cutting through Tamasin's countdown. 'EWO, any traffic?'

'Negative,' Jerry said.

'Ten,' Tamasin said. 'Pilot, your new course is one six four mag.'

Bat said: 'Confirm one six four.'

'Stand by to set your new course. Two. One. *Now*.'

Bat pulled back all eight power levers. The spoilers came out on the long, thin, mercilessly swept wing as he rolled the B52 into a 120-degree turn to the left, trimmed out, and started losing height fast. It was six o'clock Tuesday evening, Arizona time, one o'clock Wednesday morning on Greenwich Mean.

CHAPTER 3

In Van Burkart's bathroom on the eastern edge of Tucson, Arizona, Captain Rebecca Laird threw off Van's shirt, slid the door panel shut behind her, and ran the shower quickly. She sluiced herself off, jumped out, and rapidly towelled down. On the shelf she'd placed a little bottle of her usual perfume. Becks was a professional. Just as she would always leave contact numbers in case people needed her – at the risk, as tonight, of ruining a domestic evening – she would always make sure she could get at the things she was likely to need.

Van put his head round the door as she zipped up the jeans on her long legs. 'What d'you reckon it is?'

Some kinda mix-up, the duty officer had said. She hadn't understood. 'Sounds like they're scared it crashed.' She buttoned her blouse quickly, pulled on her jumper and snapped on the ponytail ring to keep her sandy hair in some sort of order.

Van was in the living room in slacks and a T-shirt. 'I'll call you,' Becks promised, and gave him a quick peck on the cheek. He was waving goodbye as she switched on the Volkswagen's engine.

*   *   *

Afterglow from the direction of California made the gentle undulations and the low, square buildings of Tucson look black, and the lights were red and yellow and very bright. The roads weren't busy and Becks was jumping traffic lights. At the Craycroft Road main gate she held up her

26

pass to the window. Then she broke the base speed limit, racing up to the control tower where the duty officer was waiting.

She'd crossed the ground-floor room that afternoon on her way upstairs to watch Bright Angel depart. With seven big men in it, it looked crowded at not quite half past seven in the evening. The man in the USAF uniform was flustered. The others, in blazers or hooded sweatshirts, showed emotions ranging from the indignant to the irate. Becks hadn't met the flustered one more than a couple of times before but she had him checked out. He had captain's bars that he'd still be wearing when they pensioned him off in another five years or so and his name badge read Hultlander. His eyes bulged behind his glasses, his puffy cheeks testified to his taste for french fries and his girth to his distaste for exercise. Officer or not, this man wouldn't hurt a fly, never mind make decisions on his own.

Relieved at the sight of Becks, he turned to the nearest of the angry men. 'Uh, this is Captain Laird. Captain, this is Colonel Powell.'

They were in civvies the way she was. She shook Powell's hand. He was Van's size and build, with a pencil moustache, but his eyes were small and hard and challenging, unlike Van's.

'How can I help you gentlemen?' Becks smiled.

'We came here to take a preliminary look at Bright Angel,' Powell said. 'We have a flight plan to take her to Perth tomorrow.'

The penny started to drop.

In plain reflex Becks began: 'But Bright Angel flew . . .' Only of course they knew about that.

'No, ma'am.' Powell was trying to keep his temper and he didn't think much of Davis-Monthan. 'Bright Angel is still out there on the flight line.'

It had been a *different* B52 today. Using Bright Angel's flight plan and callsign, altered for date and time.

Beck's brain still hadn't caught up. She turned to Hultlander. She wasn't sure which was bulging more, his eyes or his tummy. 'But which BUFF was it we launched today?'

'We don't know, ma'am.' He almost stumbled over his words.

Becks's voice sharpened. 'Well, do you have the copy of the flight plan?'

Wordlessly, Hultlander handed it over. Becks scanned it and glanced up. 'Captain's name – Powell.' Her eyes met those of the man who said he was Colonel Powell.

Equally laconically, the man flipped a dog-eared US passport at her, covered in visas and vaccination certificates. It looked as if he really was Colonel Powell. He jabbed a finger at the flight plan.

'This is not my signature, ma'am. And lookit here.' He pointed at the spaces for aircraft type and registration.

For aircraft type it gave: Boeing B52G. For serial: 59-2603.

'That is the plane,' Powell said, 'that is out there on the ramp right now.' He spoke slowly and emphatically, as if addressing a dull pupil. 'And *our* flight plan is for tomorrow – Wednesday. Not today.' He showed Becks the copy.

Becks looked at Hultlander.

'I called radar in LA and Hawaii,' the tubby man said. 'They couldn't find it.' Not bad, Becks had to admit: going for *where* it was, not *which* it was. 'LA signed it off normally, just before six our time. Hawaii wasn't even expecting it – the flight plan never got circulated that far. Looks like it just vanished over the Pacific.'

B52s didn't just vanish like that. 'Wait,' Becks said. She fought to remember what she'd seen that afternoon. There wouldn't even be pictures of it, she realized. *Photos before a mission bring bad luck.* Vietnam vet or not, there went one crafty captain. Becks caught Powell's eye. 'Today's flight was supposed to leave a smoke trail on takeoff — it didn't. But it didn't have a long, tall fin and rudder like those Ds out in the Graveyard — it was a short, broad tail.'

'H-model,' Powell said. 'Last of the line. Built 'em at Boeings in Wichita in '61, '62. The engines are turbofans, not the old straight jets. That's how come you didn't get the smoke from the water injection.' He watched Becks, hard-eyed. 'The air force still flies Hs. They have a lot of up-to-date gear on those birds — all the microchips, state-of-the-art nav systems, bombing computer . . .'

A police siren, outside the base, drifted on the night stillness. Beyond the windows all was black, and the room was chilly.

'Wait a minute,' Becks said edgily, 'let's just *find* this goddam BUFF, let's not stand around guessing what it might have on it.' Hultlander was blinking rapidly behind his glasses. Becks asked him: 'Did you call General Hartmore yet?'

'Not yet, ma'am.' Phoning the base commander to tell him something like *this* had happened came under the heading of valorous conduct beyond the call of duty.

Shit, Becks thought. 'OK, leave me to do that.' Hands on her hips, she turned back to Powell and his crew. 'Gentlemen, my apologies. We do have to get to the bottom of this and there are some urgent inquiries to make, and in view of that I'm afraid I see no purpose in your waiting here. Uh . . . especially since I am grounding Bright Angel right now until we have this thing cleared up.' She'd expected objections from Powell. Instead, he seemed simply nonplussed. She said: 'You have somewhere to stay?'

'We do, ma'am,' Powell said heavily, and glanced at his crew. 'OK, guys.'

They were filing out of the control tower as Becks started her calls.

First, security. B52G serial 59–2603 was staying right
where it was until further notice. Next, the main base
switchboard. 'This is Captain Laird, A2. Anyone who
calls in wanting any public information about anything
to do with the base, particularly aircraft movements' –
a *movement* is the standard aviation-industry term for
a takeoff or landing – 'switch 'em through to me. Any
information to go out of here is to come from me. I'll call
the PR office.' She hung up.

Without looking at the duty officer, she muttered: 'We
daren't let this get out. We can't let the public know we
lost a B52.' She glanced over. 'And, hey, let's not even use
the name, in case someone overhears us. We need a code
name.'

Unhappy, Hultlander blinked a bit. 'Bright Angel,' he
mused.

Becks snapped her fingers. 'That's it! *Dark* Angel, not
Bright Angel. That's what we'll use.' And now for the
difficult bit.

She picked up the phone. No point putting this off.
Chewing her lip, she dialled Major-General Hartmore's
home number.

He answered on the third ring, in person. 'Yeah?' No
name, no number, just the high, harsh, metallic, sawn-off
syllable.

'Sir, Captain Laird, A2, calling from the base. This line
is insecure.' First things first. She was making herself sound
brisk and efficient, she was speaking rapidly. Most of the
lines out of the base were insecure; that was routine; the
select few hardened ones were used for official calls and
anyway almost all lines to private homes were insecure.
They might have bugs on them; they would certainly emit
radiation that could be picked up and read by signals
intelligence receivers. So you made circumlocutions. 'Sir,

30

there's what looks like a serious mistake over one of today's takeoffs. I'm afraid I shall need to explain to you face to face.'

'God *damn*, Captain.' Hartmore was too professional to let anything slip on an insecure line, but he didn't mean to leave Becks in doubt as to how he felt about her. 'OK, I'll come in.' He hung up.

Becks blew out her cheeks and leaned on the phone.

The base was very quiet, very lonely. She could almost hear the dry rustle of sandy soil, stirred in the night air. Her hair was a mess. She could feel Hultlander's bulgy eyes gazing helplessly at her.

Still without looking at him she muttered: 'But who the hell *were* they on that crew today?'

'I have no idea, ma'am.'

Becks wanted to snap. She'd known he had no idea. She turned, sharply, one slim, long-fingered hand on her hip, the other still on the phone.

Innocently, Hultlander said: 'Captain Laird, ma'am, why don't we just put out a radio call on Guard?'

Guard, the military emergency channel. For a moment, it had the simplicity of genius, then Becks recognized the snags. 'Don't like that, Captain. We don't know what codes Dark Angel has, so we'd have to send in clear, and then the whole world would know. Besides, even bounced off a satellite, the transmission would be to a certain extent directional, and we don't know what the direction should be. Anyway, do you really think they'd answer?' Irritably she reached to fiddle with her ponytail ring.

'Guess not, ma'am,' Hultlander mumbled.

Becks finished fiddling. 'OK,' she said, 'that was a *B52H* that took off today, and it didn't come out of the Graveyard. Here's why: they've been getting Bright Angel ready for weeks, and we'd'a all seen it if they'd been getting *two* BUFFs ready. So Dark Angel musta come in from *somewhere*.' She jabbed a finger a Hultlander. 'Can you go check the aircraft movement logs? I want a note of any H-model that arrived in . . . well, I guess it can't be more than the last week.'

'Yes, ma'am!' It was something he could do.

Frowning, Becks left the man leafing through the reports and entered the inner office. It wasn't her own office, she didn't know where most of the things were, but she knew where the scrambler phone was.

She called the CIA in Langley, Virginia. It was a bit later in Langley: a quarter to eight here in Arizona was a quarter to ten in Virginia. She'd only ever had dealings with the CIA once or twice before, she was a bit nervous of them; but she knew what she had to ask for.

She gave her coded authority as Davis-Monthan's head of A2. 'Can you reassign one of your satellites over the Pacific? We're looking for a B52.' She gave them the details, the sign-off time from Los Angeles radar.

'No problem, ma'am,' the smooth, disembodied male voice replied. 'We'll be in touch.'

They hung up.

Slumping her long body in the borrowed swivel chair, Becks chewed her lip, thinking, worrying. Thanks to Hultlander, bumbling as he was in some ways, LA radar was now alert in case Dark Angel came back, and Hawaii radar in case it staged through there.

On the other hand, either event was a bit unlikely. Becks racked her brains.

Who the hell *were* they? – she thought. Who let them in? Who might have *seen* them? She jumped quickly out of the chair and put her head round the inner office door.

'Captain, can you get someone else to look through those flight movement logs? Right now I need you to talk to ops and get a trace on the groundcrew who dispatched Dark Angel.'

CHAPTER 4

Libya, the summer before the flight.
Desert landscapes don't give you much to relieve the eye and Tariq Talal's training camp in northwest Libya wasn't an exception. Still, you could say that cut down on the distractions when you were seventeen, scared, and forcing yourself along the assault course.

Merciless, the instructor in his boots and olive fatigues yelled in Palestinian-accented Arabic: '*Faster!*'

Sweat rolled into Adem Elhaggi's eyes and he didn't know why he was on the assault course in the first place. He was brain, not brawn; he was good at maths and physics and he'd wanted to study electrical engineering and they'd all said that was fine: when he'd finished his studies they'd teach him how to make bomb timers.

'*Faster!*'

Adem was 10 feet off the ground and quite close to panic. He'd been through the flooded pipe, and that had been bad enough; he had the fire jump to go yet and he wasn't looking forward to it; and right now he was upside down on the ropeway with a couple of kilos of live ammunition on his belt and a loaded AK47 hanging off his shoulder. He'd never have imagined how badly it would restrict movement.

Breath shallow, gasping softly, Adem grabbed forward with his hand, at the same time hurrying his foot movement.

It was his foot that missed.

One minute he was still hanging on, crying out now, still pretty certain he could get that grip back. Then as he groped for it, something else went, and then *wham*.

The first thing that reached him as his head cleared was relief that the AK hadn't gone off; he really had put the safety on properly. The second was the instructor's voice, with several quite unjustified assertions about Adem's mother. The third was pain, wave after wave after wave of it, turning him sick. He'd come down with his right shoulder slap on top of that rifle.

'Come on, boy, you're dead, clear out of it! Come on, move!'

Adem struggled. For a moment nothing happened, and the instructor shouted again, then with tears of sheer pain filling his eyes, Adem forced himself. He moved. At first it was a crawl, then he was on his feet, doubled over, limping.

The instructor called out, but this time not at him.

Clutching his shoulder, face harsh with pain, Adem turned. It was Zoheir on the ropeway now. She was seventeen, the same as him; he didn't know her other name; she was the only girl on this course. Adem hadn't expected to see girls on it at all. She had the same weight of ammo on her belt as the boys had, the same Kalashnikov slung from her shoulder, and the agile grace she showed, swarming along the ropeway, turned Adem's pain into near-despair. He'd so much wanted to impress Zoheir. All the boys wanted to.

Adem went where the instructor signalled him to. It hurt where the AK weighed on his shoulder; it hurt when he transferred it to the other shoulder; it hurt when he moved – he'd broken it, he was sure now; he wouldn't even be able to write in his exercise books for weeks.

When the instructor finally realized, he just took Adem's rifle and ammo off him and sent him walking alone through the sun to the medical office. The last thing Adem saw as he left the assault course was Zoheir, springing nimbly over the fire trench with her rifle in both hands. That was all he needed.

In the medical office Dr Jabran dropped what she was doing and looked after Adem at once, all sympathy and efficiency. She was Palestinian like Adem, a plump, stocky woman of fifty who, like the rest of the very few women in the camp, wore headscarf and chador, except on exercises, and who treated the young trainees as if they were her own kids; yet her own were grown up and living far away.

'Sit down, Adem.' She took his shirt off herself, she didn't call one of the nurses.

He sat with his eyes half closed. It didn't matter how hard he tried, this pain wasn't something he could just get used to. He could feel Dr Jabran's fingers, expertly probing. New pain jerked a sharp suck of air through his teeth.

'It isn't broken, Adem. It's dislocated.'

'Oh, good.' He was determined to sound casual, determined to be macho about it like the old hands among Tariq Talal's guerrillas; especially in front of a woman.

'This will hurt.'

'It's all right.'

But of course it was nothing of the sort. She reset the shoulder. Then she busied herself on the far side of the shadowy room while Adem let the tears dry on his face and pretended he hadn't shed them in the first place.

Back at his side, bulky in the dark chador with her brown face smiling and tenderness in her wise eyes, she had a mug of water and two aspirins. 'I'm afraid we're out of pain killers.'

'It's all right.'

'Just rest now.'

Adem hadn't thought a thing like this could make you so exhausted. At last the pain was ebbing and he drowsed, aware no more than dimly of the movements in the room, the voices. Then there was something in those voices that woke him with a start.

'What? Are they back?'

Dr Jabran wasn't in the room now, it was one of the nurses. There were four nurses at Tariq Talal's camp, two men and two women, and this was the very dark one of the male nurses; Adem knew him by sight but hadn't spoken to him.

The dark nurse grinned, his eyes crafty. 'They're back – and it was a victory!'

A terrorist action, and it had been another success. Everyone in the camp knew that Tariq Talal had been out with Ali Ben Mokhtar, his chief lieutenant, somewhere in western Europe. Eagerly Adem asked: 'What happened?'

But the dark nurse just grinned knowingly and got on with what he was doing.

Dr Jabran was in the doorway. Adem caught the sadness in her eyes.

'Violence begets violence,' she murmured wryly. 'Murder begets murder. People need me here, but . . . sometimes we should ask ourselves whether there isn't another way.'

Adem stared. Dr Jabran turned her back and left.

Walking in the late afternoon heat from the medical office to the trainees' quarters, Adem passed Tariq Talal's Command Council HQ. Zoheir was coming out. With the exercise over she was just another shape in a headscarf and chador, but those eyes were unmistakable. Involuntarily Adem remembered the shape she'd been, moving on the ropeway. Recognition lit up her face as she saw him, but she had a worried air. She was hurrying, but Adem caught her.

'Zoheir! Are they in there?'

She didn't nod. In the Middle East, a backwards nod means *no*. 'Tariq Talal and Ali Ben Mokhtar,' she murmured, voice low, troubled eyes wide. Her gaze lingered on Adem but she was too preoccupied to ask how he was. She muttered: 'Mustafa was killed.'

Shock jumped inside Adem's chest. He remembered Mustafa. Big, fit, mid-twenties, one of the best marksmen in camp. 'But . . . they said it was a victory.'

'Many of theirs were killed. Of ours, only Mustafa.'

'What was it?'

'An airport.' Zoheir hurried away. She hadn't asked after Adem's shoulder.

The pain of it hadn't gone away, but that was just something you put up with. Adem watched Zoheir's heels and the flow of her chador, then glanced at the Command Council HQ. It was a place all were in awe of. If they let Zoheir in and out of there all the time she must be even better than Adem thought she was.

In the trainees' quarters, Adem was first with the news about Mustafa. They were all Arab boys in their late teens and they laughed and joked and made fun of Adem for dislocating his shoulder. It seemed pretty friendly but Adem's tolerant smile was cautious nevertheless. He was naturally skinny; he wasn't so tough and macho as they were – hence his act – and he couldn't quite be sure they really liked him. With his books and his scientific knowledge and his engineering flair he managed to make them all suspicious of him. But this was different, Adem had a tale to tell, and they all started in with their different yarns.

All sorts of stories went the rounds of the camp, some of them more plausible than others. One that had stuck in Adem's mind recounted an attack by Tariq Talal in Berlin, one he'd carried out with typical reckless courage, and entirely alone. A US staff colonel was flying into the still-divided city via Tegel airport. There was nothing individually special about him, he was just a handy American. A couple of bodyguards met the man and took him outside to the waiting limo. Unfortunately for them, Tariq Talal was also waiting, with a Kawasaki bike, a gym bag, and inside the gym bag a Heckler and Koch HK54 chambered for 9mm. He gave them most of the magazine from a range of 12 metres just as the colonel was getting into the limo. Both bodyguards died but the colonel only lost his right arm. The Americans shot back, but not for long: there were too many uninvolved civilians around. Half an hour later the Kawasaki was parked outside Kochstrasse U-Bahn station, Tariq Talal was strolling out of Friedrichstrasse station on the east side, and the USAF was tightening up its security.

Talal still fought in the front line with his warriors and that impressed Adem.

It was night now. Outside, the clear air had a chilly bite, but the trainees warmed up at the long trestle table under the paraffin lanterns, wolfing down rice and scrawny chicken and chickpeas.

Ali Ben Mokhtar sauntered in.

Everyone turned. Ali Ben Mokhtar commanded almost as much respect and adoration in this camp as Tariq Talal himself did. He was a stringy six foot with world-weary eyes and care-stooped shoulders. There was a cynical, downward twist to one corner of his wide, thin mouth and a scraggy, full beard on his sunken face that showed a lot of white mixed in with the black. He was forty but could have passed for fifty-five.

He greeted them, a battered palm raised. 'Don't stop eating. I have a victory to report.' They'd stopped eating anyway, too excited to go on. 'Yesterday by the grace of Allah our commandos attacked the servants of the Great Satan, America, at Frankfurt airport. Many were executed by our bullets and many more were slaughtered when the servants of the Great Satan fired upon our glorious commandos, hitting instead the very infidels they were meant to protect. Our brother Mustafa died a heroic martyr's death and is now in Paradise.' Again

Ben Mokhtar raised his bony hand. 'Great is the might of Allah and great is His victory!'

Adem joined in the cheering and the praising with the rest. He was puzzled, though. That last bit about Allah, Ben Mokhtar had muttered instead of declaiming, almost as though he could hardly make himself quite believe in it. Maybe he was missing Mustafa.

Numbers were one of Adem's strong points, and it hadn't escaped him that Ben Mokhtar hadn't talked numbers. Often they didn't. Often, when they did, it was sensible to take a nought off the end of the figure they quoted to arrive at a realistic total. Adem had been at Frankfurt airport once. He could picture it, the gleaming lights, the stunningly tidy ranks of check-ins, the travellers from everywhere in the world, the police patrolling with their submachineguns. Now Adem could picture it as a scene of carnage and horror.

A mighty shout went up. Tariq Talal himself came into the canteen.

He came in slowly, with the swaggering gait of a conqueror, his chunky, bearded face smiling fatly. This was the man who struck the Great Satan and who didn't run and hide, the man who stayed boldly at the head of his loyal commandos. He was bigger than Ben Mokhtar, four inches taller and a lot bulkier; and he was five years younger than his chief lieutenant but looked more so. His Arab headdress matched oddly well with the open-necked, red silk shirt that bulged over his belly and met the wide leather belt that held up his smart Western designer jeans.

He clenched his fist and held it high. 'Victory!'

They all roared in response. 'Victory! Victory! Victory!'

He spoke to them, his voice ringing out. To Adem it seemed less like an impromptu speech, more like a harangue. Then they were grabbing their rifles, all except

Adem, who didn't like to use a gun one-handed, and sweeping out into the night.

Stars danced in the velvet summer night and the muzzle flashes of the AKs danced in time. The jubilant bursts echoed and back-echoed off the slab sides of the quarters blocks and the Command Council HQ. The crowd pressed Adem on every side and swept him round and round the buildings. People kept knocking his shoulder but he didn't mind the pain, he was too excited.

Outlined against the night, the dome and minaret of the mosque at Bir al Hadh – mere yards away from the camp's high boundary wire – had the guardian silhouette of a SAM missile. Light washed a patch by the quarters block door, like a portion of a radar sweep, and in it Adem glimpsed Tariq Talal's towering figure. He held two of his soldiers paternally, his arms round their shoulders, his size dwarfing them. One of them, Adem saw suddenly, was Zoheir. She was gazing up at Talal, still in headscarf and chador. Her face was radiant and Adem felt a sudden pang.

'Adem, take care of your shoulder.'

He turned. Dr Jabran was at his elbow, watching him with concern.

'It's all right,' Adem said. It wouldn't have been manly to tell her how much it really hurt.

She touched his arm gently. 'Be careful. It might get bumped.'

Boys in the crowd were shouting Tariq Talal's praises. He was the one who struck telling blows, he was the one who would never forsake his warriors.

Dr Jabran listened, a wry look on her face. Softly she tut-tutted. 'Violence begets violence,' she repeated, just loudly enough for Adem to hear.

Stupid old woman, Adem thought.

CHAPTER 5

Eyes critical under wiry, grizzled brows, General Bat Masterson adjusted the power levers until all eight rev counters on the B52's engines showed the same. At one stage of his life Bat had played church organ regularly, and controlling the BUFF's jets was a bit like controlling organ stops. A thousand feet above the Pacific wave crests, the big aircraft kept up a rippling twitching in the choppy, cool air.

'We know this is a real long haul, crew,' Bat said on the intercom. 'Let's divide into sleep teams. We may not all be ready for it yet, but it'll help us to stay alert later. Who wants first go?'

Nobody volunteered.

Jerry Yeaver said from the rear-facing EWO station: 'I think Russell oughta go.'

They all knew why.

'OK,' Bat said. 'Get some sleep now, Russell. Mario, I want you to get some sleep, too.'

Anxious, Jerry watched Russell Feehan's pain-taut face as the older man readjusted his seat. You weren't supposed to take off your bone dome during flight but it was the only way to get anywhere near comfortable. A B52 is a military machine, not an airliner. Russell wrapped his worry beads round his hand and closed his eyes to doze. To Jerry, he seemed to slip into sleep reassuringly easily.

Jerry ran the toe of his boot around the corner of his flight case in its stowage. That was reassuring, too, knowing it was there, with its contents. Furtively Jerry glanced over his shoulder, half-afraid Mario might have caught him. Mario scared Jerry – his certainty of always being right and his implacable anger. And then there were the things his anger could lead to, like that time in Vietnam – if what they said about Mario was to be believed.

*   *   *

Bat unstrapped and climbed out of his seat, his long, lean body stooped under the low ceiling. Mario did likewise, and for a moment the B52 was controlled purely by the autopilot. Fleetingly the men's eyes met. Bat knew that Mario didn't trust anybody, but there was trouble in store if the co-pilot wouldn't trust even his captain. Holding his peace, Bat slid down into the righthand seat, Mario's co-pilot station, and touched fingertips to the yoke as Mario climbed over the trim wheels and power levers and into the pilot's seat. To sleep in the front of a B52, you wanted to be in the lefthand seat. Fuel management is pretty much a continuous job, and the controls for that are at the co-pilot's side.

Mario toyed with his crucifix, looked severe, then settled down with his feet clear of the rudder pedals and went to sleep.

Bat went on with the fuel transfers. His face thoughtful, he lit a cigarette.

They were flying south-east. Out of sight of them to the left lay the coastline of Baja California, Mexico. On the instrument panel, in the middle above the engine gauges, Bat had mounted three watches. One was set to Arizona time, to give a reference for how long they'd been flying; one was set to zulu time – Greenwich Mean; and the third was the aircraft's own time, local for where it happened to be.

Bat blew smoke, the taste sour in his mouth. He'd given up smoking when the Vietnam war ended because Alice,

42

his wife, had begged him to. But now it didn't matter any more.

Arizona time was 1835, zulu time 0135. Here over the Pacific it was 1735 and the lights in the sky and the wash of the ocean were tirelessly beautiful. Fine cirrus veined the distant pale blue and the waves were steely and green and vengeful. The engine note, ceaseless through the bone dome, made 'white noise', and Bat was aware of a faint, pleasing tension in the pit of his stomach. He had the cigarette in the corner of his mouth as he worked the pumps, moving fuel outer to inner, aft to centre, keeping the B52 in balance. His eyes ranged methodically over flight instruments and engine gauges but he'd been doing this for so many years that it didn't take concentration any longer, it left his mind free to dream.

Alice's face came back, and it was as if she was right beside him again and they were in the Champs Elysées on honeymoon. Paris, Bat thought, the only place in the world to go to on honeymoon. But Alice had been dead almost a year. She'd never got over what had happened to Edward.

Every child is a hostage to fortune, Bat thought, but when you lose the only one you've got, your life doesn't have a lot of purpose any more.

Losing Edward had turned Tamasin into what she was.

*   *   *

'Nav,' Bat said on the intercom, 'how we doing for track?'

'On track, Bat,' Tamasin's clear, confident voice said in his headset. 'Groundspeed as planned, 330 knots. We have a wind vector of 110 degrees at no more than two to four knots.'

'Sounds good, Tamasin.'

Tamasin felt good all right. They were on their way. She turned to Chuck Brantley, portly and jovial in the ejector seat next to her, grinning as he lit another cigarette. 'I can't believe this,' she said. 'These are fantastic conditions. I can't believe the way we got *away* like that!'

Sitting back in his seat, Chuck grinned slyly. 'Just relax, honey. You can depend on old Uncle Chuck to see you OK.'

Tamasin watched him a moment, her eyes hooded, through the skeins of smoke in the dull orange lighting. What Chuck said was true. He'd had help with the legwork from Jerry Yeaver, but actually it was Chuck who'd done all the arrangements for this, activated the contacts, put the paperwork in place. All she and Bat had done – after originating the idea – was to borrow one of her company's Lears and sneak illegally into Mexico a couple of times to test radar coverage. Quite how Chuck had gone about it only he knew, and he wasn't saying. But Tamasin knew it was Chuck who'd organized the flight plan; Chuck who'd organized a *duplicate* flight plan that had led the real crew of Bright Angel to suppose they were due out on Wednesday instead of today; Chuck who'd achieved the real miracle of rigged paperwork that had resulted in this actual B52H turning up at Davis-Monthan yesterday, Monday, in place of another aircraft intended for store in the Graveyard.

She caught his eye. 'How did you get on to Jerry and the others, Chuck?'

Chuck's was the name that had come first into Bat's mind when he and Tamasin brewed up the idea. Bat had known Chuck from old USAF days as a man with untold contacts. Of Chuck's personal courage there'd never been doubt, but neither Bat nor Tamasin had expected Chuck to come back a fortnight after Bat's proposal and *volunteer himself*, for a place on a one-way flight.

Cash had changed hands – Bat wouldn't need that big

ranch of his at Pozo Lindo any more – but that wasn't the whole story. Chuck felt almost as strongly as Bat and Tamasin did about fighters who struck only when they knew the opposition couldn't strike back.

Chuck's podgy face went into dimples as he laughed, and his thick moustache bristled amiably. 'Just you rely on Uncle Chuck, honey.' He fondled her knee.

By the time Chuck had come back to Bat to volunteer, he'd already found two of their recruits, Jerry and Russell. Finding the last man had taken longer, and at one point it had looked as if Tamasin would have to fly as co-pilot. Then Mario had turned up, with a hint of trouble over habitual gambling, and another piece of Pozo Lindo had been signed away.

To Mario, Tamasin reflected, this flight was pretty much another gamble. Apart from anything else, Mario was gambling on getting out of it alive, which was more than some of them were.

'Have you ever flown a BUFF?' Tamasin asked.

'No, I only ever worked as a radar nav. And nav, at one time.' He patted Tamasin's knee. 'Guess you're the only little honey on the crew apart from our brave pilots who actually does have experience handling one of these contraptions. Yeah – I've navigated BUFFs, F4s.' That was the Phantom fighter, built originally for the US Navy and since used worldwide by air forces, not least those of West Germany and Britain. Chuck said, 'Your brother ever fly F4s?'

Tamasin was twenty-nine years old, the youngest person in the crew by some margin from Jerry Yeaver, the next youngest. Her brother Colan was eighteen months younger than her and flew Tornado long-range interceptors with the Royal Air Force.

'Yes,' Tamasin said, 'but he was hardly out of training, then.'

'Your father was RAF, too, right?' Chuck said.

45

Tamasin nodded. 'Resigned when he succeeded to the title.'

Chuck frowned. 'Is "knight" a title?'

'He's not a *knight*.' Tamasin couldn't remember how many times she'd had this conversation with Americans; and every time she did so she saw again the big house outside Liskeard with the creeper on the severe grey walls, and the walks they'd used to take on Bodmin Moor. 'He's a baronet. Both sorts get "sir", but a baronetcy runs in the family. A knighthood is just once.'

'OK,' Chuck said. 'So is going in the RAF a family tradition?'

'That's right,' Tamasin said drily, 'an ancestor of mine flew with the RAF in the Battle of Agincourt in 1415.'

Chuck's cheeks dimpled again as he laughed.

'Well, it's true, actually,' Tamasin said, 'the Penhales *have* had some centuries of the military tradition. The guy at Agincourt was actually one of Henry's cavalry. And another of my ancestors commanded a vessel in Sir Walter Raleigh's fleet. Another of them' – she glanced at Chuck – 'chased off a bunch of upstart colonials at Bunker Hill.'

'That right?' Chuck grinned. It wasn't, but it made a good yarn. 'We shouldn't oughta let you British on this flight.'

'I'm American,' Tamasin said, 'by marriage.' She hooded her eyes again, sitting very still.

'He older than you or younger, this brother?'

'Younger.'

Chuck noticed the edge to her voice and he glanced over, curious. But her relationship with her brother was one of Tamasin's secrets. How she'd always made the running, because she was the elder; how she'd always broken whatever new ground there'd been; and how Colan had nevertheless always had the attention because he was a boy. How Colan had never seemed to put any

46

effort into anything, he'd always been laid-back, never had uncertainties about what he was doing – and how everything he'd done had been better than her own achievements, every time.

These days, Tamasin tried not to resent it. But there it was, plain for anyone to see. Flight Lieutenant Colan Penhale had a career and a title to look forward to and a happy family life. Tamasin Masterson was a widow and angry about it.

*   *   *

Jerry Yeaver came down the vertical ladder.

Tamasin felt relieved to see him; Chuck had started flipping pages on a girlie magazine, deliberately provocative.

'You guys hungry yet?' Jerry said with a shy smile, his lips close to her face in the noise.

Tamasin shrugged, indifferent, smiling up wistfully as Jerry stooped over her. Jerry didn't deserve to be depressed, she reflected, not after what had happened that day at Eielson. Yet for all that, she knew something had gone wrong for him in the aftermath of that furious act of heroism.

'Sure am!' Chuck said.

'Let me come up and give you a hand with it,' Tamasin said to Jerry. She took off her bone dome, settled it on the console, and unstrapped.

Usually on a B52 crew you each bring your own food supply on board in your flight case. But that's assuming a normal B52 mission of about eight hours. This one was different and so were the food arrangements, with extra supplies brought on board and strapped down in place on the first level.

'You'll catch hell,' Chuck said, 'Mario sees you with no helmet.'

'I'm fed up with the thing,' Tamasin told him, and

47

followed Jerry up the vertical ladder, stiff after that length of time in the seat.

In the light through the windscreens the first level seemed very bright after the second. Turbulence jogged the big bomber and Tamasin put her hands out to balance herself, ducking under the low ceiling. Jerry had to stoop; she hardly did. Bat, on the right, turned and smiled at Tamasin, but his lazy friendliness couldn't hide the sadness in his far-sighted eyes. Or the smouldering anger. Mario and Russell were sleeping, after a fashion. Tamasin went forward to look outside.

At these latitudes it was still bright in the wintry afternoon. For all there was to see, they might have been a thousand miles out over the ocean; but this was reality, to Tamasin, compared with those scopes and switches below. The ocean had turned purple, flecked with little foam caps going gold in the sun, and through the skeins of cirrus the sky had turned dark blue, with a velvety quality that reminded Tamasin of a dress she'd once worn to a ball when she'd still been in the sixth form.

Bat reached out as Tamasin stooped to see outside, and held her hand. She gave his a squeeze. She loved Bat. He'd given her tremendous support after Edward's death – so had Alice – even though the loss had been as great a torment for them as it had for her. Then when Alice had died, still grieving for her murdered son, and left Bat on his own, Tamasin had supported him through his second loss.

Perhaps it was inevitable that they should become lovers – shyly, tentatively, the intimacy seeming somehow forbidden. They'd met each other's physical needs just once and afterwards had found it easier to express their love and tenderness more formally.

Jerry came up behind Tamasin and she released Bat's hand and moved aside. 'Coffee,' Jerry said, and handed Bat the beaker.

'Hey, I was going to help you do those sandwiches,' Tamasin said.

'Done them.' As Bat fixed the coffee beaker in its holder, Jerry reached over with the sandwich. It was a proper American-style sandwich, ham, cheese, lettuce, tomato.

'Sorry,' Tamasin said. Partly, she thought, Jerry's humility came from having such a lousy opinion of himself.

'No sweat.' Jerry smiled, his cheeks gaunt, eyes hollow behind the metal-framed glasses.

Tamasin took a sandwich for Chuck and clasped it against her as she climbed down to him, sturdy body agile, one hand free for the ladder rail. Chuck grinned at her, still looking at his girlie magazine, half an eye on the radar scopes. Tamasin handed over the snack and drew him a beaker from the coffee maker and went back up.

Bat had his back to her, against the evening light, working the pumps, and Jerry was sitting on the metal floor with his coffee, long legs reaching from one side of the cabin to the other, ankles crossed. He watched Tamasin. Tamasin craned her head round the gunner's station and looked at Russell Feehan. Russell was sleeping, his face that same awful grey, his lips parted. Sorrow came over Tamasin in the knowledge that there was nothing she or anyone could do for Russell's pain. Stomach cancer. The best he could hope for was a quick end to it.

But Tamasin wasn't expecting to come out of this alive either.

Jerry handed Tamasin a coffee. She hadn't felt hungry, nor had he. Tamasin sat on the metal decking with her back against the opposite cabin wall to Jerry, her leg not quite touching his.

Jerry was a nice guy to be around, she realized. Much as she loved Bat, his patrician aloofness could seem forbidding, whereas Jerry was approachable. And Jerry wasn't a macho martinet like Mario, finding fault

49

all the time; or the roving-hand sort like Chuck, likeable as Chuck was in many ways.

Tamasin wanted to know now what had gone wrong between Jerry and Sue, his wife, who'd divorced him in Nevada when he'd been based at Eielson, Alaska. She couldn't quite bring herself to ask; nor could she yet talk to Jerry – although she was starting to need to – about the heartache that had been part of her ever since Edward died.

CHAPTER 6

For all the night's cool, Captain Rebecca Laird was feeling hot and clammy in the office in the control tower at Davis-Monthan as she reached for the scrambler phone. It was two minutes to eight, Arizona time.

This call was to A2 headquarters at the Pentagon. In Washington it was two minutes to ten. A man gave his name and rank. He sounded sleepy and irritable and Becks thought she could hear a TV show playing in the background. Becks made her report: a B52, model unknown, serial unknown, crew unknown, appeared to have gone missing on a flight that appeared to be unauthorized.

The A2 lieutenant-colonel at the Pentagon wasn't very interested. 'OK, Captain, I'll log it. Meantime, you come back to us when you have some more definite facts.'

Hanging up, Becks got the feeling the guy didn't believe her and that the main reason he didn't was that she was female.

Hultlander bustled in, eyes and stomach a-bulge, clutching a clipboard. He'd been busy and he'd been organizing help. 'We have the three groundcrew, ma'am, the ones who dispatched Dark Angel! Fretwell, McGurty and Castro.'

Becks widened her eyes. 'They're here? On base?'

'No, but I have their home addresses here.'

'Let's go get 'em,' Becks said. 'Fetch 'em in right now.'

He bustled out again. Becks fiddled nervously with her sandy hair, thinking about Major-General Hartmore, on his way over now having broken off his supper – she suspected – in mid-mouthful. She was in no state to deliver bad news to the boss.

The young guardroom sergeant burst into the office. He stuck his arms straight out, thrusting a folder of photocopies at her.

'OK, sergeant, what is it?'

'It's in there, ma'am. We think we have a record of the guys who took the . . . who took Dark Angel.'

Becks took the folder. 'Yeah?'

'Just before four this afternoon, ma'am. They were in two taxis, three in one, three in the other. The names were all false, looks like. The captain gave his name as Colonel Powell. They were all kitted out, in their flight suits.'

A jetliner was sighing somewhere, distant in the desert night. Becks wrinkled her brow, glancing at the skinny sergeant. 'They got in at *four*? But they were starting the engines at a quarter past. What'd they do for a briefing?'

'Guys in the guardroom figured they musta briefed off base someplace, ma'am.' His adam's apple wobbled prominently.

That made sense, Becks realized. It cut down the number of people to see them and maybe challenge them. The sergeant added: 'One guy figured one of the flight crew coulda been a woman. Don't know if that makes any sense, ma'am.'

It didn't, yet. Becks flicked her ponytail. She felt annoyed, but not with the sergeant. Tracing those taxis wasn't an A2 job, it was a job for Tucson Police Department, if not actually for the FBI.

The sergeant left. Another NCO came in, an older man with a moustache. 'This any interest, ma'am?' He had the flight movement logs.

'It is if you have any B52s,' Becks answered.

'I do.' He placed the photocopy on the desk. 'It was a

SALT job, in from Barksdale to go into the Graveyard.'
Barksdale was a bomber station in the northwest corner
of Louisiana. The current Strategic Arms Limitation
Treaty included terms for taking older US and Soviet
nuclear-capable bombers out of service. B52s came into
Davis-Monthan from several different bases, their bomb
racks gutted, stripped of all but navigational radar. 'It's
an H-series bird, serial 60–086. Only BUFF into here in
six days.'

'An H?' She turned bright eyes on his face. Powell had
reckoned Dark Angel was an H. Becks said: 'Looks like
you could've found it.'

She got rid of the man, found a number for Barksdale
and dialled. It was gone twenty past eight Tucson time
and Louisiana was an hour ahead. She got the duty officer.
His attitude was a bit like that of the A2 officer in the
Pentagon.

'We have a record of a B52H,' Becks explained, 'serial
60–086, arriving here from you yesterday. Do you have
any record of the departure?'

Wearily, he consulted his records. 'No, Captain.' The
man was a major. Everyone Becks approached seemed
to be more senior than her and to think she'd been
overpromoted. 'The plane we flew over to you yesterday
was an H, but the serial was 60–068.' He lectured her, his
patience audibly strained. 'Looks like you have a mix-up
with numbers at your end. 068 is the plane that's to
go into storage. 086 is still operational and it's with us
here. It's on an ops training programme based here at
Barksdale.'

'What kind of training programme?' Becks asked,
suspicious.

'Conventional weapons delivery.' Free-fall, high-explosive
bombs, in other words. The major said: 'I don't see why
this interests you, Captain. Someone at your end simply
has their serial numbers confused.'

'Sir,' Becks pleaded, 'we would really be obliged here if you'd please go check on your flight line. We need to be sure which end the mix-up is.' In the receiver, the major sighed. 'And please call me back ASAP,' Becks begged. 'We do have to know quite urgently.'

She plonked down the receiver. In her frustration she dragged her sleeve across her eyes, then tossed her head, flipping back the thick, sandy ponytail. Regulation heels rang on the concrete like gunshots in the night. It was twenty-five to nine. Major-General Gus Hartmore strode into the office behind a chestful of medal ribbons, and the stars on his shoulders flashed light. The Colt .45 hung on his hip as usual.

Becks leaped to attention and then couldn't remember if she was supposed to salute when she wasn't in uniform.

In the doorway Hartmore paused just long enough to give her a look that should have shrivelled her. Then, disdainfully, he strode into the silence of the office.

'Why aren't you in uniform, Captain?'

'Sir, I was called in here while I was off duty.'

'What about the work you were staying late to complete?'

Sonofabitch. 'Sir, I completed it and then I went off duty.'

Tight-lipped, Hartmore turned his shoulder and paced slowly across the office. All six foot of her still at attention, Becks was aware that his compact, stiff-limbed body was quivering with repressed energy – and bristling with indignation because she was not only female but taller than he was. 'You completed your work. Then you went off duty.'

'Sir.' He made it sound like desertion in the face of the enemy.

Hartmore swung back. His eyes glittered. 'OK, Captain, now kindly explain why you see fit to haul the base commander in here in mid evening.'

She told him.

He paced as he listened to her, hands clasped in front of him, his whole athletic body tense, barely restrained. Becks could see him growing angrier as she talked, yet still holding it all in.

'OK, Captain, you are telling me some unknown crew of pirates has stolen a United States Air Force bomber and that while this theft against the nation took place you simply *watched*. At the time that you were watching this theft take place, you should have been at your post, where you woulda been in a position to prevent this. Do you have any comment to make?'

For a moment as she watched him listening to her story, Becks had felt a glimmering of sympathy for the man. In his mid-forties, brainy, gifted, with ambition bursting out of him, and here was a disaster that might put an end to his career. All the same, shooting the messenger was rather an outmoded idea.

'Sir, I'd'a thought that was a job for base security, not A2.'

Hartmore's thin lips almost disappeared into his face. From clasping his hands in front, he clasped them behind him, and paced tautly across the office. Light caught the polished leather of the holster of his Colt as he turned.

'You leave me to talk to base security, Captain – I'll decide what goes.' He swung to face her. 'How long you been promoted captain?'

'There weeks, sir.'

Hartmore's eyes lingered over her. There was nothing sexual in the way he looked her up and down, there was merely contempt. Maybe he felt contempt for all women, Becks thought, and maybe that was why he was a lifelong bachelor.

'OK, Captain. What we need heading up that A2 section here is a man with more seniority and experience.' He put the emphasis on *man*. 'Dismiss!'

Her back rigid, Becks snapped a salute. It was sheer reflex. Hartmore returned the salute perfunctorily and turned his back as Becks marched out. Her cheeks, white before, burned suddenly, and the desert air touched her face, sharply cool.

Where the lights from the control tower fell on the parking area, a green air force van swung to a halt.

Becks walked to her Volkswagen. Boots drubbed on the concrete as three men piled out of the van. Becks opened the Volkswagen door, but her eyes were on the men.

One of them shouted, 'Let's go!' and his voice echoed off the control tower. All three were black. Two of them wore MP uniform, the third wore jeans and a shabby warm-up top. Becks had a sudden sense that the one in civvies was one of Dark Angel's groundcrew.

CHAPTER 7

All Bat Masterson's crew aboard the B52 were awake again and on station, bone domes on, harness tight. It was 2148 Arizona time, 0448 zulu, and Tamasin was counting them down to their second waypoint. The waypoint was over the Pacific. It was at 107 degrees 15 minutes west, 22 degrees 0 minutes north, a point southwest of Tuxpán, Mexico.

'Two,' Tamasin read off, watching the radar. 'One. *Now.*'

Bat eased back the yoke and the B52 came steeply left and then rolled out smoothly on the new heading. Very shortly now they would be violating Mexican airspace.

Outside it was utterly dark; the night starless. Now the noise poured through the cabin as Bat increased power on the eight TF33 turbofans.

Chuck said: 'Coastline thirty miles.' He had his attack radar set to show a narrow path, straight ahead. It was giving him terrain heights.

Tamasin said: 'Groundspeed four twenty knots. Increasing.' She had two screens in front of her. She'd set her radar to mapping mode and it showed the coastline that Chuck had reported. To its right, the electro-optical viewing system showed the same picture as the one on the screens that dominated the pilots' panels. Its picture came from the two turrets under the B52's chin, one a TV camera, one a forward-looking infra-red sensor, both steerable. It wasn't showing land yet. Tamasin reached left for the contrast control, immediately left of the

57

mode selector. She adjusted brightness. She said: 'Four fifty knots. Keep increasing.'

Above and facing aft, Jerry was keyed up, alert, watching for radar reaching them. On this flight, any radar was a threat radar. He didn't entirely believe that if a threat radar painted them, he would spot it in time to act. There was no reason why he should doubt his abilities but he always did. He kept remembering what his commander at Eielson had said to him when they grounded him, and that made him feel useless. He kept remembering the things Sue had said before she left him.

Russell, bloodshot-eyed at the guns, watched the tail radar, eyes narrowed behind his glasses. Every so often his worry beads flipped.

Mario saw it first, the harder black against the glossy blackness of the ocean and the funeral drape of the sky.

He said: 'Landfall. *Bienvenida en Méjico.*' Not that this flight was going to be welcome anywhere in the world.

No-one was passing the time of day now. This part was the second most difficult of the operation, after getting their hands on the aircraft in the first place, and the second most dangerous, after the time-over-target itself. For this leg they had a terrain-comparison cassette – again Tamasin would have given a lot, short of her virtue, to know how Chuck had charmed it out of Strategic Air Command's plausibly deniable possession – and they slaved the autopilot to it but kept a very close eye on the instruments and radar in case the cassette lied to them.

Low down, they were jolting in the turbulence. They were three hundred feet above ground level. Quickly Tamasin fished in a shoulder pocket for the twist of paper with the airsickness pills, the ones she'd cut meticulously in half to give her just enough prevention without turning her sleepy. The pocket on the outside of the shoulder was one of the few you could get at with your harness pulled tight. She swallowed the half pill.

Chuck said: 'Terrain twenty.' He sounded like a DJ introducing a new single.

The engine note rose. The nose eased up. Then pitched down sharply as they crested the ridgeline and jammed six people hard against the shoulder harness as they burrowed back into the valley.

This was the worst thing about being down here, Tamasin thought; the only way to see what the world was like outside was that ghostly picture on the EVS. Again the B52 lifted strongly, again it pitched sickeningly down. And again. This time Tamasin had nausea acid in her throat.

*　　*　　*

Ground levels were rising quickly now as the B52 bored thunderously into the mountains of central Mexico. Bat had his face mask clipped up, he was keeping them down among the weeds. From the cockpit window you couldn't see a thing, just darkness, and very occasionally a scatter of lights from a hamlet. On the EVS the view was enough to shake you rigid. The peaks were all around, to the left, to the right, dead ahead.

But that cassette Chuck had got them off SAC was still finding them the way through.

'Radar!' Jerry said. 'Incoming radar!' He sounded tense. Mario flicked Bat a look.

In his lazy, careless Arizona drawl, Bat said: 'Whose?'

A pause.

'Area radar at Guadalajara,' Jerry said, sounding relieved. 'The airport. Sheee-it!' There was wonder in his voice. 'Those sonsabitches aren't even looking at their scopes. They shoulda called us on radio by now.' But this was getting on for eleven at night, local time.

'Nav,' Bat said, 'let's take no chances. Give me a dogleg and get clear of this.'

Tamasin said: 'Stand by.' Dim light gleamed on the transparency of her protractor as she worked on the matt-black map table. 'Your new heading will be one seven five mag. Two . . . one . . . now.'

The big jet rolled heavily to the right.

The tension Tamasin felt was almost sensual. They were *doing* something at last, they weren't just talking any more, and her part in it was crucial. She was watching the scopes acutely as Chuck stolidly called terrain. She was looking for Lago de Chapala, a big body of water amid the crags. She had it on mapping radar before it showed on the EVS.

'Start left turn on to one zero five . . . now!'

Again the seat shifted under her, lifting her now to look down on Chuck. The EVS showed faint starlight on the lake.

The scatters of lights that Mario saw from his righthand seat in the nose were bigger now. Still Bat was keeping them low, and the light turbulence kicked them around as the nose lifted and dipped in the inputs from the terrain-following cassette. Compared with the Sonoran Desert they'd taken off from, this was a busy area.

Waypoint Three was a point due north of Mexico City and they were coming up to it fast.

*   *   *

Mario kept on nagging Jerry: 'You getting any radar yet?'

Most often Jerry said no. Occasionally he said yes. Mario's questions always made Jerry jumpy because he knew, from their very first exchange, that Mario didn't trust him as a crew member or as a man. It was reassuring to touch his toe to that flight case.

In between watching the radar receivers and identifying frequencies and origins of what came in, Jerry was tuning into radio channels for a listen. Jerry always had been good at languages. Spanish was his second-best foreign language, after Russian. Arabic he had a job with and his German had gaps in, despite the great-grandfather who'd emigrated from Saxony in the first place and bequeathed the family a name – Jever – that subsequently had to be anglicized so that Poles and Greeks and other regular Americans could pronounce it right. Still, Russian was the one he'd used all the time up at Eielson, Alaska.

'Waypoint Three,' Tamasin announced.

Waves of airsickness were getting to her; she much preferred the pilot's job to this one, stuck here in the dim interior light in the belly of the BUFF. Even so, she was making a sound job of it. She'd navigated them through the narrow, winding pass south of Querétaro where the peaks either side of them ran up to the best part of ten thousand feet.

*   *   *

'Nav,' Mario said testingly, 'you still happy with course and time?'

'Co-pilot,' Tamasin said, 'confirm I'm still happy.'

It was 2240 Arizona time; 0540 zulu. Doggedly, wordlessly, Russell Feehan watched his tail radar, while the cancer ate at his innards. He would give it till the hour before he took another painkiller. One more big ridgeline, and the engine note rose as the autopilot advanced the power levers and lifted the big jet's nose.

Then they'd done it. They'd left not only the mountains behind them but the thickest population clusters, too.

As the B52 started shedding height, running down the hill slopes towards the Caribbean seaboard, Bat snapped open the clip on his oxygen mask and let it swing open. His eyes met Mario's. They hadn't even been challenged.

61

On the other hand, there'd be a lot of people in a lot of little farms and mountain towns wondering what the noise in the night had been.

Let them wonder, Bat thought, and dug his cigarettes out of his knee pocket. Mario shielded his eyes as Bat snapped the flame from his lighter. His long exhalation betrayed relief. Then in an instant of guilt he saw Alice, her face smiling as she welcomed him back from Vietnam; and after that he saw Edward, and he knew why he was here.

*   *   *

'Turn left,' Tamasin announced, and gave Bat the new heading. 'This will get us directly to Waypoint Four.' Waypoint Four was the coast crossing, the point where they headed out across the bay for the jungle peninsula of Yucatán.

The moon had come out. Stars were showing. Ahead in the darkness Mario's sharp eyes caught the glint of the faint light where it fell on surf.

Jerry's scopes were clear. The nearest town was Veracruz but it was well to the north and no radar was reaching them. This route was mostly Tamasin's work and Jerry was impressed.

'Waypoint Four,' Tamasin announced, 'right . . . now.' She was watching the view on the EVS.

They flew over water. The Bay of Campeche; part of the Gulf of Mexico; itself part of the greater Caribbean. Chuck let his face mask dangle and lit a cigarette.

'We're right for position and right for time,' Tamasin told Bat over the intercom. It was 2310 Arizona time, 0610 zulu.

'OK, nav,' Bat said, holding the mask up to his face but still with the cigarette in the corner of his mouth. 'Mario, what's the fuel burn look like?'

Mario had been watching him, Bat realized. Keeping an eye on him.

Frowning, Mario studied the gauges, and the notes he and Bat had been making on the clipboard as they transferred fuel. Fuel burn was critical to this whole mission. B52s had flown colossal distances unrefuelled before, but this was the first time anyone had gone for this sort of distance at these sorts of heights. It helped, not having bomb racks or cruise missiles under the wings – the drag those things created got through fuel at a horrendous rate; having this BUFF aerodynamically clean made the crucial difference. And Bat and Mario – and Tamasin, with her experience as navigator and as pilot, in particular on B52s – reckoned they'd worked out the right combination of power settings for the various legs to get them over their target with enough fuel for their task.

Mario looked for ways to find fault with what he saw on the gauges. 'Good, I guess,' he said grudgingly. 'If anything, looks a little better than we figured.'

It was time to slow down, with no settlements under them to disturb. Bat eased back the throttles.

Tamasin calculated the new groundspeed and reported. Bat acknowledged. They were 1,000 feet over the bay, driving eastwards through the night, the B52 solid and rolling slightly under them with its ceaseless engine noise. Smoke from Chuck's cigarette drifted around Tamasin and she cuddled Buster, the fluffy rabbit, and thought about her Cornish forebears. The one who'd sailed with Raleigh; really he'd been scarcely better than just another buccaneer, preying on the galleons of imperial Spain in this selfsame corner of the globe, four hundred years ago.

'Time to relax, team,' Bat said. 'Let's get two guys sleeping. Jerry, I guess it's your turn – Russell, can you mind those radars?' He heard *sure thing* in his headphones through the all-pervading breathing of the turbofans. 'OK,' he said, 'well, I'm gonna stay awake for this leg and take the next turn for sleeping. Chuck and Tamasin, let's have one of you sleeping. Which of you wants to stay awake?'

'Aw, c'm'on,' Chuck said on the intercom. 'We can both sleep together.'

Tamasin gave a short, humourless laugh. 'I'll stay awake,' she said. 'I feel fine.' Even the airsickness that had plagued her through the mountains had settled down.

'Suits me,' Chuck said on the intercom. He let the mask swing down and leaned across to Tamasin, the hand on her knee again. 'Sure you don't wanna sleep with me?' The smell of cigarettes clung to him.

'Not a chance,' Tamasin said wryly. Chuck settled back in his seat.

Above them, Russell and Jerry were swapping places, Russell taking over Jerry's radar watch.

CHAPTER 8

Libya, the summer before the flight.

Three weeks after the Frankfurt attack, Adem Elhaggi was in the medical office again, arguing with Dr Jabran because a bunch of the other trainees were going out on a desert exercise and Adem wanted to go with them. Dr Jabran said he shouldn't. She wasn't happy with the way his shoulder was mending. She knew it was hurting Adem even when he swore on the Koran that it wasn't.

'If you're fit for a desert exercise, you're fit for lavatory duty.'

Everybody hated lavatory duty. It was smelly and unpleasant. You had to laboriously empty out all the stuff from the quarters block into a truck mounted on a trailer, then tow it behind an ancient farm tractor to the pit, and pump it in using a petrol-driven pump that was the trailer-tank's sole labour-saving device. When the tractor broke down, which it did not uncommonly, you had to hitch up the trailer to a couple of mules. Adem had been down for lavatory duty that morning but another trainee had taken it over.

'I'm perfectly fit for lavatory duty.'

Behind them, Tariq Talal's voice boomed: 'Then maybe you should do lavatory duty tomorrow morning.'

They turned. He was in the doorway, hands on his hips, bearded and confident, with the teasing smile fattening his face. It was early evening. The desert exercise was tomorrow. The medical office was one of the handful of rooms supplied by the camp generators, but tonight the couple of bulbs were weak, like Adem's will-power when he got overtired. Light hung in bands of soft pink and brown in the sky to the west.

'All right,' Adem said gruffly, stiffening his back to meet the challenge.

Tariq Talal laughed, a big sound that made the office seem small. He strode across the floor and clapped a meaty hand to Adem's good shoulder. 'Not tomorrow,' he said. 'Not the day after, but two days after that. Tomorrow I want you to join your brothers on the desert exercise.'

Delight and excitement flared inside Adem and he gasped, wide eyes gazing up. Hand still on Adem's shoulder, Talal turned to Dr Jabran.

'Now, you can't really mean that this talented, young warrior isn't fit to take part in tomorrow's exercise?'

She looked sceptically at Talal, then at Adem. 'He may regret it.'

'I won't!' Adem burst out.

'You see?' Talal grinned. 'He won't.'

Slowly Dr Jabran smiled, her eyes watchful, her face sad. She said nothing.

*   *   *

Well before dawn they left camp. There were eighteen of them, seventeen boys in their mid to late teens, and Zoheir; the leader was Ali Ben Mokhtar, stringy, world-weary, taciturn and tough. They adored Ben Mokhtar almost as much as they adored Tariq Talal. This was to be forty-eight hours of navigation and survival, and besides rifle and ammunition they carried food, water − all their supplies. At intervals they would halt at improvised target ranges in the desert. Then Ben Mokhtar would test them for marksmanship.

Ali Ben Mokhtar was over twice the age of the youngest trainee. He had high standards and he meant them to be met. As a leader he was demanding, with little patience for stragglers.

By the end of the first day, heat had burned off the high spirits that had put a spring in their stride as they set out that morning. Keeping up was the summit of their ambition, not that there was occasion to discuss it among themselves. Adem, exhausted, felt the bitter realization that he'd bitten off more than he could chew. And that his shoulder wouldn't stop hurting.

Stars shone over him as he collapsed on his blanket roll. He didn't see them, he just went straight to sleep.

Again they were up before dawn and today was even worse than yesterday because Adem didn't feel as if he'd rested more than five minutes, the evidence notwithstanding that he'd slept soundly from eight till three.

At ten on the improvised range their shooting was all over the place. Ben Mokhtar cursed them and scored accurate groups from two hundred metres as the sun pounded down, just to show them. Adem could almost believe it when another trainee muttered sourly that Ben Mokhtar must have had that rifle of his specially calibrated for sniping.

At half past eleven they were on the march again and Ben Mokhtar was as merciless as the sun above them. Pain pounded ceaselessly in Adem's shoulder.

At twelve, in the worst of the heat, they rested, but the only shade available was what they could improvise. The bread was stale now, the water warm. Some of the trainees seemed to doze after they'd eaten but Adem couldn't, it was too hot.

At two, as they wearily gathered themselves to march again, Adem found himself shoulder to shoulder with a haggard Zoheir, her parted lips cracked and parched, her eyes mere slits in the sun, her dusty face burned and peeling. She tried to lift her rifle but for a moment it wouldn't leave the ground.

67

His own AK slung on his back, Adem stooped and picked up Zoheir's rifle and handed it to her. The movement caught his bad shoulder but he fought down the grunt of pain. His eyes met Zoheir's. She took the AK and slung it on her shoulder but she didn't look grateful. Her eyes slipped away from his and she started adjusting the heavy webbing ammunition belt at her waist.

'Zoheir, let me take some of that.'

Adem's hand was outstretched. He wasn't a tough young man, unlike some of the others on the exercise; he wasn't much taller than Zoheir and certainly no more sturdily built.

'No,' she muttered.

'I can manage it.'

'No,' Zoheir said, 'I'll manage. We all have to manage for ourselves.'

Then Ben Mokhtar was there, with a rage in his hard, old eyes like the wrath of the sun as it lashed them. 'You want extra weight, do you, boy? I'll give you extra weight! Here!'

On his belt he had eight ammunition pouches. Each trainee carried eight. Four of Ben Mokhtar's were full of fired shell casings for re-use, four still held live rounds and they were the heavy ones. Ben Mokhtar unclipped the four with the live rounds and took them off his belt.

'Here!'

There was nothing else for it. With tears of chagrin pricking at his eyes, Adem clipped Ben Mokhtar's ammunition to his own belt.

Zoheir had slipped wordlessly away. With a shouted command, Ben Mokhtar set them marching at a tough pace.

Two hours of it and Adem was finished.

They were marching in single file and Ben Mokhtar was far out of Adem's sight at the front. Adem had been third from last but now he was bringing up the rear. He was alone. He didn't even know where he was. They were out of the sand desert now and into rock desert. Boulders lay sand-blasted, radiating heat; outcrops shouldered high, shadowless, their jagged knife-edge stratum lines exposed; and the pebble floor hurt Adem's feet through his boot soles. He didn't know what time it was. None of them wore a watch; they'd been learning to tell time by the sun. Only one trainee was still in Adem's sight and he kept vanishing round the next outcrop.

On Adem's face, the skin felt hard like a mask. Parched mouth harsh, he forced himself onwards, round the outcrop where he'd last seen the man ahead.

No-one was there.

Fear pierced through Adem's weariness and rose towards panic. He hated Ben Mokhtar now. Wading through this heat was like wading through setting concrete. Surely they wouldn't leave him here? Tears pricked at his eyes.

Another turning. Still no-one.

Pausing a moment, scared and angry, Adem scanned the desert floor. For a moment he was utterly lost and the sweat of fear ran down his spine. Then he spotted the clues, a crushed sandstone pebble here, half a boot print there, pointing his way out of this terrifying bewilderment of outcrops. *So go for it, Adem Elhaggi.* He wasn't finished as long as he could put one foot after the other and, as long as he had the will, then he would carry on.

Anger drove him onward around the next shoulder of rock.

Ben Mokhtar was standing close by the rock in a tiny wedge of shade. Wordlessly he watched Adem. No smile showed on his face, but he held out his water bottle.

*   *   *

At Adem's back the rock was still very warm, but the relief of sitting slumped, supported, overwhelmed him. If Ben Mokhtar knew Adem was crying, he gave no sign. Presently Adem gave back the lukewarm water, and Ben Mokhtar put a hand on Adem's good shoulder and they stood up.

'Give me your ammunition,' Ben Mokhtar said.

Adem unclipped Ben Mokhtar's ammo pouches from his belt and handed them over.

'No, yours, too,' Ben Mokhtar said. 'I'll take four.'

More tears. Adem obeyed. Ben Mokhtar jerked his head, and they walked together through the oven heat of the desert, the pain dull, relentless in that shoulder.

Ben Mokhtar said nothing, and as they rejoined the waiting trainees, Adem knew he was still in disgrace. Yet as they walked up to the group, sitting or squatting in what shade they could find, Ben Mokhtar again put his hand on Adem's good shoulder.

'Adem,' Ben Mokhtar said. He raised his voice so they could all hear. 'You've done well. You've shown that you have strong reserves of stamina and courage. I want all of us to recognize that.'

For an instant, Adem caught Zoheir's eye. She actually looked impressed as well as concerned. Suddenly Adem had to bite his lip hard.

'But there's a lesson here,' Ben Mokhtar said. 'Helping one another is fine. But each one of us individually has a vital task to perform, and each one of us has the responsibility of achieving the individual objectives set us. Now let's go!'

*   *   *

Oddly, Adem didn't find it difficult to cover the two hours' march that brought them to the next, brief, night halt. The sun was going down as they camped, about a quarter to seven. Tomorrow they would be back at Tariq Talal's camp.

At two they struck camp. Half an hour later they were back on the march.

Everyone had been taking a hand in the navigation and now it was Zoheir's turn. Night navigation was no simple task; yet, in leading, Zoheir seemed to Adem thoroughly confident.

By half past four the late summer sun was above the horizon. That was when Zoheir halted them and compared her compass and the terrain and realized where she'd gone wrong.

They were fifteen hundred metres off the point where they should have been, which wouldn't have been too bad if they hadn't had a big, steep-sided wadi – a dry watercourse – in the way.

There was nothing else for it. Zoheir led them off looking for a way down into the wadi.

The sun was high and hot at six when they reached the point they should have passed at half past four. From there, it should have been four hours' straightforward march back to camp, bringing them past the wire about 0830, but now they were an hour and a half behind schedule and correspondingly tired. Fatigue turned four hours of marching into five hours. Zoheir brought them, dragging their boot heels, into camp under a blazing sky at eleven, and Adem's shoulder was in agony. He kept trying to hide it.

After water, the first thing all of them wanted was sleep. First, though, Ben Mokhtar insisted on a debrief. The discussion left Zoheir fighting tears of humiliation over her mistake, and they were all utterly exhausted. At last, at almost noon, Ben Mokhtar allowed them to their quarters to sleep.

*   *   *

71

Adem slept from ten to twelve, when his head hit the tiny, hard pillow, until six-thirty, when one of the trainees who hadn't been on the exercise roused him and the others for supper. Still drowsy, Adem hardly noticed what he ate. He was hardly aware of what he was doing afterwards, either, at prayers in the open air between the quarters block. Prayers were a regular feature of camp life.

The sun was no more than an afterglow in the west and the air cooled quickly. Prayers over, they dashed back indoors. Even now it wasn't time to rest; Ben Mokhtar led them to one of the rooms they used as lecture theatres. He had a lesson for them, based on the way they'd handled the desert exercise.

It was ten, the chilly night starry beyond the draughty window-frames of sun-warped wood. All the trainees were in on the lesson, not just the ones who'd been out on the exercise. Even the ones who'd been asleep all afternoon were nodding off as Ben Mokhtar emphasized his points, one bony index jabbing. Then Tariq Talal sauntered in.

He hadn't been with them during prayers, Adem realized. He grinned at them as they turned in awe, a giant towering over them, full of confidence with his beard bushing out and his knowing eyes twinkling. Ben Mokhtar fell silent, aware that he'd lost his audience, aware also that in this camp that was how things would be. Tariq Talal sought out an empty place among the benches and put his arms round the shoulders of the trainees on either side.

Adem watched. The pride in the eyes of the trainees who'd been favoured with Talal's embrace was self-evident. Then Adem's gaze fell on Zoheir's face. Adoration and awe were there, and something close to worship, but there was something else that looked closer to fear.

'My warriors,' Tariq Talal beamed.

Ben Mokhtar wasn't bothering to try and continue.

'Your desert exercise was an outstanding success. You have achieved miracles.'

Sleepy-eyed, Adem forced his tired brain to listen. Tariq Talal's speeches always had that effect: he could hold an audience spellbound. He made everything make sense. Every time Adem had heard him speak, Adem had been convinced of his rightness, magnetized by his confident smiles, swept along in the flow of his logic.

Nor were the warriors at the camp the only audience that Talal bewitched. Adem knew that Talal travelled often to the larger Libyan towns, Tripoli; Al Khums; Benghazi; Tobruk; Sabhah, down in the desert; and out there fulfilled every good Muslim's duty of almsgiving by distributing food and medicines, stuff that was hard to get anywhere in Libya. And of course he addressed the people. He had the authority of the country's leader to do so.

On the other hand, Adem reflected, it wouldn't look very good in the eyes of the people if the country's leader stopped the speeches, since he'd be stopping the free food and medicine as well.

Tonight, he realized, Ben Mokhtar must have given Talal a detailed briefing on the way they'd performed. Talal singled out each trainee by name to say how well each one had done. He praised Adem by name. He praised Zoheir. He had a gift, Adem realized, for finding encouragement even where there appeared to be failure.

'I'm proud of you all,' he said, 'but now let's look after ourselves. Let's get some sleep.'

He stood up, all smiles and bushy beard, his bulk over-shadowing them. He left, amid a chorus of adoration.

'Well,' Ben Mokhtar said in a soft, tired voice, 'that ends that, then.'

Knees bumped desk tops woodenly and feet scuffed on the floor. Standing up with the other trainees, Adem looked for Zoheir. She'd been biting her lip and rubbing at her eyes on and off all through the lesson.

She didn't look at any of them, she just slipped out swiftly into the night. Adem frowned. Zoheir might have simply been going to the women's quarters – there was no real reason to suppose anything else – yet suddenly Adem had a strong suspicion that Zoheir was going after Tariq Talal.

He turned in with the other young men but, exhausted or not, he couldn't sleep. His shoulder wouldn't stop hurting, and he couldn't find a way to lie that gave him any comfort. In the darkness one of the young men mumbled in his sleep, and Adem set his teeth and forced himself to lie still; forced himself to make no sound in his pain. Its relentlessness humiliated him. It reminded him how vulnerable the mortal flesh was.

His thoughts constantly returned to Zoheir. Again and again he wondered whether she really had been going to Tariq Talal.

CHAPTER 9

Over the sea the flying was actually almost soothing, without all that yawing and pitching. Tamasin Penhale Masterson realized she was relaxing in her seat as she worked a few minutes longer at her charts. As she turned her head slightly, she realized Chuck Brantley wasn't sleeping yet – his eyes weren't fully closed. Keeping an eye on her.

'Can't sleep?' she said.

'Uh-unh.' He didn't seem bothered.

Actually, Tamasin realized, she herself was feeling quite tired. The Mexico leg had been hard work and they'd been flying now for the best part of seven hours; although that was nothing to the flying that was yet to come. Fleetingly Tamasin wondered how Jerry and Russell had coped, up there in the rear-facing seats.

'Chuck,' she said suddenly, 'what *are* you in this with us for?'

'Patriotism,' he said, and closed his eyes and folded his hands on his paunch.

That wasn't an answer. Tamasin knew it and Chuck knew she knew it and, trust him as she might, Tamasin couldn't ward off the occasional pang of worry because of it. There was something she simply *didn't know* about Chuck. She sighed softly. She wanted to speak to Jerry, but of course he was sleeping. She felt lonely. She thought of Bat. That was *real* loneliness, she reflected, being the man they all brought their problems to; the man who had to hold them all together, and hold *himself* together to do so; the man with the responsibility.

Then the face in her mind's eye was Edward's and whenever she remembered Edward she remembered the way he'd died. Alone and far away, so that she couldn't hold his hand and give him comfort. She could manage that thought dry-eyed these days – just. But now she was the one who needed company.

Presently she unstrapped and took advantage of the slack work period to get up and go aft to the relief station. It was behind the nav and radar nav seats, next to the life raft stowage. This was what took your time. She had to virtually take all her clothes off to use the thing and she couldn't use it comfortably, anyway, it was designed for men. At least, though, someone – Bat, she suspected – had fixed it up with air fresheners. Power trembled through the airframe and the B52 seemed even noisier here than at her console. It was rocking faintly; little, hard jolts in the low chop over the sea. Tamasin added a touch of perfume and tugged at her flight suit until her clothes felt comfortable again and then went back to her work station.

She didn't sit down, she just glanced at Chuck, evidently sleeping, then picked up her sextant and clambered up top.

*   *   *

Moonlight through the cabin windows made skull-like gleaming curves on Bat's and Mario's bone domes, and the instrument panel glowed orange for the engine instruments, blue and yellow for the flight displays and silvery grey on the EVS scopes. The EVS scopes were turned off now. Russell, in Jerry's seat, glanced at her as she came up. He smiled.

Tamasin craned over and took a look at Jerry. He was restless and she couldn't tell if he was asleep or not, but she didn't feel like disturbing him. She bent close to Russell. 'How are you feeling?'

He gave her the same tough, friendly smile. 'OK, I guess. How about *you*?'

He meant it, he really did feel concern for other people. 'Nervous,' Tamasin confessed, in a quiet voice that told Russell *he* was allowed to know that but nobody else was.

Russell clasped Tamasin's hand in his. Dry and bony as his was, it still held a surprising reserve of strength. The contact helped Tamasin. 'Bat was right, to say that prayer for us out there on the ramp,' Russell murmured, close to her ear. 'We're going to glory, Tamzie dear, and the cause is right.'

Tamzie, she thought. That was what Colan always used to call her when they were little, before he could really say his words properly. She'd called him Collie, making fun, putting him in his place because he'd been such a threat to her in those days. She squeezed Russell's hand. Here he was, dying of cancer and eaten up with pain, a man of sixty-two who looked getting on for eighty, and still it was other people he thought of first. This was a difficult one to handle dry-eyed.

'Russell, what about your family?'

The clasp of their hands seemed to give her more comfort than she could give him. Even at this station of life he was a man with a lot of love to give.

Thoughtfully Russell looped his worry beads round his free right hand. 'Well, of course, Gracie, that was my dear wife, she died around two years ago. A stroke and then pneumonia . . . sorta complications.' He could sound matter-of-fact, talking about it. 'And our son and daughter, they're all grown up, they have families of their own. I'm quite happy that I'm not leaving anyone who's gonna miss me – not in any real, practical sense.'

'But . . .' A man like this would leave the world poorer for his passing.

'To die on a raid in a worthwhile endeavour' – Russell's soft voice through the jet backdrop was earnest – 'is better than to face my kids with either watching me die slowly from this thing . . .' he still couldn't say the word *cancer* even now, it was one of his few blind spots . . . 'or finding one day that I shot my own head off.' He avoided her eye. 'To my shame, I guess I really thought of that. You know I've always kept guns around the house.'

Tamasin squeezed his hand. She remembered something. 'You were a championship marksman, weren't you?'

'Right. Lotta trophies. And I still keep my hand in.' Russell grinned lopsidedly up at her. 'Reckon you guys'll be OK with me minding the gunnery around here.'

A little longer, Tamasin clung to Russell's hand. She didn't know, now, which of them was comforting the other.

*   *   *

You couldn't get your head into the blister that formed the sighting station for the star shot. It was only big enough for the sextant. This was tricky, Tamasin thought, her body braced, boots apart on the metal decking. It was coming up to midnight, Arizona time, but on their easterly heading they were crossing time zones rapidly and astral navigation never had been Tamasin's strong suit. The inertial navigation system used accelerometers and the global positioning system used satellite triangulation and either of them alone was a safer bet than star shots by Tamasin Masterson; but they were running this flight by the old Strategic Air Command rules and the assumption was that any or all avionics systems might fail, and you'd still need to know where you were.

78

So far as she could tell, they were OK for position, OK for time. She logged it and moved forward towards the pilots' seats. The two men caught Tamasin's trace of perfume. Bat moved his head slightly, Mario twisted round from his fuel transfers.

'Why, hi, nav!' He couldn't keep the challenge out of his voice, even when he smiled. 'How we doing?'

Tamasin knelt between the seats, almost touching the trim wheels, and passed a hand over her hair. She'd left her bone dome below and she thought she was going to be in trouble from Mario. 'Spot-on,' she said. She wasn't at all sure that they were spot-on, not just going by that star shot, but she didn't want another roasting.

This time, Mario seemed to accept it. Kneeling, Tamasin gazed up at the stars. There was plenty of elbow room on a B52's first level, between the pilots' seats and the gunner and EWO stations; it was just the height that was a touch cramped. In cross-section, Tamasin thought, the thing was a bit like a railway carriage, only narrower – say the width of a three-seater bench. The height was about right, if you thought of fitting two levels into an ordinary commuter carriage.

Mario shifted in his seat and fingered his crucifix. Bat turned from the controls, on his face the patrician, fatherly smile that Tamasin loved. He put his hand over hers and at once her broad, efficient hand seemed small.

'How you feeling, Tam?'

'OK.' She had half an eye on Mario. He scared her sometimes, with that reputation of his. She blurted out suddenly: 'It's just such an odd feeling. I mean . . . to be on our way, with all our affairs put in order, everything settled, everything . . . relinquished, really. It's as if we've put the whole of our lives behind us . . . as if we're sort of . . . martyrs already.' She always thought of Edward as a martyr.

'Guess I feel the same,' Bat said, and the wrinkles

gathered at his wise eyes as he smiled in the night. 'Christian warriors can also be Christian martyrs.'

She found it faintly disturbing, the way Bat brought in the religious element. Her own motivation was far less spiritual. And yet religion did come into it, in its political aspects, if only as a baffled response to the inextricable interweave of politics and religion that was Islam. The Penhales were an ancient Cornish family with an ancient Roman Catholic tradition, and Tamasin had been raised in that faith just like all the others; yet she'd never shared the intensity of Bat's commitment. She'd never found anything in Christ's teachings that encouraged His followers to go out and blow the unbelievers to smithereens.

Bat followed Tamasin's unspoken thoughts. He'd often been capable of that and it always unnerved her when he did.

'Our mission is *right*, Tam.' His big hand squeezed hers slowly, filling her with his confidence. 'I believe it would have been approved by the Church had it been possible for the Church to know about it. We have to view this in the light of a Crusade. The Crusades against Saladin were a holy war against militant Islam, and in large measure that's what this mission is, now.'

Mario's surly toying with his crucifix showed the same intensity that came out in Bat, Tamasin realized. Mario was the only person on this flight who'd won the Medal of Honour and he hadn't even done it in the air. He'd been at a forward base in Vietnam when one night the Vietcong overran the place. Mario had been the one who grabbed a submachinegun, led a dozen Americans to safety, then went back and rescued a wounded airman. It had been chaos, hand-to-hand combat in the dark, and Mario had killed four Vietcong.

The inquiry report afterwards had glossed over whether there'd been any real need to kill them.

The story that was muttered sometimes about Jerry Yeaver's brand of heroism was of a different kind.

'Bat,' Tamasin said, cautiously but with feeling, 'one bunch of militant fundamentalist headbangers, whether murderers as in this case or not, doesn't represent mainstream Islam.'

'Sure it doesn't,' Bat said. 'Millions of mainstream Muslims *don't* go around murdering and imprisoning people on a racial-religious basis. But when *these* guys murder people, they use the name of Islam to justify it. That's why our mission is a Crusade.'

'We lost two people we loved,' Tamasin said, teeth gritted. 'I'll go for the idea of an eye for an eye, but I'm not prepared to call this a Crusade.'

Mario turned. 'Honey, it's a surgical operation that Uncle Sam doesn't have the gonads to carry out officially – so we have to do it for him. *I* don't need to remind you Tariq Talal killed your husband and, indirectly, Bat's wife – who just never got over it. But Tariq Talal is also responsible for a whole lot of other deaths, and he's becoming a religious and political force where he is right now. We're out to stop that. This is a *life-saving* mission, Tamasin – we're heading out to save the lives of all those poor guys Tariq Talal wants to kill in the future.' He broke off. He pointed straight ahead through the shallow cockpit window. 'Hey, see that?'

Tamasin craned forward. In a moment she had it, the tiny glint of starlight where the surf broke on the shore of Yucatán. Not for the first time, she marvelled at Mario's eyesight.

*   *   *

Midnight, Arizona time. Tamasin felt restless rather than sleepy. She took her sextant and ducked aft towards the ladder, pausing on the way for a look at Jerry.

She was sure he wasn't sleeping but she couldn't summon the courage to speak to him.

She shinned down the ladder, sat at her station, tickled Buster for fun, then strapped in. Chuck wasn't having trouble sleeping, he was snoring away. Tamasin felt the power flood through the airframe, felt the whole thing rise perceptibly, as Bat lifted the B52 up to 2,000 feet to cross Yucatán.

Waypoint Five was midway across the peninsula, a point south of the city of Mérida. Tamasin used Doppler radar to check the drift, then computed the groundspeed. It was still as it should be: 330 knots. On course, on time. Tamasin yawned for the first time and put a hand to her mouth as the constant note of the turbofans wrapped itself reassuringly round her. She shivered a little; but Bat preferred to have the airconditioning on the cool side and she didn't bother asking him to turn it up.

She counted them down to Waypoint Five.

The heading stayed constant, cutting across the big, solid peninsula so as to bring them out over the waters of the southern Caribbean; it was just a call for a position check. Then, faintly, Tamasin was aware of a light thud somewhere. But the B52 forged on tirelessly and, whatever it was, she assumed it must be trivial.

At the flying controls, Bat and Mario noticed the thud and swapped suspicious glances. Then Bat looked at the engine gauges.

Turbine rpm started winding down fast on Number Eight. Equally rapidly, exhaust gas temperature rose. Then as the B52 yawed perceptibly to the right, towards the failed engine, the fire lights flashed on.

CHAPTER 10

Between the control tower and the women officers'
quarters Captain Rebecca Laird went from anger to
tearfulness and back to anger in the space of a four-minute
drive. In the quiet of the early night she sat alone in the
Volkswagen for a moment, patching up her face with
tissues from the glove compartment. Then she stomped
inside.

The anguished sounds of U2 came from a huge
ghetto-blaster picked up on one of Ella's air-force visits
to Singapore. That sort of superb tone was wasted on
such loud music, Becks thought; her own taste ran
more to Fleetwood Mac. Ella gave her a grin, looking
domesticated, ironing a uniform in the small kitchen while
something that smelled tasty baked in the oven. Then she
saw the look on Becks's face and realized this was early
for her.

'Hey, Becks! Did you just walk out on him?'

'Got called in,' Becks muttered, and mooched over to
peer into Yeltsin's cage. Yeltsin wasn't very interested.
'Then I just got chewed out by the boss for being out of
the office this afternoon.' She crossed the kitchen, sniffed
at the coffee pot, then opened the fridge and frowned in.
Half a bottle of tequila, some cans of Miller Lite. Becks
dithered morosely.

Ella stood the iron on its end and watched Becks. She
knew damn well there was more to it than that but she
knew better than to ask directly. She shut off the cassette
player.

'That guy Hartmore is a Grade A pain in the ass.'

'He's still boss of this base,' Becks growled, and decided. She lifted the tequila. 'You desire?'

'Gimme a beer,' Ella said. 'I won my tennis game. Listen, Becks, *any* man who hates women that much is a pain in the ass. Hartmore has a real problem. You and I don't.'

Becks pulled two cans of Miller out of the fridge. She handed one to Ella. She took a tumbler out of the cupboard, slopped a measure of tequila into it, tried to down it in one, then in the end took three to kill it. She shoved the tequila back in the fridge and snapped the top on the second Miller.

'Boy,' Ella said, watching her, one fine, black-skinned hand savouring the cold metal touch of the can.

'I *think*,' Becks said softly, 'I just blew it. I have a feeling I am now *ex*-head of A2 on this base.' She took a swallow of cold beer.

Ella dumped the can, crossed the kitchen in two strides of her athletic legs, and put her arm round Beck's shoulders. 'Hey, honey. That can't be right. Even he can't do that to a good officer without real good reason.'

Beck's lower lip started to quiver. There'd be scapegoats all right when the top levels looked into the affair, and Hartmore would see to it that his own career wasn't the only one that got wrecked.

The phone rang.

'Shoot,' Ella muttered, and strode across the floor. 'I'll get rid of 'em.' She picked up the receiver. 'Yeah, hello?' she said in a voice that all but declared: *get off the line right now.* She frowned. 'Who?' Her eyes switched on to Beck's. 'I don't know. Hold on, I'll see if she's in her room.' She covered the mouthpiece. 'A Captain Hultlander. Are you in?'

'Oh, Jesus,' Becks groaned, 'he's calling me back so Hartmore can fire me officially. I better take it.' She walked over and Ella handed her the phone.

'Yeah,' Becks announced, 'this is Captain Laird.'

'Uh, Captain, this is Marvin Hultlander, you know, I, uh, this evening I, uh . . .' He sounded even more worried and bumbling than he'd been when she drove in from Van's place. But why the first name now?

'OK,' Becks said.

The tubby captain sounded conspiratorial. 'Listen, I'm in the next room from General Hartmore and a bunch of MP guys. They may come in any minute, I might have to cut off. I just figure you oughta know this.'

'Know what?'

'Just after you left, they came in with this guy off Dark Angel's groundcrew. He's Fretwell, he was the crew chief. He says he only recognized one person off the flight crew. Have you ever heard of a Mrs Masterson, an English lady who flies Lears out of Tucson International?'

Becks drew a breath. Ella watched her, her intelligent, black face tense. 'Tamasin Penhale Masterson?'

'Right.'

'You're saying Mrs Masterson was on Dark Angel's crew?'

'Fretwell says.'

Becks whistled. She'd never met Tamasin Masterson but she knew the story.

On the other hand, she knew Tamasin Masterson's brother. Had met him. She saw it instantly in her mind's eye. Ramstein air base, Germany, while she'd been over there on her European posting; a Nato bash; and a big, hunky RAF pilot with slow movements and a laid-back grin, sex appeal and a wife not too far in the background. Colan Penhale; with just that idiosyncratic – Cornish – spelling. He'd just been promoted Flight Lieutenant, equivalent to a captain in the US Air Force. Colan Penhale flew Tornado interceptors.

Urgently Hultlander said: 'Listen, Captain, we do have a problem. General Hartmore doesn't believe Fretwell and

85

he's trying to make him come up with a different version. General Hartmore says no way can a woman crew a B52. I think right now Fretwell's starting to figure maybe he made a mistake. But right at the start he was *real sure* it was her – real good 'n' sure!' In the pause, Becks got a sudden picture of Hultlander, blinking behind his glasses. Then he muttered, 'Shit, I have to go now!' and hung up.

Thinking hard, Becks put down the phone. It was brownies, she realized, that was what Ella had in the oven. Thoughtfully she prised the soft contact lenses out of her hot, smarting eyes and set them aside safely. She glanced over and met Ella's eye.

'You heard of Tamasin Penhale Masterson?'

Ella's face hardened. 'Whose husband got butchered by those terrorists?'

'Right.'

Ella nodded. Watching Becks, she realized that, whatever this was, it wasn't for her to know about. Nevertheless she managed to read a part at least of what was in her flat-mate's mind. 'Hartmore must at least have heard of her.' Ella's voice was soft. 'On the other hand, how long's Hartmore been down here in Arizona? Not long. Could be he didn't know she was in Tucson. Could be he didn't even know she flies jets.'

But a B52, though. Maybe, Becks thought, Hartmore wasn't so dumb if he disbelieved that groundcrew chief. Meanwhile, if you wanted to know what ticked in Tucson . . .

Slowly she picked up the phone. 'Let's see if Van knows anything.' She dialled. The small kitchen had a big, four-blade ceiling fan. The whole block had been built before the days of airconditioning. But at 10 Celsius outside, the fan wasn't turning. January in Arizona. Becks thought of her family in Minnesota: five-foot drifts and the wind blowing 20 below all the way off Baffin Island.

'Hello?' Van said.

'Hi, it's me. What can I say? How can I leave a big hunk on his own all evening in a town like this? I'm sorry.'

'Duty calls,' Van said.

'I guess.'

Delicately, Van cleared his throat. 'This plane of yours – did it crash?'

Worse than that, Becks thought. 'I think maybe *I* crashed. Honey, did you ever come across an English lady Learjet captain called Tamasin Penhale Masterson?'

'Sure. She's living at her father-in-law's place. Bat Masterson. He has a ranch, oh . . . south of town, somewhere on the way out to Tubac. Pozo Lindo.'

Tubac lay on the road to the Mexican border crossing of Nogales. It was an arts and crafts colony where Van sometimes sold his paintings. 'Pozo Lindo?' Becks repeated.

'That's what the ranch is called. It's kind of old Spanish. It means "beautiful well".'

'So my, ah, friend Linda, she's called "beautiful" in Spanish?'

Van knew of old the edge in that tone. 'Look at it this way, Captain Curvaceous, in this kinda country, *any* well's beautiful.'

He'd do. 'Listen, you sexist pig, do you have any way of confirming whether Mrs Masterson is actually right now *at* this Pozo Lindo place?'

Van hesitated. 'Sure. I know Bat a little. I can give them a call.'

'Why's he called *Bat* Masterson, anyway?'

'Oh, I believe the family's in some way related to the original Bat Masterson. Bartholomew, that was. He was one of the legends of the Old West – latter half of the last century. Bat was short for Bartholomew. Gambler and gunfighter – sheriff at one time at some place in Kansas. Ended up in the 1920s working as a sports writer on a

New York newspaper.' Van thought a moment. 'I'll call Bat, then I'll call you back.'

They hung up.

Ella was getting the brownies out, and the heat from the open oven door felt reassuring. Becks lowered her bony body into a chair and reached for the can of Miller. Weariness came over her in the frustration of her anger, yet still her whole body quivered with determination.

Van rang back.

'Couldn't raise Bat.' He sounded puzzled. 'Got the ranch manager there. Seems Bat and Tamasin went off on a field study trip in the desert, so they're both not around. They had no radio with them but they had a Jeep with a tent and sleeping bags and ample food and water. Manager says they could be back maybe Thursday or Friday.'

It was still Tuesday. 'What d'you think?' Becks said.

'I don't know what to think.'

Like hell Professor Van Burkart didn't know what to think. 'OK,' Becks persisted. 'Tamasin Masterson's husband Edward was Bat Masterson's son, right? Where's Mrs Masterson senior?'

'Alice Masterson died around a year ago.'

Hardly an event unrelated to what had happened to her son. 'Was Bat aircrew?' Becks asked. 'What kinda planes was he on?'

'He's a veteran B52 captain with a lot of experience over Vietnam. He made two-star general, same as your boss is now.'

B52s. *So why hadn't Captain Laird thought of that before?*

She chewed her lip, head in her hand, conscious of Ella, hovering, ears flapping. Never mind Ella. Ella you could trust, and right now it went against human nature for ears *not* to be flapping. Those brownies smelled good. 'Van, I'm not sure I like this.' Like it or not, the implications stared them in the face. But what also stared Captain Rebecca Laird in the face was that this information would have to be passed on to a justly jumpy base commander who'd already shown how he dealt with bringers of bad news.

'I don't like it, either,' Van admitted.

'If they bust me out the air force, can I move in with you?'

'We could sure try, but I have to wonder whether any guy has the capability to make an honest woman outa you.'

'I gotta think this one out, Van,' Becks told him. 'Thanks for checking.' She hung up.

Ella crossed to her as she stared moodily, unseeing, across the kitchen. She knew better than to ask questions, she just put a friendly hand on Becks's shoulder.

'Who the hell do I consult on a thing like this?' Becks muttered.

Still Ella knew better than to say anything.

An idea came slowly into Beck's mind. Sliding her eyes sideways, she peered shortsightedly at her watch, working out what time it would be in England.

CHAPTER 11

In the night over Yucatán, Number Eight's exhaust gas temperature went off the end of the little orange numbers on the clock.

Mario Peroni muttered, '*Shit,*' but no-one heard it because, that low down, he wasn't using oxygen and his face mask wasn't clipped up. Automatically he closed the power lever and hit the fuel cutoff. Bat Masterson was simultaneously winding on right rudder trim to correct the yaw and easing back the power on Number One to compensate for the sudden unhelpfulness of Number Eight. Mario hit the extinguisher button.

The fire lights went out. Mario and Bat swapped glances. But the B52 was still thundering through the night 2,000 feet over the Mexican jungles.

Tamasin came through on the intercom, nervous. 'What happened?'

'Goddam crazy owl,' Bat said. 'You know any other kinda bird flies at night over this kinda country?'

Birdstrike, Tamasin thought. She'd had perspiration on the back of her neck but suddenly it was tingling cold. She'd never had a birdstrike, not in twelve years of flying. She remembered the tales: *eagle went in one end, the turbine blades came out the other.* But those were from guys who'd survived.

Mario was adjusting the remaining throttles. 'Nav, get us a recalculation on that route plot.'

To maintain the speeds they'd assumed, the fuel burn was likely to increase. But on this flight there were no diversion airfields; this target wasn't one they could compromise.

Chuck woke up, alert instantly. 'Hey, gorgeous, what is it?'

She told him.

At once he craned over her route charts. 'You want a hand?'

It was something in the way he said it. It was more than an offer, more than a command, more like a warning. This was the experienced expert Tamasin was talking to, the man who'd been his wing's master navigator over Hanoi. Yet still this wasn't simply an old hand's experience talking, it was the voice of a man who distrusted a colleague who was in this to kill the target, never mind whether she died in the achievement.

Chuck didn't mean to die in the achievement, but they all knew that.

'It's OK, Chuck, really I've already got a mental picture of what we want to do.'

'Honey . . .'

'I'm *not* your little fucking *honey*!' With her dark eyes blazing out from under the bone dome she forced him away from her by sheer weight of will-power. Still Chuck kept craning to see, and Tamasin felt she wanted to hunch her shoulder round the charts like a schoolkid keeping the next pupil from copying her answers.

Either she was imagining this or the B52 was trembling. Sweat prickled on her face where the inner helmet pressed against her forehead.

Movement on her right. Jerry Yeaver bent over her, one hand on the ladder rail, tall and lean with the honesty shining from his vulnerable eyes through the glasses. 'Tamasin, you want any help?'

'No,' she snarled, 'I'm a big girl now.'

Jerry didn't reply, he just vanished back up the ladder. It dawned on Tamasin, lip out-thrust as she prodded the keys on her pocket calculator, that maybe she'd upset him. Too bad.

She called Bat on the intercom. 'I've done the new fuel burn, sticking to the original attack plan. We'd be over target with about 25,000 pounds of fuel – how does that sound to you?'

In the pilots' seats, Mario and Bat swapped glances again. Mario pulled a sour face and fingered his crucifix.

'Tamasin,' Bat said, 'we have found that BUFFs can be a little hard to control when you have asymmetric power and the weight's below a certain level. Especially at the higher power settings we're gonna need for the bomb run. Can we try another plot, please?'

With the ejector seat behind her and the chart table and screens and dials and knobs in front of her, Tamasin felt she was in a prison, with no outside view and no escape. Panic clutched at her. Then she glimpsed Chuck sitting patronizingly next to her, itching to get his hands on her charts, and determination took over.

'OK, pilot.'

Hands shaking now, she ran through her calculations, forcing herself not to hurry, forcing herself to get it right. The ceaseless noise all around her was oppressive. She felt cold.

She called Bat again. 'We're going to be slowed up. To arrive with the weight right, we're going to have to arrive in daylight.' She didn't know how Bat would react to that idea.

He just said: 'Work it out, Tamasin. Give us the new timings when you have them.'

Then, with the night black ahead of the windscreen, he met Mario's eyes.

Mario leaned across the engine console, furious. With his intercom mike swinging clear, he yelled at Bat through the noise. 'Are you crazy? In daylight, that's plain suicide!'

Bat leaned over to be heard, but his voice was even. 'It's probably suicide anyway. That doesn't matter.'

'We *agreed*, Bat! We agreed all necessary risks and no more! We did *not* say let's all go right out and slaughter ourselves! We agreed each one of us is *prepared* to get killed on this thing, we did not agree any of us will *deliberately* get themselves killed – or get any of the rest of us killed, either!'

'You've flown daylight raids, same as I have, Mario.'

'Yeah! Enough of them to know in daylight we won't even get near the target!' Mario's eyes were blazing. Mario was a gambler, but he still liked to have the odds right.

'We've done it before and we'll do it this time,' Bat replied doggedly. 'We know about the local threat situation, we had a thorough briefing.' Courtesy of Chuck Brantley, he remembered.

Mario yelled: 'We might as well just dive on the goddam target, kamikaze style!'

'You know damn well we have to get the plane out of Libya at all costs,' Bat said coolly. 'We have to remove the evidence. We have . . .' Then Tamasin's voice was in their headsets.

'Can I suggest a new route?'

Bat said: 'Go ahead.'

Tamasin said: 'We *were* going to cross mid-Algeria, hit the target, and continue out over the Med, but I think this might be a better way. We'd cross the most deserted parts of the Sahara – Mauritania, northern Mali, Niger and Chad – and we'd come round the Tibesti mountains and up from Chad.'

'That's even longer,' Bat said, surprised. 'How d'you figure we can make it?'

'It's actually not that much longer in proportion to the original plan,' Tamasin said. 'Anyway, we'll be flying more slowly. What this route does have going for it is that we approach the target from the east, out of a dawn sky.'

Again Bat and Mario swapped glances. Bat said, 'I like that.'

Mario liked it, too, but he still wasn't letting it go without a challenge. 'Nav, you sure about that fuel burn?'

Tamasin repeated her calculations. She was sure.

'I still like that,' Bat told Mario. 'Let's buy it.'

* * *

Moonlight caught waves breaking on the east coast of Yucatán. They were leaving Mexico for good. In the dim light Tamasin was entering the new waypoints into the computer.

'Let's get back to some sleeping,' Bat said. 'Chuck, Jerry, your sleep got kind of interrupted – do you want a crack at some more?' They said no. 'OK,' Bat said. 'Tamasin, then, that's you and me.' He handed control to Mario and settled down in his seat.

Tamasin finished the computer inputs. She hadn't realized how tired she was. Chuck gave her a grin and she climbed out of her seat and let him out. She slid back through into Chuck's seat and Chuck took over Tamasin's place to watch the navigation while she slept. She settled herself as comfortably as she could. The last thing she noticed before drifting into sleep was Chuck lighting another cigarette and scattering ash all over her console.

* * *

On the first level, Russell was back on the guns.

'Wanna eat?' Jerry offered.

Taut-faced, Russell shook his head and wrapped his worry beads round his hand. 'Could use a coffee.'

Their eyes met. Getting Russell a coffee meant going back down to that second level and a highly irascible navigator. The coffee maker and the water supply alike were down there, on the upright installation that included Tamasin's panel and console. They faced out on to the walkway.

Oh well, he was going to have to go down there some time.

Jerry levered his lanky body out from the seat, went forward bent almost double under the ducting on the low cabin ceiling, and checked with Mario. Mario wanted coffee. Resignedly, Jerry clambered down.

It relieved him to find Chuck grinning cheerfully at the navigator's station while Tamasin slept comfortlessly in Chuck's place. Jerry drew four beakers, handed one to Chuck and clasped the other three precariously against him as he went back up the ladder.

Shoulder to shoulder with Jerry as he sipped hot coffee, Russell realized what was wrong with the younger man. Pensively he flipped his worry beads. He should have guessed what would happen when Jerry went below.

'You take it too hard, Jerry. Tamasin's a very competent young woman and she needs to have men realize that.'

'I know that.' Jerry was looking down at the metal decking between the seats. 'All I wanted to do was help.'

'Sure.' Russell persisted. 'Tamasin could've been a bit nervous, too. Could be she just sounded like she was rejecting you when really she wasn't.'

Jerry shrugged. 'Well, I guess it doesn't matter, any-way.'

'Yeah, it does,' Russell said. 'You feel bad about it.'

Jerry glanced at him, their bone domes almost touching. '*That* matters? Oh, yeah – in case I fuck up over target.'

He'd meant that literally, Russell realized, not in bitter irony. 'No,' Russell said, and put a bony hand on Jerry's sleeve. 'It matters because you are a human being with feelings and you have a right to your feelings, like you have a right to be alive.'

In a little surprise, Jerry considered. He couldn't see how he did have a right to be alive. He was no use to anyone, except for what he could do as EWO aboard this aircraft.

'What did go wrong with your marriage, Jerry?' Russell said.

In normal life, that sort of question is sensitive to the point of rudeness. When you're faced with the likelihood that the rest of your life might take no more than another twenty-four hours, you need to know certain things that otherwise you wouldn't.

Jerry recognized that. He was happy enough to talk to Russell; yet it was too much like selfishness, dwelling simply on himself. 'I guess maybe we both made mistakes. What about yourself? I mean . . .' He broke off. 'I keep thinking about your family.'

But Jerry knew, or sensed, Russell's sensitivities towards his family. He knew Russell hadn't got long anyway.

In an unconscious gesture, Russell put his hand over his stomach, where the cancer was. 'I've made my peace with my Maker, Jerry; I'm ready to go. And I'm sure going to be glad to be shot of this thing.'

Russell was content within himself. He was ready to meet death, in a way in which Jerry wasn't. Because Jerry's grim impulse to destroy himself, or to be destroyed, stemmed not even from the abandonment of hope but from helplessness, rage, frustration. Russell met Jerry's eye. 'Times like this, buddy,' he said softly through the jet noise, 'it helps if your friends know certain things you'd sooner keep quiet.' He paused. 'I heard you turned down a medal after that thing at Eielson.'

Jerry sighed. He poked with his boot at the flight case in its stowage. Reluctantly he nodded. 'It woulda been wrong. The reasons woulda all been wrong.'

'What reasons?' Russell persisted gently.

Jerry narrowed his eyes behind the glasses and concentrated on the VHF tuner. 'Sue, I guess,' he muttered eventually.

'Sue was your wife?' Russell wasn't surprised that the reason hadn't been to do with the event itself.

Jerry nodded.

'You met her at Eielson?'

'Hell, no – Castle, California. California was fine – that was where we married. Then they posted us to Eielson. I guess Sue just couldn't get along with Alaska.'

Russell began: 'I heard . . .'

'There's a lot of bullshit talked,' Jerry said angrily, and hunched forward over his console.

*   *   *

Over the Caribbean it was still the middle of the night. Methodically, as he talked, Jerry went on scanning the wavebands. There'd been little enough radar. At one point they'd had energy off a very distant search radar, evidently a US drugs watch, but it showed no interest in them because they were moving west to east, not heading from Colombia towards Texas or Florida; and they were still out of range of the ground radars in Cuba, Jamaica, Honduras and Nicaragua. At one point they got waves off a US cruiser, but again the route and track didn't excite attention and the slow, 330-knot groundspeed suggested a turboprop type rather than a jet.

It was chilly aboard the B52 yet Russell's face had small beads of sweat.

'There are things a buddy needs to know,' Russell said. 'You rescued a guy out of a KC135 that crashed on takeoff at Eielson. Right, Jerry?'

Jerry focused his thoughts tightly on his console. He switched from VHF to UHF. Nothing. Russell waited. Slowly Jerry nodded.

The KC135 is an air-to-air fuel tanker. Any aircraft taking off for a long flight is potentially an unexploded incendiary bomb, but a tanker is a lot more so than most.

'Way I heard it,' Russell said, 'you were in a car with another officer, crossing Eielson under clearance from ground control.'

Again, slowly, Jerry nodded.

'They held you at the active runway. The 135 was rolling. As it went past you a flock of gulls crossed the runway. Multiple birdstrike, they lost both the engines one side just as they got in the air. Roll's kinda hard to hold on a 135. I heard they caught a tip on a snowbank and stalled back on. Guess it was a miracle they didn't fireball there and then. But since it wasn't burning when it came to rest, you went after it in the car. Yeah?'

Tight-lipped, Jerry turned the tuner. He nodded. He could still hear the man beside him yelling, yelling, *Jesus Christ, let's get outa here*, and all the time he'd been heading towards the crash at 90mph, foot on the floorboards.

'And then the pilot was out cold,' Russell said.

'Yeah,' Jerry muttered reluctantly. 'Co-pilot and engineer trying to shift him, but they were good 'n' dazed themselves. Well, you just do what you gotta do.' The officer who'd been with Jerry hadn't thought so. He'd been in the car, two miles down the perimeter track, by the time the fire crews arrived.

'You do what you gotta do,' Russell repeated. 'On top of 31,000 gallons of jet fuel just waiting to blow?'

A mirthless smile tautened Jerry's hollow face. 'You ever heard of a guy called Rainer Werner Fassbinder?'

Russell thought for a moment. 'German film-maker — West Germany as was. Quite successful. Suicided in the mid-eighties. Yeah?'

'Right. He said one day: *Es ist besser, auszubrennen, als langsam wegzudämmern.*'

98

'Hot dang,' Russell said, 'it's a sight of time since I was in Germany.'

The B52 was bouncing a bit, shuddering.

'Translated,' Jerry said softly, 'it means: "It's better to burn out than slowly fade away".'

'You'd'a sure done that.' Then Russell leaned towards him. 'Where did Sue come into that, Jerry?'

Jerry swung towards him. All the frustration, all the desperation was in his face as he raised one gaunt hand and clenched it, not in anger but in helplessness. 'If she'd ever given me a chance to do one thing *right*! If she'd ever been content with just one thing I did for her! She wanted to be a colonel's wife, or a general's, and I . . . shoot, Russell, she *knew* this from day one – I'm not that material. That day . . . she hated Alaska. She wanted us out of Alaska. I'd'a gone, too. But along with that she was just convinced that the way I was gonna make colonel or whatever was by going into admin, getting a desk job. OK, I applied – the first desk job that came up.'

Russell watched him. 'At Eielson?'

Turning away, Jerry nodded. Wearily he lowered his head. 'When I told her, she hit the ceiling. The desk job wasn't good enough – it had to be a desk job back in the Lower Forty-Eight. That was the day . . .'

'The day the 135 came down.'

Jerry nodded. Russell could see the whole thing now. Again the B52 lurched under them, but neither man really noticed.

'Well, I went back to the colonel,' Jerry said. 'I said if the transfer wasn't gonna get me out of Eielson, I'd sooner stay flying. So the colonel said, did I *really* want to leave Eielson. I guess I blew it – I was still on kind of a high after the 135. I said no.'

'It was the truth, wasn't it?'

Jerry nodded. He looked away again. 'Well, after I withdrew the application, we had an even *worse* row, and that was it. She went. I just . . . I handled it very badly. Maybe I just didn't handle it at all.'

'You ever go out with another woman?' Russell murmured.

'God, no!'

'I don't mean while you were married, I mean since.'

Jerry shook his head. 'Not during or since.'

Russell watched Jerry. 'You oughta think about that,' he said. 'Just 'cos you weren't the right guy for *one* woman doesn't mean you're not a fit guy for *any* woman.'

'I doubt it.' Jerry laughed harshly. 'Anyway, we'll be dead in a few hours, and that sure suits me.'

*　　*　　*

From below, Chuck Brantley came through on the intercom. 'We have some weather, guys. Anyone not wearing harness better think about putting it on.'

Russell and Jerry had been noticing a bit of bouncing. Now their coffee beakers sprang right out of the holders and Russell just caught his worry beads as they slid across the console. Fixtures rattled about in the big jet's cabin.

Beside Chuck, Tamasin stirred. She'd been having a dream in which she and Edward were flying a Lear at dead of night, with Edward as her co-pilot – even though in reality he would always have been the aircraft's captain. They were lost, with no idea how far it was to their destination airfield. They picked up a reading from a VOR navigational beacon, but they couldn't relate it to their charts so Edward went aft to find the right chart. Then Jerry Yeaver came back to the cockpit instead, and there was no sign of Edward. 'It's all right, Tamasin,' Jerry had said, 'it doesn't matter if we crash.' Then came a hefty jolt, and in the dream they *had* crashed, and Tamasin came awake at once.

Around her, the B52 was like a live thing. Her bone

dome bounced on to the decking, she heard crashes and thumps, and the lights flickered. They were pitching and rolling in the powerful turbulence of a Caribbean storm.

CHAPTER 12

Wet wind blustered out of the January night against fastened window frames on the houses in Woodhall Spa, Lincolnshire. It was half past five, Wednesday morning, the time of day when only farm hands and fighter pilots are awake.

Flight Lieutenant Colan Penhale was shaving, alert as he always was from the moment he rolled out of bed. The big, gabled house looked like most of the houses in Woodhall Spa, and the men who built it, in 1902, built it to last but hadn't kept the draughts out. The en suite shower room was a recent adaptation and its light showed the form of Jane, Colan's bride, half-awake and stirring; and the cot where their daughter Katharine lay fast asleep. Katharine was three weeks old, hardly back from the maternity hospital. They'd named her after Colan's mother; Lady Penhale was a GP with a practice in rural Cornwall; she'd only just returned there after seeing the baby home. Family matters weren't uppermost in Colan Penhale's mind just then, though, he was wondering how strong today's winds were going to be around 30,000 feet over Scotland.

He was dabbing his face with a towel when the phone rang.

He thought: *blast*. Muted or not, that might wake Katharine. He crossed the carpet quickly, the towel round him more for warmth than for modesty, and picked up the phone. 'Hello?' His eye was on Jane, turning over in sleepy protest.

The voice was female, distant, American, and slightly

metallic with the distortion of a transatlantic line. 'Hello, is that Flight Lieutenant Penhale? Colan?'

'Speaking.'

'Hi, there. This is Captain Rebecca Laird, US Air Force A2, calling from Tucson, Arizona. We met two years ago in Ramstein, Germany.'

'Oh, yes, I remember.' The picture was there at once: cheerful, confident, toothy American face; sandy hair; six foot and lots of leg; a good figure. But Colan was keeping his voice down to avoid waking Katharine. Rapid mental arithmetic told him in Tucson it wasn't yet Wednesday, it was twenty-five to eleven, Tuesday night.

'Sorry to intrude,' Becks said. 'When I called your base they said you'd be up for an early flight. I was kinda wondering if you could help us with a matter we're in a little doubt on, here. I believe you have a sister living near here called Tamasin Penhale Masterson, right?'

'That's right,' Colan murmured, and frowned.

'May I ask – have you heard from Tamasin in recent days? Do you have any idea what she might be doing?'

Colan considered. 'No, no idea, I'm afraid. You should find her at Bat Masterson's ranch at Pozo Lindo. She flies Learjet taxis out of Tucson International.' It was a bit of a grandiose name for a municipal airport, but it was an international field all right. 'May I ask what is your interest?'

Momentary silence at the other end. Colan had his mental picture of Becks all right, but for all he could picture her background environment she might have been on a spacecraft.

'This is kind of confidential,' Becks said as smoothly as she could manage, 'but we have a B52 that seems to be missing, and we're wondering whether there's any way Tamasin could be on it.'

Colan had half an eye on Jane again. His voice went softer. 'You mean missing, believed crashed?'

'Ah, no.' Becks hesitated. 'Missing, believed missing.'
He cottoned on immediately.

Offhand, he couldn't remember what the unrefuelled range of a B52 was, but if there was anything dodgy about this flight they wouldn't be getting fuel in the air or anywhere else. But he knew the frame of mind Tamasin had been in the last time he'd seen her. 'And you want me to guess what Tamasin might do, 'cos if we knew, we might know what your flying machine might do . . .'

'Right.' His speed impressed Becks.

Colan said: 'Whereabouts is Bat Masterson?'

'We don't know for sure.'

Colan was liking this less and less. 'I'd find him pretty quickly if I were you – if you can.'

'Colan, tell me.' Becks cut across him, this was something she had to know. 'You and I both know there's a history to this. But why would a Learjet captain – irrespective of whether she'd been married to an F15 pilot, or of what happened to that pilot – be on board a B52?'

That was easy.

'Tamzie qualified PPL before I did,' Colan said measuredly. *Private Pilot's Licence*, Becks understood. 'She's eighteen months older than me. She soloed on her seventeenth birthday.' So had Colan done, actually. 'She's a damn good pilot, she's a professional.' Once, praise like that wouldn't have come easily to Colan. Once, they'd fought like cat and dog. The draught round Colan's shoulder made him shiver. 'Do you know what the University Air Squadron is?'

'No,' Becks answered.

'It's a reserve training corps, specifically for university students. Tamzie joined that – she was still studying, of course. They trained her on Bulldogs – single-prop trainer – she got some time on C130s.' The Hercules, the four-turboprop transport workhorse; a big aircraft compared with a Lear or a Jet Provost trainer. 'But Bat was running a B52 wing at that time, up in Alaska. One summer he wangled for Tamzie to go over on what they loosely called a USAF-RAF officer exchange – you know all these UAS students have military ranks; Tamzie was Pilot Officer Penhale. Well . . .'

'You mean she was flying in B52s *then*?'

'Well, yeah. Flying in them and flying them. She never had command of one, obviously, but she flew P2 a couple of times, she was handling pilot, no mistake.' P2 was air shorthand for co-pilot. When the P2 is the handling pilot, that's when the P1 – captain – has his feet up and the co-pilot is doing the work. Colan could picture her now. Dogged and determined, stocky and sombre, with those big eyes of hers hooded, and looking every bit the professional in her rumpled olive flying suit with the one blue-and-black band on the shoulder and the big squadron badge emblazoned on the upper sleeves. He'd been jealous of her but now he was proud. 'Tamzie's landed B52s. Not a lot of women have.' Silence on the other end. Colan said: 'Hello? Becks?'

Becks muttered: 'Oh Jesus. I figured she might be kind of a sound pilot, but I didn't figure B52 experience as well. You know what I'm wondering?'

Dead right Colan did. 'Becks – would Bat have any info on the exact siting of Tariq Talal's base? I mean the co-ordinates, not just it's in Libya somewhere.'

'It's moderately common knowledge in the US military,' Becks replied. 'I would guess the guy still has plenty of contacts who could tell him.'

'Same here.'

'What d'you figure?'

Colan pulled the towel tighter round him. He'd fixed draught excluders on that window only last October, maybe he should fit a new window frame altogether. 'If Bat and Tamasin got hold of a long-range aircraft . . .' he wasn't sure how much of this Jane was picking up

. . . 'I wouldn't put it past them to try and whack Tariq Talal. And I'm rather inclined to wish them luck. Edward Masterson was a damn good guy – he was my brother-in-law.'

'Right,' Becks answered slowly. Thoughtfully she paused. 'There's only one trouble.'

'Yeah?' But Colan knew what was coming.

'What do they do after they whack him?'

'Your guess is as good as mine,' Colan answered. He answered a bit quickly, as if he'd already made his guesses.

Becks was starting to make guesses, too, and she didn't like them. 'They'd have no place to go,' she murmured.

Colan said: 'And no fuel left to get there.'

Becks paused. 'I gotta think about this,' she said. 'Thanks, Colan.'

They hung up.

'What was it?' Jane mumbled. It was a quarter to six. A quarter to eleven in Arizona. Jane hadn't caught on. Colan had a think.

This worried him. As Tamasin's kid brother, he'd fought relentlessly with her ever since he could remember, because *she'd* fought *him*, because his earliest memories were of *her* resenting *his* very existence, because she'd *made* him fight. Maybe half the reason that Flight Lieutenant Colan Penhale was even now residing in the front seat of a hi-tech, high-performance RAF fighter was that big sister Tamzie had *taught* him how to fight, instilled in him that much calm, matter-of-fact aggression. And, as much as he'd hated her in the days when they'd been little and they'd fought, now he loved her at least that much. Certainly he'd felt almost the same anguish that she'd experienced over Edward; not the whole of it, because Colan wasn't the one who'd lost his partner; lost the one who'd been going to spend the rest of his life with her.

106

But a bombed-up B52 that had gone autonomous wasn't good news.

'Tamzie may have gone out on a limb,' he told Jane. 'But there's nothing you or I can do at 6,000 miles' range.' Stooping, he kissed Jane. Very sensitively he picked up Katharine, and in her sleep the girl wriggled against her father as he cuddled her; and she still hadn't woken as he tucked her up again.

Colan put on his uniform, bolted his breakfast, and went out.

* * *

Eastern Lincolnshire is flat the way not much else on earth is flat except maybe the Netherlands, or Africa's endless Kalahari. Woodhall Spa had some patches of trees but there wasn't much else except the old-fashioned, grand houses to break the icy wind driving the chilling drizzle. Colan Penhale was a family man but he was also a fighter pilot and he also received what on a flight lieutenant's pay wasn't an entirely superfluous allowance from a rich, titled father. The family car was the Peugeot 505 estate; that was the one that Jane mostly drove. Colan drove the commuter car. Commuting was the four miles between Woodhall Spa and the station at Coningsby and the commuter car was a twenty-year-old Triumph TR6 drophead sports. Four of the guys on the squadron drove black Toyota MR2s but Colan's car was a collector's piece and turned more heads in town than the MR2s did.

On the other hand, the soft top on the TR6 had more draughts in than the whole of that big, gabled house had.

It was still dark when Colan parked and strode through the numbing drizzle to the squadron ops room. The great, gaunt hangars against the stormy sky were a relic of an era when you'd had a touch more warning of approaching bother, and the aggravation wasn't likely to be full of nerve gas, poisonous microbes or strontium 90. One day they'd get hardened aircraft shelters like in Germany; meanwhile, Parliament was spending its money funding state disinvestment.

In the changing room a few men were about and one of them was Colan's navigator.

'Hi, Colan.'

'Hi, Salim.'

Flying Officer Salim Arshad greeted Colan with the same half-shy grin as always. He was twenty-six, two years younger than Colan, born in Britain into a family that had its roots in Pakistan. He had a ten-month-old son and tried unsuccessfully to hide how proud he was of the kid and of the wife who'd borne him.

'How's the young master?' Colan asked Salim.

'Oh . . .' Salim nodded . . . 'fine, fine.' From his slow, deep, English public-school voice, you wouldn't have guessed his Asian origins. He was clean-shaven, his complexion quite dark, with a strongly delineated wedge of jaw and dark, thoughtful eyes. He was five foot ten, the same height as Colan, but slim and graceful whereas Colan was thickset, powerful and purposeful, a muscular, John Bull image. Salim was a spin bowler; Colan in his time had played rugby. These days Colan worked out on weights; he considered it unprofessional in a fighter pilot to run the risks of injury you could meet on a rugby field.

*　　*　　*

They changed into the olive flying kit with the squadron crest on the shoulders. The two men got on well, had done from the day they'd met. Salim recognized Colan's openmindedness, not least about race; Colan recognized

Salim's abilities, and respected them. Tacitly, Colan had felt that if an Asian officer could get as far as Tornado training, he must be at least as good as the UK-origin officers on the same course, and probably better; experience indicated the latter.

They briefed. Weather: cloud was down to 800 feet over most of England and Scotland; surface winds moderate to strong; dewpoint; icing. Notams: very little; no royal flights and no nearby airfields where people were practising skydiving on a day like this. Mission: a two-hour combat sortie with tanker rendezvous, possibility as usual of some Soviet traffic.

With their *g*-suit leads swinging, Colan and Salim walked through the operations room, signed the necessary forms and checked the logs, then walked through the rain to their Tornado.

Salim climbed the ladder to the aft cockpit. Colan walked round with a torch for a careful look over the aircraft. This was a thorough inspection, even though the groundcrew had gone over the Tornado in detail an hour earlier. The wing was head-high to Colan and he couldn't reach the tail to check the rudder, but he checked everything else. Ailerons. Flap tracks. Nav lights, transparency unbroken. Missiles, on and secure; arming pins out; needles in the right sector. The engineer officer who'd done the earlier check was hanging about by the wingtip, and Colan spoke to him. He was a man Colan trusted, a man with whom now and then he'd allow himself the cautious luxury of a couple of pints of Bateman's bitter in the Gamecock in Woodhall Spa.

Colan joined Salim in the front office and allowed the ground-crewman who'd followed him up the ladder to shove all the right plugs into all the right sockets, strap him in, and take out the pin on the miniature detonation cord, the filament of explosive that would blow off the canopy if they had to depart in a hurry.

Colan took out the ejector seat pin. He started the generators.

Cockpit checks: OK. Weapons checks: OK. Intercom: OK. Colan consulted Salim about his radars: the radars checked OK. All the groundcrew were standing well back with their ear protectors on. Colan closed the cockpit canopy and ran the auxiliary power unit. Output: OK. Colan ran up the first RB199 turbofan. In the closed cockpit with the bone dome on you couldn't hear the racket it made.

Colan shut off the APU. He started the second main engine. Then it was chocks away and the Tornado rolled.

Over the long radar nose the airfield was a black expanse of rainy nothingness. Shivery wind-ripples on the pools on the tarmac reflected the nose light. The Tornado was painted pale grey to make it harder to see against sky or cloud, but out here in the blackness it was just another shape with a couple of lights on. Raindrops ran on the canopy and Colan turned up the airconditioning heat control. This had the best airconditioning of any aircraft he'd flown.

'Cobra One,' Coningsby tower said. 'Clear to roll.'

Cobra One was today's callsign. Colan was looking all round but they had the airfield to themselves. Out of the fast taxi he steered on to the runway centreline, picked a marker among the distant lights at the end, and opened the taps. The shove in the back as the burners lit was the same sensation as always, but the thrill of the acceleration had the same effect on Colan as the first time he'd experienced it. There was nothing else like this in the world.

They punched off the runway and up hard into the cloud.

Salim's deep voice was cool in the headset, unflappable, matter-of-fact. He would always sound unruffled, Colan reflected, whatever direction the aircraft was pointing or whichever side it was up. Now he was giving Colan headings and heights and Colan was flying blind in the cloud but flying impeccably, precisely.

At 32,000 feet they came out of cloud roughly over Inverness, Scotland.

*   *   *

Local time was slightly after seven. Hardly a star showed in the endless arch of black sky but Colan could see a faint glimmer in the east, off the starboard wingtip. He could just glimpse that wingtip if he twisted really hard against the harness. It was fully swept now.

This sort of flying was undemanding, hardly more than just steering the aeroplane, and Colan spared a thought for Tamasin.

If she really was on that B52 and if that thing really had gone autonomous with a bomb load, then the girl really was over her head in trouble. And yet if she *had* set her heart on blowing Tariq Talal to blazes, Colan deeply hoped she'd do it. He'd felt so helpless when Edward had died. Nothing you could do, nothing you could say to a bereaved young wife made any difference. He was gone. Nothing would bring him back. Meanwhile, governments shrugged their shoulders and did nothing, because you couldn't impose economic sanctions on a bunch of murderous outlaws who weren't even much to do with the state that gave them house room. In any case, that state was isolated diplomatically from the Western world.

Well, now maybe someone *was* doing something.

Ground radar was giving them vectors for the VC10 tanker. As the winter light strengthened, the sky was turning charcoal.

'Contact,' Salim said in his deep, unruffled voice. 'Range one four.' He'd found the tanker on the Tornado's Foxhunter radar at fourteen nautical miles.

The sky grew dove grey. A brace of distant, tiny, flashing white lights were the VC10's strobes. Colan called the tanker and they positioned astern and the small basket reeled slowly out from the VC10's rear fuselage, curved and graceful against the pearly sky and the ocean of rumpled cloud below, starting now to pick up the colours of daylight. Colan nudged the probe into the basket drogue. It was a point of pride to him to get a good contact first time, every time. They tanked up, cruising north, high over northern Scotland. They thanked the tanker crew. They broke off and Colan retracted the probe.

'Cobra One.' The fighter controller, miles away down on the ground, was a woman. She sounded about Colan's age and as coolheaded as Salim and, to judge by her voice, she'd been raised in Belfast. 'We have a bogey, track two zero five, flight level four one zero, range seven five, your vector is three one two.'

Unidentified aircraft, heading south through the Faeroes Gap. 'Cobra One,' Colan acknowledged, and stood the Tornado on its port wingtip.

Reheat punched in and they went supersonic.

*   *   *

At 46,000 feet Colan levelled the Tornado with the reheat still fully in and the speed around Mach 1.1. At those heights that gave them an airspeed of around 1,200 knots. Cloud, sliding across their path, was close enough below to give the sensation of speed, and in the early day the sky was going pale feathery brown.

'Cobra One,' the woman from Belfast said. 'Come left ten, vector two nine zero.'

At that speed the course correction was rather a subtle one.

'Contact,' Salim said, sounding almost bored. 'Ten

o'clock. Three zero miles, closing.' And closing fast. 'It's a big bastard,' Salim said. 'Maybe a Bear.'

Bear was the NATO codename for the four-turboprop Tupolev Tu 95. It served as a bomber, maritime patrol and reconnaissance aircraft.

'Hm,' Salim said thoughtfully. 'Maybe not. Going a bit quickly for a Bear.' Then he said: '*Ha*. He's got us.'

This was part of the game. You got them on your radar, they got you on theirs. No-one was messing around with a missile lock, not up here. That wasn't part of the game.

Four feeble contrails off the bogey aircraft stretched pinkish brown where they caught the rising sun. There wasn't much of them: at this time of year, contrails sometimes didn't form at all this high up, it was too cold.

'Visual,' Colan said, trying to match Salim's deadpan voice. He'd caught the flash of the bogey's strobes. A moment later he could see the aircraft itself, hard and very tiny against the sky as it went colourless in the growing day. 'Cobra One, Suitcase.' *Suitcase* was madam from Belfast. 'We have visual on a . . . ah . . .' Four jets. High wing. Clumsy fat fuselage like a flying slug. And *what* was that gubbins on top of it . . .? 'Mainstay. We have a Mainstay.'

The Soviet Ilyushin Il 86 had been around for twenty years as a transport roughly equivalent to the American Lockheed C141 Starlifter except in terms of airborne aesthetics: the Ilyushin was an ugly device. More recently, they'd bolted a big, saucer-shaped radar dish atop the fuselage, the way Boeing had done to turn the 707 airliner into the E3 AWACS – Airborne Warning And Control System. NATO had dubbed it Mainstay. It had been something of a triumph in terms of taking a Plain Jane of an aeroplane and making it look truly horrible.

113

In terms of functioning, though, the Ilyushin AWACS worked well, no mistake.

Colan brought the Tornado's speed down to formate on the Mainstay. He was frowning. 'Salim, where are the Foxhounds?'

Foxhound was the NATO codename for the MiG 31 fighter. It was a very capable aircraft and Colan had never seen a Mainstay operating without a couple of Foxhounds flying close escort.

'Got no Foxhounds, Colan.'

They must *be* there. They couldn't just *not materialize* on radar. Dammit, Colan thought, maybe it *really* hasn't got any.

'Negative on Foxhounds, Colan.'

But Colan had been flying fighters too long not to get a nasty, prickly sensation at the back of his neck.

He had the Tornado's canopy now four feet under the Ilyushin's port wingtip. Faces peered out of portholes. This sort of thing eased the tedium of a long flight out of Murmansk or wherever. One of the Russians waved. Two others clicked cameras. Salim was clicking his camera, too. Colan had spent several years of his life waving at Russian airmen in these sort of latitudes. These days, he reflected, with the Soviet leadership as it was, the relationship was rather cosier than in former times; you hardly thought of these people as potential enemies any more.

The enemies were people like Tariq Talal.

Colan waved the Russians goodbye, dipped the nose to pull clear of the Ilyushin, then snapped the Tornado upside down, drew back the stick, and went hard round and down for the cloud, still watching out for the MiG 31 escorts he couldn't believe weren't there.

But not a MiG materialized.

*   *   *

Colan flew south, let down through all those fathoms of cloud, and eased the Tornado through the rain down the approach path at Coningsby. It was twenty to ten, the daylight muddy grey. Gusts spattered cold raindrips against the canopy and Colan, as he taxied into his parking place on the ramp, was thinking first of relief of the bladder, then of strong, hot coffee. He opened the canopy and ran through the shutdown drills.

Then as the groundcrew put up the ladders against the cockpit's sides a man with a wing commander's shoulder tabs on his flying suit was crossing the windy expanse of the ramp. Their commanding officer. *Oh hell*, Colan thought, *what have I done this time?* Standing up in the cockpit, he glanced aft at Salim. Salim's dark face with its precise wedge of jaw was blank.

Well, Colan was the aircraft captain; it was his job to be first at the scene of the crash.

He went down the ladder. Salim came down behind him. Shoulder to shoulder, they saluted the wing commander. He returned the salute and gave them a smile. Colan couldn't interpret that.

'How was it?'

'Pretty routine, sir. Intercepted a solo Mainstay.'

'Good.' The wing commander nodded. 'I've just had some new orders concerning you, Colan. NATO wants you at Sigonella, Sicily, as soon as possible.'

CHAPTER 13

Another succession of crashes rang through the belly of the B52 and Tamasin was alarmed. She gave Chuck Brantley a bleary look. Chuck was in her navigator's station, looking at-home.

'Where are we?' Tamasin said. 'What time is it?'

'Ten past ten zulu,' Chuck yawned. 'Ten past three in the morning, Arizona time. Don't ask me what the local is. We're kind of south of Jamaica.'

Tamasin said: 'Had we better swap places?'

Through the engines' roar there were bumps and bangs. The B52 dropped sickeningly and then surged forward. Jerkily Chuck clambered out and held on tightly to the vertical ladder beside him. As Tamasin followed him she caught the back of her bone dome on one of the ejector seats, then pitched forward and caught the front of it on the EVS screen surround. She grazed her wrist on the control panel. The B52 lurched down and Tamasin went flying. It was only inches but she hit Chuck hard. He caught her with his free arm and steadied her. Tamasin clung to Chuck. This time, neither of them was kidding.

Her knuckles were white as Chuck clambered back across, the B52 rolling, jolting. He grinned at her: stuff like this didn't bother real, macho men. When she made for her seat it lurched up, into her, and the impact jarred her from her coccyx to her skull. Shaking, she strapped in. She peered anxiously at the nav plot, picking up their position. Chuck called on the intercom.

'Hey, Bat, Mario, can't'cha get us outa this weather?'

Mario Peroni fingered his crucifix amid the thick,

black hair and looked at Bat. Bat didn't reply, he was methodically monitoring his blind-flying panel. Sourly Mario acknowledged: 'Copy, radar.' He looked outside.

Local time was 0615. Darkness or not, Mario could make out some of the structure of the B52. When he twisted round he could see the wingtips really flapping, swinging up, swinging down; and the big, flattish engine nacelles, each with two turbofans in, swaying in different directions.

He'd seen worse in a B52 in a storm. 'What d'you reckon, Bat?'

Bat shrugged. He felt like another cigarette, but he hadn't a hand free. 'We can ride this. It's more a question of fuel burn.' He was laconic, his movements economical like his words, his leathery face tireless, timeless.

Mario checked the flowmeters, checked the tanks, checked the graphs he was making from the figures he'd logged. He wasn't really happy with the fuel burn, but then he wasn't really happy with much about this flight.

'Jerry,' Bat said, 'you have any views on whether we want to climb over this?'

'Yeah,' Jerry Yeaver said, 'we want to stay low. Soon as we climb, we're in range of ground radars at Kingston, Jamaica, and Barranquilla, Colombia, plus there's a drug spotter patrolling just south of Jamaica – looks like a US E2C radar platform. Also I'm a little nervous about showing on that OTH installation in Maine – their computer could almost certainly ident- ify us if it picked us out, clear of all the weather return.'

The over-the-horizon ground radar in Maine had been set up largely to spot drugs flights. It bounced its signals off the upper atmosphere to overcome the blocking effect of the Earth's curvature and pick up targets at very long range.

'Right now,' Jerry said, 'we have storm energy all around us, plus scatter off the ocean surface. Climb, and we'll lose both those advantages.'

Mario looked at Bat. 'We're staying down.'

Bat grunted agreement. He wanted a cigarette a lot now but he still couldn't free a hand to get one.

*   *   *

On the second level, Tamasin gritted her teeth. She could put up with this – all it took was will-power – she jolly well *was* going to put up with this. Crashes and jolts rocked them and the B52 pitched and lurched.

Chuck saw the expression on Tamasin's face. 'You need a sick bag?'

'No,' Tamasin said.

'Scared?' Chuck said.

Uppermost in Tamasin's mind, *actually*, was that they had to get their bombs to their target. They *had* to destroy Tariq Talal; it wasn't good enough to die trying. 'Yes,' she said, voice angry, shaky. 'I'm scared this crate might not make it all the way with my salutations to the man who murdered my husband!'

Chuck laughed through all the noise. He covered Tamasin's hand with his; warm, podgy, unexpectedly strong. All the time there'd been something knowing about him, something secretive. 'We're OK, beautiful. B52s sure are tough planes. Let me tell you, I have *personally* been through worse weather than this in a BUFF!'

It was cold comfort to Tamasin as the crashings and lurchings went on. She swallowed another half of an airsickness tablet. *Mind over matter*, she thought, and concentrated furiously on the nav plot. She was scared. She hated admitting it, even to herself.

She focused her mind on her memory of Edward. All the good things she remembered about Edward. Edward helped keep her going.

*   *   *

It was 0350 Arizona time before they broke out from the storm cloud. For a few moments in the clear air it was still gusty, bouncy, but that settled swiftly. Tamasin retuned the radar, unwilling to believe it, looking for further storms. She found none. She let out a long, slow breath of relief.

At the controls, Bat gave a sigh of relief, too, and glanced at Mario. Mario nodded. Bat lit a cigarette and exhaled smoke, thoughtful.

Arizona time was 0355, zulu 1055, local 0655. Dawn came up, low, pale gold, straight into the pilots' eyes. At this angle it was too much for shades. Both pilots pulled down their bone-dome visors.

'Nav,' Mario said, 'how are we for track?'

Tamasin was checking the drift already with the radar in Doppler mode. She recalculated. 'We want to come two degrees north to pick up the next waypoint.'

Spoilers nudged out on the long, thin wing. Bat adjusted the heading. Then he looked at Mario. This waypoint was the one where they'd planned a longish dogleg to the north, to avoid the Lesser Antilles and the risk of radar there, and the route was supposed to take them between Dominica and Martinique, in the Windward Islands – the great sprawl of skerryguard that made picket points in the sea between the Atlantic and the southeast Caribbean.

'Do we really have the fuel for the dogleg?' Bat asked.

Mario pulled a face. He shuffled his consumption logs, frowning at the figures. It wasn't just fuel for the target he was thinking of, Bat realized, it was fuel for the next move after that.

Bat decided. 'Tamasin, plot us out an alternative route. We have to go much more direct to the mid-Atlantic waypoint. I guess that means a cut across Venezuela.' He got the navigator's acknowledgement. He said: 'Jerry, you heard that – what d'you figure for radar on that route?'

For a moment Jerry didn't reply. He was frowning at his route charts. His toe touched his flight case, reassuring him again.

'Well . . . listen, Bat, sir, I'm really not keen. We'll be inside range of ground radars at Curaçao, Caracas . . . maybe even Port of Spain, Trinidad. And this is into coastal waters now; there'll be shipping, many of those guys'll have radars.' He twisted for a look back around his ejector seat, confirming what else he knew. 'And it's daylight now – they could just get a visual on us.'

'Don't like gambling, huh, EWO?' Mario said with harsh triumph. 'Don't like a little spice of danger now and then?'

'Sir, my brief is to get this plane to . . .'

Mario said: 'You're telling us you don't have the EWO skills to suppress a few antique radars in a couple of sleepy banana republics where no sonofabitch expects us in the first place? Is this what you wanna tell us?'

'Sir, don't you know, just *use* that stuff one time and . . .'

'You don't have the gonads for it,' Mario snarled, 'that's what *you're* telling us!'

Bat gave him a glance.

Desperate, his fragile self-confidence shattered again, Jerry went defensive. 'Sir, I can't be responsible if we have to start firing chaff at a stage in the flight like this.' Chaff was tinfoil, cut into strips half the length of the incoming radar wave. Its radar echo could swamp a receiver screen. 'We just fire chaff one time, they'll know for sure who we are!'

'Don't worry, Jerry,' Bat said in his lazy Arizona drawl

120

before Mario could reply. 'I'm taking the responsibility, and right now the priority is conserving fuel. OK, Tamasin, you have your plot yet?'

'Got a new waypoint in northeastern Venezuela,' Tamasin said on the intercom in her cool, efficient voice. 'Start right turn on to one one eight mag . . . now.'

The B52 rolled into the turn.

Russell Feehan placed his bony hand on Jerry's shoulder. Jerry bit his lip. He flicked Russell a glance but he couldn't bring himself to meet the older man's eyes. Again Russell put his head close by Jerry's to avoid using the intercom.

'Jerry, right now you are doing a better job than Mario is. Only thing is, we still need Mario almost as much as we need you.'

Jerry squeezed his eyes shut. Friendship at a time when he felt forsaken, felt a failure, was worth more to him than anyone knew. He managed a grin, and looked at Russell. Russell smiled back, out of that translucent, pain-racked face. But Russell was flipping his worry beads again and it was getting on Jerry's nerves and Jerry felt guilty because he felt that way, and he hated himself worse than ever.

What Jerry needed was whiskey. Plenty of it.

*   *   *

No-one was speaking now. They were coming within range of Curaçao radar and the tension was building. The sun climbed higher; no longer straight into the pilots' eyes. Jerry had been right, there *was* shipping about; Bat and Mario could count the fishing vessels and the little freighters; but the ones that bothered them were the giant tankers full of Venezuelan crude; they were the ones with the real radars. At 1,000 feet altitude you could hide from shore-based radar, maybe.

121

At 40,000 you could hide from the shipping. You took your pick.

They were relying on the hope that no-one who actually knew what a B52 looked like would wonder what it was doing crossing the southern Caribbean.

It was sleep break. Russell went to sleep at his station. Bat swapped places with Mario and Mario went to sleep in the captain's seat.

'Incoming radar,' Jerry said. 'It's Curaçao's frequency. Can we get down any?'

Bat retrimmed. He adjusted the throttle setting, hunting all the time for the best economy. At 400 feet he levelled the B52. Curaçao radar was still painting them and Jerry was tense but they'd had no challenge yet.

They got past Curaçao. The radar waves faded out. The sun, higher now, wasn't strong, and Bat raised the visor on his bone dome as he handled the aircraft from the righthand seat. On the bright surface of the Caribbean there was shipping everywhere.

Tamasin had vessels all over her radar scope. This low down the air was choppy, but not as choppy as it had been in the storm. Chuck was smoking again. The aircraft jolted, and ash went all over Tamasin's console, and she swore at Chuck, angrily, her voice a nagging shriek in her tiredness.

Chuck just laughed.

*   *   *

This time when the radar waves registered on the B52's sensors it was Caracas International. The signals grew stronger fast. They would grow, Jerry realized, getting tense again. The B52 was approaching Caracas, slanting in across the sea. He knew what was going to happen; he just didn't know what they were going to do when it did.

'Caracas International.' It was a very Latin-sounding voice but the English was clear, confident. 'Unidentified aircraft, range one zero kilometres, track one one eight. Identify yourself, identify yourself.'

Jerry should have known Bat would have that one ready.

Gaviota Colorada Seis, Caracas, no entiendo por qué. ¿Dónde han escondido nuestro plano de vuelo?'

Neat. Spanish, the Latin American accent Bat knew so well from Mexico, and a fake military-style callsign.

Caracas protested. No, they hadn't had Gaviota's flight plan, the flight plan hadn't been filed. What was Gaviota and where was it going? It was a good game by this time, and Bat's Spanish was up to it. Gaviota was a P2 maritime patrol aircraft and it was against military standing orders to disclose its mission. As for its flight plan, Caracas should have had that off the navy at Maracaibo.

With a dozen international airline flights converging from all round the clock, Caracas gave up.

*　　*　　*

'Four minutes to Waypoint Six,' Tamasin announced. 'That's landfall in Venezuela.'

East of Caracas the land falls away south into a long, shallow-curved, north-facing bay. Then it juts back to the north in a massive promontory with, on its far side, facing east into the Atlantic, the delta of the Orinoco river. They were cutting across the bay now at 1,000 feet on their southeasterly heading.

Gently Jerry woke Russell Feehan. Mario Peroni woke up and swapped places with Bat. Calling the countdown, Tamasin realized she was feeling very tired but so was everyone else. They crossed the coast. It was 0515 Arizona time and they'd been flying for twelve and a half hours. A normal mission was only eight hours. Zulu time would be

1215, Tamasin told herself, here in Venezuela the local time was 0815. It was beyond anything she could really grasp. Daytime scales didn't mean anything any more, and anyway everyone needed whatever sleep they could get.

Mario, fastidious, opened his flight case and dabbed his face with pre-shave lotion. He started going over his stubble with a battery shaver. The B52 rumbled over the desolate marshlands of eastern Venezuela.

'Ah, pilot, sir, we have radar.' Jerry was trying to keep the tension out of his voice. 'Looks like a military station, it . . . it is, this time it's tracking us! God *damn*!'

They were range-gated. Locked in automatically to the threat radar.

CHAPTER 14

It felt late. The smell of Ella's brownies didn't tempt Captain Rebecca Laird. She was feeling haggard. In the small kitchen Ella lounged against the sink, toying with her empty beer can. Her sympathetic presence lent Becks strength.

Now that they had a shrewd idea who was on Dark Angel, they had a shrewd idea where Dark Angel might be headed. But Captain Rebecca Laird didn't relish the prospect of telling Major-General Gus Hartmore that the B52 he'd lost was off to commit an act of war.

'Ella, honey, you haven't heard a word of this.'

'A word of what?'

'What I'm about to explain to the boss.' Forcing herself, Becks dialled operations.

The bumbling Hultlander answered. He put her through.

'Hartmore.' The thin, metallic voice was hostile, as always.

'Captain Laird, sir, A2. Sir, contacts of mine inform me that a Mrs Tamasin Penhale Masterson, who is a Learjet captain with B52 experience, is missing from her home, along with her father-in-law, who is former two-star General Bat Masterson and who is a Vietnam veteran B52 leader. They . . .'

'Captain, you were dismissed from Operations barely an hour ago after failing to carry out your duties during today. What the hell are you playing at?'

Becks gritted her teeth. 'Sir, General Masterson was the father and Mrs Masterson the wife of Edward

125

Masterson, who was butchered by the terrorist Tariq Talal, who . . .'

'Scuttlebutt I do not need at a busy moment, Captain.' Ella could hear him right across the kitchen.

'Sir, if you'd care to listen, I am trying to warn . . .'

'Quit your meddling right now, Laird, or I'll bust your ass right offa this base and, if there's any justice, outa the air force altogether!' The phone banged down.

Neck prickling, Becks cautiously lowered her receiver. She blew out her cheeks.

Ella watched her. Ella's instinct was to help, comfort, support; but something in the way Becks' face began to harden told her, this time, that wasn't what Becks needed. Becks swivelled her eyes to the side and caught Ella's gaze.

Ella nodded. 'Couldn't help but hear that, Becks.'

'Ella, where does your first duty and mine lie?'

'The country.'

It was dark outside, the night chilly, still, the stars high and bright. Somewhere in the block another of the women officers was playing a Michael Jackson tape.

'Not the base commander?' Becks said.

'Not even the President, if the President's outa line.' Ella was starting to enjoy this.

Tight-lipped, Becks turned and rooted in her bag. A car drove past outside and the little, yellow-lit kitchen clung closely about the two of them. Ella folded her arms, still clutching the empty beer can. Becks found the diary she was looking for. Not this year's but last year's.

'Who do you have in mind?' Ella asked softly.

Becks bit her lip, apprehensive, staring at the entry she'd found under Addresses. 'Guy who ran the staff college course I did last year. Senior A2 guy.' She could picture him now. Silver-haired, six foot three, not an ounce of fat on him; and that sidelong, sly smile that told you he had an eye for a pretty face. And Van hadn't been around, then. 'Trouble is, I don't think he outranks Hartmore.'

Ella grinned. 'I know what else the trouble is – he's in DC, right?'

'Right.'

Ten to eleven in Arizona was not a good time to disturb senior A2 officers in Washington. 'Gal's gotta do what a gal's gotta do,' Becks muttered. She dialled, wondering what sort of scene she might be interrupting in Major-General Andrew Maule's bedroom.

*   *   *

He answered on the second ring, his deep voice soft, imperturbable.

'Sir, my apologies for disturbing you. This is Captain Laird, at present head of A2 at Davis-Monthan.' She was straining her ears to catch any clue as to who else was in that bed.

'Stand by, Captain, I'll talk on the extension.' In the pause, it sounded as if he'd hung up. Becks kept the line open. In a few moments Andrew Maule picked up the other receiver, his voice just as deep but now not keeping quiet. 'Why, Becks, good to hear from you. And congratulations on your appointment.'

'I hope I keep it,' Becks answered, and rushed on. 'This is kind of a sensitive subject for a non-secure phone. It's about, ah . . . an asset of ours that may not be an asset any more.' She launched into it. She made up the word code as she went along.

Maule kept up with it – most of the way if not all. Across the kitchen, Yeltsin had come out of his sleeping box and was on his hind legs, gripping the cage wire, wobbling his head around to see what was going on.

'With you, Becks,' Maule said thoughtfully as she

finished. 'Sounds like you're on the right track. You did right to let me know.'

'Thank you, sir. What will you do now?' She hesitated. 'I mean . . .'

'I don't have authority to tell your base commander what to do, Becks,' Maule said smoothly. 'But I do know one or two guys I can speak to. Take my advice, now – quit worrying and get some sleep.' He hung up.

For a moment Becks let the phone dangle in her hand. Ella was behind her vision yet Becks was conscious of her presence and glad of it. Distant sounds filtered into the silent kitchen. Rap music from a stereo player. A big truck on the freeway that ran down the far side of the airfield. A compressor thrumming in a hangar somewhere.

'Oh boy,' Becks muttered, and plonked down the phone. 'That's it, then, make or break.'

In a decisive movement she stood up. Ella put her arm round Beck's shoulders, and for a moment they clung together in mutual support. Then they switched the phone through and went to their separate bedrooms.

Changing into her night clothes, Becks found her hands were shaking. What she'd done was unforgivable. Hartmore really would bust her off this base if anything went wrong now, and she didn't know whether she could handle that. A court-martial. Back to Minnesota in disgrace on the Greyhound. Would those parents she loved so much still be proud of her then? Would Van really take her in?

Then she thought of a B52, six desperate people out there in the sky, stolen thunder in the night.

*   *   *

She'd been tossing and turning sleeplessly for an hour and a half when the phone rang.

Becks grabbed it from under the covers. She was

hoping it wouldn't wake Ella but she knew it would. 'Hello?'

'Captain Laird?' She recognized that stumbling, hesitant voice. She said *yeah* and the man himself confirmed it. 'Captain Hultlander, ma'am, Operations.' No apology for hauling her out of bed; the poor sonofabitch had had Hartmore on his neck all night. 'Message from General Hartmore, ma'am.'

'Yeah?' She felt dishevelled, hot-eyed. Her heart rate zoomed.

'Ma'am, General Hartmore's orders are for you to report to your office as normal in the morning, go about your duties, and await further orders.'

Edgily Becks took it in, blinking sleep out of her eyes. 'Orders from General Hartmore?' Hartmore must be too furious to speak to her, she realized, that was why Hultlander was running his errands.

Hultlander hesitated. 'I guess so, ma'am.'

Andrew Maule must have been busy behind the scenes. Maybe he'd got someone even more senior interested, and maybe that someone had pulled rank on Hartmore. Oh boy. Captain Laird of A2 was sure going to be popular in the morning.

CHAPTER 15

If the Venezuelan air force scrambled fighters, Tamasin thought, they would without any doubt find and identify the B52 and the game would be up. Venezuela had Mirages. They could catch a BUFF. Even if the Venezuelans failed to force them down, there'd be an immediate protest to DC about airspace violation, and then Uncle Sam would know where his lost bomber had got to.

Silent, unseen, the radar waves washed over the B52. Bat Masterson could hear the Venezuelan controller on radio, calling for his ID and he knew this was the one he couldn't bluff his way out of.

'Jerry . . .'

In her headphones Tamasin heard Jerry Yeaver's voice. 'Let's see if this'll fix him . . .'

Beside her Chuck Brantley was tense, the first time she'd seen him scared. 'Jesus, not chaff! That'll tell him for sure who we are!'

Jerry said, 'No need.' It amazed Tamasin how cool he sounded.

Glancing at Jerry, Russell Feehan could see he knew exactly what was happening. Down on the ground, the radar operator wasn't taking the chance of missing the big, unidentified trace just by watching for it to come by next time on the sweep. He'd locked it in automatically with a range gate.

This way, the radar showed *only* the B52. It knew when the B52's return echo was due, and in the known intervals between returns it was switching out, sparing its operator

130

the bother of singling out the B52 manually from all the weather, the ground return, the odd migrant albatross.

Quickly Jerry found the radar's wavelength. This was what he'd trained for, this was what he was good at.

Up till now on this leg there'd been no radar transmitting aboard the B52. Its radars were in passive mode, simply registering incoming energy. Now Jerry went active. He could have just whited out the threat radar scope with barrage noise but he didn't, he went for the more subtle game, he began transmitting quietly on the same length, the same interval, as the Venezuelans' tracker pulse.

This had to be done quickly, before they could get fighters into the area.

On wavelength, on pulse. Very gently, Jerry turned up his radar transmission strength.

This was a bit much for the automatic tracker now, and it started tuning down to compensate for the gentle increase in signal strength. Down on the ground, the operator couldn't feel a thing.

Jerry went on turning up the volume. He was hardly breathing but his fingertips were steadier than he'd thought they'd be.

But he'd done it, he'd stolen the Venezuelans' range gate. Because now the tracker radar wasn't responding to the B52's return, it was responding to Jerry's signals. *Let's go,* Jerry thought, *pull the whole mother off.* He had the pulse and he delayed it a tiny fraction. Next pulse. Delay a tiny fraction more. Next pulse. Same again. And once more.

Jerry shut off the radar altogether.

'Pilot, dogleg! Nav, copy!'

Down on the ground, the radar was suddenly helpless, it was even looking in the wrong place.

Bat rolled the B52 tightly into a forty-five degree left turn. He held it for fifteen seconds and rolled forty-five

131

degrees right. Very tense, Jerry was watching his radar receivers.

'Russell, you have radar?'

'Negative, Jerry. All gone.'

Tamasin called the new heading. Bat wheeled left and picked up their original course.

Jerry let out a shuddering breath. 'OK, guys, well, I guess that kinda muddled them.'

Chuck called out: 'Wow, round of applause for the EWO, I'd say!'

Bat caught Mario Peroni's eye. Despite himself, Mario was impressed. Aft of them, Russell gave Jerry a punch on the arm and grinned at him, proud of his friend. Relief shone out of Jerry's face as he grinned back.

Then he reached shakily for his flight case, pulled it out of its stowage, and snapped it open. He avoided Russell's eye. The flask was full of Wild Turkey bourbon and Jerry took a big swallow of it. He felt bad about this; he felt horribly guilty. Guilty because it wasn't right to offer it to Russell, guilty because it wasn't right *not* to offer it to him, guilty because he'd got alcohol on this flight in the first place. Guilty because he had needs.

Furtively he glanced at Russell. He made a small gesture with the flask.

Concern in his eye, Russell shook his head.

Gulping another big swallow, Jerry capped the flask. 'Don't worry.' He shoved the flask back in the flight case and stowed the case. 'I'll be sober when we hit the action.'

Slowly, watchfully, Russell nodded. 'Sure you will.' It sounded meaningful.

*   *   *

Desolate, grey-green marshland stretched for ever: the Orinoco delta. Bat had the aircraft up to 1,200 feet and Mario's sharp eyes ranged the flatlands for birds; this was no place to lose a second engine. Now Tamasin started counting them down to Waypoint Seven.

They crossed the coast of Venezuela at 0540 Arizona time and flew over open ocean. The Atlantic. It was 1240 zulu time, local time 0840. It was a nice, bright morning and it made the pilots feel good. Russell and Jerry were aware of daylight washing the cabin, where they sat, and if they twisted round they could see sunshine. But Chuck and Tamasin were in permanent artificial light.

*   *   *

Bat called: 'Sleep break.'

It was Jerry and Chuck. Jerry swapped places with Russell so that Russell could man the EWO scopes. Exhausted, Jerry went to sleep almost at once. Chuck gave Tamasin a grin and said: 'Sure you don't wanna sleep with me?' Tamasin just grinned back. By this time she was feeling less threatened by the joke.

Desolate, brooding, grey-green like the Orinoco marshes, the Atlantic stretched for ever.

Mario examined his appearance again and added a dab of aftershave. He tugged at his collar, getting the wrinkles out of his flight suit. He fussed with his fuel transfers again.

'Do we still have enough for the mission?' Bat said.

'And some,' Mario said.

For an instant, the pilots' eyes met. Distrust was mutual and was only half-concealed.

From the outset, the deal had been agreed. The mission was paramount. After the mission, the final phase was to get out over the Med and hide the evidence in deep water. All the crew had shaken on that. Bat couldn't go back now, anyway. He considered himself dead already.

133

Mario didn't. And Mario still had family in Sicily. Bat never had known which way those gambler's instincts of Mario's would make him jump, and he certainly didn't now.

*　　*　　*

For three quarters of an hour it was clear weather.

Bat went below for the relief station and then exercised a bit on the first level and then shaved and spruced up. Tamasin left her scopes and freshened up, too; cold water on her face, another touch of perfume. She climbed up top with coffee and sandwiches and handed them round and sat cross-legged behind the pilots' seats to eat hers. The sun rocketed into the sky as they flew on east. Mario climbed out and stretched himself, and Russell came and sat beside Tamasin for five minutes. He swallowed another painkiller with his coffee.

About 0630 Arizona time, the sky clouded over. They still had four hours to go to Waypoint Eight, the next reporting station. They kept flying. Then just after 0730 Arizona time the cloud came right down over the ocean and they bored into the middle of it.

'All crew on station,' Bat said.

Below, Tamasin tightened her harness and settled Buster in his holder. In the cloud it was bumpy, and above the engine noise she could hear the same jolts and crashes as in the earlier storm. Bat glanced outside critically. He could clearly see the huge flex of the wingtips, the engines all swaying different ways.

Chuck slept on. Jerry stirred fitfully. The bumps and the lurching got worse.

Tamasin started reminding herself how to find the airsick bag in a hurry. She hated this; it was a weakness she had to hide from the men.

Bat glanced at Mario. 'What d'you reckon?'

Without looking at him, Mario said: 'We're burning too much fuel.' He paused, still scanning the flowmeters. 'Goddammit, Bat, this is the middle of the Atlantic Ocean – who the hell's gonna be running radars out here?'

Bat scowled out into the murk. The B52 dropped nauseously, lurched to the left, and bounced upwards. On the intercom Bat said: 'Tamasin, how much more of this do we have?'

Tamasin had her harness ruthlessly tight; she was taking deep breaths and the sickness was like thick slime at the back of her throat. 'Well . . .' On the radar the storm cells went all the way to the edge of the scope . . . 'It looks rough as far as I can see.'

'Roger that,' Bat muttered lazily, voice deep. 'We're going over.'

His big hand pushed the middle six throttle levers to fully open, then advanced Number One about halfway and adjusted the rudder to compensate for the altered thrust. With his left hand he eased back the big, chunky yoke. As the B52 started to rise through the wrenching battering of the storm, Bat started trimming out for the long climb.

CHAPTER 16

Tall in his olive flying suit with the squadron crest on the shoulder, the Coningsby wing commander moved warily behind his desk. Flight Lieutenant Colan Penhale stood facing him, Flying Officer Salim Arshad at his shoulder. Recently the wing commander had discovered that he needed eyesight correction for close work, and now he reached down to the desk, and fiddled with his reading glasses as if trying to frame his words precisely.

Colan prompted: 'May I ask what it's about, sir?'

'Phone call rather early today into Strike Command HQ at High Wycombe.' The wing commander gave him a searching glance. 'The Pentagon, on behalf of no less than the US President: can we send a few assets over to Sigonella, Sicily, to concoct a modest little ad hoc RAF/US Navy task force for a couple of days, and can one of the assets be a certain Flight *Loo*-tenant Penhale.' That glance wasn't searching now, more plain suspicious. 'If I had fans like you've got fans, Colan, I'd be made by now – or else dead.'

Vivid as lightning, the mental image leaped through Colan's mind. Kuwait, parched brown and burning 40,000 feet below, and around him the endless skies of the Gulf – empty. Sortie after sortie, he and Salim had flown, and never an Iraqi in sight. This time, though . . .

Innocently he said: 'Well, I really can't imagine . . .'

'No, indeed,' the wing commander said drily. 'Ours is rather not to imagine. But the fact now is that your name is known to our esteemed Prime Minister and mine isn't – not that there's any reason why mine should have been.

A thing like this is a touch political, and the PM approved it personally at eight this morning.'

In the stolen, sidelong glance, Salim was looking impressed, despite every effort.

Colan picked his words. 'Would this be anything to do with the fact that SAC seems to have mislaid a B52?'

'Don't you dare tell anyone I even hinted at any such thing.'

'We're not expected to knock this BUFF down, are we, sir?'

The wing commander stuck his glasses on his nose and looked over the top of them. The effect, from a tall, tough man in a flying overall, was quaintly comical. 'You're not expected to knock anything down unless it threatens one of your Tornados,' he said. 'You'll be briefed when you get there. You're to report to Colonel Salvatore di Carolis of the Italian air force, and the task force commander is Rear-Admiral Sigmund Berlin, US Navy. Now, our contribution to the strength is not going to be a large one, numerically, and you'll have command of it. Any ideas on what sort of force you'd like to take?'

Colan said what Salim had known he'd say. It was what Salim would have said.

'I'll need two Tornados and two Hawks, and we'll need a C130 from here for our gear and groundcrew. Presumably the Hawks'll want another Herk for theirs.' The four-turboprop C130 Hercules was the standard RAF workhorse transport.

The wing commander nodded. 'Sounds about right. We'll get a couple of Hawks from Chivenor and we'll supply the Tornados from the squadron here, plus the Herk. You'll take Salim, I imagine. Who else would you suggest as a crew from here?'

'McNair and Sewell-Baillie.'

McNair was a product of the Scottish education system and of a Clydeside family that had bequeathed him all the aggression of a Saturday night in Glasgow. Sewell-Baillie, McNair's navigator, was a languid Old Etonian whose father had made a fortune taking appendices out of rich Arabs.

'Fine,' the wing commander said. 'Go for it.' He grinned. 'Let's think of it as a useful little exercise in rapid deployment.'

*   *   *

Colan's first call was to Jane. He wouldn't be back for a couple of days; wasn't allowed to say where he was going but it wasn't Northern Ireland. Jane reacted the way she always did, her London East End sang-froid masking any anxiety she might have felt about her husband; she simply told Colan to make sure he looked after himself. It was one of the things Colan admired about Jane: she was perfectly aware that the job he did could get him killed any day, by accident, action or bad luck, yet she refused to cling; she resolutely refused to show anxiety or cramp Colan's style.

An hour and a half and a lot of strong coffee later, Colan and Salim were in the briefing room with Andrew McNair and Jeremy Sewell-Baillie and the conversation was going in short bursts between Tornado takeoffs. It only took one aircraft, the noise stopped everything.

Sewell-Baillie was saying: 'If the French get wind of what we're up to, they'll cancel our overflying clearance and we'll have to take the scenic route via Gib – tankers and piddle packs. That'll be fun in this weather!'

They were lucky enough, Salim thought privately, that the worst failing among the four of them was Sewell-Baillie's habit of showing his excitement by inventing objections to whatever they wanted to do. Sewell-Baillie was six foot, with the build of a runner, and he wore a small, trim moustache and a hairstyle like Jason

138

Donovan's. His hobby was aerobatics and he indulged it at international competitions, flying a Pitts biplane which he owned. He was single and a bit of a loner, but that didn't bother people: what counted was what he could do, and in that respect he was every bit as professional as Salim.

'The French can guess away to their hearts' content,' Colan said. 'We've told them the straight truth as far as we know it. We're doing a rapid deployment for some team games with the US Navy. Anything that arises out of that will be something that we simply happened to be ready for.'

McNair said nothing as usual. When he did speak, his Glasgow accent was far more marked than Salim's Asian inflexions. He was twenty-eight, married with no kids, a short, stocky, powerful, clear-eyed, clear-headed man who one day six years earlier had decided – not on a hangover – that he wasn't going to drink alcohol any more, ever, and simply hadn't. He'd given up boxing at about the same time, although he still did weights. He'd once had to punch his navigator and himself out of a Phantom that was rolling quite quickly and out of control. Salim thought maybe that accounted for his somewhat subdued manner.

*　　*　　*

The phone rang.

'Chivenor here,' the man on the other end said. 'Flight Lieutenant Baslow, Jack Baslow.' He had an echo of the Pennines in his voice; the West Yorkshire side. Chivenor was the RAF station where they were hoping to get the Hawks. 'Seems I've to meet you at Sigonella with a couple of our lads.'

'And some wings, too, presumably?' Colan said.

'Oh, ay, we'll bring the wings. Two Hawks, that do y'?

139

We're pulling 'em off the trials unit – the new Series 300 with the air-to-air refuelling and the radar like the 200's got. What's it about?'

'I'm afraid we shan't know with any certainty until we're there. But it seems there's a chance that we might be looking at a few Libyans.'

'Oh, ay?' Baslow sounded interested. 'That'll make a nice change.'

'Who's coming with you?' Colan asked.

'Pete Pretorius, he's the other driver. I did try to get some of the girls from admin, to make it a proper party, but the boss said no and anyway the girls aren't insured to fly Hawks. But Pete'll do. He's South African, but we'll not hold that against him.'

They hung up.

Sewell-Baillie put his well-bred head on one side. 'Was that Jack Baslow?'

'Yes,' Colan said. 'Why, d'you know him?' It was one of Sewell-Baillie's strengths that he seemed to know every other officer in the RAF and a good few in the army and navy, too.

'I met him once,' Sewell-Baillie said. 'He's a good guy – flew Sea Harriers in the Falklands, shot down an Argentine fighter – Dagger, I think it was. He was in the navy then – he switched to the RAF after that, so as not to be away from his family for too long at a stretch. Otherwise he might quite likely have made Commander by now.'

Again the phone rang. Confirmation this time of their flight plan, the French route.

After that it was one more phone call to Jane and then out to the jets.

CHAPTER 17

Libya, the summer before the flight.
Five days after the desert exercise, Adem Elhaggi was still struggling not to give in to the ceaseless pain in his shoulder.

Today he was on the firing range with Zoheir and four men trainees. The firing range was only a couple of hundred metres from the low, sandy bunker where, Adem knew, they stored the plastic explosives semi-recessed into the earth. The firing stands were like low, wooden tables made of planks, built to take a person lying full length on the elbows. Over the whole stand they'd rigged an awning framed with olive branches and thatched with desiccated, sun-browned palm fronds. Ali Ben Mokhtar was in charge of the training and Adem was already in trouble.

That right shoulder was so stiff now he could hardly move it. He forced himself again. He had the wooden stock cupped in his left hand, forward of the Kalashnikov's curving black magazine, and now he propped his right elbow, got his right hand on to the pistol grip, and fought to ignore the pain as he steadied the thick wooden butt in his anguished shoulder.

On the stand hardly six feet to his right, Zoheir fired steady, confident, single shots.

Adem tried to sight up but he couldn't get the butt seated right. Tears of sheer pain blurred his vision. He tried to tighten his finger on the trigger but he couldn't stop thinking what that recoil would do to his shoulder.

'Adem.'

Ben Mokhtar was beside him, leaning slightly forward

to peer down. Adem looked up, blinking the tears away.

'Come,' Ben Mokhtar said softly and, with a touch so gentle that it surprised Adem, lifted the Kalashnikov away from him. 'It's that shoulder, isn't it?'

Adem's first thought was to say *no*, but then he couldn't. Tears welled up again, his head hung, he bit his lip.

'Come,' Ben Mokhtar repeated, and laid a hand on Adem's good shoulder. 'You won't sharpen up your shooting until you've got that mended properly. Follow me.' He glanced behind. 'Just keep practising, the rest of you. Ten rounds, then use a new target each.'

He steadied Adem as the young man levered himself awkwardly off the stand. For an instant, Adem's eyes caught Zoheir's and he saw her concern.

From the range to the quarters blocks it was twelve hundred metres in the morning sun, but with Ben Mokhtar at Adem's side giving silent comfort, it felt less. By the time Ben Mokhtar led Adem into the medical office, Adem had recovered from the pain. Ben Mokhtar looked round, Adem's Kalashnikov over his shoulder.

'Where is Dr Jabran?'

Only the two women nurses were in the office. One of them shook her head ambiguously and didn't answer Ben Mokhtar. The other simply walked away and vanished into a different office.

The two men nurses sauntered in, glancing about, their air oddly aggressive.

'Where is Dr Jabran?' Ben Mokhtar repeated.

The darker of the two, the one who looked as if he might have come from the south of Libya or maybe even Chad, spat wordlessly through the outer door.

The other, the brawny one with the tattoo on his arm, said, 'She's not here.' Stating the obvious that way turned it almost into an insult.

'I can see she's not here,' Ben Mokhtar said with a softness that belied his anger. 'Our brother needs her help.' He had his arm protectively round Adem. 'When will she be here?'

'We don't need her,' the dark nurse said gruffly, and turned away from the door. 'We can look after our brother.' He lumbered over to where they stood, looked them over, and flapped a hand at a chair. 'Sit down. Where does it hurt?'

Pain washed over Adem in waves and he thought he was going to be sick. He collapsed on the chair. It was a mystery about Dr Jabran but the pain kept Adem too busy to give it his attention.

Ben Mokhtar did most of the work of getting Adem's shirt off. He explained to these men how Adem had hurt his shoulder in the first place. He wasn't satisfied when they tried to check Adem over; he wanted the doctor. He badgered them; he shouted at them.

Dr Jabran walked through slowly from the room at the back. She held her back very straight and walked stiffly. She wore the usual chador, and the headscarf wrapped round so that it almost concealed her face.

'Hello, Adem.' Her mouth was hidden, but the tender smile came through in her tone.

She began her examination. Adem closed his eyes so as not to pay attention.

And then she did something clumsy and the pain wrenched through him and he cried out, his head jerking away.

'Sorry.' Her dark eyes were wide.

'It's all right.' He glanced away, blinking. He couldn't believe it. Whatever else she was, Dr Jabran simply wasn't clumsy, ever.

Swallowing, he glanced at her, but she was scrutinizing his shoulder. He drew a soft breath of surprise. Three of the fingernails on Dr Jabran's right hand were completely

143

black. No wonder she was being clumsy, she must have caught her fingers in a door.

'It looks,' she murmured, 'as if I didn't quite relocate it right that first time.' She'd been perhaps too gentle. With no pain-killers left in the medical supplies, she'd been over-anxious not to hurt Adem. 'If we had X-ray facilities here I could be quite sure.'

Behind her, the dark male nurse was sneering openly.

Dr Jabran ignored him. 'I'm going to give you an injection, Adem. We have some pain-killing drugs now and this will be a local anaesthetic. Then I'm going to reset your shoulder. It shouldn't hurt.'

'Very well.' Adem glanced up.

Ben Mokhtar grinned, but his eyes were hard in the battered, grizzled face.

Then as Dr Jabran turned to fill the syringe her headscarf slipped and Adem saw that it wasn't just her fingers that were injured. She had a black eye and a bruise on her cheekbone.

Wordlessly, she swabbed the spot. She injected him. The two nurses looked on, their manner still inexplicably insolent, while Dr Jabran waited for the anaesthetic to take effect. Ben Mokhtar propped up the wall, ankles crossed, left arm cradling the Kalashnikov, eyes on the nurses. Even his baleful presence hardly seemed to cow them.

Satisfied finally, Dr Jabran reset Adem's shoulder. Anaesthetic or not, it hurt.

Dr Jabran realized it. 'Well done, Adem,' she murmured. 'You've been very brave.'

Adem smiled wryly up at her.

Adjusting her headscarf again to hide her bruises, Dr Jabran opened a wall cabinet and counted out two sorts of tablets.

'These are painkillers,' she told Adem. 'These will take the swelling down. One of each, with your meals, at

144

morning and at night.' Her mouth was hidden again behind the folds of the headscarf. 'And I want you to rest for the remainder of today and for two more days.' Her dark eyes were serious, but the blacked one was half-hidden. Again Adem's eyes glimpsed Dr Jabran's damaged fingernails. 'You won't become a fighter if you're disabled, Adem.' In her parting phrase there was irony.

'Very well,' Adem said.

He stood up unsteadily. Dr Jabran stood back and it was Ben Mokhtar who stepped forward to fasten Adem's shirt buttons and save him moving his arm. On the way from the medical office to Adem's quarters Ben Mokhtar held Adem's good hand. There was nothing erotic about it, it was simply the comradely, man-to-man contact that was given all the time in a Muslim culture. He made sure Adem was comfortable on the hard, narrow bed in the big dormitory. Then he went back to the range.

Blinds were down on the windows and flies buzzed in the half-dark. Usually when they landed on Adem he ignored them, the way he'd learnt to ignore them as a small child with his exiled family in Kuwait, the home he no longer knew. The aftermath of pain left him exhausted, and the anaesthetic jab dulled his senses, and he felt low because he wasn't completing his training properly. All the same, Dr Jabran always talked sense, he reflected: he really wouldn't become a fighter if he allowed himself to become disabled.

Then he found himself thinking about Dr Jabran.

The nurses' attitude had been rather odd. Even in a thoroughly macho society, even when the doctor was a woman, you didn't get nurses openly sneering at the doctor. Something had happened. Something had changed Dr Jabran's status here from one of respect to one of contempt. *Violence begets violence*, Adem remembered. That never had been the way Tariq Talal saw things.

145

Maybe Dr Jabran had actually argued with Talal. And maybe . . .

Those blackened fingernails. The bruises, the black eye. She'd been *beaten up*.

Yet surely not with Tariq Talal's knowledge, Adem tried to reassure himself. Surely not by Tariq Talal himself.

*   *   *

After some hours, Adem felt well enough to sit up and read a little. He wasn't going to waste a moment if he could help it. Though he'd always found the Koran heavy going he was determined to master its stories and its wisdom. The books that really absorbed him were his engineering texts. Here he could see immediate, practical applications for the knowledge the pages contained. The other book that absorbed him was Tariq Talal's own Green Book.

There were two 'Green Books', one, some years old now, by the Libyan leader himself; the other by Talal. Talal's was the one that was required reading in the camp.

It had a preface explaining that it was Talal's humble tribute to the country's leader and adding how unworthy Talal felt himself to be in assuming the challenge of expanding upon the matchless wisdom of the original. Adem wasn't sure how seriously you were supposed to take that bit. The book was easy to read because it was divided into lots of little, self-contained items: a compilation of selected verses from the Koran and aphorisms, mostly familiar but including a few from Talal's own thoughts. You could flick through it at random.

Adem did. He drew encouragement from the Koran's words on the merit of martyrdom and from its reminder that anyone who helped a widow or a pauper would gain merit likewise. Then he found a line of Talal's own.

Truly I say to you, it is more blessed to die in submission to the will of God's chosen one than to live for many lifetimes surrounded with riches.

Adem stopped and thought about that. He wondered who Talal meant by 'God's chosen one'. Then a bulky, bearded figure loomed into the doorway.

'Adem gasped. 'My father!' He hadn't expected to find Tariq Talal making sick calls in person.

'Adem!' Beaming across his tanned face, Talal strode into the dormitory. For a moment Adem braced himself, scared of the effects an embrace would have on that wounded shoulder. But Talal simply grasped Adem's wrists and gave them a friendly squeeze.

'Adem, how are you?' Talal pulled up a stool and planted his big body on it. The smile didn't leave his face.

'Much better, thank you, my father. I should be fit . . .'

'You'll be fit when Dr Jabran says you're fit. No nonsense this time, eh?' He saw the Green Book in Adem's hand and nodded. 'Good – you spend your sick time gaining wisdom.' He reached under the bed and drew out one of Adem's engineering books. 'Excellent. Have you mastered this one?'

'Not yet. I'm about halfway through.'

They talked engineering. Adem had never exchanged more than a couple of sentences with Talal before. He was impressed by how much Talal knew about engineering.

'We must all learn from the masters,' Talal said, balancing the heavy book on a broad palm. 'We must even recognize that sometimes we can learn from the servants of the Great Satan themselves. Good may yet come out of evil.'

147

'What do you mean, my father?'

'The Zionists, a curse on their name,' Talal said. 'The Israelis have made their desert bloom. Skilled engineers of our own must study and plan to make *our* desert bloom, until the sand seas turn to the green of Islam.' Then he started to talk to Adem about the desert and the animal and plant life it supported when, to the untrained eye, it seemed nothing but a dead wilderness.

The knowledge was real, the scientific interest genuine. 'My father,' Adem said, 'where did you come by all your engineering and scientific wisdom?'

The answer was unexpected.

'At the American University in Beirut,' Talal said. A cruel edge crept into his voice. 'That's where I first learned to hate the followers of the Great Satan — for their arrogance, their corruption, their dollar imperialism.'

Adem didn't quite follow what Talal meant by 'dollar imperialism', but there was a force behind the words that he couldn't gainsay.

As abruptly as he'd arrived, Talal stood up and left.

*   *   *

Next day, Adem was back on his bed and resting again, giving his shoulder a chance, confident that it really was mending.

He'd lifted the blind on the nearest window to give him light to read by. Over breakfast he'd seen Dr Jabran, in passing, and she'd told him to come back and see one of the nurses if he had any more pain; but he hadn't.

He kept on doggedly with his books.

All day long there were young men in and out of the dormitory block. Sometimes one of them asked how Adem was; mostly they were aware of him while not paying him much attention. It wasn't unfriendly;

it simply wasn't necessary to look after him all the time.

Then, to Adem's astonishment, Zoheir slipped in and made her way over to him.

It was late afternoon. Adem gazed wide-eyed at Zoheir. Women weren't allowed into the men's quarters any more than men were allowed into the women's but, in a case like this, people turned a blind eye; and anyway there were always other men about. She smiled as she approached him. She'd finished her training for the day and she was back in the chador and headscarf.

Fishing under the chador, she produced an orange. 'Hello, Adem, how are you getting on? I've brought you this.' She gave him the orange.

'Why . . . thank you . . .' He was almost embarrassed. It was as amazing as it was gratifying to discover that Zoheir was even interested in him. He looked at the orange in his palm.

'It might do you good,' Zoheir said, her smile serious, and sat gingerly on the edge of the bed, gathering her chador. Fresh fruit didn't come into the camp as often as they might have liked.

Adem's fingers trembled a little and he was very conscious of Zoheir's eyes on him. Carefully he peeled the orange. The sharp citrus smell spread across the dusty room. It cut into the smells of sweat and stale food, cigarette smoke and clothing awaiting the laundry. Adem pulled off a couple of segments and offered them to Zoheir.

'Thank you.' She sounded as if she hadn't expected the offer.

'What was your training today?' Adem asked.

'Assault course again this morning.' Zoheir pulled a face. 'The pipe was all full of water, we had to go *right under* in it, and it smelt *disgusting*. It gets all in your

149

hair.' She popped the orange segment into her mouth and raised a hand briefly to her headscarf. 'Then English this afternoon.'

Zoheir already had fluent French in addition to her native Arabic. English was going to be an addition to her skills. Theoretically the trainees weren't supposed to discuss the special skill each one was being schooled in, but there were a lot of open secrets. Zoheir knew that Adem was studying to build bombs and Adem knew that Zoheir was studying to become a radio operator and international courier.

'Who takes you for English?' It was as good a way as any of keeping a conversation going.

'Dr Jabran.'

'Oh, yes?' Adem glanced up. 'How is she?'

Zoheir's eyes met Adem's. She knew perfectly well what Adem meant. 'Better,' she said, lowering her voice. 'The bruises are going down.'

A couple of men trainees were over by the door, but they were several feet away.

'What happened?' Adem asked.

Warily Zoheir glanced over her shoulder at the two men. She glanced back at Adem, lifted her chin and tut-tutted the negative. She didn't want to speak, they might overhear her.

'Was it an accident?' Adem prompted.

Zoheir tut-tutted again. Her eyes held anger and contempt, but not for Adem.

'Was she attacked?'

Zoheir flicked her eyes towards where the men were. She moistened her lips. 'You could say so,' she admitted reluctantly.

'Was she on an operation?'

At the other end of the room a third young man walked in. He slapped one of the others on the shoulder and said something, and the three of them burst into guffaws.

Zoheir looked at them and then turned to Adem, leaning close, confidentially.

'No, it wasn't an operation. She was beaten up by Tariq Talal and one of his bodyguards.'

Adem was aghast. 'Who? Ben Mokhtar?' But Ben Mokhtar wasn't actually a bodyguard.

'Not Ben Mokhtar. Someone much younger – I don't know the man's name. There'd been some sort of a row. Dr Jabran criticized one of Tariq's operations – that one at Frankfurt airport when Mustafa got killed.'

Still Adem was shocked, gazing in disbelief at Zoheir. He was so baffled he didn't pause to wonder what there might have been to criticize about the Frankfurt airport operation. 'Well . . . surely it's more than just criticizing an operation! Surely Dr Jabran must have . . . must have shown severe disloyalty or something.' He hesitated. 'Is she apostate as a Muslim?'

'If anybody's apostate, it's Ben Mokhtar,' Zoheir muttered gloomily, eyes roaming the room as her thoughts went off at a tangent.

'What d'you mean?' Adem asked sharply.

Her eyes came back to his. She thought for a moment, then tut-tutted.

'What is it about Ben Mokhtar?' Adem persisted, and his voice gathered strength. He clasped the sleeve of the chador. 'Listen, Zoheir, tell me – one day I might *need* to know.'

'Shush,' she whispered, 'keep your voice down!'

He obeyed. 'Well, *tell* me!'

She glanced at the three men by the door, but they weren't interested in her or Adem. Again she leaned close to Adem. 'All right. Ben Mokhtar told me this one night, late, at the Command Council HQ. He's been active for many years in guerrilla operations and he's seen contradictions between what he's been called upon to do, and much of the teaching of the Koran. He said he was

151

simply inured to it and he didn't really care about the faith.'

Adem was still open-mouthed. 'But surely Tariq Talal is a faithful Muslim?'

Zoheir shrugged. 'I suppose so.'

'And surely a faithful Muslim wouldn't administer punishment without good cause?'

Again Zoheir's eyes slipped away, as if to hide her thoughts from Adem. 'Dr Jabran isn't the first person Tariq's punished,' she muttered. 'And he doesn't distinguish between men and women when he punishes them.'

She jumped up abruptly. She didn't say goodbye, she just swept out of the dormitory, moving quickly. Adem stared after her.

He still had half an orange but he didn't feel so hungry now. Slowly a suspicion grew in his mind that maybe Zoheir herself had experienced punishment at Tariq Talal's hands. Then a new question took shape. Had there *really* been something wrong about the Frankfurt operation? Had Dr Jabran found something of substance there to criticize?

CHAPTER 18

At 40,000 feet Bat Masterson levelled the B52 and then tapped ash off his cigarette. Beside him, Mario Peroni was looking happier already as the fuel flowmetres dipped. This height was much more economical for the TF33s.

Sun blazed into the flight deck and Bat put thoughts of radar out of his mind. Below on the second level, the main thing Tamasin Penhale Masterson was aware of was how smooth it all seemed now that they were out of that cloud. She was also trying to put thoughts of radar out of her mind. She sensed that the aircraft was level and she unstrapped from the hard, cold, black ejector seat. She swung stiffly to her right, into the tiny gangway by the ladder.

Daylight leaked down the hatch. Tamasin felt light-headed but it was from funny sleeping patterns, not because she'd parked the sweat-slippery weight of the bone dome on her console in Buster's care. She ducked a look at Chuck, fast asleep in his harness; stretched; flexed her knees a couple of times; then clambered up the ladder.

Her eyes met Russell Feehan's as she emerged into the dazzle. His were gaunt with pain again but he gave her the same friendly, generous smile. She realized she wanted to hug and kiss him. Instead, still blinking in the light, Tamasin reached and gave Russell's bony hand a squeeze, then went stooping forward and bent over the trim wheels and the massive bank of power levers that separated Mario and Bat.

Before, all there was to see had been grey-green ocean.

153

Now it was a fermenting seascape of bubbling, glinting cloud, brittle like meringue and as insubstantial, spreading for ever.

Mario could smell Tamasin's perfume; on the other hand, she could smell his after-shave; but he pretended he hadn't realized she was there. Weathered, square-jawed in his bone dome, Bat turned to her with sad love in his smile.

'Gosh,' Tamasin said, very English suddenly, 'it's comfier up here!'

'In some respects,' Bat replied.

So often, Tamasin thought, he and she had shared the same worry, unspoken. 'What about some coffee? A sandwich?'

'Sounds good,' Mario said, acknowledging her presence as subordinate, the way a woman should be.

Any other time, Tamasin would have been highly tempted to make an issue of that. Yet now she was growing tired of being considered an 'honorary man'; she was almost glad of a role that confirmed her as a woman. She turned, ever agile despite the constriction of the flying overall, and ducked her head aft to the rear-facing seats. Jerry Yeaver looked as if he really was asleep this time. Tamasin put her face close to Russell's to ask him what he wanted. Water, he said. She fetched that first.

With shaking hands Russell washed down a painkiller.

Tamasin knelt suddenly beside Russell, a hand up to his console as if to steady herself. She put her other hand on his sleeve. 'Russell . . . Russell, you're feeling bad, aren't you?'

He looked at her. Something in his translucent face was distorted, but his eyes were kind. 'Not too good, I guess,' he said and grinned, as if he'd just lost a friendly game of squash or chess.

For an admission like that, Tamasin knew, he must be feeling ghastly. Tears started at her eyes and she

154

reached instinctively and embraced him, her head on his shoulder. The damned ejector seat was in the way, the damn harness. The tears crawled down her cheeks.

Russell patted Tamasin's arm. There was appreciation there but also weariness.

She took his shoulders and looked at him, blinking fiercely. 'Oh, Russell . . . I feel this is all so *wrong*, having you out here!'

His smile was calm, confident. He had it all thought out. 'If there's a heaven, and I believe there is, then, why, Gracie'll be there already and we'll be back together again. If there's just nothing, then I won't be conscious to miss my friends. Meanwhile, we're on our way to wipe out a murdering gang of terrorists and we'll save a few lives when we do it. That's a good reason for dying, for a man in my state.' Then the sadness filled his wry smile as he looked at her. 'Now as for *you*, Tamzie . . . if there's one person on this crew who *really* ought not to go, it's you. You have such a lot of life and a lot of love to give – and it sure is a shame you're throwing yourself away. Oh, I realize why you want Tariq Talal wiped out – you bet I understand that. But there's kind of a bit of tragedy about it when a beautiful, talented young woman lays down her life in a mission.'

Tamasin laughed drily. 'It's no more tragic if a woman gets killed in combat than if a man does – that's just society's traditional perceptions.'

'The perception's right where there are kids concerned,' Russell replied. 'Anyway, it's just as tragic, Jerry throwing his life away. He ought not to be on this flight any more than you should.'

Silent with thought, Tamasin stood up and went to draw coffee and make sandwiches. She gave Russell his sandwich before she served Bat and Mario. Bat was flying hands-off, the autopilot managing the aircraft smoothly in the frozen mid-Atlantic air.

They had the sky to themselves. It arched deep blue over them like some endless journey. Below them the cloud flowed to every horizon in heaps and furrows and whorls and hollows, bouncing back the light like ping-pong balls. Gazing at it, fascinated, Tamasin could almost have sworn the B52 was flying in silence.

Mario, uncharacteristically considerate, gave Tamasin a glance. 'Hey, do you two want to wake Jerry and Chuck and get some sleep?'

Tamasin looked at Bat. Bat looked at Tamasin. They said no. It occurred to Tamasin, she couldn't tell why, that out of all of them, Mario was perhaps the only one who actually enjoyed being on this flight. He actually relished the idea of getting into a fight and killing some people.

'OK,' Mario said, turning rude again, 'why not let's check how the nav plot's doing.'

He was bored, Tamasin realized, he needed someone to shove around; maybe he wanted a fight with her. She wondered whether he was jealous of the attention she'd been paying to Russell. 'OK,' she said tamely, and went back down the ladder.

She glanced at Chuck, tickled Buster's chin, picked up her sextant, and climbed back up to take a sun shot so as to confirm the INS and GPS plots. She liked all this sunlight; the last thing she wanted was to be cooped up in that ejector seat again when they were at this sort of height.

Mario kept niggling at her to go back down. When she wouldn't, he turned in exasperation to Bat.

'Listen, man, you're supposed to be commander on this flight – how about exercising a little authority around here?'

Bat gave him a look, narrowed eyes glare-wrinkled from the sun of Arizona and the sun of high altitude. 'That's what I'm doing, co-pilot.' Tamasin could make up her own mind. Bat didn't want to throw his weight about.

Again Tamasin glanced at Bat but he just looked front, over his flight displays. His face was stubbled now and his lower lip jutted the way Tamasin knew it did whenever he thought about Alice. And Edward. His past life, gone now. White light gleamed in the sky and off the clouds and for a moment, eyeing it, Tamasin felt the bitterness of regret. She was going to have to go below, there'd be friction otherwise, and they could do without that. Mario had never been happy having a woman on the crew.

Climbing down the ladder, her movements were stiff, tired, resigned. At her console, she shifted the bone dome but still didn't put it on – it was too heavy just now, too uncomfortable. She compared her sextant reading with the INS and GPS. On course, on time, 0945 in Arizona, 1645 zulu time, and local time only two hours behind that as they crawled eastwards towards the Greenwich meridian. Three quarters of an hour to the mid-Atlantic waypoint.

Chuck was still fast asleep.

Tamasin almost joined him. She was nodding off over her charts when Russell's voice came on the intercom, taut with wonder. And with suppressed alarm.

'Crew, we have search radar. There's some guy out there looking for us.'

CHAPTER 19

The alarm drilled into Captain Rebecca Laird's conscious-
ness. Seven sharp. She reached from under the covers and
shut it off. The memories of the night before returned
instantly, and the knowledge that she was risking her
career.

Urgently Becks shoved off the covers and stomped to
the shower. She ran it cold over her tall, lean body, then
turned it fully hot. It was a brutal way to start the day
but it did the trick when you were still short of sleep.
Then as she faced the mirror and straightened her uniform
she wondered how much sleep Tamasin Masterson was
getting.

In the kitchen, Ella was finishing a coffee. 'Hi, Becks,
I made enough for two.' She gestured at the percolator,
smiling, confident. She rinsed her mug in the sink and
was heading out the door as Becks reached sleepily for
the cupboard with the English muffins in.

Becks ate breakfast and went to the Beetle. Grackles
were calling, harsh-voiced in the mild morning dazzle,
the males fat blodges of purplish black feathers as they
strutted on the pale, flat earth. The mountain horizon
was a silhouette in pastel blue, canyon-veined and crisp
in the clear desert air. Then a pair of A10s took off and
shattered the effect.

Bracing herself for trouble, Becks drove to A2.

*   *   *

The outer office door was open: Julio, her clerk, was there.

He was no more than a couple of years older than Becks; she'd inherited him from her predecessor. The old A2 chief might have had some idea what made Julio function but Becks never could fathom it. Julio never did a stroke more work than he had to, yet he was always first in that office, and often last out; he was always talking on the phone in an undertone, yet he hardly ever had anything to report to Becks.

Today he was true to form, putting the phone down quickly and snapping a salute as Becks walked in. 'Morning, Captain Laird, ma'am!'

She acknowledged his greeting. She was on time by the wall clock, Hartmore couldn't get her for that. 'Any phone calls for me?' She wasn't even sure what to expect.

'No, ma'am, but a whole slew of signals.'

Julio had one of those open, down-home, southern accents, and it sounded wrong coming from a dapper little man hardly five foot seven with the olive skin that betrayed Latin ancestry, and dark, crafty eyes. Becks always felt that Julio was up to something he didn't want her to know about.

She crossed the outer office. It took its sole daylight from a window looking across a corridor to another window. It was narrow and it had a sink and draining board and coffee machine in one corner. Becks's office, behind the locked door opposite the door to the outer chamber, was bigger, but not by much, and smaller still once they'd jammed a coffee table and a couple of chairs into it to serve as a 'conference area'. The communications room with its cipher telex link and satcom receiver and secure printer was off Becks' office and was hardly bigger than a broom cupboard. Becks felt claustrophobic whenever she went in there.

She unlocked the door, took the clip of reports, and went into her office. She hung up her cap, then sat at her desk. It was L-shaped, with the computer terminal on her right. It had no outside light. Sometimes Becks got so fed up with working under fluorescent tubes that she locked the office and walked around the block just to get some daylight. On the wall was a painting of Abraham Lincoln that she'd inherited from her predecessor. Opposite it Becks had placed a woodland scene from Minnesota.

Flight ops at Davis-Monthan reported on the first signal from the clip that they'd loaded Dark Angel with 48,000 gallons of fuel – the most it could take – but no weapons. There were two signals from Barksdale. One was to say the mix-up over serials might have been at their end after all; the B52H coded 60–068, which should have gone to Davis-Monthan, was still on Barksdale's flight line, and they hadn't yet found 60–086. They couldn't explain where the documentation might have come from to get an aircraft released. The second signal said they'd tracked down the weapons papers for 60–086. There were bombs on board, the full internal load, twenty-seven M117 750-pound gravity weapons, the updated variant with parachute retard, live. The air force had changed its training policy hardly two months before. Now, some training missions actually carried live weapons and this was supposed to have been one of them.

Becks squeezed her eyes shut.

The next report was from A2 at the Pentagon. They'd told the President.

Lips compressed, Becks swivelled in her chair and signed on at her terminal. She accessed the database. She typed in *B52H*. Then she typed in *range performance*.

Standard unrefuelled range for an H-model was 9,020 nautical miles. Individually they'd been known to do better than that. In 1962 a standard, operational B52H had flown unrefuelled from Kadena, Okinawa, to Torrejón, Spain: 12,500 miles.

160

Becks thought: I bet it's not *that* far from Tucson to Tripoli.

*　　*　　*

Beside her the secure phone rang and she grabbed it. The smooth, deep voice on the other end said mock-gruffly: 'Major-General Maule, Pentagon. Are you scrambling, Captain?'

'Yes, sir!'

'OK, Becks,' Andrew Maule said, and relaxed the atmosphere. 'How's it going?'

She told him what had come off the signals.

'You speak with your base commander at all today?' Maule asked. No, Becks told him. Maule said: 'Last night, A2 at senior level made an approach to Tactical Air Command.' TAC was the section to which Davis-Monthan was answerable. 'We asked for you to be authorized to carry on your work as normal – that's to say as normally as you could do in an emergency situation. You were the one who raised the alarm on this one, Captain – that's been noted – and you're in the best position geographically for running this whole thing down. Now, there's a number of agencies engaged in this thing – A2 here in Washington; SAC at Barksdale; the FBI – and we really need one office co-ordinating the entire effort.' Maule paused. 'How d'you feel about taking on the job of co-ordinating, Captain?'

Becks drew a sharp breath. Her eyebrows shot up. She couldn't believe it; she'd have given almost anything for a chance like this. 'Uh . . . what about General Hartmore?'

'General Hartmore knows we intended to raise this suggestion. While remaining on base, you would in effect be detached to A2 headquarters and reporting to me, here. All signals to me would be copied to

161

your base commander – he needs to be kept in the picture.'

Briefly Becks was baffled. She couldn't see why A2. A2, in the depths of Arizona, was a remote office not responsible for much except receiving reports from elsewhere and making sure they landed on the right desks at Davis-Monthan. 'Sir, I'm afraid I don't quite see . . . We in A2 are responsible for tactical military intelligence . . .'

'Becks,' Maule said briskly, 'there is no agency with an obvious responsibility for a case like Dark Angel. It's not an FBI job, although part of the investigation clearly comes under their ambit. It's not CIA, it's not NSA. If anything, it could be the air force police and legal department, but they aren't equipped to handle a thing like this. As we see it here at the Pentagon, Davis-Monthan A2 was the first agency to be apprised of this event, Davis-Monthan A2 used initiative and fine judgement to action this whole inquiry, and we'd like Davis-Monthan A2 to co-ordinate it to a finish.' He paused, then added, with an edge: 'That's provided Davis-Monthan A2 consider themselves up to the job.'

Becks drew a breath. 'Why . . . well, yes, sir, I'd be pleased to take on the job!' Careful, Captain Laird, don't overdo it. Suddenly she was heaping mental blessings upon the bumbling Captain Hultlander for thinking of her first. 'I'll put every effort into it, to the best of my abilities.'

'Figured you'd say that, Becks.' She could hear the grin in his voice. 'I'll message General Hartmore. Right now, there's one more thing you should know: on the basis of what you told us last night, and of what's transpired meantime, we are moving a section of US Navy fighters, tankers and electronic surveillance aircraft to Sigonella, Sicily. It's a convenient point for any action that might develop.'

'But . . .' Becks frowned. 'Why the navy? I thought . . .'

'Here's what else you should know. We have also been in touch with the British Royal Air Force and they are sending a section of fighters. RAF and USAF flight refuelling equipment isn't always compatible but RAF and US Navy equipment is – that's why the navy. Oh, and one of the pilots in the RAF contingent will be Flight Lieutenant Penhale.'

Becks made what would have been a whistle if it had been audible.

'He's there to advise,' Maule said, 'but he's also there to fly operationally. Right, I'll get a signal off to Hartmore right now. Is there anything else you need?'

Becks hesitated. 'Yeah – Andrew, can you get me everything the air force knows about Tariq Talal? His base, how many guys he's got there, record, what kinda man he is, what kinda relationship he has with the Libyan leader – you know . . .'

'Sure, Becks. We'll lay out some code names, too. I'll code it over to you, everything we have.'

They hung up.

Suddenly Becks knew what had been happening while she'd been asleep: a monumental Pentagon power struggle between A2 and Tactical Air Command, maybe some of the other commands as well. Now that A2 in the person of Andrew Maule had won the struggle, it meant to keep the centre of the action well away from interfering hands. In the depths, in fact, of Arizona.

Then she wanted to jump in the air. It was so frustrating, being absolutely elated and having no-one to share it with. Van's face, smiling, danced through her mind.

*   *   *

Quickly, chewing her lip, she set to work. More signals were coming in.

The FBI had been working to pin down who'd been on the flight. They'd interviewed all three men who'd been on the groundcrew that had launched Dark Angel, and they'd been on to the Learjet outfit at Tucson International that had numbered Tamasin Penhale Masterson among its captains.

Mrs Masterson had picked January, of all times, to take annual leave. And no-one in the Learjet outfit had had the wit to wonder why.

She was a natural. So was General Bat Masterson, and the descriptions the FBI agents had had off the groundcrew made it pretty likely that the Mastersons were two out of the six. The prayer before the crew climbed on board virtually clinched it. USAF folklore confirmed the legend that, of all commanders, Masterson was the one who throughout his Vietnam days had always held a prayer meeting before setting out on a dangerous raid.

That left four.

In the interviews the FBI had run at Barksdale, Louisiana, the names that had cropped up were those of former Colonel Chuck Brantley and former Captain Jerry Yeaver.

They'd got Brantley as a civilian contractor running his own consultancy, organizing routine paperwork aspects of B52 transfers to storage at Davis-Monthan under the arms-reduction treaty. Brantley handled stuff like flight plans, liaison with Soviet staff on the arms-reduction observation team, liaison with the Federal Aviation Administration over military certificates of airworthiness, even some flight catering. At Barksdale, even the guys in admin had found it a godsend to have an experienced, ex-service civilian, well fixed, contacts everywhere, to cope with the bureaucracy.

Becks was beginning to see how some of that documentation might have been handled.

Along with Brantley, there'd been Yeaver, but he'd been really hardly more than a legman. Barksdale security had photographs of both men, and now the FBI had copies of the photographs and they'd been back to the Dark Angel groundcrew and, yes, those sure did look like two of the guys on the crew.

It was coming unravelled, sure enough. *Why*, though? – Becks wondered. The Mastersons had ample motive. But why Brantley and Yeaver exactly? She read the next slip.

It was inconclusive. The FBI was following up Brantley and Yeaver alike to look for further interesting contacts; they were also interviewing the manager of Masterson's ranch at Pozo Lindo; but there were still two men on that B52 crew who had yet to be identified.

For the other signals, Becks ran the combinations on the communications room door and hid herself away in its cramped, fumey confines. The fumes came from the photocopier and, Becks vowed to herself, if they made her ill she'd take the air force to court.

She started with the A2 signal as she knew she could decrypt this one the fastest. There'd been no sign of Dark Angel – she'd scarcely expected one – but there were warships on the move. Becks lifted her eyebrows.

The carrier USS *John F. Kennedy* had been moved off station in the Med, along with her battle group, to take up position south of Sicily in international waters. Fleetingly Becks tried adding up the bill that Uncle Sam would be picking up for all this. Then she read the next signal and she wasn't so amused. The Soviet carrier *Kiev* had *also* been reported moving off station. On a course that would bring her into the same area as *Kennedy*.

Becks decrypted the NSA report. The US National Security Agency went about its tasks with somewhat less panache than the CIA – come to that, Becks thought, she still hadn't heard back from the CIA – and often produced better intelligence than the CIA, anyway. Its job was to eavesdrop on signals, everything from radar waves to computer emissions, and taking in radio and telephone on the way. The NSA's listening posts hadn't come up with much that was new compared with the A2 report. Frenzied activity in the Soviet Siberian command air forces, the Sixteenth Military District – after an official, but secret, US warning – but no sign of Dark Angel. No wonder, Becks thought, Siberia had been a way-outside risk from the start. Confirmation on *Kiev* and *Kennedy*, and the timings. Orders to *Kennedy* at 0700 zulu, ship under way at 0720. *Kiev* under way at 0635 after an encrypted order at 0555. Impatient, Becks dived into the Pentagon report.

It was a bit terse and it hadn't got much new in it – Becks ran her eye over it quickly. They'd told the President; the President had been on to the Soviet general secretary in case the BUFF went for Siberia; all US radar forces were on alert; *Kennedy* was off station.

What Becks really wanted was the CIA's opinion on all this. She shut the comms office door thankfully behind her, called through to Julio for a glass of iced tea, waited till he fetched it, then used the scrambler. In Langley, Virginia, it would be twenty past ten.

*   *   *

She got a helpful female voice on the switchboard. The helpful female voice passed her to a helpful male voice in administration. Becks explained. The helpful male voice transferred her to another helpful male voice in operations. Becks explained again. Operations transferred her to a different, helpful male voice, this time in science and technology. Ever helpful, the male voice in sci and tech was sorry, but they couldn't help Captain Laird here.

166

'OK, can you get me back to operations?' Becks was beginning to grow frustrated.

She got the same voice as before. 'Why, hello, Captain. I understood . . .'

'May I speak with someone senior in your office, sir?' She'd stopped minding who she cut across.

A new voice. 'Captain Laird. Yes?'

'I need to explain. I understand you're familiar with Dark Angel. Yesterday evening around eight our time I called one of your guys in operations to report it, and he promised to divert a satellite to look for it – Dark Angel. Since then we heard nothing. What happened to the data off the satellite?'

'OK, Captain.' The man's voice was deep, slow, bookish. An East Coast aristocrat, a senior guy. 'To whom did you speak?'

'Ah, he didn't give a name.' She wasn't sure whether to add *sir*.

'You checked the person's name and the person gave no name?' The deep, slow voice seemed put out that it hadn't had *sir*.

'Ah, not exactly.' Screw the sonofabitch, he was going to have to ask if he wanted *sir*. 'Things were happening kind of a little fast.'

'What things, Captain?' He said *captain* the way generals said it to remind you how far you had to go.

'Listen . . .'

'Please, Captain.' Impeccably polite while he interrupted her, unsettled her. 'Do go ahead.'

He *wasn't* getting his goddam *sir*. 'Dark Angel was three, four hours out from takeoff. We had barely discovered anything was wrong, we needed action right *then*, not in ten minutes' or even five minutes' time. We . . .'

'*You* at Davis-Monthan had *lost* an armed B52 and you wanted *this* agency . . .'

167

She rammed through, belting for the goal line. 'Listen, I'm head of A2 on this base, *I know* the stuff you guys have on your satellites. That's why I wanted that bird right then!'

'Yet you obtained no name from the person you say you spoke to?' Hard tackle.

Becks drove her teeth into her lip for an instant. If the man on the other end had been within line of sight, he'd have been lasered into a pile of dust. 'OK, *sir*, since you don't seem to believe a word I say, let's make a start and get *your* name right. Or do spooks only deal in cover names?'

He answered with snake-oil smoothness. 'Cordwain, Captain Laird. Assistant to the Deputy Director, Operations.'

Oh boy. That was equivalent to at least two rungs higher than Maule or Hartmore, and Captain Rebecca Laird's goose was good and cooked. *Well, the hell with that, she had work to do.* 'Mr Cordwain – sir – you may perhaps recognize that this is a desperate situation internationally. There could even be fighting, maybe – God forbid – a war as a result of what we're talking about. I ask you to believe me. I talked to a man in operations last night. Now, there has to be a record of that conversation.'

Silence.

Becks prompted: 'Mr Cordwain?'

'Bear with me one moment, Captain. I'm looking through files here on the system.'

Becks chewed her lip. She flicked a glance at the picture of Minnesota on the wall. It comforted her.

Cordwain said: 'I'm sorry, Captain. There is no record anywhere here of a conversation last night naming you, and we have diverted no satellites.'

She burst out: 'But I . . .'

'I don't doubt your word, Captain Laird. I guess we're looking here at some sort of slip-up.'

'Well, can we have a satellite *now*?' Desperately she recovered herself.

Still with his slippery smoothness Cordwain said: 'Authority for that will have to come from Pentagon A2 or from your base commander. I guess that's easy enough done, but after this length of time you must appreciate Dark Angel could be anywhere.'

Now Becks wanted to scream. If they'd just lent her a satellite yesterday, when she'd asked, and when they'd said they would, they'd have stood a better-than-even chance of finding the B52. 'I'll get right on to my commander,' she said. 'Thank you, Mr Cordwain.' She hung up. Tears of frustration and rage were forcing at her eyes but she bit her lip and forced them doggedly back. She took a couple of deep breaths, her eyes closed.

The artificial light oppressed her and her office was a cell. She was starting to wonder whether she could handle this after all. She shoved her chair back and jumped up. She straightened her clothes and walked through, chin high, into the outer office, carrying her empty tea glass.

'You have any more, Julio?'

'Sure, Captain Laird, ma'am.'

He was crossing the office to fill her glass when Major-General Gus Hartmore loomed into the doorway.

*   *   *

The uniform was immaculate, ruthlessly pressed as always, and Hartmore's relentlessly athletic torso looked as if it were about to burst out of it. The Colt .45 automatic sat on his hip, the leather holster gleaming; the medals stood to attention on his chest.

Julio almost dropped the glass as he snapped to attention and saluted.

Grim-faced, Hartmore acknowledged him. 'Carry on,' he muttered out of the side of his mouth.

Julio headed for the fridge. Hartmore fixed Becks with a baleful look.

'In your office, if you please, Captain.'

Shoulders smartly back, Becks led him inside. 'Sir.'

Hartmore didn't sit down, he preferred to pace. 'Gimme a briefing on Dark Angel.'

Becks summed it up. She stayed standing, her own side of the desk. On the desk she had poinsettias in a tub and as Hartmore heard her out, silent, he kept looking at them, wrinkling his nose in disdain.

Becks was still seething at the way Cordwain had made a fool of her, but she played that part right down.

She finished. Hartmore turned a sort of pirouette on his heel, briefly turning his back. He faced her, and as her eye met his Becks again caught the flash of resentment that he should be, however fractionally, shorter than a woman.

'Captain, d'you feel you're getting adequate co-operation from the CIA?'

'I am now, sir.'

Tight-lipped, Hartmore paced again, hands clenched together behind his back. 'A little late, huh, Captain?'

'Sir.'

He snapped angry eyes on to hers and off again, and Becks realized for once the criticism wasn't aimed at her. Five years in the air force had left her a convinced believer in the cock-up theory of history, but now she'd begun wondering whether something might not be getting past her. Hartmore, by temperament a conspiracy theorist, had never doubted it.

He spun round tautly again and sighed. 'OK, Captain. Keep me abreast of all developments *immediately* they occur.' They saluted. Hartmore strutted out, one strong hand shoving the Colt back where it belonged, behind his hip.

*   *   *

170

The computer screen indicated an encrypted signal arriving. Becks shut herself back in the fumes. She printed it out and did the decrypt.

It was the stuff Maule had promised on Tariq Talal.

There was plenty of it. The decrypt took a while. Tariq Talal's base lay ninety miles south of Tripoli and the nearest town was a place called Mizdah where the main road south forked and deteriorated into camel trails. Mizdah ought to be easy enough to miss, from a bomber crew's point of view, Becks thought. It was five miles from the camp and it didn't look remotely like a terrorist base. What really complicated matters was the little knot of houses, no more than a hamlet, that lay right on the edge of the camp.

It was called Bir al Hadh and there couldn't have been fifty people living in it but, if matters got that far, Dark Angel's radar nav was going to have his work cut out to hit the terrorists and miss the villagers.

Becks considered the base. It was a big area. It encompassed training grounds, musketry ranges, assault courses, even a sports field. For buildings it had two big, barrack-like accommodation blocks, with a canteen in one of them, and a prefabricated classroom block. And it contained explosives. They were stored in a bunker 800 metres south of the accommodation blocks, semi-recessed into the earth, concrete-walled and blast-hardened. To a degree.

Becks was frowning. Someone at A2 had added the comment that if that thing caught a stick of M117s, it wouldn't take more than two bombs that size to scatter the concrete roofing halfway across the Med. Then the next 750-pounder would go off in the middle of the explosives store.

Plastic explosive was generally pretty safe to handle, but you wouldn't want to subject it to an M117.

The other question was who'd been looking after the

stuff and how well. Four months earlier, the report said, a shady Arab had turned up drowned in Elefsis Bay, Greece, and four Mossad agents had surfaced the next day in Tel Aviv with secretive smirks on their faces. A2 understood, circuitously, from the Israelis that the Arab had been Tariq Talal's explosives expert.

The bit missing off the report was technical branch's assessment of how long it took for plastic to become unstable. Even so, Becks realized, this was starting to look promising.

Personnel. Tariq Talal had about a hundred people at the camp, a cadre of operations-hardened terrorists and a bigger proportion of eager young trainees. There weren't many women: the camp doctor, a couple of nurses, a handful of cooks – that was all.

Their choice to put themselves in the front line, Becks thought. All this time she'd been wondering how come Dark Angel's crew were so sure they'd find Talal at home and now, as she ran through his CV, she found out.

Whatever else Tariq Talal was, he was macho, arrogant and possessed of a demonstrative kind of courage. Where other terrorists moved secretly and never slept twice in the same place, Tariq Talal scoffed at such running and hiding from the Great Satan. *He* was the one with the nerve to stand by his soldiers; they wouldn't dare to send men against *him*.

Maybe that wasn't all hogwash, Becks considered. Tariq Talal was the chief suspect in that nasty little shoot-out at Tegel airport a few years back when Berlin had been still divided. To do that alone, even with East Berlin for a bolthole just behind you, took guts. The man liked the front line, he liked the adrenalin.

And he was smart. They knew Talal and his cronies won favour by distributing food and scarce medicines in Libyan towns, and it wasn't a long step of deduction to tie that to the occasional systematic series of thefts that police reported from Italy and southern France, thefts of lorryloads of supermarket goods and pharmaceuticals.

That sort of Robin Hood-style do-gooding got him in with the people. So that if the Libyan leader tried to withdraw authorization for Talal's visits to those towns, authorization for his speeches to the people, it wouldn't be Talal who looked like a spoilsport, it would be the Libyan leader. Talal knew how to buy popularity all right.

Difficult one, that, Becks thought, for the Libyan leader. Nice one for Talal.

The man was also brutal. That came out clearly, Becks thought, on the film of Edward Masterson's killing. A2, presumably with help from CIA archives, had tied the man to the single airliner hijacking; a yacht hijack in which the six Israelis on board had been systematically butchered; three airport attacks – the most recent of them at Frankfurt – in which ordinary passengers had been sprayed at random with automatic fire; several bombings of ground targets, most of which had killed people; and a single airliner bombing.

Grimly, Becks read the footnote considering the man's Islamic credentials.

They weren't strong, according to some tame Washington expert on the Koran and the *sharia* – Islamic law – for all the huffing and puffing and the observances. But Tariq Talal wasn't the first militant leader who'd attempted to bend a religion to his purposes instead of vice versa, and likely he wouldn't be the last.

So far, the footnote continued, he'd enjoyed the protection of the Libyan leader. Just recently, though, there'd been a touch of one-upmanship: I'm a better Muslim than *you* are. Becks was wondering about that when the fax bleeped and began its soft, effeminate rumbling.

* * *

This time it was in 'clear'. It was from the FBI, a résumé of Captain Jerry Yeaver's USAF career. His training, the B52 postings, Castle, Eielson. The extraordinary story of how he'd hauled the captain singlehanded out of a crashed KC135 tanker and then refused the medal they'd wanted to offer him. The point of the story jumped out at Becks from the last paragraph.

Captain Jerry Yeaver was recently divorced and he blamed himself for the break-up. His commanding officer had put pressure on him to take a medical discharge on the ground that he was suffering from depression and couldn't be considered mentally stable any more.

Furious, Becks stopped herself with difficulty from screwing up the fax and hurling it across the office.

That was no way to treat a good man who'd only needed help. And who was now going to die, for nothing.

CHAPTER 20

Suddenly aboard the B52 the sense of urgency was tangible. It quickly shook Tamasin out of her weariness. On the intercom Bat Masterson, flat-voiced, said: 'Russell, wake Jerry.'

Radar waves shouldn't have been coming within miles of them, not out here over the middle of the southern North Atlantic.

'OK,' Russell Feehan said reluctantly, and leaned across to Jerry's ejector seat.

Jerry came awake instantly. He moved quickly, swapping places with Russell as, below, Tamasin woke Chuck Brantley, at his radar navigator's station.

Out here, radar was a potential emergency.

'EWO?' Mario Peroni said impatiently.

'OK,' Jerry muttered. He was fixing his harness, frowning at the scopes. 'It's still in search mode. It must *know* it's painting us, why doesn't it lock us in?' He was studying the wavelength, studying the pulse repetition frequency.

Mario niggled again: 'What is it?'

Slowly, Jerry answered: 'Mainstay.'

They all recognized the NATO codename. It was the big Ilyushin four-jet AWACS.

'Range around, ah . . . thirty, thirty-two miles,' Jerry said. 'North of us. Up out of Havana or Conakry, Guinea, I'd say.'

'Could it identify us?' Mario said.

Jerry considered. 'Quite likely,' he said, 'even with all our radars shut down.'

175

They flew on. Forty thousand feet above the Atlantic Ocean, the radar waves from the unseen Soviet AWACS kept on painting them but still didn't lock on. Jerry started to get a creepy feeling.

'Does he have fighters with him?' Mario asked.

'Can't say without using active radar,' Jerry said. 'We don't wanna do that yet.'

Frowning, Bat said, 'If he's still not *locked on* . . .'

'Let's just maintain heading and height,' Jerry finished for him.

Below at the navigator's station, the creepy feeling was getting to Tamasin, too. She caught Chuck's eye. His chubby face wasn't happy. You were so exposed up here, Tamasin thought. Chuck lit a cigarette and shoved the lighter back into a pocket. On the intercom still no-one spoke.

Unseen, the Russian radar platform ghosted through the stratosphere thirty miles off their port wingtip.

For some moments now Jerry hadn't spoken, and Mario knew he was bothered. 'EWO, what *is* the guy doing?'

'Well, he's . . .' Jerry was puzzled and it showed in his voice. 'He's just kind of keeping on a parallel course with us.'

Bat had been trying to resist the temptation but now he couldn't; he twisted and stared out to the left. The sky at altitude was burning silver and the cloudscape spread its furrows out to every horizon and there was no sign of the other aircraft. He'd known he wouldn't see it, at thirty miles. Maybe there isn't another aircraft, he thought. Maybe we have a bug in the radar receivers. Maybe it's a ghost.

He shook his head, heavy under the bone dome. Maybe Bat Masterson was simply getting too tired for the mission.

* * *

Tamasin checked the time. Arizona time was 1021, zulu 1721, local time 1521. Mid-afternoon over the Atlantic. Smoke wreathed Chuck, sitting beside her with his eyes heavy-lidded, and Tamasin glanced at him, reflecting that he and Jerry must have had the best sleep break of anyone so far – four and a half hours. She didn't begrudge it to Jerry.

In the headphones she heard Mario's voice. 'This guy's flying east, right? Where's he up out of, EWO? Is he out of Conakry and heading home?'

'Could be.' Jerry paused. 'Although if so he ought to be heading more south, across our path.'

'What the hell's he doing over the middle of the Atlantic, anyway?'

Bat glanced at Mario, eyes narrowed in the glare. All this was guesswork. But Mario knew that as well as Bat did; Mario was just worried.

'I don't think we have a means of telling,' Jerry said, worried too. 'What gets me is why he hasn't locked on. He must know we're here, he surely doesn't think we're an airline flight. It's like he's goosing us but he doesn't want to kiss us.'

Bat grunted: 'Russell – you have your tail radar on?'

'Affirmative, Bat, passive mode only.' Like the rest of the B52's radars, Russell's gun control set was receiving only, not transmitting. Russell was as conscious as the rest of them that where a Mainstay was, there might be fighters around. He said slowly: 'It's almost as if the guy was waiting for us – only now we're here, he doesn't care.'

Tamasin said: 'Two minutes to Waypoint Eight.'

Radar wraith or not, they were still on their way, still with a mission to complete. Tamasin counted them down to the waypoint. The heading stayed constant. They passed the waypoint. They kept flying east.

177

Four minutes later, Jerry said: 'He's going.'

*   *   *

Tension hung in the pause and Chuck lit another cigarette.

'Yeah,' Jerry said, the relief plain in his voice. 'He's fading out to the north. He's turning right away from us.'

The wave of relief swept over everyone. Tears pricked at Tamasin's eyes and she felt exhausted again.

On the intercom, Bat said: 'OK, Tamasin, you and me for sleep break.'

She was about ready for that. She swapped places with Chuck again.

Twisting as best he could in the ejector seat, Jerry craned his neck cautiously and watched as Bat settled down in his seat and left the flying to Mario. Mario was busy. Still cautious, Jerry slid a look right, watching Russell. Russell had the worry beads clasped loosely in his hand and he wasn't flipping them. He was supposed to be keeping an eye on the tail radar but in his exhaustion and after all those painkillers it wasn't easy. Jerry watched, furtive, as Russell's eyelids grew heavy.

Softly, steadily, Jerry unclipped his flight case. He stole another swallow of whiskey.

*   *   *

It was noon Arizona time when Chuck woke Tamasin, 1900 zulu, local time no more than an hour behind that. There was pressure in her ears, she could hardly hear Chuck when he spoke to her, and she knew whichever of them was flying the aircraft was letting down in a steady, gentle descent over the ocean. She grinned at Chuck. She felt better for her sleep, short as it had been.

178

As she clambered over the seats to let Chuck back into the radar nav station she was pinching her nose and swallowing to clear her ears. Stale cigarette smell lingered. Glancing up the ladder as Chuck squeezed back past her, she realized already they were flying back into gathering night; the curve of the cabin roof and its writhing tubes was charcoal-shadowed.

The next time they saw daylight they would be over target.

Movement beside her, a tall figure. Jerry Yeaver whisked down the ladder, worked the coffee maker, and plonked two coffees on the console beside her, the light catching his glasses. She looked up with a smile, but Jerry avoided her eye. He didn't say a word, he just scrambled quickly back up, scared of her.

'Thanks, Jerry!' Tamasin called. Then as she passed Chuck his coffee she remembered the way she'd snapped at Jerry earlier, when he'd offered his help, and she felt guilty.

Bat's voice, deep and reassuring in her headphones, said: 'How we doing, Tamasin?'

They were coming up to Waypoint Nine. Tamasin said: 'Ah . . . four minutes, Bat.'

For the first time in the flight, she realized, she felt comfortable with the others, even with Mario; she felt part of the team, accepted, appreciated. Except maybe by Jerry. She'd hurt him and she wished there was something she could do to make amends.

*   *   *

Waypoint Nine was a spot over the ocean, southeast of the Cape Verde Islands and roughly due west of Dakar, Senegal. It marked the point where they turned north to fly parallel with the coast of Africa to pick the loneliest spot available to cross back over land.

'Pilot,' Tamasin said, 'your new heading will be zero one zero. Stand by for left turn in fifty seconds . . . forty-five . . .' Her voice was steady, confident, as she counted them down. 'Zero!'

Bat wheeled the big aircraft left, watching the horizontal situation indicator and the gyro compass until the new heading came up. He rolled out of the turn. From where he and Mario sat, it was the last of a fine evening of gold and magenta and crimson, shading now through deep browns to the velvet black of night. The sun had been on their tail but now as Bat levelled out on the new heading it came round and blazed balefully into the lefthand side of the cockpit, a molten ball of flame already starting to merge with the ocean. For a moment Bat reflected on what the next sun he saw might be like.

He adjusted the throttles. Tamasin called, checking the speed. This leg was a fast one, twenty minutes only, north between the Cape Verde Islands, speckled in the ocean off the port wingtip, and the busy coastline of Senegal.

Tamasin checked the readouts on the INS and GPS. 'On course, on time,' she reported. 'Confirm groundspeed is now three eighty knots.'

'Radar,' Jerry called. 'Ah . . . right on the edge. It's Dakar airport. Fading out.'

They were flying away from it.

Tamasin reported: 'Ten minutes to Waypoint One Zero.'

In the corner of his left eye Jerry could see the square black hatchway down to the second level, just behind him, but he couldn't see down it. He was worried about Tamasin, even though she wasn't friendly; she'd had hardly over an hour's sleep, and here she was pitched into intensive nav.

'Radar!' This time Jerry's voice was sharper. 'Off the coast, east of us! It's a surface vessel – could be a tanker, could be a warship.'

180

Between the charcoal of the sky and the melting purple of the sea Mario's keen eyes caught it almost at once. 'Two o'clock! Got her lights . . .' He was craning, one hand to the high panel coaming. 'That's a supertanker. There can't surely be a flatdeck out here, we'd'a picked up its radar pickets.'

'Doglegging west,' Bat grunted into the intercom, pressing the yoke back as he rolled into the turn. 'We'll get outa sight of those guys.'

*   *   *

They were down at 1,000 feet again. Turbulence over the dark waves thudded into the slab sides of the B52's fuselage and Tamasin got that queasy feeling. Tense at his scopes, Jerry listened for a challenge on radio. None came. Beside him, half-awake at the guns, Russell flipped his worry beads. Love the man as he did, Jerry was struggling not to let it get on his nerves this much. Bat rolled them to the right, back towards Africa.

Tamasin got them back on course. She said: 'Three minutes to waypoint.'

Waypoint Ten was over ocean again, southwest of Nouakchott, Mauritania. Bat said, 'Jerry, you have any radar?'

'Negative, Bat.' The one they were worried about was Nouakchott.

Tamasin said: 'One minute to waypoint. Bat, your new heading will be zero nine zero, directly due east. Stand by for right turn in fifty seconds . . . forty-five . . .'

And zero. Bat rolled them into the turn, steeply now. Facing east they were facing directly into the night, a dead black sky, no stars yet, nothing but a low crescent moon.

'Pilot,' Tamasin said, 'can we have high-speed dash power?'

181

Bat's big hand reached out. Throttle levers Two to Seven shoved forward. Bat adjusted Number One for a bit more power. He retrimmed the rudder to compensate.

'Accelerating,' Tamasin reported. 'Groundspeed four hundred. Four forty.'

Beside her, Chuck was watching his attack radar, narrow-eyed, the set active now.

'Four eighty,' Tamasin said. 'OK, pilot, that's what we wanted.'

Power trembled through the big jet. Not for the first time, Tamasin felt awed to reflect on this aircraft's capability. Hemmed in by the black screens and surrounds and the chunky pale-grey plastic switches and the red circuit tester buttons, she felt insignificant. She glanced at Buster, the fluffy rabbit, comfortable and comforting in his holder. He would bring her luck.

Luck, on this flight, would be a swift and painless death.

'Coast return,' Chuck reported.

He could see it on the attack radar, Tamasin realized, and she switched on her EVS scope. It was there at once, low and ghostly in the infra-red image.

Narrowing his eyes, Mario peered ahead into the blackness. He thought he caught a gleam of surf. Bat had the B52 trimmed out, low down, flying very fast now into the east.

'African landfall!' Tamasin said on the intercom. She was fighting to keep the excitement out of her voice but it still showed through. 'We're over Africa, guys!'

The cheers and the applause weren't quite the jubilation of the takeoff from Tucson. But mingled with relief there was also mounting anticipation.

Tamasin realized she was busting for the loo.

CHAPTER 21

What most bothered Captain Rebecca Laird as she sat in her harshly lit, windowless office was that Soviet carrier, *Kiev*. She dialled Pentagon A2 on the scrambler phone, in her mind the picture of Major-General Andrew Maule, tall and tanned and silver-haired with that sly, sidelong, sexy smile. She used formal titles for the underlings who put her through, but when she heard Maule's voice she knew he was pleased to hear from her.

'Any more on *Kiev*?'

'I've just been briefing the President on that,' Maule said smoothly. It wasn't name-dropping, it was to remind Becks that she was playing an important role in an important operation. 'We have recon assets showing *Kiev* taking up station right now southeast of Sicily, kind of between the toe of Italy and the coast of eastern Libya.' If Maule had wanted to elaborate on what the recon assets were, he would have done, Becks realized. They might be AWACS over-flights or the air force's KH11 satellites or even a submarine shadowing the carrier's battle group; if not all three. 'What the damn ship's doing there is another matter.'

'What do *you* think, Andrew?'

'Well, it's something the President's thrashing out right now with the Soviet General Secretary.' Maule paused. He growled: 'But I'd say those guys know something.'

They rang off. Becks felt tense but she was starting to enjoy the adrenalin.

*   *   *

The FBI came through on the non-secure phone. 'We believe we have a fifth member of Dark Angel's crew. This time it's a contact of Colonel Brantley's, a guy called Lieutenant-Colonel Mario Peroni. Family from New York City. Skilled B52 captain with several thousand hours' flying experience, distinguished combat record in SEA.' South-east Asia, Becks understood. 'He left the air force two years ago. He's known as a gambler and there seems to be some kinda question mark over his financial affairs.'

'Good stuff,' Becks answered. 'Thanks.'

Five of them, then. The Mastersons; Brantley, the fixer; Yeaver, the legman; and now Peroni, another combat veteran. The Mastersons were bent on revenge, Becks thought; Yeaver had his own problems; and now there was a clear implication that Peroni had been promised some cash reward.

She wondered what Brantley's motivation was.

*   *   *

Abruptly she got up. She'd spent too long in this artificial light. As she strode through the door, Julio spoke hurriedly into the phone and hung up, and then turned to her with his dark eyes placid, controlled, in that saturnine face. Maybe, Becks thought, she should get a bug on that phone; but that was a technical skill that she'd never been taught.

Pale gold light washed the flat immensity of the airfield. It must have been 70 Fahrenheit out there. More A10s took off, and a bus trundled by on one of the through roads, a long, cumbersome, old-fashioned-looking affair in air-force dark blue. Becks filled a small watering can and took it inside to the poinsettias on her desk.

*   *   *

The datalink beeped. Becks took it. The code gave National Security Agency, the radio eavesdroppers. The message was a touch late, and the NSA official had added a note of brief apology. The event had occurred about 1230 zulu time, 0530 today for Arizona. A military base in eastern Venezuela had range-gated a bogey – unidentified aircraft – only to have the range gate convincingly pulled off. The bogey had vanished. When last reliably seen on radar it had been travelling east with a groundspeed of 540 knots: a jet, then. Phone and radio intercepts from the same area indicated that the Venezuelan base commander had been given to understand by his operators that it was a big aircraft.

What the *hell* would they be doing in Venezuela? Becks went into her office. At the back she had a wall map of the world but up till now she'd kept it rolled up.

She took it into the outer office. 'Julio, give us a hand.'

Dark eyes blinking, Julio moved cat-like to her side. They found a spare bit of wall and fixed up the map. Julio found some gummed labels and they stuck them on the map, with the times and the supposed sightings.

'East from there,' Julio said, looking intellectual as he stated the obvious, 'takes you way out over the Atlantic.'

Exactly where it should be.

'Good,' Becks said non-committally, and returned to her office wondering whether to phone that jerk Cordwain in case CIA might admit to having any sources in Venezuela. Then the fax warbled. FBI again.

They were still following up any contacts of Chuck Brantley's they could find and now they reckoned they had a strong candidate for the sixth crew member aboard Dark Angel. Russell Feehan, ex-colonel, again SAC B52s, gunnery expert, age sixty-two, home state South Carolina. Wife deceased. A son in Natick, Massachusetts, a daughter in Atlantic City, New Jersey; each married, neither admitting to any idea where their father was, neither admitting to having seen Russell Feehan for weeks. One thing they both agreed on: Feehan was badly ill with cancer.

Somehow the FBI had got Feehan's doctor talking. It was an extensive cancer of the stomach and upper intestine. Feehan was in a lot of pain, he was dying and he knew it.

*　　*　　*

An hour went by. Memos to answer, reports to fire off, paperwork; but Becks was thinking about the pain in Russell Feehan's body and the pain in Jerry Yeaver's soul. And in Bat Masterson's, and in Tamasin's.

Around eleven, more from the NSA.

They'd got a couple of signals off a Soviet Mainstay radar platform on a patrol over the southern North Atlantic, probably destined for the base in Conakry, Guinea. The signal was encrypted and they hadn't cracked it yet but the code in the message preamble showed that it wasn't meant for the regular military, it was meant for the KGB.

That Mainstay had spotted something over the ocean. And NSA obviously reckoned it was Dark Angel.

NSA had one more thing, just as odd if not more so. Twenty minutes earlier they'd intercepted a cipher squirt deflected off a satellite, origin somewhere in the Urals, destination central southern Med, possibly into Libya. Again they hadn't cracked the cipher, again it was the code in the message preamble that aroused the interest.

It indicated Spetsnaz. Soviet special forces.

That was one to bounce off Andrew Maule. Becks dialled Pentagon A2.

'Can't help, Becks,' Maule said thoughtfully when he'd

listened to her. 'Unless they crack that cipher, we're all guessing.' He considered a moment. 'Only comment I can make is that we know the Spetsnaz do have several Arabic-speaking personnel, and in Lebanon we once had rumours about a team of Spetsnaz fighters using Red Crescent uniforms and vehicles for cover.'

'What about Libya?' Becks asked.

'Don't know anything for certain about Libya.'

Maule's tone held a reservation and she recognized it. 'What do you know for *un*-certain?'

'Well . . .' Maule was still debating whether to pass this on, but he knew he'd committed himself now. 'Four days back NSA also got a cipher squirt using the Spetsnaz code preamble. It seemed to indicate a team possibly entering Libya over ground, but all that's just conjecture. They haven't cracked the cipher and we have no independent confirmation.'

Becks hung up. She checked the timing for the Mainstay's signal: 1722 zulu, 1022 Arizona time, not quite an hour ago. She locked the cipher room behind her, her eyes alight when they met Julio's. She took a ruler and calculator. On the big wall map she stuck a label to indicate the position for the Mainstay intercept.

It was still looking right.

Becks consulted her watch. Colan Penhale ought to be on the ground at Sigonella by now.

CHAPTER 22

Night enveloped the B52. With the coastline of Mauritania safely behind them, Bat Masterson had climbed out of the jolting ground effect, levelled the bomber at 4,000 feet over the Sahara, and throttled back to cruise speed. Shattered rock showed on the forward-looking infra-red like broken, jagged knife blades, and Mario Peroni's sullen gaze wandered over the boulders and pebbles on the scope; this wasn't sand sea country yet.

'Sleep break,' Bat said in his laconic Arizona drawl.

It was the turn of Russell Feehan and Mario. Russell fell sound asleep at his station. Bat and Mario swapped places and again Bat flew the aircraft from the righthand seat while Mario slept soundly on the left.

Down on the second level, Chuck Brantley lit another cigarette and leafed idly through his girlie magazine. The ride was smooth enough at this height but still Tamasin felt oppression in the atmosphere; and Chuck's cigarette brought back a twinge of the nausea she'd felt when they'd been down in the weeds.

'Mind the nav for a mo?'

'Sure thing,' Chuck said with a sidelong look. 'What's she want doing with her?'

Tamasin gave him a tolerant grin and left him at his console, tucking the straps tiredly into place in her ejector seat. Aft, in the cramped space of the relief station, she renewed her perfume. Faint light caught the tough, rubberized packaging of the two life rafts, and she wondered if they would actually find themselves using the things. She edged back out into the narrow walkway between her navigation console and the pressure hull of the B52. Underfoot, the gridded metal flooring seemed to tremble faintly. Tamasin climbed up the ladder.

*   *   *

Stars shone in the eternal night through the overhead panels and Jerry Yeaver turned his head quickly to look at her, eyes frightened behind his glasses. In an instinct to reassure him, Tamasin gave him a smile. She clambered on to the metal decking of the first level and ducked under the dark ceiling piping for a look ahead.

The smell of paraffin and stale food and sweat hung in the cabin air, and a whiff of Brut deodorant from Mario. In the aching night the stars were hard and bright and without number and when Tamasin gazed up at them they reminded her of the desert sky over Arizona where she'd lived with Edward and loved him. Nevertheless it lifted her heart to see outside for a change. Bat glanced over his shoulder and his silhouetted face smiled at her. Noise wrapped itself round them.

Tamasin stooped to Bat and asked if he wanted anything. He said no, and she climbed down to the water container, drew herself a beaker, and climbed back up. The water was still cold. It made her feel better.

Then there was movement at her side and she turned.

*   *   *

Jerry Yeaver's rangy body seemed bent almost double under the low ceiling. His eyes were still wide, luminous in the deep shadow. He spoke close to her face through the steady engine note.

'You OK?'

She glanced at him, conscious at once that his concern

was genuine. 'Sure . . . thanks.' She smiled. 'Water for you?'

'Uh . . . OK.' Uninterested, he sipped from the beaker and handed it back. 'I mean, you didn't get too much sleep.'

Tamasin hesitated. After the way he'd reacted, before, it surprised her that he should have been thinking of her. 'I'm fine.' She smiled and herself took a sip. 'I guess I am a little tired, but I should get some more sleep, before . . .'

Chuck came up the ladder, and suddenly the low-ceilinged platform between the two sets of ejector seats was very crowded. Tamasin gave Chuck a suspicious look. He grinned back through the darkness, moustache bristling, and held out a podgy palm. Tamasin made out some pills cradled in Chuck's hand.

'What's that?'

'Amphetamine. Keep you awake.' Chuck eyed her, bulky in the confined space, and in a light, side gust the B52 swayed under them. 'We're gonna need this to function properly when we get over target.'

Wordlessly Jerry took one. He swallowed it with his water.

'Not for me just yet,' Tamasin said. She didn't know what it would do to her airsickness. She had a sense that the real reason Chuck was up here was to check on her.

Chuck swallowed a pill and offered one to Bat.

Bat shook his head. 'Ask me again when we're approaching the IP.'

The initial point was the marker for the start of the bomb run. And this was real now. Suddenly Tamasin felt cold down her spine.

'OK,' Chuck said, and went back down the hatch.

*   *   *

The B52 rolled faintly again and Tamasin realized in fact

it was something the aircraft was doing all the time, wallowing through the sky in a permanent dutch roll, and the only reason she was noticing it was that she was out of her usual station, standing up here in the starlight on the thin metal decking. She was so tired that at moments she felt almost disoriented; she wondered whether she'd done the right thing in refusing Chuck's amphetamine. Jerry dithered, a foot away from her.

Hardly paying him attention, Tamasin sat on the decking, her back against the side of the cabin, and stretched out her legs in front of her. She clasped her plastic beaker of water in both hands.

Jerry sighed at some private regret. He knelt down, one knee on the decking, one crooked, with his wrists balanced on the raised one.

Tamasin said: 'Are you scared?'

Her watch was still on Arizona time. It gave 1338, lunchtime. Zulu time was 1938. That was now the same as local time: they were close to the Greenwich meridian. This far south, night fell just a bit earlier in January than it did in summer; about enough to tell. Much further south than this, Tamasin reflected, and you'd get nightfall at the same time all year round.

'I guess not,' Jerry said as if his mind was on something else. He didn't seem to care; the amphetamine hadn't altered his mood or made him less nervous of her. He looked at her. 'Are you?'

Yes, she was. Not scared of dying. All along, she'd found nothing worrisome in the abstract concept of the ending of her life; especially not when she remembered Edward. But the thought of being maimed, of being alive and in agony, that scared her.

On fewer than ten fingers she could count the hours left to her to live.

Tamasin nodded her head. She avoided Jerry's eye, but he was watching her closely. She'd put her left hand on

191

her knee and Jerry reached out and took hold of it. His hand seemed a lot bigger than hers, stronger than she'd expected. The comfort he gave her flowed powerfully into her, and Tamasin squeezed Jerry's fingers, aware suddenly, frighteningly, of how much in these last hours she needed human comfort. Faintly, she discovered a sense of the comfort her own strength gave to Jerry.

Jerry's voice came strained through the engine background. Eighteen inches away with his bone dome on, Bat couldn't have heard him. 'It just isn't right for a lady like you to die, just to blow some stinking terrorist out of existence.' The speech had the ring of one that he'd prepared hours ago.

Russell, bless him, had said something similar, Tamasin reflected. Yet there'd been deeply held sexism in Russell's opinion – the sort of sexism that's innocent for *almost* all the time, the sort that spurs a man to give up his train seat for a woman – and Jerry had always believed actively in equality.

She leaned towards him, still clasping his hand. 'I've got a personal stake in this raid, Jerry. It was *my* husband, *my* lover they kicked shit out of and shot. I miss him. I'm angry – angry? I'm bloody furious, every time I think about it. I really, truly want to kill Tariq Talal, and everyone else he's infected with his perverted ideas of justice and his spurious interpretation of Islam. I want to save all the innocent people he and his bunch of bastards are plotting to slaughter. If I get killed in that process, that honestly is a small price to pay. Sure I'm scared, but it's still a small price. But what about *you*?' She squeezed his hand again. 'Where's *your* personal stake? You're the one who's got no business dying. Honestly, Jerry.'

In her hand, Jerry's hand stirred slightly, and he was looking at the decking, avoiding her eye. Then, as if apologetically, he eased his hand out of hers. It went to a bulge in the leg pocket on his flying overall. He gave a furtive glance forward, but Mario was asleep. He slid the whiskey out of the pocket and took the cap off quickly.

Nervously, he held out the bottle to Tamasin. Wide-eyed, Tamasin shook her head. It was the first she'd known about that whiskey. It broke every rule they'd agreed on for this flight, and there were good reasons for those rules.

Jerry swallowed quickly, capped the bottle, and thrust it back in his pocket. 'Yeah . . . OK . . . see . . . I guess it just doesn't *matter* if I die. I mean, really. I don't have any importance to anyone.' He was talking quickly now, almost gabbling through the jet noise. 'I don't care that it's that way, it just doesn't matter.' He grabbed the bottle out of his leg pocket again, he gulped another swallow and shoved the bottle back. 'I mean . . . right now I do have an importance, and it's what I can do in getting this bomb load on to target. Other than that, I mean . . . who cares?' He shrugged, genuinely indifferent. 'Listen, we *stole* a B52. After this, even if we survive the mission, we will never have an independent life, any of us – we'll be in jail. Who wants that?'

'You *will* insist on missing the point,' Tamasin said through her teeth.

What she hadn't expected was to realize, startlingly, that Jerry *had* become important. To her. Yet she couldn't tell him. And it wouldn't have done any good if she could have done. He should never have been on this doomed flight in the first place, he should have had a therapist to help him and someone in his life to love him. But it was too late for that now.

Abruptly she stood up. 'Got to look at that nav.'

'Tamasin . . .'

He didn't understand, she knew that and it was pointless trying to explain. ·

* * *

193

She turned her back on Jerry and hurried to the hatch, and now tears ran down her cheeks as she climbed down the ladder. On the walkway with the B52 wallowing under her she gripped the ladder rail in her left hand and mopped her face with her right. The last thing she needed was Chuck trying to comfort her. Anger burned her up, anger at her weakness, anger at the sacrifices people were called upon to make in order to accomplish a task that elected governments hadn't the will or the courage to do for the people who'd elected them.

As she strapped herself back into her ejector seat, Chuck spilt cigarette ash on Buster, and Tamasin flew at him. Typically, Chuck tried to make a joke out of it; but he had the wit to see quickly that Tamasin was genuinely angry.

She counted them down to the next waypoint.

CHAPTER 23

Wet runway stretched away, a black scar on an uncharacteristically green Sicilian landscape, and Colan Penhale
brought the Tornado over the threshold bars at Sigonella
with the RB199s idling and Andrew McNair four feet
off his fully forward wingtip, barely astern. The four
mainwheel legs touched almost as one. Give 'em a nice
formation job, the squadron commander had told them
as they left Coningsby. Italians love a bit of show.

It was 1631 Italian time, 1531 in England. Turning on
to the taxiway, McNair brought his Tornado directly
behind Colan's. The Follow-Me van led them to a
dispersal, pools of wet on the tarmac, just like Coningsby
only a bit warmer and without that permanent gale
blowing. As he taxied Colan could see ranks of parked
US Navy F18 and F14 fighters, both twin-tailed types;
a couple of KC10s, the tanker derivative of the civilian
DC10, again in US markings; and half a dozen Tornados,
the short-nosed interdictor-strike variant, wearing Italian
air-force colours.

Drizzle fell feebly from the thin overcast 3,000 feet
above as Colan opened the cockpit canopy and shut down
the aircraft. McNair's canopy came up. Colan twisted off
his harness, unplugged his leads and glanced at Salim
Arshad in the back. Salim delivered his slow, dark-eyed
smile. The route had been a doddle and the French hadn't
suspected a thing.

'OK?' Colan called.

'Sure!'

Hoses and leads swung from Salim's flying suit as he

climbed out of the cockpit with its small, neat radar displays, on to the top of the port engine intake. It was a solid piece of engineering that would easily take two men's weight. The Tornado had no integral ladder. That made getting out of it a bit acrobatic when you landed away from home base. Colan climbed after Salim, on to the flat top of the intake. This aircraft wasn't built like a tank, he reflected, not for the first time – it was built like a ship. From the tip of the massive fin-and-rudder, the size of both one of those F18s' twin tails put together, Salim walked out on the horizontal stabilizer, stooped, grasped the leading edge and swung down. At full arm's stretch there was still a few inches' drop.

Colan followed Salim.

Vans and trucks and anti-aircraft guns under netting, even a motorbike, stood round the dispersal, all surrounded by Italians in overalls or the occasional air-force uniform. Andrew McNair and Jeremy Sewell-Baillie walked across from the other Tornado, bone domes under their arms, in that rolling, almost swaggering gait that betrays the restriction of a *g*-suit. Around the two Tornados' jet exhausts, the faint drizzle was turning to a faint fuzz of steam.

'Good afternoon, gentlemen,' a tall man in an officer's cap said. 'Di Carolis.' He offered Colan his hand. 'Excellent formation landing, if I may say so.'

The rank badge was full colonel and the blue tab over the pilot's wings confirmed the name. Salvatore di Carolis was tall, hollow-cheeked and aquiline and reminded Colan immediately of the Asterix comic strip's idea of a Roman senator. His English was perfect, spoken as if he'd learnt most of it from reading Jeeves books. Di Carolis had the air of an academic, of a northern Italian who wasn't at all at home in Sicily.

He ushered them into the back of a Fiat personnel bus and the driver set course for the operations block.

'Have you heard from the rest of our lot?' Colan asked. They were plainly the first RAF arrivals.

'We're expecting the Hawks in about three quarters of an hour,' Di Carolis told him. 'The C130s in maybe an hour and a half.'

The Coningsby C130 carried all the gear and spare clothes for the four of them. There is no stowage on a Tornado. All that the four aircrew had brought with them was a toothbrush each, in a pocket, in case the C130 was diverted.

The big armchairs in the ops block were a relief compared with the confines of the Tornado cockpit. A lumbering Neapolitan in an airman's uniform brought espresso.

'Have you heard about the *Kiev*?' Di Carolis asked.

Colan raised his eyebrows. 'No.'

The Soviet carrier had dropped anchor north of Benghazi in eastern Libya, between the coasts of Libya and Crete, and was now flying helicopters and a combat air patrol using the new, navalized model of the MiG 29 Fulcrum fighter. NATO reconnaissance aircraft out of Chania, Crete, were keeping an eye on the situation and the Sixth Fleet had a couple of frigates shadowing the battle group, but no-one could do better than guess what the Red Navy thought it was up to. On top of that, Long-Range Aviation was sending up Mainstay AWACS aircraft with MiG 31 escort out of the Ukrainian bases, on a pattern running south over Romania, Bulgaria and Greece to fly racetracks over the area bounded by Sicily and the Gulf of Sirte.

'What about the *Kennedy*?' Colan asked.

'She's under way,' Di Carolis said. 'She has not quite reached her station.'

All this Russian stuff bothered Colan somewhat. He started worrying what Tamasin had got herself into. If this was going to end up as a massive east-west stand-off, it was going to undo an awful lot of the good that had been done lately to foster world peace, not least by the Soviet leadership.

Light was fading as the Hawks arrived. Colan watched the formation landing. Rain was falling now as Di Carolis went out to collect the crews. He was back forty minutes later with Jack Baslow, Pete Pretorius and their navigators. Baslow was a weathered five nine, balding on top, with a wiry build and an aggressive, confident air; at thirty-one, he was the oldest of them. What Colan knew of Baslow he admired: a man who could more than hold his own in air combat but who had the humility to put his family before his career. Pretorius was different: twenty-seven years old, six four, and so big he could hardly fit into a Hawk's cockpit. He had a clipped, Afrikaner accent, a languid quiff of gold-blond hair, and a voracious appetite for girls.

It was six. Di Carolis took the RAF crews into the canteen. Service catering had improved over the years, Colan reflected, but this was impressive. He ate spaghetti and locally caught swordfish, thoroughly enjoying himself.

He didn't drink. None of them drank, they didn't know whether they might be flying tonight. The RAF's rule of thumb was to allow twelve hours between 'bottle and throttle', and it was a rule they took seriously.

Coningsby's C130 landed. Shortly afterwards so did Chivenor's. Then at twenty past seven a corporal called Colan to the phone.

'Captain Laird is calling from Davis-Monthan, Arizona.'

CHAPTER 24

At 2310 zulu time the airconditioning aboard the B52 quit and nothing Jerry Yeaver was able to do made any improvement, so they sat at their stations and slowly started shivering as the cold of the desert night percolated into the cabin of the bomber. Waypoint Twelve had been at 2215 zulu, over Mali, a spot on the desert some miles north of Timbuktu. Now Tamasin counted them down to Waypoint Thirteen, a point in the southern tip of the Tassili, the rocky table land in the remote south of Algeria.

Still they flew east. In her sweaters, Tamasin hugged herself.

'We have roughly three hours to the next waypoint,' Bat Masterson said, in his deep lazy voice. 'This leg is the last any of us can expect any sleep.'

It was 2350 zulu, 1650 in Arizona. The night beyond the bomber's windows was a wasteland. Night in the Valley of the Shadow of Death.

Chuck was awake for the waypoint. He insisted that Bat and Tamasin had their sleep. Jerry and Russell said the same; even Mario agreed. Bat nodded off reluctantly at his station. Russell dozed. Jerry watched the radars. Tamasin swapped places with Chuck and huddled up in the impossibly uncomfortable seat to try and sleep. She gazed at Buster, but Buster wasn't a substitute for human contact, and now Tamasin had a terrible need for human warmth, physical comfort. When you were this tired, your spirits hit rock bottom. Tears prickled at Tamasin's eyes in her eternal loneliness, and she realized she was afraid of the coming battle; afraid, too, of her own death in a way she hadn't experienced when she'd been ready to die as a way of rejoining Edward.

Aloof now, Chuck didn't even seem to want to paw her.

*   *   *

Movement caught Jerry Yeaver's eye, on his right, and he turned to see that Russell had woken up. In the orange glow from the console lighting Russell's face was strained. The two men's eyes met.

'You OK?' Jerry said. 'You want anything?'

'Drop of water.' Russell's husky voice was a whisper.

Jerry fetched it. Shakily Russell uncapped his pain-killers. He swallowed. Still Jerry was watching him, concern in his eyes behind the glasses, and Russell grinned wryly as he set the water beaker back in its holder.

'What's on your mind, Jerry?'

'Your kids.'

Russell shook his head. They'd been over this. 'Sooner or later you got to leave it *all* behind. Anyway, they wouldn't want to put me through this . . .' he had that old rueful, twisted grin . . . 'pain, humiliation. But as for *you* being on this flight . . .'

This was something else they'd been over.

Bitter, Jerry slipped his whiskey out from his leg pocket. 'You have to contribute.' He avoided Russell's eye. 'You have to be productive. I don't have anything to offer any more.' Quickly he took a gulp from the bottle, its level no more than a quarter down, and quickly he capped it again.

Then Mario was bending over him, shoulders squared.

'You goddam snivelling drunk, I'll throw you right the hell off this plane!' He grabbed for the whiskey. He missed, Jerry was shoving it in his pocket already.

Mario slammed the back of his hand across Jerry's face. 'I'll tie you in the goddam bomb bay and drop *you* on the Ay-rabs, and I hope you're alive when they get you!' Jerry was cowering, Russell leaning forward suddenly, and Mario flung his left fist across and punched Jerry in the face. 'No wonder they threw you out the air force, we don't have room for spineless jerks!' Jerry's bone dome cracked into the metal of the ejector seat, his glasses fell on the console and slid to the decking. 'I'll kill you right now and . . .'

'I'll kill you sooner, co-pilot.' Russell's voice cut through the jet noise like steel. 'We need Jerry's skills more than we need yours. What are you doing off station?'

Mario's fist was drawn back for another punch but he paused and stared hard-eyed at Russell, surprised at the strength in the old colonel's voice. 'She's on autopilot, for God's sake.' He'd been going to the relief station. He curled his lip at Jerry, slumped with one arm raised in defence, blood pouring from his nose, his eyes streaming. 'As for this asshole . . .'

'You get about your job, co-pilot,' Russell said harshly, 'we'll get about ours. Just learn to work in a team like the rest of us. Prima ballerinas like you are what we don't have room for!'

'Huh!' Mario said, and stared angrily. 'Well, I guess we're stuck with each other.' He pointed at Russell, his hand turned palm up. 'But you better not screw up over target – either of you!' He vanished down the ladder.

Russell reached over to give Jerry a wad of tissues. As Mario clambered back up, Jerry was still trying to stem the blood from his nose. Suspicious, Mario strode back to his fuel transfers.

Russell reached down and picked up Jerry's glasses. He put them on the console. He put a hand on Jerry's shoulder. 'Easy, buddy. Mario's all on edge.'

The other element remained tacitly understood. Unlike Jerry or Russell, Mario wanted to survive this mission. He was scared now that he might not and that made him, unlike Jerry or Russell, afraid of dying.

Slowly Jerry turned his head, holding the blood-soaked tissues to his nose. Then he saw the deep lines on Russell's face, the twist of the jaw.

'Russell, get a painkiller.'

Russell smiled grimly. 'Later.' He squeezed Jerry's shoulder. 'Listen, buddy, make me a promise. No more till after target, OK?'

'OK,' Jerry whispered.

Russell stuck out a hand. They shook. Pain came into Jerry's eyes again.

'It's all . . . no damn good, anyway . . .'

Russell picked out Jerry's words from the ceaseless sounds of flight. Russell knew that the feeling of intense depression is a mixture of fear, despair, hopelessness and rage, turning to frustration because you feel yourself powerless to act; and all that is combined with implacable self-loathing. Yet still you can forget it, for a while, if you think there's something you're called upon to do, that no-one else can do. If you can seize the feeling that, even just for a few moments, someone else needs you, then you can put it aside.

Again Russell put his hand on Jerry's shoulder. 'Ease up on yourself, buddy. It's true what I said. We could make it with one pilot if we had to, we couldn't without the EWO.'

For a moment Jerry didn't respond. Then, almost reluctantly, he nodded.

At 1940 Arizona time, 0240 zulu, they were on schedule. Waypoint Fourteen was in Chad, south of the mountain range of the Tibesti. Bat had the bomber up to 5,000 feet because of terrain and it didn't make it any warmer.

On the intercom he said: 'Synchronize watches, crew, let's set Libyan time right now. We have, ah . . . zero four, four zero.'

Mario climbed out of his seat and went down the hatch. At the relief station he shaved and spruced up and put on lashings of deodorant. On the way back up he tried to get Tamasin into an argument about the navigation. She didn't quite succeed in ignoring him.

Bat was the next one down for a shave. Then Tamasin let Chuck out. The amphetamine seemed to have brightened Chuck's mood. Whether that was a good thing Tamasin wasn't sure. He grinned at her as he passed back into his seat, and fondled her thigh. Then, as he sat at his console, he switched on the intercom.

'OK, fellas, there's this guy goes into a bar with a dog, and he says . . .'

Russell clambered stiffly down the ladder. Tamasin caught his eye and gave him a sympathetic smile. Maybe as much as anything Russell was seeking refuge from awful jokes.

Jerry didn't come down – much as he needed a shave. He hadn't much energy left for things he wasn't forced to do.

'Ten minutes to Waypoint One Four,' Tamasin announced. This one was southeast of the Tibesti. 'Stand by to turn left to the north.'

She ducked aft, briefly, while Chuck monitored the countdown. She hardly needed to renew her perfume but she was trembling now and she needed things to do. She brushed her short hair in the tiny mirror, she fiddled with her earrings. When she strapped back in they still had six minutes to run.

*   *   *

'Pilot, stand by for left turn. Your new heading will be three five six.'

Bat grunted: 'Confirm three five six.'

Tamasin settled her bone dome on her head, its weight oppressive in the metallic grinding of the jet noise. In the cold her fingertips were going numb and the orange displays in front of her danced in the blackness. Stale cigarette smell irritated her nose and stale coffee lingered in her throat. The B52 wallowed gently under her like a great ship on an ocean swell.

'Two . . . one . . . zero. Turn now.'

The harness held Tamasin tightly as the big jet rolled. She was looking down at Chuck. A faint shudder passed through the aircraft and then Bat was rolling level on the new heading.

'Pilot, start letdown,' Tamasin said. 'New height five hundred AGL.' Above ground level.

Chuck straightened to his task, the attack radar probing ahead. Weightlessness lifted Tamasin against her harness as the B52 started to sink. Chuck said: 'Terrain ten o'clock in three zero miles. You are clear on the nose.'

Tamasin frowned over her charts. She checked the GPS plot. She checked INS. Apart from that birdstrike on Number Eight, not a thing had gone unserviceable on them. Only airconditioning, and that hardly mattered at this stage of the flight. She checked her watch, checked the console clocks: 2025 Arizona time, 0525 local.

On the intercom she said: 'OK, we're over Libya.'

CHAPTER 25

Libya, November, before the flight.
Until the rain started falling in earnest, Adem Elhaggi
had been convinced that the safest way to drive a car in
the Libyan capital of Tripoli was to get on the road going
out. Now the rain was splashing all over the windscreen
and the spray made the highway hard to see.

Adem wasn't too familiar with driving a car, particularly in cities. That was why Ali Ben Mokhtar, beside
him now as they drove south, had insisted on Adem
doing all the driving. Adem was tired and it was a good
150 kilometres from Tripoli to Tariq Talal's camp but at
least his shoulder had pretty much healed up now – he'd
had hardly a twinge from it all day.

Zoheir lay curled up on the back seat, dozing. It had
been a tiring day.

They'd been in and out of odd little offices all day,
in back alleys that only Ben Mokhtar knew. It seemed
to Adem that these offices must have some sort of
connections with the Libyan government, because in all
of them they'd deposited passport-style pictures, mostly
of Zoheir but some of Adem; and later they'd collected
bundles of official-looking documents.

What Adem had ended up with was Libyan and
international driving licences. They looked impressive.
They belied his inexperience with a car. He hadn't seen
Zoheir's papers but he knew they must be connected with
her intended role as international courier.

The headlights of the oncoming traffic dazzled Adem.
It was the first time he'd driven by night and, with the rain

teeming down, visibility was frighteningly bad. But the car was one he felt comfortable with, an old Peugeot 305, tough and well suited to North African roads.

Ben Mokhtar sat slumped on his right, watchful, wordless. Zoheir might almost not have been there.

Dimly ahead through the spray were the tail lights of a big truck. Adem discovered that he was hesitating.

The road was a twin-lane expressway, in Libyan terms one of the best in the country. Trailing just clear of the huge wake of spray from the lorry Adem was driving at around 75 km/h and for this road it wasn't fast, even in rain like this.

'Get past him,' Ben Mokhtar muttered.

Adem nervously checked his mirror. He pulled the Peugeot into the lefthand lane. The view wasn't much better. Adem accelerated, conscious beside him of Ben Mokhtar's weary impatience, his tired scorn.

Spray blinded him and fear jumped in his throat. Then he was past, and he relaxed and put his headlights on to main beam. He glimpsed the speed, 100 km/h.

Under the sheet of rain plastering the road surface, one front wheel caught a pothole.

In his hands Adem felt the steering wrench, and he corrected instinctively before he could wonder what had happened and then the rear wheels swung and they were sliding on the rain-washed surface, sliding diagonally. Terror rose inside Adem as he realized he wasn't controlling the car any more. He needed help, he needed Ben Mokhtar, yet Ben Mokhtar didn't seem to react. Light blazed through the whole inside of the Peugeot as the truck's headlamps loomed up to them and Adem found that he'd taken his foot right off the accelerator and now the truck's two-tone horn blared, scaring him again, and *still* Ben Mokhtar hadn't reacted.

But Adem had, and the Peugeot was running straight again, only an awful lot more slowly.

'*Allah Allah*,' Adem muttered.

The truck blared its horn again and the spray poured over the Peugeot as it swept past. Adem changed down a gear and then cautiously accelerated. A couple of cars overtook him. Adem didn't know what he'd done now to get out of that. A four-wheel skid, he realized, that was what it had been.

'Good,' Ben Mokhtar muttered, still evidently unruffled. 'You turned with the skid. That's the right thing to do. Now let's keep moving.'

Adem found he was breathing in big lungfuls, his palms trembling on the steering wheel. Yet this had to be done. In the mirror he glimpsed Zoheir, sitting up, gazing forward, eyes wide and lips parted. It wasn't going to impress her if he lost his courage just because he'd once lost control of the car. He'd got it back, after all.

The cars that had passed him were long gone. Gritting his teeth, Adem accelerated after the truck. This time he overtook it without incident.

Ben Mokhtar grunted approval. In the back, Zoheir settled down again.

The road narrowed. The traffic had thinned. Even the rain was easing up a bit but the landscape lay dark and damp as Adem drove south, on into the desert. It dawned on Adem that he'd got the hang of driving at night in the rain. He sensed in the same way that Ben Mokhtar had confidence in him.

The realization made him bold enough to ask: 'Ali, what *is* this operation that we're being prepared for?'

Ali Ben Mokhtar grunted and wouldn't say. The next question came similarly unbidden; a reflex impelled perhaps by months of pondering and fretting and worrying.

'Ali, what was it that went wrong with the Frankfurt operation – when Mustafa died?'

Ben Mokhtar grunted again. After a moment he lit a cigarette without offering one to Adem. Adem only smoked when he could get a cigarette, which wasn't often. Ben Mokhtar blew smoke through his bony nose and then, out of the corner of his eye, Adem saw him glance into the back of the car. In the driver's mirror, Adem could see Zoheir curled up asleep.

Glancing right, Adem caught Ben Mokhtar's eye.

'There were four of us,' Ben Mokhtar muttered, and Adem could tell the reluctance in his tone. 'Mustafa was the best marksman among us – not that this called for any marksmanship, we were just supposed to scatter the shots at any target that crossed our paths.'

For *target*, Adem understood *air traveller*.

'Mustafa was supposed to signal the attack by being the first one to shoot. We were spread out in several places in the terminal area but we could all hear it as soon as any one of us opened fire. The reason Mustafa was supposed to shoot first was that he'd been given the most exposed and dangerous sector of any of us.' Ben Mokhtar dragged on the cigarette and its tip glowed. 'In the event, someone else fired first.' Adem could just about hear the words through all the noise from the engine and the wet road. 'Mustafa was at once exposed to the danger – the Frankfurt police had a machinegun in an overhead gallery and they shot him with it. Even so' – a sardonic edge grated in Ben Mokhtar's voice – 'even that action was successful, for us. The police machinegun crew killed three travellers as well as Mustafa.' He part-opened the window to flick ash but the wind scattered it all over the inside of the car.

Zoheir hadn't stirred.

'Who was it, then, who fired first?' Adem said.

Ben Mokhtar didn't reply. Adem glanced over. The road ran straight in the rain and dark. Ben Mokhtar with his world-weary expression was looking straight ahead but, as he sensed Adem's eyes on him, he returned the young man's gaze.

Adem gasped. 'You don't mean . . . you mean it was Tariq Talal who fired first?'

Sighing faintly, Ben Mokhtar dragged a moment on his cigarette. 'There's enough people know it, I suppose,' he said cynically. 'Just don't go spreading it all over the camp.'

Thoughts tumbled through Adem's mind. Maybe the plan had been meant to function that way, after all. Maybe Mustafa had volunteered for the danger. He'd always been brave. That was why he'd been so popular with the young guerrillas in the camp.

Then as Adem remembered how popular Mustafa had been, suspicion crept into his mind. Had Mustafa *really* known what Tariq Talal planned to do? Had that *really* been just an accident?

*   *   *

The rain had stopped by the time Adem parked in the camp, but all the sandy surfaces had turned to mud.

'Well done,' Ben Mokhtar said as they got out stiffly into the chilly damp of the winter evening. 'You drove well.'

Zoheir gave Adem a quick, shy smile and vanished into the darkness. Ben Mokhtar took back the car keys. Shivering in the cold, Adem made his way across to the quarters block for some supper. He was late. There wasn't much supper left.

He'd hardly swallowed a couple of mouthfuls when they summoned him to Tariq Talal's Command Council HQ.

Two of the bodyguards escorted him. Adem felt excited. He'd never been into the Command Council HQ before. This was a rare privilege; maybe he was going to get a pat on the back for something he'd done on the errand into Tripoli.

209

A different bodyguard opened the door for them, cradling a Kalashnikov, his face dour. The rooms were brightly lit by the camp generators that could always be heard in the background. Brightly woven, traditional Arab rugs covered the floor; there were sofas and chairs, a polished table, a TV, a stereo player, a big fridge-freezer. Convector heaters made the rooms pleasantly warm, and it struck Adem that it was only right and proper that the leaders should enjoy more comfort than the led; the leaders had suffered hardships enough in the past.

Adem's escort opened a door and Adem followed him down a flight of narrow, concrete stairs. Suddenly it was chilly again. Adem had heard about this system of cellars under the Command Council HQ. These were what they called the 'operations rooms'.

Tariq Talal was waiting. He didn't look friendly. He wasn't wearing the silk shirt and Western designer jeans today, he was dressed in sandy-browny desert camouflage fatigues, and the heels of his jump boots echoed off the concrete as he paced. He had three guerrillas with him, similarly dressed; hard-eyed Arabs in their twenties whom Adem didn't know.

Talal dismissed Adem's escort with a jerk of his head. There was a wooden table and wooden chairs, and a map on the wall showing Europe and the Middle East. Talal didn't invite Adem to sit. None of them was sitting.

Suddenly Adem was scared, but he still didn't know what this was about.

Talal turned sharply, scraping a heel. 'Let's hear it, then, Adem Elhaggi!'

'Hear what?'

'What you got up to in Tripoli with Zoheir.'

*   *   *

Blood pounded in Adem's temples. He fought for something to say, anything. He could almost have wished for some transgression to admit, yet there was nothing.

Two of the Arabs moved in on him. All three of them were bigger than Adem, and Tariq Talal with his bearded head brushing the ceiling was the biggest of them all. The one closer to Adem had beard stubble. The other was a stringy man with a cruel mouth and a squint. They both smelt of sweat.

Beard Stubble grabbed Adem by one shoulder and shoved him into the wall.

Adem cried out. 'I don't understand! I don't know what you mean!'

Squint grabbed Adem's other shoulder, the bad one. He kicked Adem's shins.

'You know perfectly well what I mean,' Talal said. He hadn't moved.

'Insolent dog!' Beard Stubble muttered, and shoved Adem again.

They were in front of him and to his left. Gasping, bewildered, terrified, Adem started backing away to his right. They moved with him, shoving his shoulders.

He protested: 'But I . . .'

'I saw it!' Talal's voice boomed, echoing. 'I could see the way she was looking at you when you got out of the car. What were you two up to behind my back in Tripoli?'

This was madness. The thought flashed through Adem's mind that this must be what they called paranoia. Talal was imagining things.

Beard Stubble shoved Adem again. '*Answer!*'

'There was nothing!' Adem cried out. 'Nothing happened in Tripoli!'

The third Arab, the one who hadn't moved yet, levered himself off the wall and sauntered over to Adem. He was taller than the first two and he had hollow cheeks with a hint of meanness. He shouldered Beard Stubble aside and gave Adem a shove that sent him sprawling further through the echoing concrete chamber.

'Nothing you've forgotten?' His voice was a mutter, throaty, threatening, low.

'Nothing! Nothing!' Fear rang in Adem's voice.

The tall Arab shoved him again. This time his shoulders hit the end wall. He was feeling sick, even though he'd eaten hardly anything.

'Relationships between guerrillas' – the same chilling undertone – 'are expressly forbidden.'

'There wasn't a relationship! There was nothing!' Adem was terrified.

'Insolent dog,' the tall Arab muttered, and kicked Adem's ankles out from under him.

Concrete slammed into him. A boot hit him and blasted all the air from his body. Adem was sobbing aloud, arms hunched, protecting his head. More boots hit him.

'There wasn't a relationship!' he cried out in panic. 'Ask Zoheir if you don't believe me!'

*   *   *

For some moments after they stopped kicking him Adem lay there, huddled, still protecting his head. A boot scraped. A match ripped in the echoing silence, and the soft exhalation followed it as somebody lit a cigarette. Slowly Adem let his aching arms fall. Tears stood in his eyes as he lifted his head.

Tariq Talal took the cigarette out of his mouth and gazed contemptuously at Adem. The way he stood over the young man exaggerated his height. His voice was smooth but more menacing than the tall Arab's.

'Is that what you want – you want us to call Zoheir here for questioning?'

In shock, Adem realized what he'd done. He'd just invited a beating-up for Zoheir. Suddenly in his mind

212

he could see Dr Jabran, the last time he'd seen her. That bruised face, the blackened fingernails.

'No! No, don't call her!'

'So there *was* a relationship?' Talal towered over Adem, determined to have a confession out of him.

Adem froze up. He didn't know what he should do.

The tall Arab caught him by his collar scruff and hauled him upright with one hand so that his sheer physical strength terrified Adem. Then they were all beating him again.

'All right! Stop!' He didn't know what to do any more. 'I'll tell you, I'll confess!'

Tariq Talal murmured: 'Stop the beating.'

* * *

But for the tall Arab, pinning Adem one-handed to the wall, Adem would have fallen again. His ripped clothes had vomit on them. His eyes met Tariq Talal's; the guerrilla leader's were merciless. Desperately Adem fought through the panic in his mind for something to say, anything. Anything that wouldn't make trouble for Zoheir.

'All right . . . it's true . . . I'm evil and I'm a bad Muslim and unworthy to be trusted as a guerrilla.' He'd got it now. 'I . . . it's true . . . I had . . .' For a moment he thought he was going to cry again but then suddenly he was dry-eyed. Dry-mouthed, too.

Talal took the cigarette from his lips. 'You had what?'

Adem forced the words out. 'I had lascivious thoughts of her when we were in Tripoli.' He moistened his lips. His cheekbones were aching and his teeth felt loose. 'But then when I tried to touch her hand she withdrew it, and she repelled all my advances.' He waited for retribution.

Silence vibrated in the concrete chamber. The tall Arab's breath smelled.

213

'You say you had lascivious thoughts,' Talal said studiously. 'What were your lascivious thoughts?'

Adem squirmed. Two thoughts were immediately clear. For one thing, Talal plainly regarded Zoheir as somehow his personal property. For another, he enjoyed hearing sexual language employed by others.

And this was too embarrassing for Adem now; he couldn't take his false confession any further.

'I'll give you three to start talking,' Talal said, and drew on his cigarette again. 'One. Two. Three.'

But Adem had dried up, helpless.

'Beat him,' Talal said.

*   *   *

The beating probably didn't last as long as Adem thought it had. He didn't know why they'd stopped, he just lay there, battered on the concrete floor. Talal spoke, a brief, surly interrogative.

The voice that answered was Ali Ben Mokhtar's, sour, bored. 'What purpose is all this serving?'

Adem didn't look. He wanted to close his eyes but he was too scared. Harshly Talal shouted: 'This young scoundrel needs to be taught a lesson!' It echoed off the chilly walls.

It surprised Adem when Ben Mokhtar snarled back, just as ferociously. Of the brief, blazing row that followed Adem took in little; he just lay there and shivered. 'What's the *point*?' he heard Ben Mokhtar say. 'What's the *point* of treating a gifted young fighter this way?'

A moment's pause. Adem's eyes drifted shut.

'What do you want, then?' Talal said, voice sullen.

'Let's get him to the medical office and see what these heroes of yours have done to him.'

Somewhere Adem's nightmare had turned to a dream. He didn't believe what he was hearing.

214

Talal said something indistinct. For a moment, nothing. Then a strong, stringy arm wrapped itself round Adem's shoulders and Ben Mokhtar lifted him to his feet.

They made for the door. Ben Mokhtar was doing most of the work. Then Talal signalled with his hand and the tall Arab blocked their way. They turned, facing Talal. Adem dropped his gaze, terrified of his leader's anger.

Talal commanded: 'Look at me, Adem Elhaggi.'

Lips parted, forcing himself, Adem lifted his chin. All down his throat he could taste vomit, and his legs were caving under him.

'Lasciviousness is an abomination to Allah,' Talal said sonorously. 'It will not be tolerated in this camp. If you offend again you'll find out what *real* punishment you deserve.' He paused. 'You will be responsible for morning lavatory duty until further notice. All right, my brother.' He gave Ben Mokhtar a nod, dismissing them.

Adem wasn't conscious of the walk through the cold. The next thing he knew he was in the medical office.

*   *   *

Ben Mokhtar left Adem with the nurses. The two men took Adem's shirt and jeans off and began treating the cuts with antiseptic; the women were busy elsewhere. The brawny male nurse with the tattoo began swabbing something on the bruises. It stung.

That atmosphere was there again, Adem realized. The tension, the resentment. The tattooed nurse was hardly speaking to Adem and the dark one not at all. Adem felt uncomfortable. At least, though, that was an improvement on feeling he was about to be beaten half to death.

Dr Jabran hadn't appeared. Normally she'd have turned up by now.

Adem was worried and he blurted out suddenly: 'When is Dr Jabran coming?'

The tattooed nurse picked up another swab and dipped it in clear spirit. He said nothing. From across the surgery the dark nurse said bluntly: 'She's dead.'

Shock took the breath from his throat. In disbelief, Adem simply gaped.

The tattooed nurse turned to Adem and swabbed another bruise. Adem gasped and bit his lip in the sharp pain. He waited. But these surly men weren't going to volunteer anything, and he asked: 'What happened?'

'She was executed at dawn today,' the tattooed nurse muttered. 'She was a filthy spy.'

New shock pounded in Adem's mind. He'd have expected an accident, maybe even sudden illness. 'A *spy*? You mean for Israel?' He gasped. 'For America?' Either possibility baffled Adem. Dr Jabran had been Palestinian, same as him; she'd shared the same loyalties. Or so he'd thought.

'Neither,' the dark nurse said from across the room. 'For the Libyan government.'

It didn't make sense. Adem's mind reeled.

*   *   *

Back in the canteen Adem found his supper, hardly touched. Someone had thoughtfully put a pan lid over it. Adem looked at the food a moment, then pushed it away and walked stiffly into the shadowy dormitory with its hissing paraffin lanterns. When he'd undressed and got on to the hard, narrow bed, he had to pull the blanket over his head. He was starting to feel tearful, starting to realize that he actually missed Dr Jabran.

Spying for the Libyan government made no sense.

Libya was their host, Libya gave them support and encouragement in their mission to train here and study to be guerrilla fighters against the Great Satan. Libya

216

even supplied the bulk of their arms and explosives and equipment. Tariq Talal and his lieutenants were supposed to be co-operating with Libya. It made no sense for Libya to be sending spies into Talal's camp. Even if they were keeping a quiet eye on the camp – even in the unlikely person of Dr Jabran – it made no sense for Talal to be worried about it.

Unless Libya was planning something sinister, something Adem hadn't even suspected. Or unless Talal in turn was planning something . . .

It was too difficult. Adem began worrying how the camp was going to manage now, without a doctor.

CHAPTER 26

Sigonella's switchboard had put the call through to a cubbyhole of an office in the block that housed the officers' mess. As he picked it up, Colan Penhale reflected that if it was just gone twenty past seven in the evening here in Sicily, in Tucson it must be twenty past eleven in the morning.

'Hi. Becks?'

'Hi, Colan, good to hear you. What's new?'

Colan thought for a moment. He ran it through: arrivals – the Tornados, the Hawks, the C130s.

Becks said: 'Heard any word about fleet activity?'

Colan told her about the *Kiev*. 'Are they supposed to be any sort of threat?'

'We don't know yet,' Becks answered. 'I guess it would be unusual if they were anything else.' She gave him her own news: the FBI's reports on the crew members; the NSA on the mysterious Mainstay cipher signal. She summed up. 'For starters, we strongly suspect the Mainstay signal *was* about Dark Angel, as we strongly suspect Dark Angel *is* headed for Tariq Talal. OK, this crew. The Mastersons want revenge for Edward and it looks like they don't care if they live or die. Feehan has cancer, Yeaver is a depression case – they don't want to go on living. Peroni is in it for money, he's an adventurer and gambler who's prepared to seize his chances as they come. Brantley's motivation isn't so clear, but we suspect it's a bit similar to Peroni's. Colan, how does that square with what you yourself know of Tamasin and Bat Masterson?'

Colan thrust out his lower lip, thinking.

'I think you're right about Tamasin. She's never been the type to . . . to self-destruct, but she's quite capable of charging recklessly into a thing and being, really, indifferent to what might happen to her. I mean, I can't see them, say, doing a kamikaze and diving Dark Angel on to Talal's camp. On the other hand, I *can* see them taking every risk short of suicide to make sure of the target.' He thought for a moment. Wind threw rain against the darkened window but still this wasn't cold like Coningsby. Fleetingly he wondered what the weather was like in Arizona. 'Listen, Becks – Tamasin and Bat are both pretty experienced aviators. You build up a certain set of instincts, flying for any length of time and, I'd bet, when the shooting starts, they'll find instinct taking over. They'll just naturally find themselves *impelled* to get away. Anyway, they've got better sense than to want to leave any actual evidence of that B52 anywhere the Libyan government can find it and exhibit it.'

'It still sounds like a suicide mission to me,' Becks objected.

'You can never be quite sure how people will react when they're faced with imminently being killed, until it actually happens. Bat's experienced that, Tamasin hasn't, but Bat will be flying the aircraft, not Tamasin. Tamasin is very determined, very courageous and very skilled, but Bat's in charge and he's a combat veteran whose instincts have kept him alive *this* far.'

'OK,' Becks said. She sounded dubious. She said: 'How d'you figure Bat will go in for his attack?'

In the corridor, two Italian orderlies were disputing a point. It sounded as if they were about to get their knives out.

'We can't do more than guess that one,' Colan replied. 'We don't even know which direction he's coming in from. We can't be sure that Mainstay signal related to him –

for all we know, he could have gone straight west from LA, via India and Saudi Arabia. Anyway, I'm no bomber pilot.'

'Eastwards is more logical,' Becks argued. 'The Caribbean, the Atlantic and the Sahara probably give the least risk of a radar intercept, and anyway we have these indications from Venezuela and the Mainstay.'

'It's certainly more logical,' Colan admitted. He thought a moment.

Becks went on: 'So we're assuming he'll come in over Algeria.'

'Why Algeria?'

'It's the most direct route. They want to minimize the distance flown so as not to be too light on fuel.'

Colan considered. 'Convince me,' he said.

'OK,' Becks said. 'Bat will attack at night. It's the way he's used to. I have had detailed info sent over from Barksdale on 60–086, this particular bird he's flying, and it has all the aids – infra-red, all the radars, low-light television, laser target designator. The sensible way is to take advantage of night, run in from the west, make the hit – with all those optical aids, he'll have close on daylight-quality vision – and then make his getaway over the Med. After that, well . . .'

'I'll buy southern North Atlantic and the Sahara,' Colan said. 'I'm not sure I'll buy a night attack. He'd have to hit Talal at, what . . .?'

'Around 0200 local,' Becks told him. She'd worked that out already. 'That's one tomorrow morning for you and five in the afternoon here.'

Four and a half hours away. Close, Colan thought.

'Night is the logical time for it,' he mused, 'but it's that bit *too* logical. Don't forget there are very strong personal feelings involved here. If I were Bat, I'd want to see the whites of the eyes of the guy I'm attacking.' He paused. 'I've got a hunch.'

220

'Go on.'

'There's a lot of radar and SAMs to the north of Tariq Talal's camp, there's not much south of it. He'd never overfly to the north, not till his exit run. What he *might* do is overshoot to the south, swing round to the east, and come in out of a dawn sun.'

'And *then* head out to the north? OK. Sounds good, Colan.'

But as they hung up Colan didn't think Becks was convinced.

*   *   *

In Sicily it was twenty to eight. In Arizona it was twenty to twelve, the day bright, the mountains blue and jagged against the empty horizon.

Becks frowned, wondering whether to report what they'd said to Andrew Maule. Or Hartmore. She hadn't heard a peep out of Hartmore since he'd come in here with his gun on his hip. Hartmore worried her a bit, if she were honest.

Hartmore's trouble was that he took his job and himself too seriously. Strutting around with a gun on his belt wasn't just a symptom of being a pain in the butt, it was a symptom of being a guy with one monstrous ego. True, he couldn't mess around when he'd got a billion-dollar air base to run. That ego, though, was a big worry.

What bothered Becks was the realization that Hartmore's self-importance made him vulnerable and that losing a B52 this way could put an end to his career, the only thing he cared about.

She tried Andrew Maule's number. She didn't get him, he was out at lunch. For the first time, Becks realized she was hungry. Alone in the office she stretched. She was tense, conscious of the harsh artificial lighting and the faint whiff of photocopier from next door. She adjusted the comb in her sandy blonde hair and set it a fraction higher. The enclosed room was unnaturally quiet, insulated. There were damp patches on her blouse, the taste of coffee in her mouth and her stomach was rumbling.

She loped to the door and blinked in the daylight. Julio half-concealed the action of setting down the phone. One of these days Becks was going to find out what the guy was really up to: drugs or illegal betting or smuggling Mexicans into the country.

'Julio, you wanna go get some lunch?'

'Sure, Captain Laird, ma'am.' But he shuffled a lot of papers around before he finally went.

Becks watched until Julio reversed his ten-month-old Jaguar away from her beloved, battered Beetle, then poked through his papers with interest. She didn't find anything. But then, if Julio was flogging off air-force property to some Mexican crook in Nogales, he wasn't the sort of guy to leave evidence around. Becks picked up Julio's phone and dialled the University of Arizona.

Van wasn't there. Becks cursed mentally, answered politely, and set down the phone. A shadow moved in the corridor – a man's bulky figure – and she jumped. Shoulders stooping, Van walked into the office with a big grin bristling his beard, and carrying flowers.

'*Van*! Hey, what bonehead let you in here?'

Actually, most of the guards on the main gate knew Van Burkart, and in any case Van knew enough other officers on the base to get one of them to let him in so as to surprise Becks.

'That's a fine welcome for your one and only true love,' he complained, and wrapped his arms round her. The hug was vigorous, vital. Human contact. It was what Becks needed.

Crushed against him, delighted and relieved, Becks dragged her lips away. Van was holding the flowers behind his back but Becks had a job to get away from even the single arm that held her.

'Hey, get off, man, anyone could come in here!'

Van laughed and let her go.

Half annoyed, she straightened her clothes. 'Listen, dodo, I *run* this office, I am supposed to maintain an officer's dignity.' She swirled away from him, hunting for a vase. She found one, put water in it, and arranged the flowers, crooning to them in an undertone. Over her shoulder she said: 'Whadda you want, anyway, goddam unauthorized civilian? I oughta have you thrown off base.'

'This is a stick-up. I'm here to kidnap you and force food down you.'

*   *   *

The Porsche was parked outside. They got into it. Van drove out past the Craycroft Road guardhouse. On the corner by the traffic light a hundred yards away there was a mini supermarket and a bar. Van parked on the unpaved verge and they went into the bar.

In the bar it was very dark, spacious, low-ceilinged. Becks had gone from artificial light to bright daylight and now into artificial shadow and her eyes couldn't take it any more, she was as good as blind. Van led her to a table.

They ordered club sandwiches; beer for Van, mineral water for Becks.

'What would you say,' Becks murmured slowly, 'if you knew someone who had a loved one murdered by a terrorist, who then appropriated an item of military equipment and went to whack the terrorist?'

'This item of military equipment...' Van tilted his head ... 'it would have its original owner's name on it?'

'Right.'

223

'So it would look like the original owner, not the aggrieved bereaved, was off to whack the terrorist?'

'Right.'

Thoughtfully Van bit a chunk of sandwich and chewed. 'Since we are of course talking pure hypothesis, let's say the item of military equipment is a missile submarine and the intention is to nuke the terrorist in bed. That's heavy, a thing like that gone autonomous. You could set off a war. Wouldn't want that. You just don't *do* that, run around stealing missile submarines.'

Becks twisted her glass round, making fingerprints in the condensation. Her lean back was arched forward but her long legs were stretched out under the table to play footsie with Van. 'But suppose they did it, suppose they took out the terrorist without much related grief?'

Van looked up. He grinned at her through the charcoal shadows of the low-ceilinged bar. 'I guess I'd say, right on, brothers and sisters . . .'

CHAPTER 27

Tension shivered in the metal of the B52 and the aircraft jolted in the light turbulence as it wallowed across the Libyan Desert at 500 feet.

'Let me out,' Chuck Brantley told Tamasin.

She was busy. 'Why?' she snapped.

'I have pills to hand around.'

'What sort of pills?'

'Amphetamine, honey,' Chuck said, unruffled, 'so we all stay alert when we need to be alert.' He paused, grinning. Through the jet noise he said smoothly: 'Plus a little something in case we end up on the ground, alive, with those Ay-rabs a-comin' to git us.'

She jerked him a look, her eyes wide, round. 'Cyanide?'

Narrow-eyed, Chuck nodded.

Tamasin grabbed his wrist. 'You're not giving one of those to Jerry!'

Chuck laughed. Tamasin had never heard that ugly sound from him before. 'I'm giving one to everyone, honey, so just move over or I'll kick you over. Jerry won't take his until after the raid.'

Against the ejector seat harness she twisted to face him. 'You bloody fool, how do *you* know what Jerry'll do with a thing like that?'

'Jerry's a man, cutie pie,' Chuck said in a voice like a razor. 'He's an adult, he can make up his own mind.'

Tamasin grabbed for his hand. Chuck evaded her. 'You really want to see me fight?' she said through her teeth. 'You'll be sorry.'

Chuck sighed patronizingly. 'OK. I'll give one to everyone except Jerry. Now can I get out?'

Grudgingly Tamasin made way.

Twisting his tubby body surprisingly dexterously in the narrow space, Chuck turned to the water supply and drew two beakers. He climbed the ladder. Through the windscreen the pre-dawn sky was very dark and the cabin was chilly. Chuck stooped to the pilots.

'Amphetamine, when you're ready.'

Wordless, almost surly, Mario took his with the water Chuck gave him. Bat accepted his with a curt nod of gratitude and swallowed it.

Then Chuck gave them the cyanide capsules and they tucked them into easily accessible pockets.

Chuck refilled the beakers. He went to Russell first. Russell took his amphetamine and then with a wry grin pocketed the cyanide. Chuck went to Jerry.

'How ya doing, man?'

'Just let me at 'em,' Jerry muttered. 'This whole thing's going so slow.'

He was very tense, Chuck realized. It was a state of mind Chuck recognized from the days when they'd been together, doing the preparations for the flight. It was a state Chuck quietly fostered because, in it, Jerry would react the way Chuck wanted him to. Chuck had hidden his amusement when Mario had come down, cursing and grumbling about Jerry being a drunk; he'd known immediately how recklessly Mario had been exaggerating. Jerry was all right. Jerry had always danced when Chuck pulled his strings, and he'd dance again for Chuck now.

'You want more amphetamine?'

'I guess.'

Chuck gave it to him. Then, with contempt for his promise to Tamasin, he gave Jerry the cyanide capsule. 'Don't for God's sake let Tamasin know you have this. She's getting real cranky.'

'Sure.'
Chuck went back down.

*   *   *

Fatigue weighed heavy on Bat and he gazed narrow-eyed into the night with the bone dome pressing on his head, and waited for the amphetamine to take effect. The tremor of the airframe reached him, and he put out his hand and shook a cigarette loose from the pack. One last cigarette. Bat drew deeply on the pungent smoke and let it out slowly through his nose. No more cigarettes now, they'd be into the action. He thought about what Alice would have said, and the bitterness of his loss came back to him, the way he'd watched her weaken and die while he'd loved her and been powerless to save her. Powerless to save Edward when the terrorists had caught him. His breath shivered a little as he inhaled.

Not long now before he placed those bombs on target.

*   *   *

After Tamasin had let Chuck back to his console she didn't sit down straight away, she went aft one last time for the relief station and to put on a last spot of make-up, a last touch of perfume. This flight had been a bit like a metaphor for a life, she reflected as she peered at herself in the dim light in the little mirror. The takeoff had been like a birth. There'd been childhood squabbling in the first leg, unformed personalities asserting themselves; teenage anguish in the dangers that had threatened them from one end of the Caribbean to the other; then relationships had settled down. The Mainstay, tracking them spectrally, had contributed to a sort of midlife crisis; afterwards they'd

227

settled down to middle age, as it were, and then latter years.

Now they were preparing themselves for the final crisis. Death itself.

Strapping herself back in at the console, Tamasin realized almost in surprise that at last she'd overcome her fears. Death was a passage that she was now ready to navigate; provided only that she could kill Tariq Talal first. She checked her charts, checked the plots, checked the time. Local time was 0529. Local time was all that mattered now.

*   *   *

Up top with his back to the pilots, Jerry was monitoring radio wavebands as well as radar. He was getting cipher squirts, he wasn't sure what from; and a bit of Arabic, too fast for him to begin to follow, from a radar station on the coast near the town of Al Khums; and cleartext voices, some in American-accented English, some, puzzlingly, in Russian.

Russian was Jerry's strongest foreign language and he knew what this was about. He was listening to two separate sets of carrier operations.

'Bat, I'm getting a lot of voice off radio. Seems we have two flatdecks operating offshore, one US, one Soviet. Seems also the Libyans are really on the alert.'

Bat glanced at Mario with a frown. He didn't like that.

'OK,' he said. 'The US ship will be the *John F. Kennedy*. The Russian, if that's a carrier, could be the *Tbilisi* or the *Kiev*. We'll be the ones they're looking for, you can bet on that.'

Mario whipped round. 'Somebody talked!'

'Uh-unh.' Bat was unruffled. 'We never needed a leak, once someone figured this plane was missing and had

228

FBI track *us* down as crew. No bets on where we'd be going.'

'EWO.' On the intercom Mario's voice was edgy. 'Does Libyan radar have us yet?'

'Negative, co-pilot,' Jerry said.

It was 0538. For six minutes they flew without speaking.

Then at 0544 Jerry said tautly: 'Radar, search radar.'

Bat and Mario swapped glances. The sky was still very black in front of them. Down on the first level, alarm jumped inside Tamasin's chest. They hadn't even reached Waypoint Sixteen yet, the last before the initial point.

'No gate yet,' Jerry said. 'Still searching. Looks like they *must've* seen us.' He paused. 'Shit, it's a . . . it's another Mainstay!'

Mario said: 'Does Libya have a Mainstay?'

'Don't know,' Bat said. 'Chuck, do you know?'

Chuck said: 'Negative, they don't.'

Mario snapped: 'OK, what're we gonna do?'

'Keep flying,' Bat growled, 'till we see good cause for doing anything else.'

Tamasin was trembling. Partly it was the effect of the amphetamine, partly it was the tension of the approaching battle. This metal angularity, these scopes and switches and dials, they'd been her home for all these hours but now they were her prison. The weight of the bone dome oppressed her.

Chuck smoked. Russell flipped his worry beads, eyes hooded but alert as he watched the tail radar. Mario muttered about the fuel state. Bat was fiddling with the trim, still keeping the groundspeed on 330 knots. He never had quite managed to get the bomber properly balanced after they lost that Number Eight engine.

Biting his lip, Jerry watched his scopes as the Mainstay's radar painted them relentlessly and the unseen crew did nothing about it.

0600.

Very soon now they would be in range of ground radars, Jerry realized. His breathing had gone shallow. Again his mind flicked to the flask full of Wild Turkey.

0605.

'Fifteen minutes for Waypoint One Six,' Tamasin said, and hesitated. 'Jerry – have you got a big ship on your radar?'

'I do. It's the Russian one.'

0610.

Tamasin said: 'Ah, ten minutes to Waypoint One Six.'

Apart from Tamasin, no-one was speaking. Chuck crushed out his cigarette and this time didn't light another.

0614. Suddenly on Jerry's radar there was movement.

'Ah, we have two . . . three . . . four, confirm *four* fighters up off the Russian carrier. They're . . .' his voice went hoarse, his throat dry . . . 'heading south. Coming in good and fast for the Libyan coast. Ah, pilot, looks like this could be it.'

CHAPTER 28

The briefing was over. Behind him on the stairs as he led the aircrews up out of the underground chamber at Sigonella, Colan Penhale heard Pete Pretorius saying something smart-arsed in that clipped South African accent and one of the Hawk navigators laughing in response. Colan didn't feel like laughing. Jack Baslow, with the Falklands badges on his flying suit, didn't laugh either.

Salim Arshad, silent and confident at Colan's shoulder, lent support to his pilot.

They didn't like it, either of them. Still no positive trace for Dark Angel. Still no real idea what the Russians were up to. Still too many restrictions in the rules of engagement. No intrusion into Libyan airspace. No weapons launch unless the Libyans fired first. Radar lock-on only if a Libyan aircraft offered provocation. Nothing, not so much as a hint, of any provocation by the task force against the Russians.

Pity, Colan thought. *Kiev* had MiG 29s and he'd have enjoyed finding out how good those really were when flown by experienced Russians.

Colan's training against MiG 29s was limited to exercises with German pilots flying the fighters Bonn had inherited from the East after unification.

McNair strode up to Colan as they walked down the corridor, with the rain flipping spots on the dark panes and the overhead lighting catching them. His thickset figure was dogged and aggressive as always. 'What'll we do if Sandbox catches Dark Angel over

231

their patch and has a go at them?' Sandbox was code for Libya.

'Let 'em get on with it,' Colan said. But he avoided McNair's eyes.

McNair gazed at him suspiciously for a moment. 'Well, maybe they'll make it clear,' he said. 'D'you think our friends in the Hawks followed your words of erudition on tactics?'

The situation briefing had come from Rear-Admiral Berlin, the task-force commander. Colan had delivered the briefing on tactics for the fighters.

'I'm happy,' Colan said.

McNair knew he was anything but. Yet McNair shared his confidence in the Hawk crews.

Colan led Salim into the double room they'd been given in the officers' quarters. Still Salim didn't speak, and Colan realized where the man's thoughts were – with his wife and kid, same as Colan's. Colan gestured to the phone.

'After you,' Salim said. A thin smile lingered on his square-cut, dark features, and his deep, black eyes were thoughtful.

Colan pulled off his boots and flying suit, sat on the edge of the bed in his underpants and olive T-shirt and dialled his home in Woodhall Spa.

'I'm fine,' Jane answered him. 'Katharine's fine. How about *you*?'

'Missing you,' Colan muttered. 'Apart from that, fine.'

'Have you heard any more about Tamzie?' Her concern was apparent from her voice. Jane was very worried about her sister-in-law.

'Nothing definite.'

Jane burst out: 'Is Tamzie *really* up there?'

Levelly, Colan said: 'It looks a lot as if she is.'

For a moment he heard only silence on the other end.

Then Jane sniffed, and he knew she was having trouble. 'I feel so *sorry* for Tamzie,' Jane said, voice high as she fought with her emotions. 'Don't you think I really should phone your dad to let him know?'

'At the moment,' Colan said, 'there's nothing to let him know. We're all going on guesswork.'

They hung up.

Salim was by the other bed, also in T-shirt and underpants, watching Colan, one hand on his hip. His dark eyes held concern. 'How d'you feel, Colan?'

It made no difference that no-one had proved it yet. Both of them knew damn well Tamasin was up there.

Colan stared at the curtain. It was chilly in the room and a fly was diving round the motionless ceiling fan. Without looking at Salim, Colan said: 'I'm going to get her out of it if I can.'

CHAPTER 29

Through the pre-dawn darkness Bat Masterson and
Mario Peroni held the B52 grimly steady on its northerly
course. Russell Feehan, with a slow turn of his head,
checked the time, 0615 local, and went back to his
sleepy watch on the tail radar. Every few moments he
gave another flick to his worry beads. Jerry Yeaver was
oblivious. Down on the second level, Chuck Brantley was
trying to think up a wisecrack but not succeeding and,
beside him, Tamasin Penhale Masterson was staring at the
radar with the hairs prickling at the back of her neck.

As she watched, the *Kiev* launched a second wave of
four fighters. Streaking south savagely towards the B52.

On the intercom Jerry said: 'Eight fighters approaching
from the north.'

Mario said: 'Libyan fighters?'

'Negative. Russians.'

Then Jerry doubted himself. He would always doubt
himself. Maybe he'd misidentified the carrier; the *Kennedy*
was in the area, maybe it was her. Maybe they were
about to be attacked by *American* fighters. Sweat stood
on Jerry's face in the cold.

Tamasin said: 'Waypoint One Six in three minutes.
Stand by for left turn on to three zero five mag.' Jerry
couldn't understand how she kept the tension out of her
voice.

0618.

Traces showed on the radar scope and Jerry's breath
stopped in his throat. A land airfield.

Voice cracking, he said: 'Libyan fighters. Five, uh,

234

six. Looks like Base Hotel, the one just south of Ben-ghazi.'

But which way were they heading? Jerry needed whiskey.

'Eighty seconds,' Tamasin said tonelessly. 'Seventy.'

Jerry wasn't even blinking as he watched the radar.

In a shudder of breath he said: 'North. They're heading north.' Away from the B52. 'They're going for . . . they're intercepting those jets off the carrier.'

Eight traces in two waves were heading south fast, closing on the coast. Six opposing traces were heading north, closing with the intruders. Amazement dawned on Jerry as he realized that every radar eye was looking north to the intruders and *away* from the B52 sneaking in from the south, out of the last of the night. And that Mainstay was still painting them with its radar. He couldn't believe the luck.

'Zero,' Tamasin called. Waypoint Sixteen.

*　　*　　*

Bat rolled the B52 into the turn. Jerry was hardly aware of the shuddering wallow as the big aircraft levelled back out – he was staring at his scopes. Tamasin was keyed up, jittery from the amphetamine as they all were, and now she switched on the EVS scope.

This place was called Jabal Zaltan and there were oil wells everywhere. That meant technicians, engineers, people who knew what a jet bomber looked and sounded like. It meant telephones, radio.

'Radar,' Bat called coolly from the top deck. 'Weapons release checklist.'

'Roger, pilot,' Chuck said. He started running through the drills with Tamasin, Tamasin reading off the list, Chuck making the checks. To Tamasin he seemed very cool, as he had been throughout the flight, totally under control, cracking a joke now and then as he went through all the green-light items.

Tamasin was the opposite, she was tense, really afraid. This was the real thing, there was no getting out of it now and as she felt her fingers shaking she felt also the blockage high in her throat so that she could scarcely breathe. *No, she thought, no. I'll do it, I'll do it.* She had to get this right. The raid was the only thing that mattered, the raid was everything. It was her dying tribute to Edward. Edward who'd met his terrible death on his own, without her. She thought: *bring me luck, Buster, bring me luck.*

Chuck put a hand on her knee. It wasn't lascivious this time, it was fatherly and strong and she almost loved him for it.

'EWO,' Bat's slow, deep voice said, 'what about those fighters?'

'*Kiev*'s guys have sheered off.' He was sure it *was* the *Kiev* now, he'd been listening to the Russians on radio, the pilots, the fighter controller. 'The Libyans are tailing them, maybe twenty miles or more behind.'

0630. Still half an hour to the initial point. Bat and Mario were peering out into the darkness over the Libyan Desert and the stars were going out.

Tamasin thumbed the mike back on. 'Primary entry control point.'

They were into the battle zone.

*   *   *

Bat advanced the middle six throttles, adjusted Number One, and the noise of the surviving engines deepened. Quickly Bat wound on aft elevator trim. Wallowing, the B52 began sinking through the cold, pre-dawn air. Mario watched the radio altimeter, the one that gave them height above ground level.

'Nine hundred . . . eight fifty . . . eight hundred . . .'

236

They wanted to be 250 feet above ground.

Tamasin said from below: 'Groundspeed is correct at four eighty knots. Heading is correct, maintain heading.'

Bat trimmed out. They had 250 feet. It was 0640, still not yet first light, still twenty minutes to run to the IP. At this speed and height now it would be harder for Libyan radar to find them, even given the size of the return a B52 made. Harder still for fighters. Through the windscreens Bat couldn't see a thing, he was flying off the low-light television image on the EVS scope.

Mario snapped irritably: 'We're not going to have much fuel left after the attack.'

'Let's get through the attack,' Bat grunted. 'Then worry about fuel.'

With his instinct for the weakest, Mario switched his attack to Jerry. 'Hey, EWO, what about the start countermeasures point?' That was the next stage of the raid, as they bored deeper in towards a defended target.

'No ground radar has us yet, co-pilot.' Jerry's voice had a ring of wonder to it. 'If we switch on all the ECM, we'll be sending out so much transmission they're *bound* to find us.'

'*You* don't take chances with *our lives* at a point like this!' Mario snarled. 'Get those mothers working!'

Bat said evenly: 'Co-pilot, this decision is for the EWO. Jerry, use your judgement, OK?'

Again Mario snapped: 'What about the fighters?'

Engine noise washed around them and the sky was still dark. The cold aboard the bomber was working deep into Russell Feehan's bones as he gazed methodically at his tail radar scope. Bat had the jet at 250 feet above the desert, his palm nursing the chunky plastic of the control yoke with its proud, 1950s-style logo on the boss.

'They're orbiting off Benghazi,' Jerry said. 'Those Russians are keeping close around the *Kiev* right now.'

Below, Chuck Brantley was narrow-eyed, staring at his

radar for ridge lines in their path, ready to pass advance warning to Bat. It was 0645. Mario glanced up from his EVS scope. Beyond the windscreens, the sky had started to turn charcoal.

'We have radar!' Jerry said sharply. 'It's . . . it's an E2C. That has to be US Navy. It has us gated.'

'*Now* how about your countermeasures?' Mario called triumphantly.

'That's a US E2C,' Bat said drily. 'Do you really think it's relaying information to the Libyans? Let's keep that ECM off.'

'Yes, *sir*!' Jerry called.

Bat and Mario swapped a glance. The same thought reached both men simultaneously: their steadily mounting disbelief that they'd got this far, that they were getting away with it. Neither spoke, yet the same thought was in both their minds as it was in Jerry's: but for that first lunge towards the coast by the *Kiev*'s fighters, the bomber would almost certainly have been picked up by now on Libyan radar.

'Someone in the oilfields musta heard us,' Mario niggled.

'I guess,' Bat said carelessly, and looked ahead again.

*   *   *

In the approaching dawn the desert was cool. Apart from the familiar wallowing as the B52 thundered on, low down over the land at high speed, little disturbed its flight. Below, Tamasin turned her face right, away from Chuck, and brushed away a couple of tears. Pure tension, nothing more. She didn't mind dying, she expected to die, it was just such a scary process to go through, that was all. Beside her Chuck was concentrating on his scope, watching for high ground ahead in the narrow radar beam, but this terrain was low sand dunes and it offered

238

no threat. And Chuck, like Mario, meant to get out of this alive.

0650.

Tamasin said on the intercom: 'Ten minutes to IP.' Hearing her in the headset, Jerry again marvelled at how cool she sounded. He wasn't cool, he was shaking, he needed a drink, he was terrified.

0652.

Eyes on his radar, Jerry said: 'Libyan fighters heading back south. Recovering to base.'

0655.

Tamasin announced: 'Five minutes to IP.'

0656.

Jerry said: 'They're all heading home now, all those Libyans.'

Mario said: 'What about that Mainstay? And the E2C?'

'Mainstay's still painting us. E2C has us gated. They're just watching . . .' But Jerry didn't like it. None of them liked it.

0657.

Tamasin announced: 'Three minutes to IP.' She hoped the others couldn't hear that shiver in her voice. She said: 'Pilot, stand by for left turn on to two six six mag.'

Reaching across the console next to her, Chuck, lower lip thrust out under his bristling moustache, loaded the tercom – terrain comparison – cassette for the raid. Now the autopilot would have advance warning, through the computerized terrain data, of every ripple and turn of the section of desert they were about to fly over. It had been made from readings supplied by USAF satellites and Bat didn't know how Chuck had got hold of it. None of them knew.

0658.

'Ground radar, guys!' Jerry called, almost in relief. The Libyans had finally noticed them.

CHAPTER 30

A big bird of prey soared over the jagged peaks of the western mountains – eagle or hawk? Captain Rebecca Laird couldn't tell as she flashed her ID at the Craycroft Road guardhouse. Van Burkart drove on through in the Porsche. 'Where to, Captain Curvaceous?'

'Uh . . . make it my apartment.' She was checking her watch, working out how long she had. 'I have to get a shower before I go back there.'

Van knew the way.

He parked and then followed her inside. Ella wasn't there. 'Why are you following me around, Professor Burkart?' Becks said, but made no move to prevent him.

'I'm a normal adult male,' Van said. 'Any normal adult male would follow *you* around, short of active, serious discouragement.'

'Such as this?' Becks said, and banged the bedroom door on his foot.

'Ow, goddam!' Van howled, and shoved the door open again. 'No, honey, that kind of teasing merely inflames passion.' He pushed the door shut behind him and then grabbed her.

This time as their open mouths met Becks didn't even attempt to resist.

*   *   *

Showered, and in a clean uniform and tingling all over, Becks gave Van a peck on the cheek as he dropped her at her office. Julio was on the phone again, slumped in front of his terminal and scrolling thoughtfully through what looked like a spare-parts list full of multi-digit numbers.

Becks went through into the inner office. Five past two in Arizona, five past four in DC. Becks phoned Andrew Maule, but this time as she punched the numbers she wasn't thinking of Maule's tanned and craggy features and silver hair.

Maule ran briskly through the situation in the Med. 'The Libyans now have all their radars turned to the north. Also they're putting up Foxbats in singleton forays across the Gulf of Sirte, on flight paths that are way more provocative than anything we or the Russians are doing.'

The MiG 25 Foxbat was a big brute of a single-seat interceptor. Soviet air forces had been flying them since 1970. It had been flown up to 98,000 feet and could keep up a speed of over 1,500 knots, but there were those who said it fought best in a straight line. There were those who said that about Tornado F3s, too.

'So what *are* the Russians doing?' Becks asked.

'Just getting on everyone's nerves, I guess,' Maule said. 'Making a real pain in the ass of themselves. Excuse me, Captain.' He feigned shock at himself.

'Why, General Maule, *sir*! You go wash your mouth out with soap and water!'

Cheerfully, they hung up. Yet for a long time now nothing much had happened and Becks was getting a periodic urge to scream.

Boring old Davis-Monthan, she thought, you delivered the goods in the end. This was the toughest challenge she'd had in her career.

She readjusted the comb in her hair, then called Cordwain at the CIA. In Langley, Virginia, it would be twenty to five. 'Sir, I'd like to know anything that's new off the satellite search.'

Cordwain was as supercilious and dismissive as before,

his nasal voice taking lordly pleasure in putting a humble USAF captain in her place. 'We have essentially nothing new off the satellite search, Captain Laird. We were alerted at a very late stage. You shall have anything relevant as soon as we can get it to you.'

Becks wondered: so who decides what's relevant? Sitting back in the artificial light, imagining the winter sun out there, low over the hard line of the mountains, she found herself wishing she hadn't given up smoking.

Julio knocked and entered with coffee, a secretive smile in his dark, permanently half-closed eyes. 'Ah, thank you, Julio.' Becks gave him the best smile she could muster, but she couldn't help wondering what sort of trouble he wanted her to get him out of.

She checked her watch. Ten to three. Ten to eleven in Sicily and Flight Lieutenant Colan Penhale would be asleep, gathering his strength for an early start. Becks didn't like it, but she knew it was time she brought Hartmore up to date.

She dialled. 'Sir, do you have a minute?'

'Go ahead, Captain.' Hartmore's voice was tense, sour, critical.

She listed what they'd found out. It didn't seem to amount to much.

Hartmore thought for a moment. The brief silence that came over the line was grumpy. 'Where's your best intelligence been coming from in all this?'

Becks realized Hartmore was making her nervous. 'NSA, sir. They have come up with some really valuable signals intercepts.'

Hartmore snapped: 'Why not Pentagon A2?'

'Sir, I've had some crucial background off A2 and they're keeping me up to date with positions in the Med.' The enclosed room was pale beige. Becks was fed up with it, fed up with the faint chemical whiff from the photocopier next door. Something was humming softly, maybe a light. She focused on the brilliant red of the poinsettia on her desk.

'Why haven't CIA found it? They have all those satellites.' Neither needed to spell out what *it* was.

'They say they were alerted too late.'

'Get on to them, Captain. If we don't find that goddam plane, it's a national disaster.' He hung up.

Becks sighed. Hartmore wasn't the one who had to keep badgering a senior CIA figure who preferred to play things his own way.

Then she reflected that behind the bluster Hartmore was a very worried man. Beneath that immaculate uniform and the hard façade, he was vulnerable.

*   *   *

She didn't bother calling Cordwain when she'd only just spoken to him, he could wait. She spun her chair right around, wondering what to do.

No bright ideas. Hardly thinking what she was doing, Becks slowly reached for her keyboard and created a new file on the screen. Methodically, unhurriedly, she began entering in chronological order every note she'd made, every movement, every report she'd logged since the crisis arose yesterday evening. It seemed so much longer ago.

Then she noticed it.

It was the *Kiev*; it was the movement reports she'd logged for the Soviet carrier. She had the US President ordering the *Kennedy* off station at 0200 today East Coast time, in other words 0700 zulu. She had the *Kennedy* actually moving off station at 0720 zulu. She had reports from CIA, confirmed by readings off those KH11s of USAF A2, that showed the *Kiev* coming off station at 0635 *zulu* – almost half an hour before the US President had even issued his order. And, by all the indications, the *Kiev*'s captain had even known, in advance, where his destination lay.

If this was true, then the Russians had known where to expect the action before the Americans. A tingle ran down Becks's spine.

She grabbed the phone. She got Andrew Maule. *Check it, please check it*, she begged him. *Could be I entered my times wrong.*

'I'll get back to you, Becks.'

She waited. She felt excited. She had a sense that she wouldn't have long to wait, and she was right. Andrew Maule you could trust.

She snatched the phone the instant it rang. Maule's voice sounded genuinely impressed. 'Very good spot, Becks, well done. Your timings were dead right.'

'Jesus,' Becks muttered, and paused. She was starting to feel scared. 'I know I . . . I kinda spotted it, but honestly I find it almost difficult to really *believe*. I mean . . . if the Soviets really *did* know where to send the *Kiev*, I guess there's something real weird going on.'

CHAPTER 31

Adrenalin surged through Tamasin and she thought: *this is it*. 0658 local time and the Libyans had found them at last. She carried on gamely with her countdown. Inside two minutes to initial point.

'Pilot, maintain speed, four eighty.' Her voice on the intercom was stretched taut.

Jerry Yeaver opened up the ECM with a massive belt of spot noise. High-energy transmissions on the Libyans' radar frequency swamped the screens. Down at the ground station, the circular scopes in the darkened room whited out, energy boiling on the receivers.

That wouldn't last long, Jerry knew – they'd be after them in two shakes on another frequency. He hoped fervently that this radar station wasn't the latest Russian frequency-agile sort. Those things jumped bands faster than Jerry Yeaver could white them out.

'Initial point,' Tamasin said. 'Left turn on to two six eight mag.'

It was 0700, on the dot, the sky turning from charcoal to feathery brown.

'Pilot,' Chuck Brantley said, 'radar: tercom on, green light.'

As Bat Masterson rolled the B52 level on its new course, the big bomber was now being guided through the autopilot by Chuck's pre-recorded cassette of the terrain contours. Bat set the height for 100 feet above ground level. At 380 knots, the effect was going to be sensational. Bat could override the tercom any time, the way he'd overridden the autopilot, to fly all the turns manually.

Tamasin monitored the speed. Still spot-on. What a pilot, she thought, what a crew. It seemed almost a shame that they would never fly again together as a team.

From the front seats, Bat Masterson and Mario Peroni saw the dawn light wash sandy gold over the hill tops, the whole desert landcape solidifying around them, taking shape, coming alive. They were following the line of a *wadi*, a dry watercourse – what in Arizona they'd have called a *wash* – and most of those hilltops either side were above the B52 now. They bored massively in, in a rolling ball of stolen thunder. Unseen behind them, dust leaped and danced and trailed in the wake from the seven jets.

Nonchalantly Chuck called: 'Terrain one eight miles.' That was back-up for the pilots in case the tercom failed.

Noise percolated through Tamasin's bone dome and crowded in against her head. Her head ached. Light turbulence jolted the B52 woodenly but Tamasin was too scared to feel sick. She had the radar switched to mapping mode and she was concentrating on being able to pick out the target when it showed up, but she hadn't seen it yet. Chuck just sat, imperturbable.

The wadi was rising. Bat and Mario could see ripple after hazy ripple of grey hill. Bat had his left hand lightly on the control yoke but the tercom was doing the work. Alert, Bat and Mario kept watch.

At the tail-gun controls, Russell Feehan was in agony but he didn't want a painkiller, didn't want to slow himself up.

Jerry was jumping frequencies with the barrage noise. There were surface-to-air missile sites close to the camp and if the ground radar caught the bomber the SAMs would get a lock. This was a duel with the Libyan ground radar and sometimes Jerry was ahead with his frequency jump, sometimes he was behind. He could never tell what the next frequency would be. At the controls he was tense,

246

breathing quickly; he'd even forgotten he needed a drink. The task remained: to make sure the Libyans never got more than a glimpse of the B52 on their scopes before he whited them out.

Chuck started the countdown to bomb release. 0703, five minutes to run. 0704, four minutes.

Search radar pulses washed the B52. Instantly Jerry recognized the Fox Fire pattern off an old-model MiG 25 Foxbat interceptor. Libya flew MiG 25s. The jets from the *Kiev* were the newer, more formidable, MiG 29 Fulcrums.

'Ah, now we have a Foxbat. No lock yet. Some way out but . . . shit, is he coming in *fast*!'

The Foxbat was still supersonic. If it didn't slow down pretty soon it would overshoot the bomber by a huge margin.

Bat and Mario swapped glances.

Mario said: 'Sucker him in.' This was the last thing they needed, inside four minutes off bomb release.

Bat cut out the autopilot, pressed the yoke back to hold height, and rolled left. He counted five seconds and rolled back to the right. Five seconds. Back to the left again. Five seconds . . .

'He slowed right down!' Jerry said. 'He's getting us pretty consistently!' Still fighting off the ground radar with spot noise, Jerry started to reach for the chaff release trigger.

The Foxbat pilot was turning with the B52, trying for a lock so he could launch his missiles.

On the high ground the daylight fell gold and pink but the wadi was still shades of hazy grey and Bat had no easy task on his hands as he rolled back to the right, striving to avoid its walls. Dust boiled behind them and Bat knew the MiG pilot would be hard put to make visual contact.

Unruffled, Chuck went on calling terrain as the seat tipped left and right and left again under him, rolling, wallowing, rolling. Tamasin, in mounting terror, clung to her console and struggled to monitor her scope.

'He's in the six!' Jerry warned.

He was using the clock code, picturing the aircraft at the centre of a clock face. Six o'clock is directly behind. It's the prime position to destroy the aircraft ahead of you.

'Terrain right ahead,' Chuck said. 'Two minutes forty to bomb release.' He was keyed up yet nonetheless relaxed. He knew what the job was and what the problems were. His hand rested on the console, poised to grab for the laser designator the instant he saw the target on the EVS scope. This B52 was a lot cleverer than it had been in the days when it had flown Linebacker missions over North Vietnam.

It needed to be. Right next to Tariq Talal's camp stood the civilian hamlet of Bir al Hadh and Chuck couldn't afford to put his bombs on that.

Bat pulled the B52 level and lifted it over the terrain obstruction, clear in the dawn light, and the height gain decelerated the bomber. That put the Foxbat closer.

Chuck said: 'Two minutes twenty. Reduce speed in two zero seconds.'

Russell said: 'Got him on the tail radar. Right on the edge.'

Chuck's voice rose a little. 'Target identified! I have target on the attack radar!'

With a start, Tamasin realized that on the edge of the wadi, her mapping radar was also painting Tariq Talal's camp. They were in striking distance of the man who'd butchered Edward. Butchered so many other people, too.

Freeing a hand from radar jumping to try the radio frequencies, Jerry got Arabic, a clipped burst of words turned metallic in the transmission. A moment's pause, and another voice gave maybe three words. Jerry could hardly have followed the words even if he'd been prepared for them, but he knew what was happening.

The Libyans still ran their air force the way the Russians used to in the 1970s and early 1980s: their combat pilots were rigidly directed by fighter control on the ground. What Jerry had overheard was the Foxbat pilot asking fighter control's permission to attack the B52.

He flung a look at Russell. 'Get him now, Russ, before he locks us in.'

On the intercom Chuck said tautly: 'Pilot, reduce speed.'

Bat said: 'Copy, radar.' They were at 450 knots, decelerating.

Russell thumbed the trigger. A two-second burst.

It was 0706:15. The B52's tail gun was a rotating, Gatling-type weapon with six barrels delivering rapid-fire 20mm cannon rounds. On the edge of Russell's radar scope the Foxbat was still there and now Russell aligned the gun painstakingly. And fired again.

The trace for the Foxbat bloomed large suddenly on the radar screen, split in two and vanished.

'I think, that . . .' Russell seemed to stumble over words.

It was 0706:25. 'You did,' Jerry confirmed excitedly, 'yeah, great, you got him!'

'Good work, gunner,' Bat said impassively, and then Chuck cut across him again.

'Pilot, get this speed back, we're gonna be too fast to hit the target!'

'Copy,' Bat said, easing back the levers. 'EWO, you found any SAM sites yet?'

Jerry was searching busily. 'Still looking, sir, doesn't look like they have their radars switched on yet.'

0706:40.

Chuck called: 'Bomb doors open.'

One minute fifteen seconds to bomb release, and Tamasin remembered that opening the bomb doors

249

practically doubles a B52's radar image. Stealth technology hadn't been dreamed of when this aircraft had been on the drawing boards. With next to nothing to occupy her, Tamasin was jumpy, tense.

Above her, Bat and Mario weren't tense, they were working as a team, the way each man had, years before, with his crew over Vietnam. But this wasn't anything like Vietnam. In those days they'd done their bombing from 40,000 feet and the people on the ground hadn't even heard the jet engines before the seven-fifty-pounders began bursting around them.

'Speed is correct,' Chuck said, 'correct at 380 knots.'

Tamasin was thinking: *when I die, I'll be with Edward.*

The B52 crested the rise, 100 feet above ground at 380 knots with a dust storm boiling behind it, and the sound of stolen thunder exploded across a desolate landscape. This terrain was flat, almost treeless, its undulations low, the sandy soil turned pinkish gold in the low sun, grey and charcoal where some feature cast shadow. Mario saw scrubby bushes, here and there a cypress, some telegraph poles and now, directly on the nose, a group of low, barrack-like buildings, the earthen slopes of a bunker, some trucks and cars.

Bat Masterson realized they were looking at Tariq Talal's camp.

CHAPTER 32

Light showed in a chink of corridor as the billet door opened and an Italian officer put his head into Colan Penhale's and Salim Arshad's room.

'Good a-morning. Time a-to get up.'

Awake immediately, Colan checked his watch. 0445 Italian time. Nice to know they were punctual, it was the first rule of efficiency. In Libya it would be 0545. Maybe an hour to first light.

Dark Angel obviously hadn't attacked yet. That would have been the first thing the Italian officer told them.

Wordless, thoughful, Salim got up, in his underpants, and began shaving. Colan had packed a tracksuit bottom. He went to the basin next to Salim's, grunted a greeting and also began shaving. Salim answered with a similar grunt.

A quick shower, then they dressed: underwear, T-shirt; then the internal *g*-suit with its system of inflatable bladders; zip-front woollen jumper; then the Gore-Tex immersion suit. The LSJ – life-saver jacket – with its Mae West buoyancy aid, its rescue homing beacon, all the bits, that would come later. Colan went to the window and squinted out. He grimaced. So much for Sicily. At 0455 now it was still densely dark and the chilly night was full of drizzle.

Salim read his thoughts. 'Just like home, isn't it?'

*   *   *

They made for the canteen. Jack Baslow, the Hawk pilot,

and his navigator were the only ones there, Baslow's Falklands badges judiciously understated. The others appeared almost immediately. McNair and Sewell-Baillie, the other Tornado crew; McNair stocky, with an assertive swing of his shoulders that to Jack Baslow looked like nerves; Sewell-Baillie loping like a greyhound on a leash. Pete Pretorius, the other Hawk pilot, with his navigator, the rangy South African flipping his blond quiff out of eyes that looked bloodshot.

Colan was beginning to sense a pleasurable feeling of apprehension.

On offer for breakfast there were hash browns and pancakes in honour of the Americans and croissants and brioches in honour of the Italian hosts. Baslow was tucking into a plateful of hash browns with the relish that betokened a combat veteran; Colan wondered if he'd had quite the same appetite, bobbing up and down in a carrier on a South Atlantic swell. Colan himself could hardly manage a croissant; or Salim a brioche; although both men knew very well that they needed something at least to line their stomachs.

Colan and Salim each drank one small, cold orange juice and one small cup of coffee. A full bladder was the last thing they needed up there.

With a glance at his watch, Colan made for the phone. In Sicily 0508 was 2108 in Arizona, long gone the time Captain Rebecca Laird ought to have been home; but on a day like today, Colan was betting that she wouldn't have left her post at Davis-Monthan.

He was right.

Her voice was eager, anxious. 'How are you? What's happening there?'

Colan hated to disappoint anyone as desperate as that for news. 'Thought you might be able to tell me. We've only just got up.' He sympathized with Becks. All she'd had to do all this time was to sit around and await developments.

Everybody was going to be disappointed, he thought, if Dark Angel had crashed in the ocean, or in the middle of the Sahara somewhere, and never turned up at all.

'Well, they're flying that E2C off the *Kennedy*,' Becks said mournfully. 'But they don't have anything to report yet, only a mess of provocations by Libyan fighters.'

'I'll have to get into the briefing now,' Colan said. Salim was signalling to him.

He hung up. It had been good to hear Becks Laird's voice.

*   *   *

Droplets of drizzle clung dully to the window panes in the long, echoing corridor. They crossed a paved strip in the open night. It was wet. It had small puddles underfoot just like Coningsby. As Colan followed Salim his eyes switched across to the left, to the rows of parked aircraft, the US Navy F18s, the Italian Tornados and the heavy metal: KC10s, C141s.

And a brace of helicopters that hadn't been there last night. Big ones, the HH53 Super Jolly that the Americans had used in Vietnam for rescuing downed aircrew. Colan hadn't seen camouflage like that before, more black than green. He started frowning as he followed Salim into the floodlit hangar beyond.

The hangar was busy; lots of technicians working on lots of aircraft with military markings. The briefing room was on the far side. Colan stumbled around the equipment trolleys, deep in thought. The hangar doors were open and he came in sight of the HH53s again. A technician straightened up from a job and Colan caught his eye.

He pointed. '*Di dove sono quelli ellicotteri?*' The

question wasn't difficult. The hard part would be understanding the answer.

The man shrugged. '*Io non so, signore.*' He spoke to the man next to him.

Salim had turned, in the personnel doorway leading off the hangar.

'*Francoforte,*' the second technician said.

Salim was looking at Colan a bit pointedly. '*Grazie,*' Colan said, and strode after Salim. Rhein-Main air base, then, the big place on the south side of the international airport. Rhein-Main was hardly five minutes by chopper from the small town of Oberursel. On the edge of Oberursel was the US Camp King, and that housed one of the biggest CIA stations in Europe.

*　　*　　*

Colan and Salim were the last to arrive at the briefing and Rear-Admiral Sigmund Berlin looked pointedly at his watch. 0516.

The languid Italian, Colonel Di Carolis, gave them the weather briefing. A depression over the North Atlantic was affecting weather all the way out to here. Cloud was eight oktas, base 800 feet, tops 18,000 feet, moderate icing. Surface temperature nine degrees Celsius, sea temperature twelve degrees. 'Don't ditch if you can help it.' Wind three to four knots, 270, backing 210. The edge of the cloud lay roughly on an east-west line a touch north of the Gulf of Sirte. 'So once you're clear of cloud you can assume the Libyans will want to know about you.' All Sigonella's beacons and navaids were serviceable but the instrument landing system at one of the diversion airfields wasn't working. Di Carolis listed the no-go areas. He listed the expected civilian flying. He noted that airline crews had been warned to avoid exercises north of the Sirte.

Berlin took over. The operational briefing and the mission briefing.

Kennedy still had her standing E2C AWACS patrol and her F14 CAP. F18s were ready to launch, tanked up and equipped for 'buddy-buddy' air-to-air refuelling.

Then, after a brief knock on the door, a young Italian lieutenant hurried in with a signal slip. Colan and Salim recognized the officer who'd given them their morning call.

It wasn't quite half past five. Puzzled, Berlin read the signal slip quickly and looked up. 'OK. It seems Libya has put up fighters from bases around Tripoli and Benghazi, heading northeast. Looks like they're going for the *Kiev*.' He nodded to the young Italian. 'Thank you, lieutenant.' As the man hurried out again, Berlin had his head together with Di Carolis's.

He faced the aircrews again. 'I guess that's an odd direction for Dark Angel to come in from, if this *is* Dark Angel. Anyway, we've had nothing off the E2C.'

He got on with the briefing. The *Kiev* had been flying helicopters all night, and a CAP like the *Kennedy*. They were obviously keeping an eye on the *Kennedy*. Similarly, the *Kennedy* was keeping an eye on them.

Another knock at the door. The lieutenant returned.

'Hm,' Berlin grunted as he glanced over the signal. He looked up. '*Kiev* has launched two waves of Fulcrums and sent them south, as if to threaten the Libyan coast. If we got some times, we could figure out who is reacting to who.'

The lieutenant left once more. Berlin resumed his briefing. Whatever the *Kiev* thought she was doing in relation to the Libyan coastline, she'd offered no threat to the *Kennedy* and there'd been no suggestion of hostile behaviour. The US President had queried it with the Soviet leader. The Soviet leader had told him the *Kiev* was in international waters and the Soviet Union could send its vessels where it liked, subject to international law. Moscow wasn't bothering Washington, why should Washington bother Moscow?

Word from the Pentagon was that, so far, there seemed no reason to suspect any threat from Soviet forces; on the other hand, it wasn't the least bit clear what the *Kiev was* doing.

Berlin continued. The mission of the task force was to locate, intercept and arrest Dark Angel. The RAF callsign would be *Bulldog*. Bulldog One was Penhale; Two, McNair; Three, Baslow; Four, Pretorius. The E2C was called Trapper. Fighter control was Prickly Pear. Libya was Sandbox. The rules of engagement were as outlined last night. Strict visident: they would use IFF checks – electronic identification friend and foe – and if the return indicated a bogey aircraft they would hold fire until they'd actually seen the thing. In no circumstances was the RAF/USN contingent to fire first.

As usual, Sewell-Baillie was the one who raised the query. 'Does that still apply if we find Dark Angel and it's under a shooting attack?'

'Correct,' Berlin said. 'Radar lock-on only unless the Libyans shoot at the task force.'

Salim slid his eyes right and met Colan's. Both saw the potential moral dilemma. Now Colan didn't know whether to wish he'd never been brought in on this or to be glad he wasn't sitting it out at Coningsby.

'One more thing,' Berlin said. 'We do not mix it with the Russians. If there's a threat, break off. We can afford a clash with the Libyans but we do not shoot at the Russians.' It was the end of the briefing.

*   *   *

Colan and Salim took their places in the crew bus with the others and put on their LSJs. The bus lights reflected on the wet tarmac. Colan checked his watch: 0542. They reached the Tornado dispersal.

Cold wind rippled wetly off the Med. The RAF groundcrew had borrowed an Italian minibus and there were technicians all over both aircraft. The engineer officer loomed out of the weak drizzle, a stocky little man with rain spots on his glasses and his hands jammed into his anorak pockets; Colan and Salim knew him well.

'She's ready to go, boys!'

As Salim climbed into the Tornado, Colan made the external checks. The aircraft was fully armed. Four Sky Flash missiles lurked semi-recessed into the flat under-fuselage; four AIM9L Sidewinders hung from the wing pylons. Missiles on and secure. Arming pins out. Colan squinted at the tail, then at the wing, and followed Salim up the ladder.

Drizzle had dripped into the cockpit. Colan leaned his head over the side as the technician clambered up to strap him in. He called out to the engineer.

'I'll close this hood as soon as our friend here's finished.'

'Roger!'

The technician worked quickly. Colan was testing intercom with Salim as the young NCO plugged in Colan's leads. The NCO climbed down and moved the ladder. Colan set the batteries going and then closed the hood. He set the auxiliary power unit running and then ran through the radio check. McNair strength five. Baslow fives. Pretorius fives also. Colan checked with fighter control.

Prickly Pear was a US Navy officer with a deep, cool voice from the Mid-West. He sounded reassuring. Colan got stuck into his checklist. Then at 0554, Prickly Pear came back.

'Uh, Bulldog Section, this is Prickly Pear. Trapper

reports Dark Angel positively identified, over southern-central Sandbox and headed north at this time.' The transmission clicked off.

In the rush of adrenalin, Colan couldn't quite trust his voice to stay steady. 'Bulldog One, roger that.'

Suddenly Tamasin was within reach of him. He could actually *do* something about her.

'Hang in,' Salim murmured. He'd heard. He knew what was going through Colan's mind.

Forcing himself to stay cool, professional, Colan ran through the rest of the checks.

CHAPTER 33

Bomb racks in a B52 hold the M117s horizontally in vertical stacks. When the bombs leave an aircraft travelling at 380 knots, for a few instants they also travel at 380 knots; and to lay them from low down you need the parachute retard.

It was a hell of a speed to come on the target from 100 feet up, Bat Masterson thought.

At the radar nav station all the green lights were on. Chuck picked out the barrack-like buildings on the EVS scope and grabbed for the laser designator, at the same time looking for Bir al Hadh. He found it out to the right, a cluster of low-roofed houses just north of the barracks. He set the designator on the barracks and, with the *ready* tone in his headset, saw it instantly as the readout snapped *release*. So little time at a speed like this. Chuck slammed the release trigger. One. And two.

'*Bombs gone!*'

If the inputs to the laser were correct and all the retards worked they should now be ahead of the shockwaves when the bombs hit. Chuck was glued wide-eyed to the EVS. Tamasin had never seen him so tense.

With the barrack blocks rushing at him, growing larger like some computer-game visual, Mario Peroni saw little people suddenly spilling out across the sandy dull earth. This was the closest he'd ever been to a target and it didn't look real. From the ground a single light winked, yellowish silver, and he thought *machinegun*, then, *can't be – assault rifle* – but it hardly mattered. A thing like that wouldn't do much to a B52. Mario was tired and stiff, as

259

they all were, too tired to be more than mildly excited. He was conscious, as Bat was conscious, that they were all of them behaving like the experienced, practised team they were, ably backing up Chuck Brantley. Chuck was the man doing the real work now.

Russell Feehan was absorbed in his tail radar. He was genuinely indifferent about the MiG he'd shot down. He had constant underlying pain, it gripped the whole of his abdomen, yet he'd had it so long he was hardly conscious of it any more. Beside him, Jerry Yeaver had no thought of himself or his depression or the wife who'd left him, his mind was focused purely on the wavebands. He'd found two of the SAM batteries Chuck had warned them about; their radars were searching but even now they hadn't found the B52. Jerry hadn't used his ECM yet, there'd been no real need. In a tiny corner of his mind he was surprised at himself, at the cool way he was going through his drills, even with the alcohol in him, even in this his first and only time in combat. He spared a thought for Tamasin. She must feel good, he thought, finally getting her revenge on Edward's murderers. Then he wondered whether maybe she felt scared.

Tamasin wasn't scared, she was terrified. At the nav console, with nothing but the ghostly image on the EVS and the panels crowded around her in the dim light with their switches and dials, and the ejector seat handle that of course at this height she could never use, and with the whole assembly rocking and roaring and jolting around her, she felt airsick as well. That was bad enough but what made it worse was that she had to hide it. They weren't to know she was terrified. They had to understand a woman could do every bit as well as these goddam macho hero men.

But she'd realized something now. Simply handling a B52 in the air, simply pulling your weight on the crew as nav, that was one thing. Taking the thing into some place where people wanted to kill *you*, *personally*, that's right, *you*, and still doing the job properly, that was another matter entirely.

And they hadn't even been shot at yet. Even that MiG hadn't been allowed the chance of a crack at them.

But they were there now and their bombs were slanting in and the buildings vanished off the EVS as they slashed over them.

Into the mike, Tamasin called tautly: 'Pilot, left turn, pick up two zero zero mag!' In her mind's eye she still saw that last glimpse off the EVS, the buildings, the people running, live people, who right now had eighteen 750-pounders coming at them.

But these were the people who'd butchered Edward Masterson; who'd killed dozens of other innocent people in dozens of attacks; killed people because of their nationality, not because of anything they'd done; or killed them sometimes irrespective of nationality, killed them merely because they were on an American airliner that got blown up by a Tariq Talal bomb.

Well, this time the bombs were coming courtesy of Tamasin Penhale Masterson.

Chuck announced: 'Bomb doors closed.'

The B52 wheeled massively into the turn to the south and they were clear of the target, probably invisible from the ground already but for their dust trail.

Tamasin was straining her ears, thinking: *surely they can't all have been duds? Surely they can't have loaded practice rounds after all?* The noise that still swamped her was the B52 itself and she couldn't hear the thunder of the explosions.

'OK, crew,' Bat said lazily, 'we took a little small-arms fire there. Check in. Co-pilot, seems like you're OK. Nav?'

'I'm OK,' Tamasin said.

'Radar?'

'Check,' Chuck said.

'EWO? Gunner?'

Jerry and Russell both checked.

Tamasin realized she was still attending to the navigation. Personal autopilot, she thought; it was happening almost subconsciously. 'Pilot, eight zero seconds to IP for the second run.'

'Roger, nav,' Bat said.

Jerry Yeaver was still surprised at the way Tamasin's voice sounded in his intercom. It amazed him how a woman without even simulated combat experience could operate so coolly under fire. She really wasn't afraid. Not like him.

Tamasin gave Bat the turn. Bat brought the bomber left. Mario was checking systems suspiciously but there was nothing off line that he could find. Tirelessly Russell watched the tail radar. Jerry scanned the wavebands.

Tamasin announced: 'One five seconds to IP two.'

Chuck reminded them: 'Only two minutes for this last run, guys.'

'Pilot,' Tamasin said, 'left turn, pick up three six zero mag. Turn *now*!'

They wouldn't be coming out of the sun this time. One of the lessons Bat had dinned into Tamasin was that if you have to hit a target twice, never come at it the second time from the same direction. Around her the little black cage with the switches and dials and scopes tilted steeply again and she was looking down on Chuck as gravity shoved her into her unusable ejector seat and she felt the bomber shudder as Bat rolled it out to head due north.

Chuck reached for the switch on his console. 'Bomb doors open. One ten seconds. One hundred.'

Orange flashed on Jerry Yeaver's console as the first SAM battery caught the suddenly double-sized trace of the B52. He told the others: 'One SAM station up!' Then

262

he retuned the bomber's transmitter to the SAM site's frequency and gave it full belt.

0713:15 and they'd lost the surprise but it didn't matter, Bat Masterson thought as he held the B52 steady and fast and low down. Tariq Talal still wouldn't be expecting them from the south. 0713:20.

'Shit,' Mario muttered, 'we sure hit 'em good!'

The smoke was grey and brown, lifting and spreading out in the near-windless early morning, and Mario couldn't see a trace of the buildings any more but here and there at the base of the smoke he could see the tiny red gleams of a dozen fires. Eighteen M117s they'd laid down on that barracks complex and at least some of them had found their mark.

'We missed the munitions,' Bat said. He held his breath as he searched for a sign that Bir al Hadh was still standing.

Smoke drifted and parted and Bat glimpsed flat roofs, that slender minaret. He breathed out.

'We'll fix that, right now,' Chuck's voice said in their headsets. That massive plastic-explosives dump, and the arms and ammo. They knew where it was.

Jerry said urgently: 'SAM launched!' He couldn't keep the fear and tension out of his voice any longer. If that thing had home-on-jam guidance it would come straight into them. 'Another SAM launched! Another . . .'

The missiles were out to the right. Mario actually saw the bright yellow blaze as the boosters lit, he could see the red tongues of the rocket exhaust.

'Ah, I have visual, one, two SAMs . . . three . . . we have four SAMs, visual.'

Bat held the bomber steady towards its target. He'd had lots of SAMs fired at him over North Vietnam but he never had learnt to enjoy the experience.

CHAPTER 34

Just outside radar range of the Libyan coastline Bulldog Section met the tankers. Four of them, one for each fighter, US Navy F18s. At 18,000 feet each jet towed a contrail, glittering silver against the hard blue dome of sky, and the sunlight tapped impatient fingers on the white cloud below where it hid the sea. When Colan first saw the tankers they were coming from the left at right angles, just where the briefing had said they'd be. Without opening his radio Colan wheeled his fighters to the right to come up behind the F18s. None of them was going to use radio now until strictly necessary. Radio signals would get picked up. As Colan closed behind his F18 the basket reeled out behind, and Colan thunked the Tornado's probe into it. A good contact, first time, every time. Colan took pride in that. The fuel started flowing. Colan glanced right.

McNair's Tornado eased in and made contact. Baslow's Hawk 300, sun silver off the cockpit hood beyond, was fuelling already. Colan looked left, for Pretorius.

Space opened, visibly, between the Hawk's probe and the F18's drogue. One missed contact. Holding his Tornado steady astern of the tanker, Colan watched Pretorius try again.

The big South African nudged the little Hawk in towards the tanker, his head a black globe with the visor pulled down on his helmet. The probe jabbed in. Too hard, and the drogue bounced away, and again the Hawk dropped a yard back. Pretorius tried again.

Gently now. Colan was thinking him through it and

he still wasn't going to open that radio. *Pretend it's your girlfriend.* Pretorius closed the Hawk cautiously with the F18 and the probe slid into the drogue. *Contact.*

They fuelled.

Baslow finished first. Colan heard the Hawk pilot's radio fizz open, the double click of the mike that was the agreed signal, and as Baslow broke contact and eased back from his tanker Colan's own tanks were full and he was clicking his mike.

Throttled back at 400 knots Colan took the section down for the cloud.

*   *   *

Visibility vanished at 11,000 feet but the fighters were in battle formation, spaced out over easily three miles, and they had their radars on; passive mode only so far, receiving but not transmitting.

They came out of cloud at 6,000 feet but there was more of it below, a thin layer from 1,200 feet down to 800 feet. Colan levelled them at 700 feet with the grey cloud now over them and the sea steely and swelling below. No white caps yet, Colan noted. Above them the cloud thinned out and then suddenly the sky was empty, blue. It made the sea seem almost black.

Colan looked out for the others. He glimpsed Pretorius and McNair but couldn't see Baslow. At Colan's left hand the twin throttle levers were big chunks of tough metal and he eased them back in the slots in the pale grey console to hold formation.

'Turn port,' Salim said in the headset. 'Zero eight zero. Let's not get too close to those Libyans.'

Dead right, Colan thought, let's let *them* come to *us* and sort it out. For the first time, he used radio. 'Bulldog, turn port, go!' With a touch of back pressure to hold his

265

height he rolled the Tornado steeply to pick up his easterly heading.

This was the northern boundary of the Gulf of Sirte. No land in sight, no shipping, just the bluey-black, surging surface below. Colan looked for Pretorius and found him, looked for McNair and Baslow and didn't see either of them. But that was how it was, flying battle formation.

'Salim?'

'Listening out,' Salim muttered, absorbed in his radars.

Colan had a moment now and he ran through what they knew.

Dark Angel had finally shown on radar, in southern Libya, heading north for its target. All that could stop it was the Libyan air force: the US Navy-RAF task force wasn't going to fly over Libya to head them off. Yet instead what had happened was that the Libyan air force had gone tearing off to Benghazi to chase the Russians away. The *Russians*.

Colan thought: those Russians knocked on Libya's front door and then ran off down the street. So no-one was watching when Dark Angel came through the back door and burgled them.

Interesting, that.

*   *   *

It was 0610 Italian time. Colan had the panel clock set to Libyan time, 0710. On the radio Salim heard Trapper, the E2C AWACS. Code of the day for the *John F. Kennedy* was Boston and that was who Trapper was calling.

'Looks like Dark Angel arrived home!'

'Roger that,' Salim murmured. Salim didn't often get excited, but now he was starting to feel tension in the gut. It was pretty clear what the wordcode meant. The B52 had hit its target.

Colan acknowledged.

The brief was for Bulldog Section to fly a racetrack pattern and now the four fighters were curving back round to the north. Glancing up, Colan realized the cloud was moving across them to the south, faster than forecast. Soon it would be right across the whole Gulf of Sirte.

'Salim, can you pick up Sandbox coastline on your radar?'

'Yeah,' Salim said, 'just the coastline. I can't reach as far as Tariq Talal's camp.'

The section carried on flying the racetrack pattern, taking it easy, 350 knots. Salim went on sweeping the coastline with the radar. They continued that way for ten minutes. 0716. 0717. 0718.

The radio fizzed open. 'Bulldog, Trapper.'

'Bulldog.'

The E2C crewman said: 'Dark Angel heading out north, approaching the coast. Sandbox has fighters up.'

'Bulldog,' Colan acknowledged. 'How many fighters?'

'Hard to say. Looks like plenty. Trapper, out.'

*   *   *

Colan kept flying. The cloud had swept right in and the sea was steely grey, still with that thin speckling of little white caps. The Tornado cockpit was simply a comfortable flying office with its bank of dials in front and an oblong metal shelf on the left with the throttle quadrants. On the right was another metal shelf with all the systems switches; then the head-up display projected the essential flight data on to the windscreen so you didn't have to look down inside the cockpit in the middle of a battle.

For all his training, for all his professionalism, Colan was feeling tense.

0720. Salim murmured: 'Sandbox fighters. Around that coastline. I've got at least . . . eight, no, ten.'

'Roger,' Colan said. The section kept flying. 0721.

'Got them,' Salim said without emotion. 'It's Dark Angel all right, there's nothing else big enough on the display. It's almost at the coast, it's got a couple of fighters a bit off the six.'

Not quite on the B52's tail, Colan understood. This was beginning to get quite difficult. 0722. Bulldog Section kept flying. 0723. 0723:30.

'SAMs coming up now,' Salim said. 'Dark Angel's manoeuvring.'

That was the understatement of the week, Colan realized. He could picture a desperate pilot yanking two hundred tons of Boeing engineering around the sky, tipping it from one wingtip to the other and back again and hoping the whole assembly didn't come apart around him. There'd been a trace of tension in Salim's deep, dark voice. 0724. 0724:20. 0724:40.

With his voice deliberately steady Salim said: 'I think Dark Angel took a SAM hit.'

CHAPTER 35

All she could do was wait. Tamasin was clutching Buster and her emotions were a whirl of confusion. Her wide eyes scoured the EVS scope but it didn't show the missiles streaking up and over at her, all she could see was a blurry smudge of smoke that might have concealed anything. Over Libya it was 0713:45. Bat Masterson was still pressing home his second bomb run and upstairs Jerry Yeaver would be jamming like a lunatic and Tamasin was trying to work out whether she cared. Partly she was terrified, she couldn't deny that. Partly she was elated because they'd already destroyed a massive part of Tariq Talal's camp and the EVS picture confirmed it. Yet the rage within her was as fierce as it had been the day Edward was killed, and she still wanted to die, was actually *ready* to die now that they'd delivered their riposte to Tariq Talal. Nevertheless it scared her, this idea of dying, scared her by its very imminence. And the worst nightmare of all hadn't left her and never would: the dread of being trapped and maimed and in agony, perhaps burnt and disfigured in an aircraft fire, before she went.

Jerry Yeaver was far too busy to think anything. And as Jerry's hands flew over the panel, launching chaff, firing infra-red flares to distract a heat-seeker, Mario Peroni was still watching the incandescent trails of the four missiles.

The first one blazed past and vanished. 0714:10.

'One gone ballistic.' Jerry's voice was cracking. 'Two gone ballistic.'

At launch, a surface-to-air missile is guided by radar or heat-seeking. When the guidance stops working the missile behaves like a projectile fired from a gun, it goes ballistic: unguided, it obeys the laws of its own residual energy and of gravity.

Chuck said: 'Fifty seconds. Forty-five seconds.'

Jerry said: 'Three . . . and four. All gone ballistic.' And *he'd* done that, he'd saved the bomber, he'd fired off the chaff that had confused the seeker heads.

Chuck said: 'Bombs gone.'

*   *   *

At the controls, Bat Masterson said nothing. Nothing was going to bring back the family of his that Tariq Talal had destroyed. Yet through his eternal sadness a bitter jubilation was growing because the blazing havoc beneath him signified the destruction of Tariq Talal. On the first run he'd seen those heroes with their little AKs firing rifle bullets at the B52. This time he had no impression of any such thing – any heroes left were running for their lives. In the smoke and haze it was hard to be positive but Chuck seemed to have got his first two sticks of bombs squarely on the accommodation and stores buildings and there was hardly a wall still standing.

0714:45. Chuck said: 'Bomb doors closed.'

In the same instant Bat realized they were going to fly directly through the smoke where it rose over the wreckage. As they punched into it and the turbulence jolted them, his vision blurred grey in the hot air boiling upwards from the fires.

0715:10. Mario was awestruck. 'Man, we blew the whole bunch to . . .'

The plastic dump went up, just behind them.

*   *   *

It was like something you only got in the middle of

a thunderhead. The shockwave slammed into the B52 and the tail kicked up and the whole big aircraft surged forward, slanting nose-down through the air, now ballooning upwards as the airspeed decreased perilously fast towards aerodynamic stall. As one, Bat and Mario hauled back the yokes. The second shockwave hit them. They'd lurched right up now to 800 feet and this time, as the pressure pattern rocked it, the bomber pitched sharply nose-up.

Bat rammed the yoke forward again. 'Mario, give us some trim!'

They must have laid that whole stick right on the dump.

Mario grabbed to his left and spun the big, old-fashioned trim wheel. Bat, the muscles standing out on his left arm as he held the yoke forward, reached right and shoved the seven surviving power levers up to the stops. Power flooded the aircraft.

The nose came down and they were level at 1,100 feet. They'd averted the stall.

Eleven hundred feet was too high. Bat hauled back the power levers and muttered, 'Two fifty, Mario, let's go.' Again Mario spun on the trim wheel and the B52 started wallowing its way down towards relative safety.

Bat's eyes met Mario's. In Mario's Bat recognized that reckless, gambler's look. Mario was excited, he was poised to make a move.

But Bat Masterson was still the aircraft captain and he couldn't believe the way things had worked out. It was 0717, their bombs had gone, the target was wiped out, and the B52 still hadn't got a scratch on it apart from that birdstrike over Yucatán. Maybe a few little bullet holes, nothing more.

They were sinking through 400 feet now and Mario was getting ready to intercept target height. Bat opened up the intercom.

'OK, crew, magnificent effort — we sure paid our respects to old Tariq Talal there! And we saved Bir al Hadh. Check in now. Co-pilot OK. Nav?'

'Check,' Tamasin said. She had a shake in her voice.

They all checked, Chuck Brantley, Jerry Yeaver, Russell Feehan.

'Nav,' Bat said, 'give me a heading.'

'Zero five zero mag,' Tamasin said. 'That line strikes the coast just east of Al Khums. It's the nearest we can find to a gap between SAM sites.' But Tamasin's eyes were full of tears now and she didn't know whether the gap in the SAM chain was the right thing for this crew to look for.

It was Chuck who'd found out about that gap.

*   *   *

Ninety nautical miles separated the camp from the exit point on the coast. Roughly seven minutes' flying left if they kept up this groundspeed — 480 knots. The attack was past, the course was set, and now the sense of anticlimax swept over Tamasin. In sheer nervous reaction the tears broke loose, unbidden, unwanted. She turned her face away from Chuck and fought the crying till it stopped.

You couldn't help thinking in terms of a future, you never could. Yet she knew there could be no future for any of them, not now, not after stealing a B52 and committing an act of war.

Bat knew how Tamasin was feeling. He got her working. 'Count us down to the coast, Tamasin, give it to us in minutes. While you're doing that, plot us a heading for the deep-water ditching zone.'

Quickly Tamasin checked the nav plot. 0717:30.

'Six minutes thirty to the coast, Bat.'

Chuck had been watching the narrow-band radar, with

272

the B52 dropping gently back down a different wadi, its walls higher than the bomber was flying, and now he gave Tamasin a sharp look, hard-eyed.

Mario said harshly into the intercom: 'Forget the deep-water DZ, navigator. You plot your heading for the following co-ordinates: Thirteen degrees, zero minutes east, thirty-five degrees forty minutes north. Navigator, copy!'

Confusion whirled in Tamasin's brain. The co-ordinates were for a spot only a few miles east of the Italian island of Lampedusa, and the waters there weren't anything like deep enough. 'Co-pilot, that's the opposite way from . . .'

'Navigator, you're talking to the ship's captain now!' Mario said. 'I'm taking over this plane.'

0718.

Chuck had grabbed his flight case but Tamasin was hardly aware of him.

Steely-voiced, Bat said: 'Crew, hear this. *I* am the captain of this flight and you'll take my orders and not anybody else's. Navigator, we'll fly a heading for the deep-water DZ, but first we'll hit the SAM gap on the coast. Work on it.'

On his console Chuck was spreading out a half-million aviation chart covering the southern central Med.

Mario snarled: 'Listen, we all had enough of this let's-die-heroes'-deaths horse shit! I have an RV set up off Lampedusa that can get us all out of this. Nav, you just gimme a heading for *my* RV!'

0718:20.

Doggedly, Tamasin said: 'Heading once we cross the coast will be zero one five mag.'

'Zero one five mag,' Bat copied.

With the chart open in front of him, Chuck said: 'Correction. That heading will be three four six.' Chuck was the man who'd been wing master navigator.

Tamasin wrenched her angry little body against the harness, lunging her head at Chuck. '*Chuck, you bastard, you keep out of this!*'

Chuck laughed in her face.

He'd been bent on surviving, too, Tamasin remembered. Desperation filled her. Now Bat had one heading and Mario had the other and there was going to be the most colossal battle for control between the pilots once they crossed the coast.

Up top, Jerry thought: Jesus, we're going to live after all; I can't handle this. Then he remembered his cyanide capsule.

0718:40.

Russell Feehan's slow voice on the intercom said: 'Two fighters off the six. Searching.'

*   *   *

Again Tamasin's stomach went hollow with fear. The feeling fought with the leap of elation in her at the thought of dying and being with Edward again. She could face him, now that she'd avenged him. If things got that far.

'Small traces,' Russell said, deadpan. 'I guess Fishbeds.'

Fishbed was the old MiG 21. Small, agile, fast; dated yet still deadly. This B52 was dated, come to that.

Bat said: 'Keep counting us down, Tamasin.' Bat sounded deadpan, too.

'Gunner,' Mario snapped, 'don't forget we have to get this plane right outa Libya whatever happens.'

Russell didn't bother to reply.

Jerry was pounding out the barrage noise, looking for the MiG 21s' frequency, desperate for a drink now he knew he deserved it, yet too busy to free a hand for the flask.

0719. Tamasin said: 'Five minutes to the coast.'

0719:10. Russell said: 'Jerry, we have radar lock.'
The MiGs had got them.

'Shit,' Jerry muttered, and went on searching. He hit the chaff trigger. Bundles of tinfoil punched off the bomber and Jerry knew the MiGs' radars would now be all over the place. He gave Russell a swift, searching look but Russell gazed grimly into his scope. Jerry wondered whether Russell was in a lot of pain but then wondered if it mattered any more.

0719:30. Russell said: 'Missile launch. Atoll, Atoll. Four of them.'

Either those pilots were really desperate, Jerry thought, or they'd had stupid orders from the ground. The Atoll was a smallish, dogfighting missile; it was radar-guided but, with that amount of chaff in the air, Jerry knew exactly what would happen.

0719:50. Jerry said: 'Went ballistic, all of 'em. Goddam fools loosed off too early.'

Chuck joked: 'Fighter control's on our side.' It was crazy, running those fighters so rigidly from the ground.

Tamasin said: 'Coast in four minutes.' She was in a permanent present, she had no future and her past didn't exist. She couldn't face the impending battle with Chuck and Mario; the Libyans were enough.

His face drawn, taut, Russell muttered: 'Sonsabitches're closing in.'

'Standing by with flares,' Jerry said. He didn't want to fire too early. He didn't really know why he was doing this, except that they wanted to crash in the sea, not on the land where any wreckage would be found. Actually, though, he realized, the adrenalin felt good.

0720:15. Russell said: 'Lead MiG is closing . . . Atoll! Second Atoll!'

Russell had them on his tail radar. It was the only way to tell: these Atolls were different, they were the ones with

275

the infra-red seekers and they'd locked on. Undaunted, Jerry fired the flares.

High over the bomber, the Atolls screamed harmlessly out to sea.

'They're gone,' Jerry said. 'And he's out of ammo.'

'But hopping mad,' Russell murmured. 'Here he comes, right in, and I guess he'll use guns.'

*   *   *

With all those scopes and switches, it was almost like a video game. The roar of the jets and the wallowing of the B52 as it rocked in the ground effect might not have existed. Differences forgotten, Bat and Mario were concentrating on holding the aircraft level and on course and roughly inside the 200–250 foot height band. It was calling for a lot of muscle power from two tired pilots. Sun sparkled on the dull, distant sea and the scrub lay dusty in the semi-desert. Mario kept glancing at the fuel gauges. Precious little left now.

As they came out of the wadi and over the flat, coastal plain Tamasin was searching ahead for the best gap in the coastal SAM chain and trying not to think about MiG 21s making a guns attack. 0721.

'Coast in three minutes!'

Pain pulsed in Russell's stomach like a knife in the gut but he kept focusing on his tail radar. It showed the two MiGs closing in line astern with the leader now six hundred yards off the six. Five hundred. Four hundred. This was a game of nerve. It was a game to see which of them could last the longest before shooting.

And Russell was perfectly happy to chicken out first because now the MiG was in easy range of the radar-guided Gatling. Russell gave it one long blast of 20mm and blew it apart.

'Shit,' Jerry breathed, in awe. Two MiGs in one day

to Russell Feehan. No bad achievement for anyone, and rather impressive for a man of sixty-two.

On the radar, as the returns from the scraps of the lead MiG dispersed, the second one's trace swerved around suddenly – one pilot shaken rigid. He banged off his infra-red Atolls, wrenched away hard, high and right, and left the missiles to it.

Jerry hit the launcher. Flares blazed into the sky and swooped away from the B52. The first Atoll curved away.

Oblivious, Tamasin in the shuddering cage below announced: 'Coast in two minutes!' It was 0722.

The second Atoll bored into Number Two engine's jet pipe and exploded.

CHAPTER 36

Libya: *that day*.

For six weeks solidly now Adem Elhaggi had been on lavatory duty. He knew all the routines backwards, he'd even stopped gagging on the smell, but he hadn't yet learnt to enjoy it.

He wore battered leather gloves and was wrapped up in denim jeans, sweaters and a scruffy old zip jacket but, with the sun hardly over the horizon at not much after seven in the morning, his unprotected ears were freezing. He'd been the first person up and about in his dormitory but the chilly morning air had swept away the last traces of sleepiness from his eyes. The others would be sitting over breakfast now. Adem hoped they'd leave some for him.

Climbing off the ancient French tractor, its engine still running in case, once stopped, it refused to restart, Adem swung the hose arm out over the malodorous sump. At the edge of his eye he could see the quarters blocks, a good couple of thousand metres away, beyond the low mound of the explosives store. Adem primed the pump a couple of times and then pulled the starter handle. He had to pull it twice more before it fired up.

He wasn't carrying weapons, not even a knife. You never did, for lavatory duty. Camp security consisted of guards at the main gate and a frequent dog patrol on the long, vulnerable perimeter. Tariq Talal's and Ali Ben Mokhtar's nightmare was a surface attack by Israeli special forces.

278

The thought of an air raid had never entered anyone's mind.

Over the chug-chug-chug of the pump motor the racing roar of many jets exploded across the desolate landscape. Mouth wide open, Adem wrenched around. It was so close. It had sprung out of nowhere.

Dawn sun dazzled him and there was nothing in the sky but then, with a suddenness that paralysed him, something huge and black with great, outstretched wings like the angel of death burst out of the wadi to the east and rose terribly against them. Dust trailed and boiled behind it in a yellow-brown blur. Adem didn't understand. Any self-respecting aircraft came at you out of the sky, it didn't leap up from under your feet. He was still scanning for the others, there must be more of them to be making this amount of din.

Tiny black objects fell from the huge black thing as it thundered at the camp, swelling terrifyingly fast in size and noise. Flower-like shapes bloomed from the black objects and slowed them down behind the massive black aircraft. They were hemispherical, khaki-coloured, and the dawn light turned them translucent, and Adem realized they looked just like the brake parachute he'd watched once on a MiG 25 landing at an air-force base. They were fascinating and beautiful but Adem still couldn't make sense of what he was seeing. He knew, as if he'd known all his life, that the huge black thing was a bomber, and he thought first, *Israeli*, then, *no, American*, then, *no, Russian*; then the horror of Dr Jabran's death came back to him and he thought, *surely not Libyan?*

By the quarters blocks, people were firing guns, yet in all the noise you couldn't hear them.

The great black aircraft was impervious, it was like some mythic monster and Adem, agape as the thing streaked over them swamping them in its thunder, sensed that only witchcraft could counter the terrible sorcery that was being wreaked now.

He couldn't take his eyes off it. It rolled into a turn and as he turned with it he clearly saw the savage sweep of the long, thin wing. He completely missed the moment when the bombs hit.

The first thing he was conscious of was pain; the shock wave that slammed him face first against the trailer had been silent. Now, asprawl on the gritty ground, his ribs hurt and all the bones of his face felt bruised and the echo still rang in his head; yet he knew instantly that if he'd been on the other side of that trailer he'd have been blown clean into the sewage pit.

Then came the explosions. Wave after wave after wave of them. With his eyes squeezed shut and the blood running from his nose over his lips Adem clapped his hands over his ears and huddled prone and terrified as the very earth rolled and heaved under him. Maybe this was some nightmare. Maybe in a minute he'd wake up.

But it had eased now. Blinking, eyes pricking, Adem lifted his spinning head.

The nightmare had changed. He wasn't in the same place any more, this landscape wasn't the one he'd last seen as he gaped at the black bomber, sweeping overhead.

Slowly it dawned on him that the reason he could see the roofs and the minaret of Bir al Hadh was that the buildings that used to block the view simply weren't there any more. The quarters blocks. All his fellow warriors. In the place where they'd been were flames and smoke; sandy earth lay in heaps where the land had lain flat. The bomber had destroyed the whole camp.

Then Adem realized he had to do something.

The pump was still working, emptying the contents of the trailer into the sewage pit. Hands trembling, Adem unhitched the tractor. Its rackety old engine was still running. Pain from the old shoulder injury stabbed into Adem as he swung up into the saddle and shoved into gear.

The thing moved maddeningly slowly.

*   *   *

Short of the remains of the quarters blocks, Adem threw the tractor into neutral and jumped off. Hardly a wall was still standing and the smell that reached him was the harshness of burning, the sharp, sour tang of explosives – and something else, something sweetish that he'd never smelt before. He ran forward, then halted. For a moment he couldn't tell where anything was any more. Or had been. Helplessness engulfed him. Then he saw that one of the shattered walls had tiles on, naked now to the eerie winter morning; and under the tiles was a sink and draining board. He knew what it was, the remains of the kitchen next to the canteen where Adem Elhaggi should have been eating his breakfast if he hadn't been on lavatory duty.

Dust haze hovered above the rubble that had been the canteen. There must have been twenty trainees under that rubble.

Shakily, Adem stumbled forward. It was difficult even to believe what he was seeing. The ground was pitted with craters and great mounds of sandy soil stood everywhere. Adem couldn't even tell where the space between the quarters blocks had been.

He stopped short. Two men lay naked on the ravaged earth.

Adem's first thought was that they must have been dressing when the bomber struck; then he saw that one still wore a sock, and he realized that the sheer force of the blast had stripped the clothes from their bodies. He didn't recognize either man. One was face down and had a raw, red socket where his left arm should have been. The other was face up with his eyes open, staring, and his lips parted and blood running from his mouth, nose and ears. Panic rose inside Adem as he realized he had no idea how to help them. Then he realized they were both dead, anyway.

In a terrifying rush of jet noise, the bomber came back.

*   *   *

The impact as Adem landed face first on the shattered soil jarred the old ache in his shoulder. He'd gone for the nearest thing resembling cover, the rim of a bomb crater, but even as the loose earth skidded under him he began wondering what sort of protection that would be against a power that could shift such quantities of soil. Smoke from a fire drifted over him and Adem lifted his head. He thought: *when I die, I'll be a martyr and I'll go to Paradise.* Yet he actually wanted to *see* the thing before it sent him to martyrdom and he gazed up, open-mouthed.

It was compelling. He couldn't take his eyes off it. It came on him from the direction of the sewage pit and he saw it clearly: the long, black fuselage; the great, swept wing; the pods under the wing that he realized were the jets; Adem even picked out the blisters in the angry nose. He couldn't remember having so much as seen pictures of a thing like this; it was extraterrestrial, it was out of science fiction. It had majesty in the powerful way it swept over him.

Some instinct told Adem the thing had dropped more bombs and he got his head down fast.

Big shudders pulsed through the earth and Adem

knew he'd been right. It was nothing to what came next.

In frightening silence the giant hand of the shockwave lifted Adem bodily clear of the ground. He was prone in mid-air with his eyes wide with incomprehension when the noise filled his whole body and all the air went from his lungs. The explosion was deep, oddly dull, and it turned suddenly, shockingly, into a sharp, savage pain in both Adem's ears. He wanted to cry out but he had no breath to do so. Earth slammed into him, the surface of the crater, and there was agony in his lungs as they collapsed, still with no air in them. He was asphyxiating. So this was what it was like to die. The pain of it was a worse humiliation than the terror.

*　　*　　*

Stuff was hitting him, falling out of the sky, some of it mushy, some of it hard. And he wasn't dead after all.

Pain stabbed in his ears and throbbed in his shoulder and ached in both lungs as they pumped and pumped and pumped. Then Adem realized what was happening. It was sandy earth raining down on him from that last and biggest explosion. And it would bury him alive if he didn't hurry.

In a desperate, scrabbling crawl, Adem struggled out of the crater. For a moment he was on all fours, then he straightened his back. He was still gulping air, even if it was full of grit and dirt and smoke.

The day had turned a dark, dingy grey. Soil was still pattering down around Adem and his clothes and his hair were covered in filth and there was sand and slime in his mouth. Tears made tracks through the dirt on his face. He thought, *I want to go home*, yet he knew that the home he'd had long ago with his parents, that was gone and that this, his new home, didn't exist any more.

He couldn't think. He was ready to die and nothing mattered any more. He caught sight of the old tractor, a few hundred feet away, lying on its side between him and the still intact homes and mosque of Bir al Hadh. It puzzled him. He could have sworn he'd left that tractor the other side of the crater.

Rising to his feet, Adem looked all round.

The bomber had gone. Where the explosives store used to be there was a roaring column of smoke and dirt boiling higher and higher into the dulled sky and the way it swelled and mushroomed made Adem wonder for a chilling instant whether the bomber had used a nuclear weapon.

If it had, though, there wouldn't even have been this little left.

He turned, blinking dirt out of his eyes. The only buildings left standing were the half-dozen houses and the mosque at Bir al Hadh, but those wouldn't have much glass left in their windows. Gusts of wind plucked at Adem's hair. It was desperately cold, he realized suddenly, and he clutched his battered arms round his aching chest. With the pain throbbing through his head, ears, shoulder, he thought of Dr Jabran. But she was no help, she was dead; Tariq Talal had had her executed. All that grit down his throat. He needed water. Talal never had hired the replacement doctor he'd promised them.

His face running with tears Adem, without knowing why, stumbled through the churned-up earth towards the old, overturned tractor.

Amid the heaps of soil, three bodies lay in his path.

Nausea churned in Adem's stomach and he forced his eyes open again, forced himself to look. They might actually be alive.

All three had been stripped partly naked in the blast. Adem crouched beside the first one. It was a man and he still had his jeans on but he was bleeding from the mouth and his right hand was a mangled, bloody stump. Maybe he'd been holding a rifle when the blast hit. Adem held the man's left wrist. A pulse still fluttered. Right, Adem would *have* to find some way of helping him.

First check the others.

The second man lay on his back in boots and undershirt, eyes closed, face peaceful, not a mark on him and stone dead. Pressure waves from the blasts could do that, Adem remembered, it could happen with artillery shells or air bombs. Trembling, he went to the third inert figure.

It was Zoheir.

Horror filled Adem. Zoheir was unconscious and there was blood matting her fine, dark hair where it tangled over her ear. Adem grabbed her wrist. For a moment he thought she had no pulse; then he found it and, as he fought to think straight, he saw that she had no more visible marks on her than the dead man beside her. The blast had left her wearing one sleeve of a shirt and the top and one leg of her jeans and yet, despite the tatters of her clothing, she retained her innate modesty. She was beautiful, too, even in this state.

'Zoheir! Zoheir! Oh, Allah, Allah . . .'

His own voice reached him thickly through the dizzy singing in his head and the ceaseless, sharp pain in both ears. Not far off, fires were crackling, and there were secondary explosions from the plastic dump. Zoheir moaned faintly, and her arm stirred. Her eyelids seemed to twitch but didn't open.

'Zoheir!'

Adem was crying, desperate to do something, not knowing what. He knelt upright, praying to God out loud, and looked all round, searching in his helplessness for a miracle.

For an unbelievable moment it looked as though God had answered his appeal. Trundling into sight cautiously amid the heaps of destruction came a Libyan regular army vehicle, on its sides the Red Crescent of the ambulance service.

*   *   *

Adem was still jumping up and down, shouting, waving his arms, when the Red Crescent ambulance pulled up a few feet short of him. The driver stayed at the wheel and kept his sunglasses on. Four men in desert-camouflage fatigues climbed warily out of the back. Two of them were carrying what looked like folding-stock Kalashnikovs but it never occurred to Adem to wonder why, he just called them over to where the casualties were lying.

'Help them, please help them!'

A broad-shouldered man, taller than Adem, with a thick, black moustache strode up. Adem knelt beside Zoheir and held her hand. Still her eyes didn't open. The man with the black moustache crouched on the other side of Zoheir and the swift, efficient way he examined her told Adem that if this man wasn't a doctor, at least he had medical knowledge. He grunted softly and turned to the man with the peaceful face. After an even briefer check he examined the man with the mangled hand. He straightened up.

'Leave this one, he's dead. See to the other two.' He spoke Arabic but the accent wasn't Libyan.

Then from the direction of Bir al Hadh, Adem heard the sound of another car engine.

He turned quickly. It was a Mercedes saloon, lurching soggily towards them over the wrecked earth. It jolted to a stop, all the glass gone from its headlamps and windows. All four doors flew open. Adem stood up. The Red Crescent team turned.

The first man out of the Mercedes was Tariq Talal.

Adem couldn't believe it, far less understand. Tariq Talal's Command Council HQ simply wasn't there any more, there were three huge craters almost overlapping one another where the building had stood. Even the cellars had gone. Talal was in his Western clothes today, designer jeans, mohair sweater, and his tangle of black hair and beard emphasized the way he looked: shaken, angry, afraid, but not really hurt. The two men with him wore fatigues and jump boots. They were the tall Arab and the squint-eyed man who'd beaten Adem up that day he'd been to Tripoli: bodyguards of Talal. The fourth person in the car was a woman. Adem had never seen her before. Like Talal, she wore Western clothes, jeans and sweater, and the weepy way she clung to Talal suggested a wife or mistress. A replacement for Zoheir, Adem thought suddenly, in the same moment realizing where they'd come from: Bir al Hadh. Talal hadn't been at his warriors' side at all. And if he hadn't chosen to replace Zoheir, maybe she'd have been the one to be safe in Bir al Hadh when the bombs hit.

'We're taking this ambulance,' Talal said. 'Get us away from here, get us somewhere safe.'

*   *   *

Impassive, the Red Crescent team stood there. Adem was open-mouthed.

'Come on,' Talal said. 'There might be another attack.' He took the woman by the arm, leading her to the ambulance.

He was in shock, Adem saw. He hadn't taken it in that some of the casualties here were still alive. 'But, my father!' Almost without realizing it, Adem had interrupted, pointing at the three bodies. 'Our brother is alive and wounded, and our sister Zoheir!'

287

'Stay out of this, you worthless whelp!' Tariq Talal said without interest, without even looking at Adem. 'Quickly, now!' He pushed the woman into the back of the ambulance.

Hands on their guns, the two bodyguards in their fatigues watched Adem warily.

He stood, agape, watching the Red Crescent team let them get away with it. The bodyguards got in the ambulance. The Red Crescent crew got in after them. The doors slammed. Inside, someone spoke to the driver. He glanced at Adem, then started reversing. And the miracle was over, the godsend had gone. The ambulance turned, then drove forward. It wove away from Adem through the craters and heaped earth.

Tears blinded Adem. He turned. He was alone again with one dead and two dying guerrillas and one of them was Zoheir. All the pain came back inside him and his ears were singing. Dizzy, he dropped on his knees and took Zoheir's hand. It was pointless. Anything he could do was pointless.

A man came limping up out of the havoc behind him. Ali Ben Mohktar.

CHAPTER 37

Thirteen hours now Captain Rebecca Laird had been in this lousy office and she'd had enough of it, yet with the action at this stage she couldn't just leave. Ten past nine at night and the sky star-studded and Julio long since gone. She hadn't thought she'd miss him.

She knew Hartmore was in his office, one of very few people right now at Davis-Monthan, and she called him, he'd told her to phone whenever there was anything.

'You called Sigonella?' There was something about the way he said that. It puzzled Becks but she couldn't put her finger on why.

'Yes, sir. The aircrews are briefing right now.'

They hung up. Loneliness encircled Becks, the artificial light oppressed her. She took out her contact lenses, mopped her eyes as they watered, then put the lenses back in. Delving in her bag, she checked the result in her make-up mirror. She went into the outer office, a single spotlight over Julio's work station, and then right out, into the corridor. She leaned on the windowsill, peering into the darkness. She needed sleep. She needed anything except to be here, waiting, waiting.

A car horn in the emptiness seemed to echo. Becks got an acute sense of the ghostliness of that aircraft graveyard, huge and silent out there under the sharp desert moon.

Headlights swept around the corner, pointed at A2, closed in to the wall, and went out.

*   *   *

Becks tensed. She couldn't see outside properly and there was hardly anyone in the building. She never kept a gun in the office and anyway her pistol scores were terrible, range practice was a thing she ducked out of whenever she could.

Van Burkart loomed into the corridor with an armful of paper bags and a wall-to-wall grin. Becks gasped.

'Van! You can't come in *here*, this is supposed to be secret!' Somehow, coming in here felt more forbidden by night than it did by day.

Stooping, beard bristling, he strode triumphantly up to her. 'I have special permission, Captain Curvaceous. Jeff Sluter's on at the guard house.'

Sluter was a major and was yet another of Van's network of contacts. Ignoring all protests, Van strode into the outer office and set down his paper bags. Becks walked in behind him.

'Van, what the hell am I gonna do if Hartmore comes over?'

Van seized her by the shoulders, swept her against his powerful body and kissed her fiercely on the lips. He straightened up, fished in his pocket, and pulled out a folded form. 'There. I am officially signed in by Major Sluter.' He released Becks and sat down at Julio's work station with the determined air of a sit-in protestor. 'Now quit worrying, Captain. Any old ape gets let in *this* far, so don't give me this Top Secret crap.'

'Well, you sure aren't going any further in.'

Van shrugged. 'Pull the blinds down, we could manage OK in here.'

Becks widened her eyes, on her face a mixture of horror and relish. 'Van, we can't . . . we can't do *that* right here in my office . . .'

Van laughed out loud and started setting things out from the bags he'd brought. He'd been to a Taco Bell. He had tacos and refried beans and a pack of Bud to soak it down. Becks sat at the spare desk in the outer office and wolfed the food Van gave her.

On a sudden thought, she grabbed the phone and called Ella at their flat. 'Hey, Ella, can you make sure Yeltsin has enough food and water?'

'Sure,' Ella said. 'I'll keep an eye on him. You're working late.'

'Mm-hm.'

Ella lowered her voice. Carefully she said: 'It'll be over by midnight. Bird can't stay in the air longer than that.'

Becks cursed under her breath. 'Is this all over the base already?'

'Wouldn't say that,' Ella replied, choosing her words. 'But up in air traffic we have noticed a certain interest in B52s. But you know us, we don't go around spreading rumours.'

'Just don't,' Becks begged her. 'This has to keep confidential.' They hung up.

Becks met Van's eyes as he chomped a bite of taco. Behind the glasses, Van's eyes held a knowing look that was a lot more intelligent than the knowing looks she so often got from the usual incumbent of that seat.

Softly Becks said: 'You know?'

'Can guess.' Van took a swallow of Bud. 'Bat and Tamasin Masterson are definitely missing.'

Becks rested her eyes on his. She turned to face front and nodded. She took out her contacts and blinked a bit. She closed her hand round the cold can of beer but then didn't lift it, she was thinking yet again about Tamasin Penhale Masterson.

From the start, Becks realized, she'd identified with Tamasin. Tamasin was like her, a woman in a largely male world, in a sense even having to prove her own competence. And Becks felt exhausted, despite that night's sleep. She wondered how much more exhausted Tamasin must be.

291

'Guess you could argue,' Van said, 'that the US itself had a duty towards its citizens to go in there and clean that terrorist base out.'

Becks had spent hours debating that one with herself. 'Depends whether you class Edward Masterson's murder, and the others, as acts of war or common crimes. We have A10 tank-buster aircraft out there – we don't send them in to take out high-crime neighbourhoods in Phoenix or LA.'

'No, 'cos you can't isolate the good guys from the bad guys. Rule One for a terrorist who wants to collect his pension is to mingle with the good guys all the time. Tariq Talal at least has the balls to stand up and show his face – that's why he has such a strong following. He's also pretty confident of the protection he gets from the Libyan authorities.'

'What that crew's done is illegal,' Becks muttered. 'Maybe immoral, too.' She brushed back a stray lock of hair.

Cynically, Van said: 'I guess that depends whether they win.'

* * *

Ten o'clock came. Probably Colan would be airborne now, Becks thought. The datalink beeped. Becks rushed into the inner office and this time Van stayed outside. The terse message was in cipher and the origin code showed Pentagon A2. Becks ran the decrypt, fingers trembling now. She went back through. She avoided Van's eyes as she sat at her desk.

'Professor, you're a civilian, I never told you a word of any of this.' She picked up the phone. She got Hartmore.

'Go 'head, Captain.' The base commander's voice was slack, its habitual rigid authority missing. He sounded tired.

292

'Pentagon A2 reports Dark Angel positively identified and flying over southern Libya.'

'Uh-huh.' Hartmore paused. 'Any idea whish way she flying?'

Sudden realization shocked Becks. She'd never seen Hartmore go near alcohol and yet that slur in the voice told its own story. 'North,' she said, and hung up quickly. She stole a glance at Van. He was watching her, fascinated. She clapped a hand over her mouth but she couldn't suppress a giggle.

Van raised his eyebrows. 'Hey, what gives?'

'Hartmore,' Becks giggled past her hand. 'He's gotten bombed! And he's the one guy on this base who never touches a drop!'

For a moment Van stared. Then he laughed out loud, his big voice booming in the lonely office.

*   *   *

Twenty minutes later the datalink broke the mood again. Again Becks dashed inside. It was Pentagon A2 once more, but it didn't carry cipher this time, just a single codeword. A word Becks had agreed on with Andrew Maule.

She was tense, biting her lip as she returned. Again she avoided Van's eyes, she simply sat down and dialled Hartmore. 'Captain Laird, sir.'

'Yeah?' Hartmore sounded bored.

'Pentagon A2 again, sir, the codeword.' She hesitated. 'Dark Angel hit the camp.'

For a moment, nothing. Becks braced herself for the explosion. She prompted him: 'Sir?'

Hartmore seemed to sigh. 'Oh well,' he said wearily, quietly. 'I guess it doesn't matter.'

Another long pause. Becks was wondering what to say to him when without explanation the phone slowly clonked down, in her ear.

CHAPTER 38

The Atoll explosion jarred through the B52 and bits flew off in a stream of fire – chunks of the jet pipe, of nacelle, piping, pump gear, shards of turbine blade. The whole aircraft swung to the left and, in her little black cell, Tamasin felt the bomber wallow and lurch and stagger. The displays blurred in front of her.

The heavy, powerful roll was hard to control and now Bat and Mario were working hard to survive a little longer.

Bat called out: 'It's Number Two!'

The inner engine in the outer port nacelle. The one they'd lost to the birdstrike was Eight, on the other side of the aircraft. Bat was using differential spoiler to damp out the roll, winding on the trim with his right hand to compensate. Mario grabbed across the mass of levers on the huge throttle quadrant, chopped back Number Two, cut the fuel feed, and then eased back power on Seven to even it out. Number One was already throttled back to balance Eight. Mario hit the fire-extinguisher button. Bat got the B52 back under control and trimmed into a steady climb. Instinct had taken over. Deep down in his mind Bat was back over Vietnam, getting a crippled BUFF back above the 2,000 foot mark so as to give the nav and radar nav some chance of survival.

This gave them the option, anyway.

Groundspeed was down around 300 knots, still decreasing. Bat asked Mario: 'How we doing?'

Mario said: 'I shut down Number Two. Fire is out.'

Fear gripped Tamasin by the stomach as she realized

what had happened. She was frozen. Then some of the stories came back to her that she'd heard from air-force pilots, how you couldn't rely on a single missile hit to down another fighter, let alone a monster this size.

The B52 was still flying.

Jerry called: 'We have SAM, *two* SAMs, uh, *three* . . . two up from port, two starboard.' It was 0722:40. Jerry opened up jamming. He punched out the chaff and flares.

Tamasin shut her eyes. This time there would be no escape. With a long, shuddering breath, she made herself relax because there was nothing to be done. She concentrated on hoping that she would die instantly.

Chuck put a hand on her knee. 'You'll be OK, beautiful.'

Her eyes were closed and she hardly minded him groping her. 'At least they won't get me alive.' Her voice through the jet noise came high, soft and shuddering, and the jet noise wasn't constant any more, it was surging, booming, fluctuating.

'Jammed out one on the port,' Jerry called. Then: 'Jammed out both on the port.'

But the two on the starboard side still had lock-on.

Grey sea filled the windscreen and the cloud rose in a great, murky bank on the far northern horizon but they hadn't reached the coast yet. Flat-roofed houses speckled the yellow-grey landscape beneath them and there were miniature trucks on tiny roads lined with little cypresses. A bus, bicycles, donkey carts. People were on their way to work but they were stopping to look into the sky and Mario didn't just know why, he could *see* why.

The two blazing missile trails were the brightest thing in the whole morning landscape, coming up from the right.

'Visual, two SAMs, two o'clock!' Mario's voice was tense, angry.

It was 0723:30 and at 3,000 feet they were practically over the beaches.

With the chunky plastic yoke hauled back into his stomach, Bat rolled the B52 violently to the right, head-on into the SAM attack. He had the wing almost vertical and the whole aircraft shuddered. If Jerry's jamming didn't break those radar locks, maybe this would. More bits were whirling off the disintegrating Number Two engine. Tamasin clutched at her console as every loose scrap of paper slid off it. Chuck was grinning down at her. Russell Feehan could have been looking down at Jerry Yeaver but he wasn't, he was focusing on his guns. Steadfastly, Jerry kept on firing off more chaff and flares.

One missile lost lock.

Jerry called: 'That's one, went ballistic!'

The second one was turning with the B52, curving, slanting over and in on the bomber.

Mario was following Bat through on the controls, lending Bat his strength to drag them round. They were on a wingtip and for a moment Mario thought they were going to go beyond vertical.

'OK,' Bat gasped, 'other way!'

Together, they rolled the yokes over and kicked out their legs for full left rudder. This was the most violent manoeuvring Bat had ever put a BUFF through. The aircraft rolled back through level and now Tamasin was looking down on Chuck as they stood on the port wingtip. Mario was wobbling his head around, heavy under the bone dome as the *g* force came down powerfully and he saw that they were crossing the coast, they were emerging over water, the place they needed to be.

Hanging on to his harness, Chuck gasped: 'Wow!' He looked up at Tamasin. Around them the B52 was shuddering. It started to tilt back slowly out of the fierce turn.

Against the *g* force, Mario pushed his head round and

up, scanning the sky overhead. The orange-white of the missile flame arced, dazzling against the hard sky, and dived down on them. Mere feet from the B52, the SAM warhead detonated.

CHAPTER 39

Grey cloudbase brushed the clear canopy on the Tornado and the greeny-grey sea surged slowly. Colan Penhale waited nervously as Salim Arshad scanned his radars.

Colan prompted: 'Yeah? *Was* it a SAM hit?'

Maybe Salim had misread his radar. Maybe a B52 could survive a SAM hit. It was 0725:30.

'Dark Angel's still flying.' Salim had a trace of puzzlement in his voice. 'Maybe I was wrong about the SAM.'

Colan had an immediate – and accurate – picture of the B52, damaged, limping out to sea with a dozen Libyan fighters after it. He drew a mental picture of Tamasin's face. He tried to guess what crew role she might have taken.

'Salim, who else is in the area?' His voice was taut.

A pause.

'Golden and Silver are off east of us,' Salim said. 'We're the closest section.'

Golden and Silver sections were F18s. With missiles, this time, not just a load of Jet A.

The seascape was murky. The cockpit was quiet around Colan and the salt spray blurred the wave tops. Colan couldn't see Salim but he got a strong sense of his crewman's presence. 0726. Colan made up his mind.

'Prickly Pear, Bulldog.'

'Go ahead, Bulldog.' Prickly Pear was the ground-based fighter controller.

'Prickly Pear, I'm requesting clearance to take Bulldog Section off station and intercept and escort Dark Angel.'

'Stand by.'

*　　*　　*

The two Tornados and two Hawks were on the edge of the Gulf of Sirte and flying east at a lazy 350 knots. Colan cupped the stick lightly in his right hand. The grip had trim controls on it. He had the Tornado nicely in balance.

'Bulldog,' the voice in the headset said, 'Prickly Pear. Cleared as requested.'

Without waiting for Colan to ask, Salim said quietly: 'Your vector is two ten magnetic.'

'Bulldog,' Colan said on the radio. 'Two one mag. Starboard turn, go!' Then he snapped the Tornado into a roll that took them well past vertical, and hauled back the stick to level out, tearing south-west. It was 0726:35.

*　　*　　*

Ten seconds elapsed.

His voice still steady, Salim read off his radar. 'Four bogeys up out of Sandbox, attempting to intercept Dark Angel. Big traces. Foxbats, they're Foxbats.' The massive, superlatively powerful MiG 25 interceptor.

Colan radioed: 'Bulldog. Dash speed, go!' They'd agreed 500 knots for dash speed. The Tornados could have doubled that if they'd used reheat but the Hawks had no reheat and they'd have been left standing. If Colan split his formation it would be because it made sense tactically.

He couldn't believe his fighters would make the intercept now, not given the speed a Foxbat could travel, overhauling Dark Angel.

0727.

Salim said almost casually, 'We've got some Soviet Fulcrums now.' The MiG 29, the one the *Kiev* carried, the one Colan had wanted a look at. Better in a scrap than a Foxbat. Colan didn't bother asking how Salim knew the traces on his scope were Soviet Fulcrums. 'Maybe eight miles short of Dark Angel. Hm. They're moving into the Libyans' six.'

Colan was trying to keep calm. Libyans *and* Russians crowding round Tamasin's aircraft.

0727:15. Salim's voice went sharp. 'The Fulcrums have locked radars on to the Foxbats! What are those crazy Russians doing?'

Colan half-turned his head. It surprised him, too, but he didn't often hear that amount of emotion in his navigator's voice.

Salim said: 'Well, that did the trick. The Foxbats have broken off.'

'What about the Fulcrums?' Colan muttered into his oxygen mask.

A pause.

Salim said: 'Also moving off. Looks as though they're recovering to the carrier.'

Bulldog Section was at 700 feet, boring in south-west. They'd been 155 nautical miles short of Dark Angel when they'd come off station, roughly eighteen minutes' flying. They were covering eight and a quarter nautical miles every minute. But the B52 was flying very slowly.

'Thirty sea miles,' Salim murmured. It was 0727:40.

If those Libyans kept off, Colan thought, they'd have done it, they'd catch Dark Angel.

Salim said: 'Foxbats moving back in on Dark Angel. Fulcrums are . . . heading out east, they're out of it.'

This was going to be touch and go after all. Deliberately Colan radioed: 'Bulldog. Nutcracker, go!'

This was the one he'd briefed them on yesterday at Sigonella.

*   *   *

Colan sheered off to the left and throttled back and then, as he levelled out, peered around in the murk. A Hawk slid up out of the grey spume and positioned itself two hundred yards off Colan's port wingtip. The pilot glanced towards him but Colan couldn't see his face. It was Pete Pretorius. Colan couldn't see the other two aircraft, nor would he. They'd gone the other way. Splitting the team this way put the big South African, as the least experienced pilot of the four, with the formation leader while McNair, not so senior a Tornado pilot as Colan, had the wily veteran Jack Baslow to back him up.

Salim had his radar in search mode. 'Two five sea miles.' It was 0728:05. From the radar it was clear that the B52 was struggling.

'Two zero sea miles.' It was 0728:35. 'One five sea miles.' 0729:05.

They came clear of cloud again. The cloud rose up in a great, grey wall behind the fighters. The sky above the sea was huge and blue and hazy and something about the morning air gave it a liquid quality, so that the sea now lay almost luminescent. Colan caught only the odd white cap now but as yet no spindrift. Liquid as that sea looked, though, hitting it at jet speeds would be like hitting concrete.

0729:30.

'They've found Dark Angel again,' Salim said. He paused. 'One zero sea miles.'

Something went tight in Colan's throat and now he didn't see how the hell they could make it in time.

CHAPTER 40

Even above the jet noise Tamasin heard the missile explode. It was like a very close thunderclap. In the B52's steep, shuddering lefthand turn she was looking down terrified on Chuck. The aircraft jolted savagely and shuddered harder and she knew what was coming next. Stall then spin. Something hit her right ankle, the thud of a blow, a stinging pain, blood wet in her boot. Things were crashing and rattling and a ferocious, icy draught sprang out of nowhere and tore all around them so that the maps and papers leaped and flew in the air. Tamasin was petrified, frozen into her ejector seat. Maybe it had been a missile, maybe an engine had exploded. Either way, this was what you went through just before the crash. She wondered whether she'd still be alive when they smashed into the sea and whether she'd drown.

Then under her the aircraft rolled level and pitched slowly nose down. She couldn't believe it, they were back under control.

Her watch showed 0725.

Bat's voice came on the intercom. 'Crew, check in. Nav?' His voice sounded strained.

'OK,' Tamasin managed. The idea of imminent death scared her. She wasn't going to cry, she bloody well *wasn't* going to.

'Radar?'

'Why, hi,' Chuck said, 'things sure are fine down here!'

Tamasin's ankle was hurting dully. Bat said: 'EWO?'

In a choking voice, Jerry said: 'I'm OK but Russell's

302

dead, Russell's dead!' It shook Tamasin to realize that Jerry was crying.

Bat said: 'Mario's dead, too. Jerry, you stay at your post, but I'm gonna need some help from Tamasin and Chuck. C'm'on up right now, you two.'

Tamasin yanked off her oxygen and radio leads. She grabbed for the seat harness twist-release.

With fear in his voice for the first time, Chuck objected. 'Hey, Bat, why don't we just eject?'

Tamasin ducked out of her seat, stocky, tough, agile. She could guess Bat's answer. They were too close to the coast and the Libyans would get them. In any case, they were below 2,000 feet and if Chuck tried to go on his own and leave the rest of them to it he'd smash himself apart when he hit the sea. The wallowing was setting in again, worse than before. Icy wind stormed gale force into Tamasin's teeth as she poked her head through the hatch and her ankle was hurting fiercely, something had definitely hit it. Then as Tamasin levered herself with her elbows up into the tempest inside the cabin, she smelled something burning.

*   *   *

Jerry didn't look at her. His eyes were wide behind his glasses, straining at his scopes, and the harsh, stubbled lines of his face had tears running down them. In the wind, Tamasin could hardly breathe, and the shrieking filled her brain. With the decking rolling under her she crawled out of the hatch, her bone dome heavy, the disconnected oxygen mask swinging at her throat. The bright colour splashed across the opposite side of the cabin was blood, she realized, Russell's blood, but it was the thin smoke filling the cabin and the blue sparking from the cables on the cabin ceiling that jammed the breath in her throat. All over the cabin there were shrapnel holes and the wind was ripping and screeching through them. The air up here was freezing in savage jets that drove the air out of her body. Tamasin realized Bat was bringing down the speed so as to reduce airflow through the shrapnel holes, but with the aircraft in this state he wasn't going to risk getting too close to the stall. Tamasin forced herself upright against the wind, her sturdy body hunched under the ceiling, and yanked the survival knife off her boot. It crossed her mind that she might be inviting an electric shock, or that she might be destroying something vital, but she had to stop that fire. The cables were hot where she grabbed them but not hot like a casserole fresh out of the oven and she grasped them just long enough to saw through them with the knife blade. She was gulping air.

The sparking stopped. Chuck materialized at her shoulder. Tamasin turned to glance at him and in doing so she glimpsed Russell, slumped over the gun controls, and her stomach turned over. A chunk of missile had almost severed his neck, and his head hung askew in the red-spattered bone dome. The horror of it was the blood, still pumping. Tears welled up in Tamasin's eyes but she had no time to weep and Russell was beyond help, anyway. Through the icy maelstrom of air she fought her way forward, Chuck's portly body crouching behind her. She stooped to Bat's shoulder.

He flicked his eyes at her but he kept his face forward. He was ashen, grey. Tamasin had never seen a person's face that colour. This was a man she loved. The colour of Bat's face made the blood look redder where it spattered his cheek. He had more blood soaking into his flying suit, on his shoulder, on his chest, on his leg. Blood lay in bright spatters all over the pale grey engine console. Mario's eyes were open, staring sightlessly into the gale and there was blood all down his chin, flooding from his mouth. He had wounds on the throat and chest, Tamasin realized, horrible wounds. Even his crucifix ran bright red. Like Russell, he must have died instantly. Horror filled Tamasin at the sheer quantity of blood everywhere and she wished now she'd never got herself into this savage male world. Yet this was the very sacrifice she'd *wanted* to make for so long, for Edward's sake. She forced herself to overcome the revulsion and the disbelief, fight down the physical nausea surging in her stomach.

'Get Mario outa there!' Bat's voice was grim and strained and Tamasin knew his grating shout through the wind noise had cost him heavily in strength. 'Tamasin, you gotta take over!'

*   *   *

In all the tearing shrieking she could scarcely catch even that desperate yell, yet she understood; yet nevertheless she didn't know where to start. It was hard enough to get *oneself* into a B52 pilot's seat, over those big trim wheels and all the engine levers.

Jerry's radar was working intermittently, which was better than not at all. It told him there was a single fighter in the wide six, looking for them, close to finding them. Jerry didn't know what ECM he still had working but he hadn't time for systems checks. He yelled Bat a warning. Bat didn't answer. Jerry yelled again and this time twisted to peer round over his shoulder.

Bat had his hands full controlling what was left of the B52.

Chuck shoved Tamasin out of the way and reached out for Mario. That suited Tamasin. His face grim, Chuck

305

fumbled for the release on Mario's harness and wrenched. He was leaning over the throttle quadrant and the position was all but impossible. Bat reached under Chuck to hold the power levers in case they got knocked. Chuck took hold of Mario under the armpits and grunted. Blood was all over him.

'C'm'on, hey, Tam! Lend a hand!' Chuck's yell was angry.

Tamasin hardly heard him but the meaning was clear. Jammed against the cabin wall, she half hooked herself over Mario's seat back, her hips brushing against Chuck's body. She caught Mario's right armpit. Chuck hauled. Tamasin twisted and bent and then as the B52 lurched under them, Tamasin held Mario under the thighs to keep him from catching the power levers or the trims. It amazed her how powerful Chuck was.

Between them they got Mario over the console. His blood was everywhere – slippery sticky on their hands, wet on their flying overalls. Chuck was sweating and swearing and cursing and Tamasin knew it was at her; she hadn't been helping nearly enough. They set Mario down on his back beside the cabin wall. Tamasin was trying not to look. Bat was swearing and cursing at Tamasin, too, his face like blotting paper as he struggled with the controls. The B52 was wallowing its way slowly down towards the top of the Med.

Forcing herself, Tamasin pushed through the blasting air to clamber over the console and into the co-pilot's seat. She had to sit down in Mario's blood, pools of it. She clipped up her oxygen mask and plugged in the lead, then she could breathe again. She plugged in the intercom and then strapped on the seat harness. She adjusted the rudder pedals for reach and then looked fearfully to her left, at her father-in-law.

In the intercom he said, 'Take it, Tamasin.'

Blood spots stood sprayed across the horizontal situation indicator and the attitude-director indicator. They'd even gone across the inside of the windscreen. Tamasin took a firm grip on the yoke and moved it left as the B52 wallowed right. Again she caught Bat's eye.

'I have control.'

* * *

In utter relief, Bat slumped back in his seat with his eyes half shut. Now Tamasin was flying the B52.

Chuck didn't have a quibble with that decision.

Tamasin ran her eyes over the panel. All the instruments seemed to be working. The speed was down to 180 knots and with all these draughts they weren't going to be flying any faster. The B52 kept trying to roll and it was taking all Tamasin's time simply holding that great wing level. Jerry was on the intercom and he sounded panicky.

'Bat, do you copy? Bat, we have two Foxbats closing in, I can't jam their radar out any more.'

'Just do what you can, Tamasin,' Bat muttered.

Into her mask, Tamasin said, 'OK, Jerry, I have the aircraft – we'll manoeuvre if we have to!' For the first time she noticed the fuel emergency lights on the panel. They were almost all on. This aircraft was running on fumes.

Chuck understood. He turned and stumbled aft, got Russell's harness loose, and dumped the man's body out of his seat. They'd all respected this man, maybe loved him, but right now reverence was misplaced. Chuck strapped into the gunner's seat and plugged in the intercom.

'OK, Tam, Jerry, I have the guns.'

CHAPTER 41

In the dimly lit A2 office at Davis-Monthan, Becks met Van's eyes. His were round and curious behind the glasses. Hers were troubled.

Van murmured: 'What's he say?' He meant Hartmore.

Becks fixed him with a look. 'Said it didn't matter. I don't understand . . .'

Of course it mattered. Hartmore knew it mattered. He was the one who'd called it a national disaster, he was the one whose career was most at stake for letting the thing get off the ground in the first place.

He was the non-drinker who was now legless drunk.

'I don't like this,' Becks muttered. And they both thought of that Colt .45 Hartmore wore on his hip.

Van stood up briskly. 'Off station, Captain.' He pulled out his car keys.

*   *   *

Exhaustion washed over Jerry Yeaver and he knew they were going to die any minute but that didn't matter so long as he could just sleep. He was too tired even to bother about the sharp, tearing, smarting pain in his left shoulder, or the blood he could feel sticky on his back. The B52 lurched under him and on the scope the two Libyan MiG 25 Foxbats were in the bomber's six, still searching with their radars. Doggedly, Jerry kept trying to jam them out but now he was starting to suspect that his ECM gear might have antenna damage.

*   *   *

308

The lefthand Tornado and Hawk were up to 1,000 feet to match the Foxbats' height and bearing in on them now at 500 knots as they approached. The distant sky was clear, feathery blue and with the sea swelling green and powerful under him Colan Penhale could sense the rush of movement even at this height.

Salim said: 'I'm picking up a MiG 21 singleton, edge of the scope, southerly, out at eight o'clock.'

'Sandbox or Ivan?' Colan said.

'Sandbox.'

'Rog,' Colan said. Then: 'Foxbats, two ten o'clock.'

Salim's attack radar was already on.

The Foxbat pilots had their radars on, too. They saw two bogeys coming at them from oblique port and another two from oblique starboard, closing at a phenomenal speed. The two Libyans had drilled in what to do in a head-on pass or a pursuit attack, but they'd never seen a nutcracker before.

Colan Penhale had.

Sun gleamed on McNair's canopy coming head-on at them a touch over their height so as not to collide at the point of the crossover and it gleamed again on Baslow's; you could hardly see the fighters for the cloud of condensation in the high-subsonic shockwave pattern. Then Colan and Salim had overshot them with a closing speed of 1,000 knots and Pretorius yanked left and peeled away hard from Colan's wing.

'Bulldog Four.' The clipped Afrikaner vowels rang clear on radio. 'Pursuit climb.'

Baslow's relaxed Yorkshire voice said: 'Bulldog Three.' Baslow was doing the same as Pretorius. The two MiG 25 pilots, shaken rigid, were pointing radar noses at the stratosphere and standing on their reheat flames.

Colan rolled the Tornado half-inverted and yanked it round on a wingtip into a climbing turn as viciously tight as a Tornado would go. His bone dome became a massive weight and he strained to keep his head above his shoulders. Briefly both crews lost vision. Then as the gravity unloaded and the Tornado climbed, Salim came fast out of the grey-out and focused swimming eyes on his scopes. Two big traces, two little traces. That made it easy. The small ones were the Hawks, the big ones the Foxbats.

Colan locked up the first MiG on the radar, the Tornado starting to close. The fight was going very fast, the way it will at jet speeds.

'Bulldog One, tallyho.'

Almost at once there was Andrew McNair's deep, Glaswegian growl on the radio. 'Bulldog Two. Come and gerrit, Jimmie.' He'd locked up the second MiG.

The MiGs were going up almost vertically in full radar illumination and in an obvious state of panic because they should have split up and turned by now. Yet, as Colan knew, with the Tornado climbing as hard as the MiGs, any turn now would bring them back inside missile range of the Hawks, prowling the cloud top below. Suckered, a real beaut. Distant against the dazzle now, Colan saw the bright pale red diamonds of the MiGs' reheat plumes.

They winged over. It should have been suicide. They were at 24,000 feet and from the near-vertical climb the MiGs dropped into a near-vertical dive.

'Bulldog One,' Colan murmured, 'let's press this one home.' He chopped back the throttles, hauled the stick right back, kicked the rudder and hauled nose-to-nose at the MiGs as they plunged back past him.

Salim's body went weightless, then the g shoved him into his seat. Then the straps were holding him against his ejector seat and he stared straight down as the Tornado headed for the sea. The lead Foxbat swung, corkscrewing in the reckless dive as if its pilot thought he could get away from that radar. Colan kept on down. This was the point at which, a quarter-hour or so earlier, the Soviet navy had broken off its attack.

Colan decided to show that the RAF was more tenacious.

* * *

Slow pain wrenched raw at Jerry's shoulder and gradually he was finding it harder to ignore. In the noise all round him he could feel the B52 reeling, staggering, but that was just a part of what little remained of his life. It amazed him that the two Foxbats had broken off. He'd thought they would definitely destroy the bomber. He was scanning the wavebands, partly out of routine, partly out of idle curiosity. He was now getting English voice off one of the frequencies and slowly through his exhaustion it dawned on him that there was something odd about it.

Holding the B52 as steady as she could in the slow descent, tail high and wallowing, Tamasin could just see Bat Masterson, struggling with his pain. Her ankle was hurting. Maybe they really should try for Italy or Sicily after all, maybe they should force-land there. On the ADI there was still the heading they wanted for deep-water ditching.

Jerry realized what he was listening to. This was *English* English. On the intercom he said in amazement: 'Hey . . . the British are here!'

Tamasin's heart leaped.

* * *

Deceleration forced Colan against his harness as the dive brakes took effect. He glimpsed McNair, out to his right, and then in astonishment saw a silver flash as the canopy shot off the trailing MiG. The chunky black

311

shape that sailed horizontally out after it was the pilot, in his ejector seat.

Colan just glimpsed the pilot separating from his seat, then he was down and past and, an instant later, the lead MiG appeared in plan view against the steely sea. Colan hauled the Tornado out of the dive. Gravity rammed him down in the seat and his vision greyed.

Inside his helmet McNair said: 'Was that mine or yours?'

Maybe the man had lost control of his MiG. Maybe he'd got tired of waiting for a missile launch. Hardly a stupid move, Colan thought, to get out before he got blown to bits. The surviving MiG, tiny on the horizon, bent around and headed south.

'Colan, we don't want to get over Sandbox,' Salim warned.

Dead right they didn't. 'Bulldog, break off,' Colan said, and pulled away high and left. His head and arms felt heavy in the climbing turn. These days they put the ejector seat handle between the pilot's legs because, with all that g, you couldn't guarantee being able to reach up for an overhead handle. Colan levelled out. On radio he said: 'All Bulldog aircraft, re-form three zero.' That meant the height: 3,000 feet.

Colan craned around, searching the sky. He couldn't see any other aircraft.

'They're all here on radar,' Salim said.

'What about Dark Angel?'

'Got it.'

'Give me a vector.'

'One zero two mag,' Salim said. They'd shifted well to the west of the B52. 'Colan, that Fishbed single-ton's still around, I've got him closing now on Dark Angel.'

*   *   *

312

The MiG 21 Fishbed was on Jerry's scope and gaining. With his shoulder hurting Jerry said tautly: 'I can't jam him out any more.'

'Got him locked,' Chuck Brantley said, beside Jerry at Russell's old place at the guns. 'Tail radar seems to be working OK.'

'Don't shoot too soon.'

Chuck ignored him, he hit the trigger on the 20mm Gatling. On his scope Jerry saw the small MiG yank away to the right and then swing back in. Again Chuck fired, again the MiG swerved just in time. For the third time the MiG 21 lined up in the B52's six and now there was the warning tone as the fighter's radar found lock. Hardly breathing, Jerry hit the flare launcher but there was no sign of anything happening.

The MiG fired two heat-seeking Atolls and broke off as Chuck fired again and missed. On the radar Jerry saw the whole thing.

*   *   *

Three thousand feet over the Med Colan glimpsed the twinkle of McNair's canopy, the Tornado a quarter of a mile to the left and barely visible.

'Fishbed singleton's broken off its attack,' Salim said.

A soft, grey shape came arrowing out of the dazzle and took up position forty yards off Colan's left wingtip. Sun flashed off Pretorius's face mask and Colan could picture the big grin on the big Hawk pilot's face. Colan still couldn't see Baslow's Hawk, but Baslow was like that.

They closed on the B52.

*   *   *

Sheer terror gripped Tamasin as she waited for the Atolls to hit and she just sat there with her hands full of B52.

313

The huge double thump was like a sonic bang except they felt it rather than heard it. The yoke wrenched in her hands and the big bomber tried to roll out of control. Bat woke up and grabbed his yoke, helping Tamasin get the thing back, and now the fire lights came on in engines Five and Six; both the ones in the inner pod, starboard side.

And now suddenly Tamasin was far too busy to panic.

Voice strained, Bat said, 'I have the wing.'

'Rog.' Tamasin left Bat fighting the yoke and grabbed across to the left to the power controls. The same vicious draughts were still knifing through the cockpit and the blood splashes were drying dark on the quadrant. Tamasin pulled back the Five and Six power levers, both together, her right hand still on the yoke in case Bat's grip weakened. She shut off the fuel. She hit the fire-extinguisher buttons.

'OK, Bat, I have it.'

'You have it.'

The draughts were like spears of ice and the cabin was chaos. Blood was all over the panel, splashing in the footwell. Horrific visions spread through Tamasin's mind. If she failed to hold it on one of these rolls, they'd spin in. Or that weakened wing would disintegrate. She leaned forward and craned out to the right, looking aft. Red flame glowed in the Five and Six intakes. Maybe the whole wing would catch fire.

She swung round to Bat. Their eyes met.

'We'll never make Italy now,' Tamasin said. 'We can't try ejecting, either, it's not sensible. I'm going to ditch.'

'Go ahead,' Bat gasped.

No-one had *ever* tried to ditch a B52 before.

Chuck came on the intercom, furious. 'Hey, we're still flying, aren't we? Let's *keep* flying! We gotta make it for Italy!'

314

Wearily, Jerry said, 'It was never in the deal that anything much mattered once we hit the target.'

'Well, *I* sure as hell matter!' Chuck snarled at him. 'And I'm getting outa this!'

Chuck still hadn't given up his determination to survive, Tamasin realized as she fought to damp the rolls. It dawned on her dimly that there was something that Chuck knew that no-one else did. She was too busy controlling to pay much attention, controlling the aircraft, controlling her terror, controlling that pain in her ankle.

'None of us matters,' Jerry said. 'We did it, that's all.'

Chuck said: 'That's your business, if you want to die! I don't!'

Jerry did want to die, Tamasin sensed, even now; and she had a vital realization that it was wrong that he should do so. She was even starting to sense that she herself would rather live. The cockpit smelled acrid with smoke and the freezing winds knifed through it and the aircraft was so hard to hold and the rudder pedals were slippery with Mario's blood. Yet within Tamasin the life instinct itself had come into play and it was impelling her, even now, to keep the bomber flying and not simply give up and let it crash.

'We slaughtered Tariq Talal, Chuck,' Jerry said. His voice on the intercom was strangled, the way it had been when he told them about Russell. 'But we did it in a stolen jet! We don't have anything to live for any more – even *you* don't!'

'Quitters can die, but I'm no quitter,' Chuck sneered. 'You go ahead and die, but don't try and make me die with you!'

Tamasin looked left, pleading. '*Bat* . . .'

But Bat Masterson was too far gone now to stop these two from quarrelling.

* * *

315

It was there, a black smudge low over the greeny-grey sea under the overcast and flying slowly. On the radio Colan said: 'Prickly Pear, Bulldog.'

'Go ahead, Bulldog.'

'Visual on Dark Angel. Bulldog.'

The fighters closed quickly on the bomber. The B52 was at 800 feet, sinking steadily, evidently under some sort of control but rolling and yawing visibly. Colan's face hardened as he brought the Tornado closer, out to the right. The smudge the bomber was leaving was a hazy, oily trail of smoke, and now Colan could actually see fire, in both the engines in the inner starboard pod. He held the Tornado a moment on the right behind the B52 and then rolled in under the six barrels of the 20mm Gatling, still twitching menacingly, the sting in the tail. Pretorius slid his Hawk across with Colan. McNair and Baslow were higher and a good way back, wary in case whoever was on that tail gun mistook them for MiGs. Now as Colan brought the Tornado alongside the B52's nose he could see the damage to the cabin. No question, people in there were hurt. He closed a little more, searching for a look at the pilots.

The captain, in the lefthand seat, was lolling back against his ejector seat. He didn't seem to be taking much interest. The co-pilot, on the right beyond the captain, craned forward suddenly over the yoke and peered out at Colan. The way their eyes met, across the distance, reminded Colan of the remote way he would get eye contact with Soviet crewmen when he intercepted them up over the Faeroes Gap.

In their bone domes and oxygen masks, neither pilot recognized the other.

CHAPTER 42

Desert night laid chilly hands on Captain Rebecca Laird's face as she swung down into the Porsche. Van snapped on the ignition and the engine rasped off the dark walls. Van wrenched out of the parking slot in a blaze of headlights.

'Which way?'

'Right,' Becks told him. Van accelerated hard in low gear. 'Easy,' Becks called over the noise, 'it's really close!' Then: 'Here, here!'

Van yanked in beside the base commander's Cadillac.

Becks flung off her seatbelt. 'Wait here. He'll go ape if he catches a civilian in the command block.' She gave Van a look so fierce he knew she meant it.

A single light was visible on the first floor. The porch was bright-lit, harsh. The sentry was fully six foot six, black and helmeted. He had an M16 but Becks would have risked a bet that it wasn't loaded. The sentry barred her way.

'Sorry, ma'am, I can't let you in. General Hartmore's working late and he's left orders not to be disturbed.'

'Well, I'm working with him and I have to see him right now.'

'Sorry, ma'am, I have orders . . .'

'Have you any idea who I am or what you're talking about?' She stepped right up to him, shoulders back, elbows bent, aggressive. Even drawn up to her full six foot, her nose only came to his chin. The flush spreading across her face was as much embarrassment as it was anger, but she was going to have her way. 'I'm head of

A2 on this base and I have an urgent and highly sensitive communication that I can't trust to a phone line. Much as I'd like to bust your ass off this air base, I won't get the chance if you don't let me through because General Hartmore will do it for me!'

'Ma'am . . .'

She just walked round him. Then she was at the stairs, and she ran.

She half-expected to find Hartmore's door locked, but it wasn't. She didn't rush in, that might have startled him, she just opened the door gently and slipped inside.

Hartmore was lounging in his swivel chair. The whiskey bottle on the desk in front of him was down to its last inch. Becks couldn't believe the state Hartmore was in. His uniform jacket hung open, his collar was unbuttoned, his tie knotted halfway down his chest. He'd ripped every single medal ribbon off his uniform front and scattered them across his desk. His face was mottled red. He looked slowly towards Becks, his eyes dull, unfocused.

The Colt wasn't on his belt, it was in his hand, and now as he raised it he seemed unsure whether to point it at his own head or at Becks.

*   *   *

Guard was the international military emergency channel, 243.0 megaHertz, and with his Tornado just ahead of the B52's wing Colan used it.

'B52, this is Bulldog One, hi.'

The voice in his headset seemed to almost spit at him. 'Piss off, Poodle One, and let me get this thing down in one piece!' It was a strangled voice, high – a woman's voice. Tamasin's voice. He couldn't believe it.

'Tamzie! That's no way to talk to your brother!'

Silence. Colan looked right. Tamasin craned forward again and looked left. Even now they were too far apart to recognize each other. Colan couldn't see the tears spilling suddenly down over Tamasin's cheeks and over her oxygen mask.

How she managed to fly the thing she could never tell. She was blinking ferociously just to see out.

'Collie . . . this thing's a terrible handful, I can barely hold it!' Her voice had gone higher.

'Tamzie, we're getting rescue choppers out to you.' It was impossible not to identify with her in her struggle, impossible not to feel the wrenching tension in the gut or to run through in his mind all the hazards she faced.

'What good's that going to do?' On the radio her voice was a wail of protest. 'They'll just put us all in jail till we rot.'

Colan said: 'Have you got casualties on board?'

'Two dead, one wounded.' She didn't know about Jerry even now, he hadn't felt it worth mentioning. She didn't bother counting her own wound, either.

They were down to 400 feet. The spoilers kept coming in and out on the B52's long, thin wing as Tamasin fought to correct the rolling. She was struggling now to nail the right approach speed, struggling to get the nose up on an aircraft that would rather fly nose-low, to get it into the proper tail-down attitude for ditching. The monster had a mind of its own. Trimming down alongside Tamasin, Colan remembered that at light weights, like now, a B52 could be almost uncontrollable even with all eight engines working.

Tamasin reached to the left for the flap lever and then dithered. If those flaps were damaged, if even one bit of them failed to come down, they'd flip upside down and crash nose-first. There was no way to tell from the state the panel was in. Not worth the risk.

She'd never tried a flapless landing in a B52 before.

On the radio the E2C AWACS came on. 'Bulldog,

Trapper. Big formation of Sandbox fighters approaching you on zero eight four and closing.'

Colan thought: *that's all I need.* 'Bulldog. Rog, Trapper. Tamzie, what's your intention?'

'I'm going to ditch.' Her voice was strained as she fought the yoke, all alone. 'We're running on fumes as it is. Just tell me, are my Five and Six engines still burning? Oh, Collie . . .'

'Stand by, Tamzie.' A touch of back pressure on the stick and Colan was looking over the curve of the long, dark fuselage, twisting to peer back. Salim was peering back, too. 'Affirmative,' Colan said, 'they are, but it doesn't look as if it's spreading.'

The radio opened again. 'Bulldog, Prickly Pear. Golden and Silver approaching you in support.'

Those F18 sections from the *Kennedy.* 'Bulldog.'

Inside the bomber, with no view out, just the smell from the burning all round him and the icy, razor-sharp winds, Jerry Yeaver was exhausted but tense, and instinctively aware that Chuck was poised to make a move. What kind of move, Jerry couldn't guess.

Colan radioed: 'Good luck, Tamzie, I'll be with you all the way.' He was off the bomber's nose again, back on the left.

'Good old Collie,' Tamasin said, her voice tortured. Then she had another massive yaw-and-roll to fight as the B52 sank through 200 feet and the speed stayed roughly around 140 knots.

One hundred and fifty feet. Tamasin peered out at the wave tops, Colan's Tornado a hard, grey presence at the edge of her vision, the B52 wallowing around. Her arms felt done for; every time her foot slipped on the rudder she saw Mario again, those eyes. One hundred feet. Get the aircraft parallel with the wave tops, she remembered, go in tail down and nose high.

She could see the surge of the swell, but there weren't enough white caps to tell her which way the waves lay. Even so, catch a wingtip on a wave crest and she'd ground-loop. The high wing would give her a good chance, but when she went in the aircraft would float on the wing and that would put the cabin under water. Fifty feet. She wanted to shut the throttles but if she took one hand off the yoke the bloody thing would roll and catch a tip. No-one had *ever* ditched a B52 before. Maybe it couldn't be done. Greeny-grey waves surged and the overcast was high, looming and cold. Colan's ghostly presence haunted the edge of her vision.

The hell with this. Tamasin hauled back one-handed on the yoke, her right biceps bulging under the flying suit. The nose came up and the speed bled off past 135 knots — inside limiting speed for the drag chute. With her left hand she grabbed for the lever: *deploy.* As the massive parachute billowed astern and the deceleration pushed her against her shoulder straps she grabbed to her left and shut off the surviving power levers.

She felt weightlessness as two hundred tons of Boeing engineering sank the last few feet to the sea. And then *slam, slam, slam.*

The massive jolt jarred her so hard into her harness that both shoulders got friction burns and the huge, long *boom* echoed in the empty bomb bay and in fleeting jubilation she knew she'd got it right, she'd come down rear fuselage first. Then the whole vision vanished in a wall of white spray and chilling water jetting in the shrapnel holes everywhere, drenching her, and the chunky, blood-slippery yoke finally yanked itself right out of her hands as the aircraft jarred and rocked and shuddered around her. She hadn't expected such a violent deceleration.

It surprised her a lot, as they stopped moving forward, to realize the B52 had stayed in one piece.

*   *   *

That surprised Colan, too. He was high, left and aft of the bomber and he saw the spray burst out as the rear fuselage touched, and then pour back in a huge, spreading, creamy V; and it shook him, the ferocious way the water braked the massive aircraft. Colan watched in fascination as the four engine pods each trailed a separate V and thick, grey steam poured out from the fierce heat of the jets, like an old-fashioned locomotive. Behind the aircraft the drag chute filled with water and collapsed.

Then the Tornado and the Hawk had overshot the ditched bomber and were curving round tightly to return to it.

'Bulldog,' the radio said, 'Trapper. Sandbox fighters closing, speed four forty knots, range one six miles.'

From that range, they could launch missiles.

*   *   *

'Bulldog Two from One,' Colan radioed. 'Take Three and Four, climb clear, fly top cover while I orbit.' For a moment, Colan searched his mind, wondering whether this was pointless heroics. It wasn't – this way, Colan could act as decoy while the other three bounced the Libyans.

'Bulldog Two,' the throaty Glaswegian voice said. You always acknowledged.

Pretorius pulled his Hawk away and vanished, climbing steeply. Colan hadn't even seen McNair and Baslow. He peered down as he circled the B52.

The hulk was settling. Three hatches on the top of the cabin had come open, one forward, two aft: the co-pilot, gunner and EWO stations.

322

Salim muttered into his mike in a show of impatience. *We've got Libyan fighters coming at us, Flight Lieutenant Penhale.*

Colan steepened the turn, peering, worrying. *What the hell's happening down there?* Still no-one out.

'Bulldog, Trapper,' the radio said. 'Sandbox fighters one zero.'

'Bulldog.' Colan was getting anxious, impatient. With all those holes in, the B52 couldn't keep floating for much longer. The Tornado cockpit was cool but Colan was sticky under his flying kit.

Vivid yellow, a life raft appeared out of the port aft hatch – the gunner's.

Salim said in his cool, dark voice, 'Colan, we're getting attack radar off two Foxbats.'

'Rog,' Colan said. Foxbats couldn't dogfight, although Allah only knew what the Libyans might try to do with them. Gazing down, Colan saw a single figure wearing olive climb out of the gunner's hatch.

'Colan, there's six of them now.' Salim's voice was urgent. 'We'll have to break.'

The life raft inflated. The single figure climbed into it. Just one. No-one else climbing out. *God,* Colan thought, *they all bought it when they hit.* The raft with the single person in it floated away from the sinking bomber.

Through his teeth Salim told Colan: 'Bloody well break *now*!'

CHAPTER 43

Libya, just after the raid.

Where Ali Ben Mokhtar had been when the bombs went off was anyone's guess. Straightening his back as he knelt with Zoheir's hand in his, Adem Elhaggi gazed up at the older man. Ben Mokhtar's clothes were blackened, dirty, tattered; his face was bloodied, as were his head and one arm; and something about his left eye looked wrong. Yet despite the haggard air, Adem could see Ben Mokhtar was bent on survival.

'Ah, Adem, Adem. They're all dead, then, all except us.'

'No, these two are alive!' Desperately, Adem gestured. 'Tariq Talal . . .' Tears flooded his face again, he could hardly get the words out. 'There was an ambulance, but . . . but Tariq Talal *took* it!'

Wry, battered, Ben Mokhtar's world-weary face didn't change. Wordlessly, he limped to the Mercedes that had carried Talal. It still stood with all four doors open, the glass gone from its windows and headlamps. Ben Mokhtar peered in the lefthand side a moment, then slid behind the wheel. Adem jerked up his head as he heard the engine start, wondering what was happening; but Ben Mokhtar cut the engine at once and levered himself stiffly out of the car again.

'Come, Adem.'

Ben Mokhtar knelt. Grunting as much in pain as in exertion, he lifted Zoheir's shoulders. Adem took her knees. They lifted her up and manoeuvred her into the back of the Mercedes. Her head lolled and her eyes didn't open, but at least she kept breathing. Adem returned with Ben Mokhtar to fetch the guerrilla with the mangled hand. He didn't open his eyes, either, as the two of them lifted him into the back of the car beside Zoheir.

Wearily, Ben Mokhtar shut the car's rear doors. 'There's a hospital in Mizdah. You'd better drive.'

Mizdah was less than a dozen miles away. Adem glanced at Ben Mokhtar. He was holding his arm. They got into the car, Adem at the wheel. Adem poked with his foot for the clutch pedal and for a moment thought it had been blown off in the blast.

'It's automatic,' Ben Mokhtar said. 'Start it up, put it in drive, and it'll go.'

It did.

* * *

In the jolting interior of the Red Crescent ambulance, Tariq Talal on the sideways-facing seat was stooped and cramped, his great bulk awkward, clumsy in the confinement. Seven people were crowded into the small space: Talal, the woman, the two bodyguards, the Red Crescent leader and his two aides with their cut-down weapons. Talal craned his neck but then realized he couldn't see out. He turned, angry and aggressive.

'Where are we going?'

The ambulance turned, bumped once, and then ran straight and smoothly. They'd reached asphalt.

'We're going to a place of safety,' the Red Crescent leader said softly. 'As you requested.'

Talal glanced at him. There was something about his accent. It wasn't Libyan. He was a big man, sleepy-eyed, his fit, muscular body bursting out of his fatigues, his moustache thick and black but neatly trimmed in a manner that suggested efficiency. Talal glanced at the other two Red Crescent men. They had their heads together, eyes warily covering their passengers, and they were muttering together in an undertone against the background engine noise.

Whatever language they spoke, it wasn't Arabic. For the first time Talal took a proper look at the weapons the men were carrying and wondered, also for the first time, what Red Crescent men were doing carrying guns in the first place.

The guns weren't ordinary AK47s. They were the cut-down MPiK 47, as specially adapted for the East German National People's Army in the 1960s when the Cold War had very nearly turned hot. That wasn't the sort of weapon you saw very often in Libya and Tariq Talal didn't like it.

Alarmed, Talal turned to his bodyguards. 'Brothers, draw . . .'

The two Red Crescent men shot one bodyguard each and the noise swamped Talal's voice. They hadn't meant to do it this early, but if it had to be, then too bad. They used a burst each, eight to ten shots that left no room for doubt about the outcome. They'd loaded hollow-point rounds with reduced charge and muzzle velocity and the result was as intended: the bullets all lodged in their targets' bodies, not one went through and hit the vehicle. What they hadn't done was to fit silencers and the noise, in that cramped space, was enough to cave your skull in.

Talal gaped, eyes bulging, mind uncomprehending. The woman screamed, the effect soundless as in some nightmare. She grabbed Talal's arm at the very moment that he recovered enough to grab for his pistol.

Lifeless, the bodyguards had slumped into each other. They were toppling forward but hadn't yet hit the floor. Blood had gone everywhere and some of it was still spraying, bright pink.

Both the Red Crescent men shot Talal. This time the

bursts were briefer but the results were assured just the same.

Talal's eyes bulged further, his look of astonishment growing. He jolted back in his seat and his head cracked into the metal behind him. He jolted several more times as more bullets hit. Then there was blood spilling from his mouth and his eyes no longer focused.

The woman was screaming continuously, her face stretched taut with terror.

The Red Crescent leader, the big man with the moustache, had an old French 9mm automatic and he lifted it, one hand cupping the other, even though at that range you could hardly miss. Clinically and dispassionately, he put a single shot between the woman's eyes. She died instantly.

The two men with the East German machine pistols glanced at their leader. They couldn't hear a thing and nor could he; ideally, they should have had ear protectors; but the men saw the leader's lips move, his face still sardonic, businesslike.

'Sorry, madam, but it had to be. You just kept the wrong company.' The words were in Russian.

There was blood everywhere, all over the inside of the ambulance, on their clothes, on their guns, all over the ejected bullet cases on the floor. The sharp reek of firing flooded the vehicle. Turning to one side, the leader slid back the communications panel, put his face to it, and called out a codeword. He saw the driver nod in acknowledgement, then the ambulance was accelerating.

Half an hour later they were at a deserted construction project that hadn't been worked on since the money ran out. It stood beside an irrigation canal that wasn't in use yet. The moment the ambulance stopped, the three men piled out through the back doors. The driver emerged a fraction later.

The leader knew where the cement mixer had been

parked, because he'd parked it there. He ran to it and started it up.

The driver ran round to the back of the ambulance. He helped the two gunmen lift out the bodies. There was sacking – they knew where that was, too – and they rolled the bleeding bodies up in it. Close to where they'd halted, building work had begun for a sluice on the canal, and they took the bodies down the bank and laid them side by side in the foundations.

There was ample cement now but they had to ferry it over in wheelbarrows. It took about a quarter of an hour; then Tariq Talal and his two bodyguards and his woman were shoring up the base of the sluice. With them the leader placed the sophisticated, miniaturized ground-to-air radio they'd been using. It had served its purpose now; it had picked up the signals from the Mainstay AWACS flights that had told the squad exactly where the B52 had been, and when. Consequently they'd known precisely how far to stand off when the bombs hit, and when it had been safe to get in to make sure of Tariq Talal. By burying the radio they would remove any risk of its falling into Libyan hands.

They laid out the concrete, flat and tidy like the rest of the works. Then the killers were back aboard the ambulance and moving fast.

Ten minutes down the road, they halted. The landscape was deserted and the roadside ditch was quite deep. The driver got out and steered the ambulance from outside, the engine still running. The other three pushed. When the ambulance crashed over into the ditch, it fell on its side but its engine still kept running. The two with the machine pistols stood by the roadside in their blood-soaked fatigues and kept watch. The leader and the driver lifted the petrol cans they'd unclipped from the sides of the ambulance before pushing it in the ditch. Amusement lingered on the leader's lips as he thought back to the shambolic state of security at the Libyan army depot where they'd stolen the ambulance so easily two days before. He'd be surprised if that disorganized bunch of Bedouin had missed the vehicle even now. He took the rear end and the driver took the engine end and they tipped petrol all over the ambulance and then the leader lit it. It caught with a *whoomp*, fiercely enough to make them both jump back. They tossed the cans into the flames. Inside the cans, the remaining fumes caught, and fire spouted from the filler tubes; one can burst open.

For a moment, the team stood back. Quite soon the fire would die down. Then the remains would be just another rolled and burned vehicle and people would mutter *mash' Allah* as they drove past it and hope it didn't happen to them. You saw all too many rolled and burned vehicles on Libyan country roads.

The leader turned, to make his low voice heard over the fiery roar. 'Let's go.'

Their pace was that of a brisk jog. All these men were super-fit. Ten steady minutes brought them across scrub and then through olive groves and over rough ground to an abandoned, lonely farm.

A helicopter was settling on its oleos. They were forty seconds late. The helicopter was in desert camouflage and you couldn't see its military markings properly. It was a Mil Mi 24, NATO codename Hind, not a type commonly seen aboard Soviet aircraft carriers but that was its destination.

This was luxury, a chopper ride back, compared with the gruelling overland slog these men had endured on their way into Libya five days before.

The four killers scrambled on board. The leader was last. He was still on his feet, ducking in the cabin, and the air loadmaster still slamming and securing the door, as the Hind lifted off. The leader dropped into a canvas seat. He didn't bother with the harness, he just braced himself as beneath him the metal flooring tilted and tipped, then settled into the nose-down attitude of helicopter fast cruise. He looked round, one hand reaching questioningly.

Someone passed him an intercom headset.

He plugged in. He knew this aircraft, he knew where the sockets were. He called the captain. 'Any worries about radar or local air force getting interested?'

'No,' the captain said. 'Radar and the air force are all after that B52.'

His voice came over the cabin speakers and the killers all laughed heartily. The loadmaster strapped back into his seat, looking the men over, impressed despite himself. He'd trained enough times with the Spetsnaz – special forces – but this was the first time he'd been with them on an active operation.

*　　*　　*

Wind rushed icily through the empty windscreen on Tariq Talal's Mercedes and Adem's fingers grew numb as he drove. Ben Mokhtar twisted round to look at Zoheir and the wounded man. The two unconscious bodies were bouncing a bit as the car moved and Adem hated that but there was no way to help it.

'Who were they?' he said suddenly. 'The ones who attacked us?'

Wryly, Ben Mokhtar said: 'It was an American B52.'

Just as suddenly, rage filled Adem, boiling up within his chest as if it might explode out of his head. 'Those sons of Satan! Those murderers! Why do these whoremongering sons of dogs come here, slaughtering and maiming in a country whose affairs don't concern them?'

'What do you expect?' Ben Mokhtar snapped. In his voice rang the sharpness of anger, and Adem glanced at him with alarm and without understanding. Their eyes met. 'Listen, Adem,' Ben Mokhtar said, 'what do you think *we've* all been training and planning to do? Slaughter and maim Americans, that's what. Do you really suppose we're the only ones who hold such ideas?' He sighed, hanging his head as he shook it wearily. 'Anyway, it never mattered who they might have been. Our group has killed many people and made many enemies. Violence begets violence, Adem. Murder begets murder.'

They were passing the first low, shabby houses of Mizdah. Again Adem glanced in surprise at Ben Mokhtar. Of all the people to have used the words of a woman Tariq Talal had had shot for spying, Adem hadn't expected it to be Ben Mokhtar. For a moment he saw Dr Jabran in his mind's eye. It amazed him to realize Ben Mokhtar actually seemed to be endorsing Dr Jabran's appeal to common sense to avert violence.

'That was what Dr Jabran said,' Adem murmured slowly. Telephone poles lined the street and there were thin stray cats slinking out of their way, then Adem found the direction sign, *Hospital*. Ben Mokhtar said nothing and Adem glanced at him again. 'My brother, why was she killed?'

Ben Mokhtar seemed too weary to reply.

Adem slowed for the left turn. He crossed the opposite lane, the only traffic a bus in the distance. 'Was Tariq Talal planning something to do with *Libyan* politics? A coup? Is that why the national government was spying on us?'

Ben Mokhtar sighed. 'A woman friend of Tariq Talal's was pregnant,' he said. 'Dr Jabran refused to abort her.'

They were at the hospital. Adem pulled in by a sign that said *Casualty*.

CHAPTER 44

No point break-turning when a hard turn would do. Colan hauled back the stick and stood the Tornado on its port wingtip. The g-suits inflated with a wham. He'd been on the north-to-south leg of his orbit and the MiGs were coming full-tilt from the south, so that put Colan's belly towards them and left him blind and he half-rolled on to the starboard tip to watch for them. They would go for him because if they went for Dark Angel instead they knew Colan would have them. In any case they couldn't have been getting much radar return from Dark Angel with just the tail sticking out of the water.

Colan had endangered his aircraft now, he'd done everything in the book that fighter pilots weren't supposed to do.

Salim said: 'Two Acrids launched.' He was punching out chaff.

'We don't psych that easy,' Colan muttered. The MiG that had fired wasn't yet visible and the shot was outside the missile's parameters, it was just meant to shake them. Colan virtually knew what was going to happen. Coming at them at this speed, the MiGs had far too much energy and they couldn't bleed it off with a high yo-yo or they'd be into cloud and out of sight, nor with a low yo-yo, or they'd be into Davey Jones's locker.

He held the Tornado in its level turn to the south.

Both MiGs came into sight, closing at a colossal speed, and Colan rammed on full reheat to catch them and the hell with the fuel burn. The MiG pilots saw Colan an instant later because their poky little cockpit canopies

332

didn't give them anything like the view Colan and Salim had, and they both bent into a level right turn, desperately striving to kill speed.

What they saw was the slippery grey shape of the Tornado hard-turning into them, and that meant danger.

The lead MiG zoom-climbed and vanished instantly through the cloud. The wingman was a fatal fraction slower.

'*Lock*!' Salim yelled with the MiG trapped square on the radar. This time they'd been fired on first and, as the trailing MiG pulled up for the cloud, Colan yelled, '*Fox One!*' and hit Sky Flash release.

The Sky Flash leaped off its rail and snapped straight upwards after the MiG.

On the radio, McNair's voice, then Pretorius's, taut, crisp. Above the cloud four MiGs were coming in and McNair's men had bounced them. Colan had the stick back. A deep, rich American voice announced:

'Golden One – you guys leave some for us, OK?'

US Navy to the rescue. Colan punched through the thin cloud layer and burst out into the blinding sunscape. A black oily cloud trailing its shadow over the cloud top was all that was left of the Libyan wingman.

His leader was a speck on the horizon.

The dogfight was to the left of Colan and as he half-rolled inverted and climbed to make sense of it he realized what the Libyan fighter controller had done: he'd served up his MiGs on toast to the RAF. He'd wanted top cover for the low duo at 2,000 feet, which was fair enough until you realized he'd sent desert-camouflaged jets slap over a blinding white cloud background and the RAF had been up in the sun. Old-style Russian methods; you needed ground control's permission just to fart. Gazing down on the dogfight, Colan knew no-one was even shooting yet. He radioed.

'Bulldog aircraft, we're under fire, now we can get the retaliation in!'

He thought he could see what had happened. There were four big MiG 25 Foxbats and McNair's bounce had split the formation neatly in two. Now Baslow and Pretorius in the Hawks were engaging one Foxbat each but McNair had the other two to contend with and potentially the Tornado was in trouble. The encounter had turned into a looping and rolling contest. It was a knife fight in a telephone box, and any old Tornado hand will say that's one of the things you don't do in a Tornado; even over Iraq they hadn't planned much on this sort of stunt. But Colan knew damn well it was one of the things you didn't do in a Foxbat, either. There was only one snag. They'd been at it for the best part of a minute and the RAF hadn't started shooting. Suddenly the Libyans realized they'd been ordered not to.

A fighter pilot doesn't go into a dogfight defensive, not if he wants to collect his pension. McNair's men had started with every advantage they needed, but now the Libyans had the psychological edge.

Colan saw it as McNair's two gave up trying to get away from the Tornado and instead went after the Hawks. He was just too far out of it to do more than yell a warning.

The nimble Hawks were flying angles tactics. The Foxbats were saving themselves with brute energy. Baslow was tight in behind the Foxbat he'd engaged; he was angling for lock. Pretorius was too far out.

McNair's two Foxbats came in on Pretorius from his eight o'clock and he turned hard into them – he had to – and they'd cut him out. Baslow saw it from higher up and he'd almost got position for a boresight missile shot but he left it. He broke off and dived down after the two hunting Pretorius. Colan pulled through his loop hard enough to inflate the g-suits again and aimed at the MiG Baslow

334

had left but he was still too far out. McNair in the other Tornado was closer and he locked up one of Pretorius's two on radar just as the other Foxbat launched an Acrid at Pretorius. The missile looked practically as big as the Hawk it was fired at.

Pretorius broke, in a vicious, rolling turn.

Both Foxbats turned with him and McNair knew that if the first missile didn't hit, the second Libyan would destroy Pretorius. He growled: '*Fox One!*' and launched a Sky Flash.

Baslow was slanting in fast.

The Acrid exploded in a yellow white blaze and Baslow vanished but then reappeared. Then McNair's Sky Flash hit the second Foxbat below on the rear fuselage. Pretorius still had the Hawk in a six-*g* turn but he was running out of energy and Colan was after Baslow's original MiG, slipping away now from its formation, and he glimpsed it in the edge of his vision as flame blazed from McNair's target.

He'd thought the thing would blow up altogether. It didn't, it stayed in one piece and trailed orange flame, rolled over and curved towards the cloud. The canopy flew off as the pilot punched out. Then it was down through the cloud and gone.

Baslow curved around in a shallow-banked level turn, thin brown smoke streaming from his Hawk. Chunks of casing from the Acrid had hit him all over and now he had an injured navigator.

'Bulldog Three. Think I'll bugger off now.'

'Roger, Bulldog Three,' Colan said. You always acknowledged.

He wanted to send Pretorius with Baslow but there were other things on his mind. He was still too far out from the Foxbat he'd been trying to hit and now it was going after McNair.

'*Bulldog Two, your three-nine line!*'

Three o'clock was directly right of a pilot, nine o'clock was left, but only so long as the jet was flying level. By the time you'd radioed, the guy you were warning might be upside down.

'Bulldog Two.'

And by the time McNair acknowledged, he *was* upside down, in a break turn that bled the Tornado's energy perilously fast. All three surviving Foxbats were still in this fight and now the one that had fired the Acrid looped over and came down to block McNair as he strove to get away from the other two. Colan rolled beyond vertical, going nose-to-nose for the one that had looped.

'Padlock that bastard, Salim.' *Keep an eye.* That Libyan was a damn good pilot.

'Will do,' Salim said, imperturbable. But it was easier said than done.

McNair flashed across Colan's nose and an instant later so did one of the Foxbats and Colan took the gun snapshot. '*Fox Three!*' The big 27mm Mauser blazed briefly but the burst missed; that didn't matter, he'd rattled the Libyan pilot. The MiG broke off its attack on McNair.

'Bulldog Four,' Colan radioed. 'Get after Three and fly escort.'

The MiG Colan had fired at rolled back in, looking for McNair again.

'Bulldog Four,' Pretorius's clipped voice said. 'Rog.'

The one Colan was after was easing down towards the cloud top, building up speed in a shallow-banked turn. Colan was off its eight in a lead turn, nose off the Foxbat's tail and he was closing, concentrating on getting into Sky Flash parameters. But this Libyan was the crafty one and it was Salim, keeping constant lookout as a good nav should, who saw what the Libyan had done.

'Bogey in your eight, high!'

The Libyan had trailed Colan across the front of one of

his mates who was after McNair and now he'd abandoned McNair and come after Colan. *Where the hell was the US Navy?* Colan rammed the throttles back through the reheat gates and stormed up at the MiG as the one he'd been after started to pull back up.

McNair snapped his Tornado through vertical with Sewell-Baillie rubbernecking like a maniac and McNair got lock on the one attacking Colan as the MiG and the Tornado slashed past each other, nose to nose.

The Glaswegian growl went: 'Fox One.' The Sky Flash leaped off its rail, out from the flat belly of the Tornado.

Colan had his head screwed right round over the ejector seat and the Tornado standing on a wingtip as the MiG rolled fast belly up to him and twisted away hard, diving. As the whole scene slid away from Colan in the parallax of fast fighting he saw the Sky Flash turn with the MiG, harder than the MiG could wrench away. It hit. The MiG was diving, nose almost vertical, into the cloud and Colan saw the bright blaze of the distant explosion and then there were shapeless black bits showering away and down and vanishing. Colan was rolling back the other way now, hauling back up towards the sun. He glimpsed McNair's Tornado. That would be worth a case of champagne, but maybe McNair owed him one, too. Inside the Tornado cockpit it was still uncannily quiet. You didn't hear the bangs, you never felt the force of the explosions. As long as it was other people exploding.

'Salim, can you see them?'

There should still have been two MiGs around.

'I can see one bugging out.' He was twisting his head all around.

Still heading into sun, Colan barrel-rolled briskly about the axis of his climb. Still they saw nothing.

'Bulldog, you mean sonsabitches,' the American voice said. 'You sure cleaned up on them.'

Again Colan and Salim rubbernecked, but they couldn't see Golden Section's F18s. If they couldn't, probably the Libyans couldn't either. Salim switched to search mode on the radar. He got four traces, he ran an IFF check, to tell friend from foe electronically.

'It's them. They're flying top cover.'

Thank heaven for that. Colan radioed: 'Bulldog Two, escort Three and Four and recover.' As McNair acknowledged, Colan glanced anxiously at his fuel readouts and then called the E2C spotter. 'Trapper, this is Bulldog One requesting tanker romeo victor.' RV was code for rendezvous. 'You'll have to find me, I can't go looking for you.' He cut off.

'Steer one one seven for Dark Angel,' Salim said. He'd read Colan's thoughts.

'Rog.'

Colan closed the throttles and held the stick warily as the Tornado sank into the cloud top. He was searching, eyes keen, as the fighter broke through over the steely, heaving Mediterranean.

It was closer than he'd expected.

*　　*　　*

It was the cropped, stubby tail that caught Colan's eye, still sticking up from the sea surface. Even when you knew what to look for, the thing wasn't easy to find. It was barely afloat, on the empty tanks in that great, savagely swept wing, black amid the blackish-greenish swell of the sea, and the single life raft bobbed, drifting further away, 300 yards clear of the bomber now. One life raft, one survivor.

Sharply, Salim said: 'Break right, bogey in the six!'

Angry, alarmed, Colan stood the Tornado on its starboard wingtip. He tried to look out through the top of the canopy but he couldn't raise his head for the gravity.

'It's a Fishbed,' Salim said. MiG 21. A good dogfighter, like the Hawk.

Colan saw it.

It wasn't interested in Colan's Tornado. A hundred feet over the wave tops, it was tearing in with the high-subsonic condensation clouding its tiny delta wing. Too late, Colan realized what it was after and in desperation he rolled the Tornado after the MiG 21. He saw the whole thing. The bright blaze of the cannon, flame flickering, and the white threads of water ripping up around the life raft. Then as Colan yanked the Tornado savagely into the MiG's deep six, the life raft just wasn't there any more.

In the shock, Colan for a moment couldn't believe it. Under his face mask his lips were parted.

That had been murder, that hadn't been a kill in battle. In all probability it was Colan's sister who'd been murdered.

CHAPTER 45

Around Jerry Yeaver the B52 was rolling, surging, completely unlike the motion of flight. They were down. Tamasin had actually done it, ditched them in the sea. Jerry just didn't know what happened next.

On his right, Chuck Brantley moved fast, yanking off his harness. 'Let's get outa here, right now!' He jettisoned the hatch over his head. Jerry realized Chuck was terrified that the bomber was going to sink straight away.

Silence was singing in Jerry's ears. He wanted a drink. All his life, it seemed, he'd been longing just to hear silence.

Chuck was out of his seat and past Jerry's, scrambling down the ladder. The life raft stowage was on that second level. Jerry twisted his harness release, undid his helmet strap and with huge relief dumped the bone dome on the console. Chuck had vanished. Jerry levered himself out of his seat. He was weary, he was stiff, he could hardly move. This silence; he loved it.

'Tamasin! Hey, let's go!'

She was slumped over the yoke with her shoulders smarting savagely from the friction burns and the same singing in her ears as in Jerry's. Through it, thickly, she could hear water lapping. She could see the light slap of the waves shooting spray up against the blood-spattered windscreen. Her ankle hurt. She looked at Bat.

His eyes were half-closed and he didn't look at her. His harsh face was that of an old man, chalky, haggard, lined. He had his hand up to his chest and his flying suit was covered in blood and Tamasin knew he was badly hurt.

Her instinct was to get him out, get him to safety.

She jettisoned her hatch. Somehow she was aware that Chuck and Jerry had jettisoned theirs and that she ought to do the same. She yanked off her bone dome and dumped it in the footwell and pulled off her harness and then clambered out, over the throttle quadrant. She hadn't had time to worry that the B52 might sink. Her shoulders were hurting but that didn't matter. She leaned close to Bat and his eyes flickered open. She unfastened his harness.

'Bat . . .'

Jerry was there, at her shoulder. The decking was slick with pools of water.

'You did good,' Bat said. His voice was a throaty whisper. 'Real good, Tamasin.'

'Help me, Jerry,' she begged.

Jerry clambered right on to the throttle quadrant. It didn't matter what happened to those levers now. He put his arms around Bat. Bat had taken a bad hit on his right thigh, Tamasin realized, as well as on his chest. He was losing blood fast.

'You guys don't worry about me,' Bat said nonchalantly. 'I'm going where I'm gonna go.'

'We want to be with you, Bat,' Tamasin pleaded. 'You've got us all this way.'

Jerry lifted Bat bodily. He did it as gently as he could, but the pain still got through to Bat and he grunted, his face twisted. For an instant, in his mind's eye, Jerry saw the face of that KC135 captain. *Es ist besser, auszubrennen.* But he wasn't going to burn up now, he would have to rely on Chuck's cyanide. Lapping sounds of water made Tamasin realize they *were* sinking, but only slowly so far. She took Bat's weight from Jerry. She was guiding Bat. Pain got to Jerry, the pain where that missile fragment had hit him in the back of the shoulder, and he gasped aloud. Tamasin supported Bat

341

and manoeuvred him out on to the decking. They were trampling on Russell and Mario but they couldn't help that.

A life raft package flopped out of the hatch and on to the decking. Chuck scrambled out of the hatch after it and crouched down to look it over. He said, 'Shit,' shoved the life raft aside and vanished down the hatch again.

Tamasin was holding Bat. 'We won't leave you, Bat!'

Wincing in pain, Jerry eased himself out of his cramped position on the throttles. His boot splashed in shallow water. He couldn't get aft because Tamasin and Bat blocked his way and he didn't want to step on Mario. Tamasin could feel the B52 growing heavy as it settled in the sea. She could hear the water pouring in below. They hadn't much time.

A wave broke over the cabin. Icy water splashed in and the floor swayed under them.

Chuck threw the second life raft on to the deck and scrambled up after it.

It dawned on Tamasin that something was wrong with the first life raft, but she was too busy with Bat to bother. 'Help me, Jerry.' Between them they got Bat into a sitting position on the decking. They kept bumping a heel or an ankle into Mario but there was nothing else for it. Bat's breathing was getting throaty.

Chuck picked up the life raft, trod carelessly on Russell, and propped the raft on the gunner's console.

Jerry turned. 'Hold the raft, Chuck. I'll get Bat and Tam out.' Then he saw it, and he broke off, open-mouthed.

Chuck was wearing a Mae West. *None* of them had carried Mae Wests. The Mae West had the latest radio locator fixed to it and Jerry knew instantly that Chuck was expecting rescue. He had friends out there.

Chuck grinned. 'You're staying here, Jerry Yeaver, you're going down with the ship. Thought that was what you wanted.' He chuckled. Then from the thigh pocket of his flying suit he pulled a Smith & Wesson Bodyguard .38. Double action, two-inch barrel, five shots.

It was like being at the runway intersection at Eielson again, watching in disbelief as the KC135 crashed on takeoff. And then knowing exactly what you had to do.

Jerry jumped him.

Chuck fired in alarm and missed and then fired again and hit Jerry. The big .38 slug caught Jerry a glancing blow under the ribs and spun him around; he floundered against the cabin side, a man too big for that small space. Tamasin twisted her head round, over her shoulder, too shocked to scream.

As Jerry slumped on top of Mario, head up, indignation on his face, Chuck fired a third round at Jerry and missed. Then he shot Tamasin.

He hit her once, then his fifth shot smashed into the instrument panel. Tamasin cried out, anger and protest and pain in her voice, and collapsed on top of Bat even as she strove to support him.

Jerry shoved himself upright and rose to a crouch.

When the bullet had hit him it had been like a wham from a hammer but now there was only dull pain and raw smarting and Jerry didn't know how bad it was and didn't care so long as he could keep moving. Suddenly he had work to do – dying could keep. He was eyeball to eyeball with Chuck and there was fear in Chuck's eyes and no lead left in his gun. Just as close on the other side, Tamasin was in pain and squirming, moaning, fighting for breath, and now Jerry knew his priorities.

'Asshole!' he told Chuck, almost carelessly, and crouched quickly by Tamasin's side.

Bat was stirring, trying to help, but Tamasin's weight pinned him down. The entry wound on Tamasin's flying suit was red-rimmed. The bullet had entered her shoulder, roughly at the join with her left arm: Chuck had shot her in the back. Jerry took her by her right shoulder and under

343

her left ribs and lifted her clear. Pain kept stabbing in his side but that didn't matter. As Jerry turned Tamasin on to her back he saw the exit wound, a messy gash in the pectoral muscle, at the front of the armpit, just over her breast. She was conscious and her eyes met Jerry's.

'Jerry . . . oh, help Bat, I can't help him any more . . .'

In Jerry's mind now everything was different. They needed him.

Quickly he looked over his shoulder. Chuck had gone and with him that second life raft. Jerry saw the big rip in the other raft that could only have been made by a missile fragment. The sea swelled and the decking surged under them. The cabin was full of kerosene fumes from what remained in the tanks and now, mixed with it, was the tang of shooting and the sour smell of blood.

The B52 was sinking beneath them.

CHAPTER 46

Professional piloting is one thing, personal feelings are another, and Colan Penhale knew damn well they weren't to be mixed. But this was different, this was murder. Anger took over and he didn't care.

He had the Tornado at 300 feet over the greeny-grey swell, just in sight of the MiG 21 Fishbed that had destroyed the raft, and he selected Sidewinder instead of Sky Flash and banged in full reheat. Power walloped him in the back. Very rapidly he closed the gap with the MiG.

Salim was clearing the six and knew better than to interrupt.

The MiG snapped into a tight turn left and climbed steeply. Colan turned with it and then the MiG pilot realized he'd got the RAF in his deep six but by then Colan was getting the growl in his headset. Infra-red lock for the Sidewinder.

They punched into cloud but Salim had the MiG on radar and then the Sidewinder lost lock. Screw that, though, this was one Colan meant to settle with the 27mm Mauser. This was personal. They punched out the top of the cloud. The MiG snap-rolled right and, barely a thousand yards behind, Colan snapped the Tornado beyond vertical after it, with the g-suits thumping inflated and the singing in his head. Then he saw his quarry yank left and so yanked left in turn after the MiG: a tiny vicious hard shape, brown and yellow against the silvery white cloud, with its sharp pointed delta wing and its long snout. If the MiG kept this up there was a theoretical

345

chance it might actually get away but not with Colan in this mood. Rolling right, rolling left, 600 yards and closing, and Colan got Sidewinder lock again and this time held it.

But the time for the Sidewinder was if the little swine got back outside guns range. This was personal.

And there's no kill like a guns kill.

Corkscrewing fast, the MiG drilled down in a shallow curve through the cloud and Colan corkscrewed angrily down with it and they broke through the cloudbase. Visual again. Three hundred yards and the MiG hauled left, wings vertical, black between the grey of the cloud and the grey of the sea, and at two hundred yards Colan kept with it. One hundred and fifty. He got the MiG's wingtips in his gunsight. *Fox One* was the call when you fired a Sky Flash, *Fox Three* when you fired the gun, and Colan called that now. And jammed down the gun button.

Both aircraft were turning hard, but the MiG was rolling.

In grim satisfaction Colan saw the bullet strikes, right down the MiG's fuselage. Its nose dropped below the horizon. It went on rolling and there wasn't any smoke as the nose dropped right down and it hit the sea and disintegrated. It didn't make one splash, it made dozens of them.

Salim checked radar rapidly in case anyone was after them. No-one was.

'Uh-oh. Now we're in deep shit.' They'd destroyed the MiG without having been under attack.

Colan just said: 'Find us Dark Angel.'

Salim scrutinized his scopes. Colan waited. He'd levelled out of the turn, he was flying south slowly and now, as he waited for Salim to find the B52, his stomach went taut.

'It's not there,' Salim said tonelessly.

'The co-ordinates, then!' It took a lot to get Colan angry with his navigator.

'Maintain heading,' Salim said. 'OK, orbit around here.'

Salim was good, he'd impressed Colan yet again. As Colan eased into the turn and looked down, he could see the big oil stain on the water, could see the bright orange drag chute still floating, and now a long plank of dark metal that looked like half a B52's wing. It was starting to sink.

The flush of rage had gone. Now Colan felt cold and old, bitter with frustration.

Salim said sharply: 'Three o'clock low!'

Colan racked the Tornado hard over into a steep righthand turn and craned down to see what Salim had found.

*   *   *

Nothing in all that Hartmore had done to Becks, nothing of the humiliation or the antagonism towards women that he'd shown towards her – none of that prevented her from feeling immensely sorry for the man. Yet this was dangerous. That sentry's M16 might not have had bullets in it, but Hartmore's Colt .45 certainly had.

Softly, Becks closed the door behind her. 'Gus,' she said. She moistened her lips. She'd never dared to use the base commander's first name to him before.

The gun wavered in his hand. A fully loaded M1911A1 weighs well over a kilo.

'Do be careful, Gus,' Becks said. She judged the distance between her and the gun as about fifteen feet. This was a talking job, not a jumping job. Meanwhile, Becks was well inside lethal range.

Hartmore raised his head. He glanced at her but avoided her eye. 'I am going to shoot myself.' He spoke slowly, taking care with his pronunciation the way a person does when very drunk.

'No, Gus, please. You don't want to do that. Nobody wants you to do that. I certainly don't.'

'What is there for me any more?' His voice shook. It shocked Becks to realize he'd been crying. She'd thought he was one of those who couldn't.

'Oh, Gus – you've been all on your own.' This wasn't hamming. She meant this much sympathy.

'Doesn't matter,' Hartmore slurred, and let his hand fall with the weight of the gun in it. 'I lost a BUFF. I lost a bomb load. I let those assholes get outa here and start a war. Best if I just blow myself away right now.' A tear crept out of each eye.

'It won't come to that. Really.' Daringly, Becks took a pace away from the door. Hartmore glanced at her and his gun hand twitched, and Becks halted. She said: 'Don't you know it was *meant* to happen?'

He jerked her a look. His face screwed up. '*Meant* to happen? What're you talking about?'

She took a second pace towards the desk. Ten feet to go. 'Those two carriers, out in the Med. *You* know, Gus.'

'*Kennedy* and *Kiev*. Sure.' He sounded very slurred but he was listening.

'*Kennedy* moved off station today at 0720 zulu. *Kiev* left station *three quarters of an hour* earlier! And those Russians knew where to go. Those guys knew about Dark Angel before we did. There won't be any war, Gus. Those Russians wanted Tariq Talal taken out.'

Hartmore stared at her. 'I don't unnerstand.'

'Gus, I don't think any of us does, yet.' Another pace forward. Her face, her whole lean body was pleading. 'Gus, please, won't you put the gun down? You're all right, really you are.'

'They played a trick on us.' Despair shivered in his voice. 'It's still all my fault.' His gun hand swung loosely.

348

'No, Gus.' Becks bit her lip, nerving herself. She was six feet from the Colt but Hartmore cherished that gun, it was like an extension of himself. Touch it and she'd be threatening his masculinity.

So she ignored the Colt altogether. She just walked right round it, right up to where Hartmore sprawled in his chair in the tatters of his uniform, and dropped on her knees beside him, her body hunched over, so he wouldn't have to look up to her. She rested her left arm on his thigh, her eyes big and round as she gazed at him. He was still holding the gun.

'Even if you'd known about the whole Dark Angel conspiracy and you'd let it go ahead, you'd'a done the right thing.' Lightly, she stroked his thigh. 'The worst thing you coulda done woulda been to stop Dark Angel. But you didn't. You're all right, Gus.'

His lips trembled. 'You really think that?' His voice was a whisper.

'I *know* it.'

Again his lips quivered. Becks reached up and put her arms round him, she put her head on his shoulder. 'Stay with us, Gus.' Hartmore didn't reply. But in a moment Becks felt a hot tear land on her neck and she felt rather than heard the dull thud as he released the big Colt.

CHAPTER 47

Water was lapping audibly in the second level and the raw salt smell washed round them. Jerry Yeaver knew they didn't have long.

He told Bat crisply: 'I'm getting Tamasin out that hatch and then I'm getting you out. Then I'll see if there's anything I can do.'

Bat's voice was weak but it still had steel in it. 'Jerry, the syrettes.'

Jerry had almost forgotten the syrettes. Morphine ampoules, all the crew carried two each. Jerry fished out one of his own. There wasn't time to unfasten clothing, he simply injected Tamasin through the fabric of the flying suit, into the upper thigh. In a moment, the tension that twisted her face eased off.

'Thanks, Jerry . . .' Her voice was a whisper.

He got his arm round her shoulders. She was still losing blood. He lifted her, and her soft grunt told him the morphine hadn't altogether killed the pain. He got her across to the gunner's console, still running with blood. Pain tore at him as he lifted her on to the seat, but he was relieved at how easy she was to shift around. Cold, wet air blew in. Jerry hadn't realized how much taller he was than Tamasin.

'Tam, can you . . .?'

'I'm trying, Jerry, I . . .'

She had her head and shoulders out of the hatch and she was reaching with her good right arm for grip and balance. Jerry got his shoulder under her rump. He gave a shove. Tamasin came out on top of the

350

fuselage. Quickly Jerry stuck his head out, looking for her.

To his surprise, the B52 wasn't even floating on the wing yet, it was floating on the engine pods, holding it out of the water like miniature catamaran hulls. That wouldn't last, though, those pods must be filling with water even now as the swell rocked them. Jerry caught Tamasin, steadying her.

'Can you hold on, up here?'

Laboriously, she swivelled herself round to face the hatch. The blood was dark where it kept on soaking into her flying suit. Her face was pale and her eyes looked dazed with the morphine.

'I'll manage,' she said.

'I want you to help when I get Bat up.'

'I'll manage.'

The pain pulsing in Jerry's side somehow didn't matter. He watched Tamasin a second, eyes concerned behind the spatterings of sweat and grease and dirt all over his glasses. Then he gave her hand a squeeze and went back down.

Bat's eyes were half closed, his face ashen, he had blood on his lips.

Jerry knelt by him. 'You want the other syrette?'

'Later . . . when I'm out . . .'

Jerry got his arm under Bat's shoulder. The pain speared into his side as he lifted. He managed, but only just; Bat was at least the size of the captain from the KC135. The decking underfoot wouldn't keep still and Jerry could hardly brace himself to stay upright as he supported Bat's weight. He went the same way, up through the gunner's station. But there wasn't room for two of them through the hatch, and Jerry had to contort himself and get Bat's arms and shoulders out while Bat grunted, trying to fight the pain.

'Tamasin – can you hold him steady?'

From outside he heard a drowsy: 'I've got him.'

He told her: 'Stay there!' Then he ducked through the cabin, past Russell, past the damaged life raft, and round to the EWO station. Pain was ripping at his side but he forced himself out on to the fuselage.

It was damp and cold out here on the lonely swell with no land in sight. The grey sky was immense after their confinement in the bomber's cabin.

On the gently curving fuselage Tamasin was prone on her side, shivering a little, grasping Bat's sleeve with her good right arm. Jerry crawled the short distance to her and caught Bat under the armpits. He lifted. Nothing happened, the angle was crippling. Again in his mind's eye Jerry saw the snow banks and the icy sky of Eielson, the KC135 askew on the runway and waiting to blow. There was no more time to lose now than there'd been that day in Alaska. He hauled on Bat; there was no way to do this without cruelty. Eyes squeezed shut, Bat grunted. Jerry felt the man's weight shift. Then, despite every effort, Bat jerked his head and moaned aloud and now Tamasin, with what little strength she still held on to, was pulling on him, too.

He came out face first, that great trunk sprawled limply on the fuselage. Jerry got him on to his back. Jerry's breath was heaving. Bat's face was a mask of agony. Once more Jerry hauled, and got Bat's whole body out from the hatch. He could hardly see now for the tears of pain filling his eyes but he saw Tamasin kneel up and, with her good arm, cradle Bat against her breast.

Chest heaving, Jerry dug out his other syrette and gave Bat the lot, in the upper thigh. Then, stiffly, he levered himself back through the hatch to the console and over his seat into the cabin.

*　　*　　*

352

He picked up the damaged life raft, inspected it then, wincing hard, shoved it through the hatch. Tamasin had Bat in her arms and she just stared without comprehension. As fast as he could despite the tearing pain, Jerry clambered down into the second level. He knew what he needed. Sheer cold shocked him as he sloshed knee deep and freezing into the water steadily filling the aircraft. Jerry took what he wanted and then climbed back out. And this time it really hurt and he really thought he wasn't going to make it. Yet he had to make it, because Tamasin mattered.

Under him the aircraft was settling faster and he could just see the water lapping towards the square hatch between the levels. The pain caught at his breath and made his head spin, but what really upset him was the water in his boots, turning lukewarm as it sloshed around his toes. As an afterthought, Jerry picked up his whiskey.

He turned and looked at Russell. In his mind he said goodbye to his friend. Then he shoved the stuff he'd brought out on to the top of the fuselage and levered himself, gasping, after it.

*   *   *

The big, cloudy sky surrounded him and the salt sea swelled for ever. The engine pods had gone under and now the wing was settling down. He'd only just made it.

Dark blood was soaking the front of Tamasin's flying suit and her face looked drained and pale, her shoulders slumped with the relaxing effect of the morphine. She was still holding her tough little body erect, kneeling to cradle Bat in her good arm. How much longer she could keep that going Jerry didn't like to guess. He could see how badly Tamasin was shivering. Even Bat was playing his part, holding a grab loop on the damaged life raft

353

without knowing why, knowing only that Jerry must have had a good reason for pushing that thing out.

Death was hovering over all three of them, and all three were ready to meet it. But they still had some choice over how they died, one sole thing provided. Jerry was the only person who could offer them that choice.

On Jerry's belt was a lanyard. He fastened it through the metal loop on the water bottle he'd rescued from the submerging cabin. The other things he'd brought were in his pockets. Jerry set to work. Salt spray got into the wound on his side and he caught his breath but kept working. Tamasin was crooning to Bat in an undertone, giving him the love and comfort she'd have given to Edward if she'd been able, and now she saw Bat release the life raft as Jerry pulled on it. Jets were dashing overhead with their angry, tearing, rushing noise but Tamasin didn't look at them. She raised her head, her short, charcoal hair sticking out in wet spikes, and realized with amazement that Jerry was working on the damaged life raft. He'd fetched a roll of electrical tape. He was *mending* the damn thing. She couldn't believe it.

He'd fixed the first hole. He cut the tape with his survival knife. He put several layers on it. Doggedly he turned the life raft over. There was a second hole and Jerry patched it, again placing several layers of tape, working methodically, shivering all over yet careless of the cold, oblivious to the way the B52 was sinking under them.

A wave washed over the edge of the fuselage, the water running shiny and cold right over their refuge. Tamasin had her arm round Bat, whispering to him; his eyes were half-open and he was struggling with his breath but he was still alive. Dubiously, Jerry inspected his work.

'There could be holes I missed. Ah, shit, let's go!'

Lips tight, Jerry shoved the raft into the water, holding on by the grap loop. The buoyancy was supposed to activate on contact with salt water, and for a moment the suspense daunted him.

Then the raft inflated. He *had* found all the holes.

More water washed over the fuselage but the wing was holding the hulk afloat. Gripping the grab loop, Jerry knee-walked close to Tamasin. His face was turning grey, its thick-stubbled lines etched with pain. He eased his arm round Bat's shoulders.

'Now get in.'

For a moment Tamasin didn't want to release Bat. Then she saw what Jerry had in mind and she let go her hold on Bat and clambered into the raft. Now Jerry had the raft in one hand and Bat by the shoulders in the other arm. Spray stung him, cutting into his wounds, but he didn't care. Bat caught Jerry's eye and his lips moved as if in praise. It amazed Jerry how this man could continue to be an inspiration to them, even in this condition. Neither he nor Tamasin had yet paused to wonder why Chuck should have shot at them. Tamasin, with her face gaunt and determined, reached one-armed for Bat, but the agony in her left shoulder knifed through the haze of morphine and she gasped and didn't succeed.

'Hold me,' Jerry said, voice distorted with his struggles and with his own pain. 'Just keep the raft close up here.'

With her good right arm, Tamasin grasped Jerry's collar. Tears of anguish stood in her eyes. Again with an effort like that day at Eielson, Jerry hoisted Bat bodily and now, with the weight all up one end, the raft tilted and Tamasin thought it must capsize. Then Jerry had Bat's shoulder over the taut, broad, rubberized rim of the raft. The rest was just pushing and pulling.

A length of the starboard wing broke away with a *graunch* of metal. Not long now.

'Jerry!' Tamasin said. She had her good arm round Bat again in the bottom of the raft and her voice was shivery.

The cold and the wet were getting to Jerry as the

swell surged and the hulk rolled. His flying suit was soaked, from his waterlogged boots to his thighs, and that hampered his movement. For a moment he wasn't sure he could do it.

But Bat and Tamasin needed him. He knew that. That made the difference.

On the starboard side the wing tanks were filling quickly.

Jerry reached out with his right hand. Pain caught him in the shoulder and he couldn't make it, and he tried with his left hand. Salt got in the gash where Chuck's bullet had torn him and again he couldn't make it.

'Jerry!' Tamasin cried out. 'Jerry, *please*!' But she couldn't help him.

He forced himself through the pain; because of them, because they needed him. He pulled himself over the thick, tough rim and into the cold puddle at the bottom of the raft.

For a moment he couldn't move, he had to get his breath and recover. He hadn't cared before, but now he did, because of them. He forced himself through the exhaustion. He knelt up in the bottom of the raft. Wordlessly, he pulled something out of one of the big pockets on his flying suit and held it out to Tamasin.

She gasped. It was Buster. Jerry had gone back for Buster. She couldn't believe it. A smile lit up her face. She wasn't able to take Buster from him, and with a wry grin he tucked the furry rabbit into her lap as she cradled Bat, comforting her husband's father as he lay dying.

The hulk of the B52 rolled over slowly on its side. With mortal majesty it pointed its port wingtip high in the air, water streaming off the engine pods. It slid down beneath the greeny-black swell and out of sight, taking Mario and Russell with it.

*   *   *

356

In the raft there was a paddle and Jerry used it. Every individual pain in his body speared at him. Water boiled where the B52 had gone down, and a wave slopped right into the raft. There was more jet noise, but Jerry hadn't the energy to look up, he needed all his strength to paddle clear. His soaked clothes were freezing but, behind him, he knew Tamasin was shivering, too.

He glanced back at her. The movement pulled on the fierce, raw smarting in his shoulder and in his side, but he didn't dare use one of the syrettes – the drug would slow him up worse than the pain. Tamasin's eyes met his, hooded, still half-alert through the daze of morphine and blood loss.

'Jerry . . .' Her voice was weak, but she knew Jerry wouldn't leave her. 'Jerry, what *is* that up there?'

Jerry screwed up his eyes through the spatters of muck and salt water on his glasses. A circling, grey, dart-like shape with a big tail and the soft grinding growling of a couple of throttled-back turbofans.

'Tornado, I guess.'

'Jerry, that's my brother!'

Simply knowing Colan was there had made things suddenly, startlingly, different. It had been worth staying alive to see him. It still was.

Jerry's eyes closed in sheer exhaustion. He heard a thudding, booming noise and he forced them open. The water was whirling into eddies, making the raft swivel around. Jerry looked up slowly into the grey of the overcast.

He saw dark camouflage on a cigar-shaped body with fierce eyes of windscreen under a massive, chopping rotor. HH53 rescue helicopter.

Now Jerry remembered what would happen if he survived.

*　　*　　*

357

He turned to Tamasin. She was cradling Bat's head on her shoulder. Jerry's fingers had no feeling as he fumbled at the pocket where he'd put the cyanide pill Chuck had given him. He was so cold, cold to his bones, he could have slept for ever; even the salt water on his wounds hardly hurt him. If he swallowed that pill, he could have his wish.

But Tamasin needed him, for the comfort he gave her while she gave comfort to Bat. In the long run it didn't matter what happened to him, it didn't matter if he died free or in jail. Tamasin was more important, even in these final few moments of freedom. Later, too, it would make matters easier for her if he was there to face the judge alongside her.

He got the cyanide capsule loose. With a flip of the wrist he tossed it into the sea. He put his hand over hers as she held Bat's shoulder; Bat was almost gone. Not for the first time, it surprised Jerry how small Tamasin's hand was. She raised her face and looked at him and, for all the dulling of pain and morphine in her eyes, he could tell that she'd understood. Neither spoke.

Spray blasted inside the raft and the HH53 settled on the swell.

EPILOGUE

Getting into a car with the steering wheel on the right was a novel experience for Captain Rebecca Laird and she wasn't at all sure how she was going to handle it, especially with having to remember to drive on the wrong side of the road. At least the hired Sierra had automatic transmission. It was one thing less to contend with.

She'd flown from Tucson to LA and from LA to London Heathrow and she'd had a night in a hotel to recover but still she was jet-lagged rotten. She spared a half-amused thought for Julio, in jail awaiting court-martial. It was air force M/T spares he'd been selling off to a dubious freight depot in Tucson.

The M25 and the A1 had been easy enough, with the lanes separated, but the fun had started at Stamford, where the route changed to twin-lane. Yet gradually Becks was getting the hang of it.

At Sleaford the low hills gave way to endless flatness under a gusty grey sky. Arizona had flat floors virtually from Flagstaff south to Mexico, but this was different. In Arizona you always had a mountain horizon however far that desert bottom stretched, but this had nothing to relieve the eye. And the colours were so different, gentle greens and mud-browns instead of Arizona's dramatic blues and pinks and ochres. It was late March. This chilly, rainy English air really was refreshing after too much time in Tucson, but the wind was gusting and Becks kept the speed down.

Tornados arrowed overhead as she passed the great pile of Tattershall Castle, their flight purposeful. Not far now.

Amid the first low houses of Coningsby village Becks took the lefthand fork for Woodhall Spa.

Woodhall Spa consisted of long, straight avenues and haughty trees, lined at a discreet interval from the roadside with big, half-timber or fake half-timber houses. Their heavy roofs looked very English to Becks; never mind all the places she'd travelled in Europe, this was the first time she'd been in England. It was worth a week of her vacation to see the place – and to satisfy the curiosity that had been nagging at her ever since the operation ended. The houses had pine and cedar in their gardens. Flight Lieutenant Penhale's house was one of them, and Becks bet herself the half-timber on this one wasn't fake.

She pulled the Sierra into the driveway as instructed by Colan on the phone. Chilly gusts caught her as she unfolded her lanky body from the car. She was in civvies today: navy slacks, patterned woollen jumper, a smart cream leather zip jacket that she'd haggled for in Mexico; and she had her hair down.

Colan Penhale answered her ring. He was exactly the way she remembered him from that time in Germany: not tall but solidly built; not quick to smile but sincere; his eyes searching. They shook hands. Becks followed Colan past oak and glass furniture in the hallway to the kitchen at the back. It was warm, with the lingering aura of years of cooking by people who loved to cook and loved the people they cooked for. Two women and a man were dancing attendance on a baby girl. The man was tall, thin, pale and bespectacled, with a gaunt look that suggested physical hardship – just about the way Becks had expected Jerry Yeaver to look. At first, Becks couldn't tell which woman was the wife and which was the sister; but the moment Colan did the introductions it was obvious. Jane Penhale was in jeans and cardigan, an efficient, slender, pretty and bright-eyed young woman. Tamasin, demure in a dress, with Katharine, the baby, on her knee, had Colan's stocky build, dark hair and sombre, searching eyes. Those eyes betokened a person who'd done some tough living. Tamasin was three years older than Jane but the gap looked much wider. Her arm wasn't strapped up any longer but the stiff way she was sitting suggested that the pain hadn't entirely left her.

Jerry Yeaver was on his feet and keeping close by Tamasin's shoulder. It was as if he needed her protection as much as he needed her to need his own.

With a smile, Jane Penhale poured coffee. They sat around the wooden table, awkward, embarrassed.

'I sure never expected it to turn out this way,' Becks said.

Tamasin murmured, 'None of us did.'

Becks glanced across the table at Jerry. She was trying to convey friendship, but trust didn't come easily to the pale, rangy airman. He met her eye but just grinned shyly. Becks prompted: 'I'm still not clear on what actually happened when the chopper picked you up.'

'It was a CIA chopper,' Tamasin said. Under the table she was holding Jerry's hand. She'd let her dark hair grow out a bit but even so it looked short, aggressively efficient.

Becks now knew about that chopper. She'd also heard all the reasons why a CIA aircraft had been first on the scene. No-one in Tucson believed a word of it. The one person in Dark Angel's crew who might have been able to shed some light on the matter was dead.

It had been Chuck in that life raft the MiG had shot up. They'd not found a trace of him, or of the raft.

'We never touched down in Italy,' Tamasin said. 'We thought they were going to land us there and throw us in jail, but they didn't.' She glanced at Jerry. Jerry gave her a grin of encouragement; but he was still fighting down the memory of the abject depression he'd felt in those awful hours. 'They refuelled us off a C130 off Genoa,' Tamasin said, 'in the air. We went straight over Switzerland to Germany. Even then they didn't land us at Frankfurt, they put us straight into Camp King at Oberursel. Medical care first, then one hell of a debrief.'

Becks glanced at her a moment. The kitchen was quiet and Katharine was trying to play with Tamasin's coffee cup, making little noises of complaint when Tamasin moved it out of reach.

'And Bat?' Becks said.

Tamasin glanced down. In her mind's eye she could instantly see the paramedics on the helicopter, working desperately; she could see herself, in the raft, helpless with pain and protesting as they took Bat out of her arms. 'It was too late for him. He died aboard the helicopter. I did everything I could to comfort him . . .'

Wordlessly, Becks nodded.

Tamasin's voice sank to a mutter. 'We were in the hospital wing for days. Then we were in sort of unofficial custody for weeks and all the time we kept expecting to be charged and arrested. But in the end they just sort of said if we kept quiet about it, they would, so they more-or-less smuggled us from Oberursel over to the USAF base at Mildenhall and just let us go. I'm not even sure, myself, what happened on the public front.'

'Maybe I can fill in.' Becks brushed back a stray strand of sandy blonde hair. 'It's not in dispute that Tariq Talal and most of his guys died in a series of explosions at a base that on anyone's admission was full of guns and ammo for terrorist training – also a dump of plastic explosive. That plastic had actually been about for a number of years in the kind of conditions where it might not have been entirely stable. When the camp blew up, the first thing that happened was that the Libyan leader – who's never been a good friend of the West – jumped up and down about the US sending a bomber to hit the place.'

Colan's eyes were thoughtful and he was hardly touching his coffee.

'So the US said "Prove it",' Becks continued. 'So the Libyans said, if it wasn't a USAF operation, what were all these manoeuvres off the Gulf of Sirte, unprovoked aggression, our planes getting shot down, et cetera, et cetera. So we said no-one attacked your planes till they attacked us first, and the manoeuvres were an exercise to counter moves made, first, by the Soviet navy. And we could *prove* the Soviets moved first, and anyway they weren't denying it.' Becks grinned. 'Also we said, if we wanted to take out Tariq Talal: (a) we wouldn't have used a slow old B52 and (b) there wouldn't have been, as the Libyans claimed, just one aircraft.'

Colan was nodding. That made plenty of sense to a flyer. In the hallway, Becks could hear the smooth action of an ancient grandfather clock.

'So then the Libyans ask the Russkies what they thought they were doing,' she said, 'and the Russkies tell the Libyans to go climb a tree. International waters. Since when, not a lot has been heard outa Tripoli.'

Tamasin cuddled Katharine, but her hooded eyes were serious. 'The newspapers must have wondered,' she said.

She was a very still person, Becks thought, glancing at her. It was natural, it wasn't because of that ghastly wound she'd suffered. Becks found herself wanting to fiddle with the clips in her hair. 'Right,' she said. 'But Libya wouldn't let any of 'em in to see evidence of any bombing attack, they'd'a seen too much else besides. CIA has meantime come up with two bits of information which, if true, add an interesting light on why the Libyans shut up so soon. One: Tariq Talal had a network of supporters inside Libya that was so strong it was a threat to the position of the Libyan leader himself. Two: they had evidence linking Tariq Talal with subversion and terrorism in Azerbaijan – part of the Soviet Union.' She glanced at Jerry's haunted eyes, but Jerry still wasn't trusting himself to say anything. 'You can see where that leads.'

Thoughtfully Tamasin nodded. 'So Libya actually wasn't even sorry to be rid of Talal . . .'

'Once the first knee-jerk reaction was over,' Becks said.

'And the Russians had an active interest in scotching him.' Tamasin thought for a moment, one hand effectively keeping Katharine out of mischief. 'God! That Mainstay!' She turned to Jerry. 'We wondered all the time why that flew along with us and still seemed to ignore us!'

Jerry looked at Tamasin. His confidence was coming back. 'They knew,' he said softly. 'And those fighters off the *Kiev*, when we were coming up outa the south of Libya, the ones that went for the Libyan coast and got all those fighters scrambled to meet 'em. They *wanted* us to hit that camp . . .'

Colan, head on one side, murmured: 'What's this I hear, then, about a Congressional inquiry?'

'Ah,' Becks grinned. 'There were two inquiries, one by the air force, one by Congress.'

'Oh, yeah?' Colan was looking intrigued.

'Well, the air force *had* to run *its* inquiry,' Becks explained, ''cos the original crew of *Bright* Angel had complained, and 'cos we at Davis-Monthan had gotten agitated about what appeared to be a missing B52. The Congressional inquiry was a much more high-level affair, aiming to figure out whether the operations off the *Kennedy* that day had had anything to do with this series of explosions and loss of life at Tariq Talal's camp.'

Thoughtfully Colan said, 'Did you hear a rumour that there was a satellite film showing a Hind landing aboard the *Kiev*?'

Becks met his questioning gaze. 'That's not rumour, that's fact. We don't know for sure where the Hind came from, but it could have been Libya. It's certainly really unusual to see a Hind on one of those flatdecks. But we have no idea at all what it was doing or what the significance was.' She grinned apologetically. 'That's fact, too.'

Colan's eyes were steady. 'Still on rumour, wasn't there something about the base commander at Davis-Monthan?'

'Ah, yeah.' Becks glanced at him. 'General Hartmore. He's OK. He was sick for a day or so just after the incident but he recovered, he's still in command there.'

It was right that he should be, Becks thought. A medical discharge, or even extended sick leave, would have broken him, and she found no advantage in seeing people broken. And she'd supported him, she'd helped smuggle him out of that office so that hardly anyone knew what he'd done to that uniform.

He'd had the decency, too, to realize what she'd done and to alter his attitude towards her.

'What did these inquiries turn up?' Tamasin asked watchfully.

'It was interesting,' Becks replied. 'The USAF inquiry found no evidence that a mysterious B52 flight ever took place. A B52H did at one stage appear to have gone missing from the inventory at Barksdale, Louisiana, but later examination of the paperwork revealed that *that* bird was destroyed deliberately in gunnery practice.' She caught Colan's eye, tongue in her cheek.

'Neat,' Colan murmured.

Tamasin said, 'What about the Congressional inquiry?'

'Ah, yeah,' Becks said. 'Well, curiously enough, it was the day after this mix-up with the B52 that Tariq Talal's camp blew up. That was the day the Libyans protested about American aggression – and, interestingly enough, Soviet aggression – and the day when records show intensive flying off the *Kennedy*, plus operations by a

US Navy-RAF task force in which weapons were fired. And we're talking now Libya and the Med – a third the way around the world from where the mix-up with the B52 occurred. So we now have the spectacle of all these Congressmen looking for ways to prove the USN-RAF task force took out Tariq Talal, and not one of them wondering how far a BUFF can fly without refuelling.'

Jane Penhale smothered a laugh. Tamasin grew tired of holding Katharine and Jane took her back.

Colan said slowly: 'So if no-one's alleging that anyone actually stole a B52, there wouldn't seem much point in charging anyone with the theft of one. Unless, presumably, someone forgot themselves so far as to suggest that there might be a different theory.'

'Also, *presumably*,' Jane added, 'no-one's alleging the theft of a bomb load, either. Or its use.'

Tamasin looked at Jerry. He grinned, but there was anger at the back of his eyes. 'It was Chuck. Chuck was the key to it all. He set the whole thing up – paperwork, ammo, bombs, fuel, flight plan, target intelligence. I was with him on a lot of it – he knew right where to go, for everything.'

'But the *idea*,' Tamasin said intensely. 'The idea came from Bat and me.'

'It was all they needed,' Becks told her. 'Someone to just *have* an idea like that.'

Colan objected. 'You're not going to tell me there was some conspiracy just waiting around on the assumption that sooner or later Talal was bound to waste someone whose relatives had access to a B52?'

The future Lady Penhale raised an elegant eyebrow at her husband, her arm keeping their daughter out of harm's way. 'Does that matter? These relatives *did* have access.'

'Until you and Bat went to Chuck,' Becks told Tamasin, 'there *was* no conspiracy.' She tapped an index finger in emphasis on the old, wooden table. 'The way I figure it, going really mainly on rumour – and that's the best we're gonna get in a deal like this – is that Tariq Talal right then was a serious pain in the butt to the whole of the US Government, intelligence services and military. Had been for some while.

'OK. You guys went to Chuck. Chuck went to his CIA contacts – with Bat's plan. When *those* guys saw it, it was too good an opportunity to ignore. They gave Chuck everything he needed to put the plan into operation.'

'It always was down to Chuck,' Jerry said. He glanced at Colan, and Becks recognized the trust that had built up between the two men. 'Anyone who wanted a thing fixed *had* to see Chuck. Bat knew that, Bat had to go to Chuck like anybody else.'

Becks tilted her head. 'Jerry – how *did* it work?'

'Chuck was recent ex-USAF,' Jerry said. 'He had the consultancy going, doing contracts for the military, liaison with civilian authorities, all that stuff. He had contacts everywhere – always had done, all through the time he was in the military. Get you anything, Chuck could.'

'Right,' Becks said, one palm flat on the table. 'CIA. They always gave Chuck all the resources he needed.'

Jerry nodded, eyes pale behind his glasses. 'So, well, seems there was a short time interval between the time Bat and Tamasin approached Chuck originally with the idea, and the time Chuck came back and said it would work.'

'Almost a fortnight,' Tamasin said. Under the table she squeezed Jerry's hand; but the way she sat showed how stiff that shoulder still was. 'We thought he'd just been figuring ways of doing it. In hindsight . . .'

In hindsight, Becks reflected, maybe there were people in official positions to approach. And discuss, secretly and deniably, an operation that would never in a million years receive Presidential sanction.

'First I heard about it was when Chuck approached me,'

Jerry said, 'not long after he'd come back to Bat to say it was on. I was outa the air force, out of a job, out of a marriage, staying with my folks in Seattle while I figured what to do with myself. Chuck had heard all about me – the air-force grape vine. I hired on with the consultancy and started doing the initial legwork down at Barksdale while Chuck was recruiting Russell and Mario.' He had to swallow, once he'd introduced that thought. 'Then after that the whole thing ran like clockwork. What never dawned on *me* was the help Chuck was getting, getting ahold of all these things. And those CIA choppers – they were for Chuck, they were to get in real fast, before the regular air-force rescue teams, and get Chuck out. Chuck was the one the paramedics asked for first when they reached the raft. *We* were just an embarassment to them.'

'It doesn't alter the fact that Chuck had the guts to take his chances along with us,' Tamasin said. 'He couldn't *know* he was going to survive the raid.'

'Right,' Jerry said, 'but *that* doesn't alter the fact that he shot us up. He meant to silence you and me, Tam – so there'd be no-one around afterwards who knew the real story and who might speculate some.'

'Well, *was* he trying to silence us?' Tamasin answered.

'OK, what else was he doing?'

Tamasin and Jerry looked into each other's faces. Becks watched Tamasin, intrigued. 'OK,' Becks said, 'what *was* he doing?'

'Looking after Number One,' Tamasin said drily, 'the thing he was always best at.'

Becks stared. 'Yeah?'

'Look at it Chuck's way,' Tamasin said. 'He's in a ditched BUFF, it's sinking under him, he knows he's got a reception committee in the offing, he's got Jerry and me fussing round Bat, and he's got one good raft – the other's had a chunk of missile through it. He wouldn't *mind* helping us, in the right circumstances, but not at his own expense. He's not prepared to trust Jerry on his raft' – she gave Jerry a glance – 'in case Jerry makes some sort of self-destruct move that threatens Chuck's survival. As for Bat and me, Chuck simply can't see us getting out the hatch before the thing sinks. I couldn't, either, at one time, before Jerry got going. And Chuck isn't prepared to hang around long enough for the thing to sink. Then what happens? Jerry makes a move that Chuck reads as threatening him. Of course he's going to shoot – Number One's at stake!'

Becks considered. 'Sounds good, Tamasin. CIA wouldn't'a needed you two dead anyway – you're good and gagged as long as they have that threat of a jail term over you.'

'We were up there anyway to see fair play,' Colan reminded her, 'in the Tornado.'

Becks leaned her chair on to its back legs and twizzled her coffee mug round. It had stuck to its coaster and the coaster twizzled round as well. 'CIA screwed me around,' she said, 'at least in the early stages. There's a reason for that.'

Shyly Jerry nodded.

'We note also,' Colan said, 'that the Russians haven't made a fuss. But then, there's Azerbaijan. And I'm still intrigued about this Hind aboard the *Kiev*.' He met Becks's eye. 'Is it true that the Soviet leadership knew where the action was going to be, even before the US President did?'

Becks nodded, on her face a hard grin. 'Way I see it, CIA left the President out of this all along – it woulda been vetoed. But they knew they'd need the Russians at least to not take any action once they saw what the game was, so they had to bring them in on it. In essence, once they set up the plan, it *had* to include the Russians.'

Katharine succeeded in what she'd been trying to do all

this time. She upset her mother's coffee cup. Jane swore and grabbed for the kitchen roll.

Tamasin, her eyes still hooded, gave Becks a direct look. 'Well,' she said, 'with the KGB as well as CIA on our side, how the hell could we lose?'

THE END